Praise for *Palace of Tears*

'A wonderful historical novel . . . The Blue Mountains is a place ripe for fiction, iridescently spooky and timeless.' —*Sydney Morning Herald*

'A rollicking, epic tale.' —*Adelaide Advertiser*

'A tap-dancing debut novel, beautifully and lyrically written.' —*Australian Women's Weekly*

'Passionate palatial page-turner . . . a Gothic fiction masterpiece.' —*Tasmanian Times*

'This big, sprawling saga . . . brings together the sophistication of global modernity and the Australian bush, and combines the glitter and glamour of consumer culture with the homeliness of a small regional community.' —*Newtown Review of Books*

'An entertaining, colourful and informative novel . . . Leatherdale brings to life the grandeur and flamboyance of the pre-war and post-war eras.' —*Write Note Reviews*

Julian Leatherdale's first love was theatre. On graduation, he wrote lyrics for four satirical cabarets and a two-act musical. He discovered a passion for popular history as a staff writer, researcher and photo editor for Time-Life's *Australians At War* series. He later researched and co-wrote two Film Australia–ABC documentaries *Return to Sandakan* and *The Forgotten Force* and was an image researcher at the State Library of New South Wales. He was the public relations manager for a hotel school in the Blue Mountains, where he lives with his wife and two children. *Palace of Tears* is his first novel.

PALACE *of* TEARS

JULIAN LEATHERDALE

ALLEN&UNWIN
SYDNEY • MELBOURNE • AUCKLAND • LONDON

This edition published in 2016
First published in 2015

Allen & Unwin
83 Alexander Street
Crows Nest NSW 2065
Australia
Phone: (61 2) 8425 0100
Email: info@allenandunwin.com
Web: www.allenandunwin.com

Cataloguing-in-Publication details are available
from the National Library of Australia
www.trove.nla.gov.au

ISBN 978 1 76029 259 1

Internal design by Kirby Armstrong
Typeset in Minion Pro by Bookhouse, Sydney
Printed in Australia by McPherson's Printing Group

10 9 8 7 6 5 4 3 2 1

The paper in this book is FSC® certified.
FSC® promotes environmentally responsible,
socially beneficial and economically viable
management of the world's forests.

For my mother, Helen

PART 1

Angie

CHAPTER 1

Angie
Meadow Springs, January 1914

The promise of fire was in the air that morning.

Crouching inside the hedge, Angie could feel it in the dry, oven heat that pressed against the skin of her face. She could feel it in the beads of perspiration that bubbled on her forehead and the bracelets of moisture clamped around her wrists. She could hear it in the gushing of the hot, violent wind high in the branches of the gum trees overhead.

Later, what she would remember most clearly was the shimmer down in the valley. Beyond the cottage garden and the cliff, she could see the familiar haze that hung over the gum forest and farmland. But the view from the garden had altered: behind its smoke-blue veil, the valley now rippled and flashed. An ancient seabed millions of years ago, it seemed to be flooded again with a bowl of bright silver water. It was an illusion of course, a trick of the heat and light. How beautiful, thought Angie. Beautiful but frightening. For on a day like this, she knew, a mirage was another portent of fire.

Here, inside the giant photinia hedge between the cottage and the hotel was Angie's favourite hiding place. It had been this way since she was small, her secret cave of coolness and red-green dappled light from which she could watch the world come and go. She shared this secret with no one. Except Robbie. She shared everything with Robbie.

Angie was much taller now and had to squat low in the bed of leaf mulch underfoot, making sure to hitch up the hem of her expensive linen dress. How Freya would howl if she soiled that! She held her wide-brimmed summer hat in her lap to make sure it didn't snag on the branches; she would repin it as soon as she came out of hiding.

Through the glossy leaves, Angie spied on the preparations next door. There was her father, in his dungarees, wiping the sweat from his face with his red handkerchief. Freddie and three of his boys from stores had already pitched a big white marquee on the lawn and were now assembling trestle tables in its oblong of shade. Meanwhile Mr Carson and his team of waiters struggled to pin up paper streamers and coloured balloons, which were torn out of their hands by the hot gusts of wind roaring over the cliff edge. She laughed to herself to see poor chubby Benedict, painfully squeezed into his too-tight tunic and trousers, lose a race with a rogue balloon that bounced six times across the grass and then soared high over the valley, free from his beefy clutches.

When would the guests arrive? she wondered as the hedge shuddered under another onslaught of wind. Overhead, a sulphur-crested cockatoo, blown off course, shrieked indignantly. This wind brought no relief, only blasts of more heat and clouds of dust and dead leaves.

What a day to hold a party!

The trestle tables were now covered in snowy-white damask, held down with pewter tablecloth weights in the shape of koalas and kangaroos. A gold sash festooned each chair. Mr Carson paced back and forth, overseeing his waiters as they painstakingly measured each table setting with their little rulers and laid out the Palace's best silverware embossed with the hotel's elaborately scrolled 'P'. Mr Hawthorne, the general manager, emerged from his office to speak briefly with Mr Carson before hurrying away in that brisk, self-important way of his. There was no sign of Mr Fox. Or of Robbie and his governess.

Angie counted the chairs. A formal sit-down lunch for eighty people at noon on one of the hottest days in January. It was such a Mr Fox thing to do. She looked out to the shimmering valley again and sniffed the air. Nothing. Shielding her eyes, she scanned the horizon. Again, nothing. In her eleven years, Angie had already lived through two bad fire seasons. She knew the local wisdom: it was only a matter of time before this hotel on the cliff top would be destroyed by fire. Fox's Folly, they called it. As if building a luxury hotel in the Australian bush was not insanity enough, what lunacy had possessed Adam

Fox to choose this of all places, where, each summer, winds came rolling out of the valley and drove waves of flame up the gorges on either side?

Angie loved Mr Fox's magnificent, absurd hotel. In fact, it was her one true great love. But, to her secret shame, the idea of a fire, the grand commotion of it, also excited her. And if she was to be really honest, today Angie was so cross, so fed up with everybody and everything, she would probably cheer if a wave of fire swept over the cliff and engulfed the Palace and all its guests.

A trickle of sweat ran from her hairline down past her ear and under the lacy edge of her collar. This wretched heat made her itch and squirm but it was not the reason for her temper that morning.

No, that was something else entirely.

She was furious with Robbie. It was a fury unlike anything she had ever felt, a knot of anger that had lodged in her chest and would not let her breathe freely. It pressed its fingers against her temples, making them throb and ache. The fact was that her so-called closest friend had invited nearly everyone in Meadow Springs to his thirteenth birthday party. Everyone, that is, except Angie. She was humiliated. And deeply hurt.

'Weak. Just like his father,' said Freya when she found out. Her mother's outrage at Angie's public snubbing only made her feel worse. Her mother had a gift for making anything that upset Angie into a drama about Freya.

At first Freya had insisted it was a mistake. Maybe the invitation had been lost or overlooked. She asked her husband

Freddie, the hotel's storeman, to make discreet inquiries with the head housekeeper. Mrs Wells usually handled such matters. *No invitation*, came the reply. It seemed that all the staff and their families had been asked to attend. Except Angie and her mother. Poor Freddie stammered when he delivered the news to his wife and quickly made an excuse to withdraw to his storage sheds on the other side of the hedge.

When it was clear that morning that no invitation was forthcoming, Freya had stormed about the cottage in one of her worst rages in memory. At such times, she reminded Angie of an avenging angel, her uncombed copper hair like a fiery halo about her pale face, her clenched fists raised as if to smite those who had offended her with lightning bolts of wrath. Angie knew better than to say anything; that would only stoke her mother's self-righteous anger.

'The nerve!' cried Freya, still in her nightgown, as she paced the cottage veranda. The salmon-pink battlements and slate-grey dome of the Palace next door could be glimpsed through the trees, above the green barrier of the garden hedge. 'Who do they think they are? Jumped-up pedlars! We were here first. This is our valley. *Ours.* And they have the nerve to come and build their ridiculous castle here and carry on like lords of the manor! How dare they!'

Angie had heard this speech – or versions of it – many times before. She sincerely hoped that her mother's shouting was being drowned out by the noisy wind in the gums.

Freya paused for a moment then charged off into her daughter's bedroom, and returned holding Angie's linen summer dress with its high, ribbed collar and embroidered skirt. 'Get dressed. You are going to Robbie's party.'

'But . . .' The word escaped her mouth before she could stop herself.

'But nothing!' shouted Freya. 'You have as much right to be there as anyone. You are his oldest friend. And the brightest and prettiest of these cow-faced *mädchen*! Why wouldn't he want you there? I will not let that *woman*' – she spat the word out – 'humiliate us like this. I will not!'

'That *woman*' was Adelina, Adam Fox's wife. The White Witch, Freya called her, much to Angie's shocked delight. A woman of mystery, a distant and threatening figure. Stories about the Foxes circulated freely in Meadow Springs, which was hardly surprising given they were the richest family in the Blue Mountains and their hotel one of the most famous landmarks on the eastern seaboard. Angie had heard these stories many times throughout her childhood but still did not know which were to be believed and which were the stuff of gossip.

Adam was the only son of Patrick Fox, Irish immigrant and fortune-seeker whose top-hat shop in the goldfields of Bendigo had led to a string of drapery stores in Melbourne. Adam took over running the family business at age twenty and guided it through the stormy seas of the 1890s depression. Even more ambitious than his father, Adam then sank his entire inheritance into a one-off venture in 1895: a palatial emporium, modelled on the grand Galeries Lafayette fashion store in Paris. It occupied a whole block in central Sydney and boasted chandeliers, marbled bathrooms and the city's first electric escalator. A popular expression for someone with overweening confidence became 'you've got more front than Fox's'. With a flair for self-promotion, Adam emblazoned MR FOX HAS EVERYTHING YOU NEED on coaches, billboards, awnings and even a giant hot-air balloon tethered in Hyde Park. When the balloon came adrift in a high wind and wrapped itself around the flagpole of the department store of his major competitor, Fox lit an extra candle of thanks to the Holy Virgin in St Mary's. Blessed by higher powers or not, his store was a gamble that paid off handsomely as Adam Fox's became a household name.

Everyone knew that his delicate young wife came from a rich, well-established Melbourne family. Rumour had it that her father, also a baron of commerce, only accepted Adam's proposal of marriage when Old Man Fox sweetened the marital contract with a favourable secret commercial one. As it turned out, the marriage was an excellent investment in its own right. When Adelina inherited her father's fortune four years later, Adam used it to build his great folly in 1900: the Palace. Despite the naysayers, the Palace proved a resounding financial success over the next ten years and Adam continued to expand and refurbish the hotel using loans secured against his wife's substantial fortune.

It was well known that Adelina, as pale and fragile as antique porcelain, had managed to bear Adam a son thirteen years ago before lapsing into a state of near chronic convalescence. She was rarely seen in public – usually shrouded in white and seated in a bath chair – and when the family visited the mountains in the summer she spent most of her time secluded at the Foxes' private house in Meadow Springs. It was said that she struggled with deep melancholia after the birth of Robbie and that, in her weakened state of mind, she had become convinced her husband had married her only for her money and accused him of cruelty and disloyalty. Her one consolation was her son, whom she smothered with an overbearing, suffocating love. In her bedridden absence, it was the young governess, Miss Blunt, who became her eyes and ears, charged with vigilance over Robbie's welfare every moment of his day.

Adelina's ongoing illness distressed Fox. Not just as a loving husband, so the local gossips insisted, but also as an entrepreneur. Fox's hotel was founded on the reputation of its hydropathic spa, modelled on the famous health retreats of Europe. Here, guests paid handsome fees to take the healing waters from the local spring (actually imported in steel drums from Baden-Baden in Germany) and a remarkable variety of water cures under the care of a specialist doctor. These expensive health regimes even included the latest fad of 'sun baths', whereby ladies and gents were persuaded to lie naked in shallow sand pits, segregated from each other and protected from public view by screens, to be healed by the purifying rays of the sun. While Fox genuinely hoped for his wife's recovery for her own sake, the failure of the Palace's spa to find her a permanent cure was a persistent source of embarrassment.

Whatever the truth of these stories, one thing became increasingly clear to Angie as she got older. The White Witch did not approve of the girl from the cottage as a playmate for her son. There was little doubt it was Adelina who had made sure Angie was not invited to Robbie's thirteenth birthday party.

This was a new and disturbing development. Despite her tearful pleading and threats, Adelina had failed for seven years to stop Robbie from seeking out Angie's company during his summer vacations. With a flick of sandy blond hair hanging over restless brown eyes and an impish grin in a sharp-chinned, freckled face, Robbie Fox was a portrait in miniature of his father. He also had his father's air of reckless Irish charm. He had found so many artful ways to manipulate and lie to his mother and governess that it made Angie think he would do a fine job of running his father's business one day.

Angie did not *love* Robbie Fox. That was ridiculous. He was just the skinny boy from next door who filled her summer holidays with adventures and pranks and games. He was the bush naturalist who caught yabbies and frogs from the creek and kept them in a glass tank in the garages. Who organised sports for the children of hotel guests – skittles and hoop races and leapfrog – and was always the captain at cricket. Who fell off the roof of the machinery shed trying to retrieve a cricket ball and sliced open his knee on the iron sheeting. Who got a belting from his father for the joke he played on Chef Muntz with a blue-tongue lizard, almost giving the poor man a seizure.

He was just Robbie. But she planned to marry him anyway. And forgive him for not inviting her to his party.

The canvas of the marquee flapped loudly with yet another gust of wind. Mr Carson and his waiters were now trimming the elaborate flower arrangements on each table: baskets of white and red blossoms tied with silk ribbon. Nearby, bottles of champagne chilled in steel buckets and rows of crystal flutes glinted in the sunlight. A band were setting up near the marquee and spent as much time swatting away flies and rescuing windblown sheet music as they did tuning their instruments.

You cannot be serious?

Angie laughed out loud and clapped her hands at what now appeared on the terrace. Mr Fox had ordered an ice-carving of the number '13', flanked by translucent statues of an emu and kangaroo in imitation of the national coat-of-arms. She watched Freddie anxiously ushering his boys as they bore the heavy carving down the stairs and across the lawn into the marquee. Its glassy surface caught every surrounding detail, twisting them into ribbons of colour like the insides of marbles. The heat would gnaw this comical sculpture into a puddle in no time.

What a show-off!

The ringmaster. That was Freya's nickname for Adam Fox when she was feeling uncharitable, describing the hotel as his 'big top' and the guests as his 'menagerie'. Fox certainly had something of P.T. Barnum's aptitude for publicity and shared his predilection for the bizarre and novel. Apart from his business trips to Europe and the United States, Fox loved to travel for adventure and sent home crates of curiosities from Siam, Malaya, the Dutch East Indies, Japan, British East Africa and Madagascar which filled the cabinets and crowded the walls in his hotel.

Strangest of all was Fox's prize purchase last year from a crew of Arab fishermen in Libya. COME SEE THE REAL MERMAID trumpeted the advertisement in the local papers. Angie's father was responsible for unpacking the seven-foot-long corpse, dyed mahogany brown from being pickled in a tank of formaldehyde on the boat out from Africa. Laid out on a bed of wood shavings in the shed at the back of the Palace garages, this mythic monster attracted huge crowds. Freddie gave Angie a quick private viewing before the doors were opened to the public. Angie recoiled at the sight of the bare-breasted mermaid with her hollow eyes, flaccid flesh and sliced-open belly. She had been gutted like a fish, with her spinal column placed alongside her in the manner of a scientific specimen. A sob rose in Angie's throat. Whether this magnificent creature was real or not, there was no denying the pathos of this tawdry display.

The ringmaster, the showman, the impresario, Adam Fox also liked to collect people. The Palace soon became a mandatory destination for famous and wealthy foreigners on the Australian leg of their world tours as well as a mecca for a clique of home-grown celebrities. Fox's Folly was the place to see and be seen. From her hole in the hedge that separated her family's cottage and the hotel grounds, Angie had spent hours of her childhood admiring this fantasy world of wealth and sophistication. It held an overwhelming fascination for the young girl and filled her with a compelling, almost dizzying sense of entitlement.

From her hiding place among the leaves, she loved to spy on the guests as they arrived in coaches and cars or took the short walk from Meadow Springs railway station over the road, always with that same look of gawping wonder at the sight of the Palace. Swathed in heavy jackets and travelling cloaks, they crunched their way up the gravel driveway, accompanied by the porters' trolleys of valises and steamer trunks.

On hot summer afternoons, she watched the ladies in their puffy white dresses and enormous gauzy hats playing croquet on the front lawn to the tuneful clack of the wooden balls. Their husbands, meanwhile, lounged on the terrace smoking cigars or took the waters in the pool outside Dr Liebermeister's clinic. On crisp autumn mornings she smiled to see the excited honeymooners climbing into the hotel's natty Panhard et Levassor motor with a hamper to go on a daytrip to the limestone wonderland of the Jenolan Caves further west. In the winter evenings, when snow fell like icing sugar sifted over the wedding-cake frosted hotel, snatches of music and laughter drifted towards the cottage and Angie kept vigil at her bedroom window on the distant lights visible through the trees.

Sure, her father, Freddie, was the king of his domain in the hotel's sheds and vast cellars where all the machinery and supplies were stored. He loved it when his daughter visited him at work and he would show her the latest barrels of German beer stacked in the dark or the new American lawnmower he had just unpacked from its casing. But she yearned for more.

She yearned to enter the forbidden realm of the hotel itself.

It was Robbie who knew every secret corner and passageway of the Palace so intimately that he and Angie could creep about undetected by Hawthorne or Wells – though of course half the thrill was the danger of almost being found out. It was Robbie who had discovered the perfect hiding places for them both behind the marble statuary in the gallery or the huge leather Chesterfield in the billiard room. How Angie treasured the memories of those secret excursions. They afforded her even more confidential glimpses of this other world's plush, glittering life.

Most unforgettable and coveted of all was the night of the Coronation Ball held in honour of King George V's ascension to the throne. It was the year Angie turned seven. Squeezed in next to Robbie in the storage area behind the main stage beneath the frescoed dome of the casino ballroom, Angie watched spellbound as the hotel's palm court orchestra played waltzes and mazurkas, a storm of music only inches from her face. At this distance, she could even read the polished plaque screwed to the glossy black haunch of the Bechstein grand: *'In gratitude to the Palace staff – Baroness Bertha Krupp von Bohlen und Halbach, December 1908.'* The brief visit of the German armaments heiress – one of the richest women in the world – had made quite an impression in Meadow Springs.

The casino was garlanded with bunting and flags and all manner of patriotic paraphernalia for the occasion of the Coronation Ball, including a large triumphal oil painting of the Relief of Mafeking. The gold and blue dome echoed with the cacophony of swooning violins, squeaking shoes, the tinkling peals of female merriment and trumpet blasts of male laughter.

For months afterwards Angie's feverish dreams were inhabited by beautiful, poised women in silk chiffon gowns – orange, cerise and jade – whirling in the arms of bright-eyed, clean-shaven men, their lustrous black hair matching their spotless black swallow-tail coats, all under the brilliance of the casino's three-tiered crystal chandelier.

There was only one way she could gain the keys to this fairytale kingdom. She would have to make Robbie fall in love with her and propose marriage. Was it wrong for her to want to marry Robbie out of love for his family's hotel? It was not a cruel plan. She had every intention of making him happy. There were worse reasons for a marriage. Just look at Robbie's parents.

A wasp hovered menacingly in front of her face before being blown out of sight. She stretched out her left leg to ease a cramp in her calf muscle. When was this ridiculous party going to start? Her plan was to slip through the hedge when the festivities began and mingle with the guests before they were seated for lunch. It was possible the White Witch would make one of her rare public appearances as a special effort for her son. 'Nobody will challenge you,' promised Freya, 'I know the Foxes and the last thing they can stand is a scene. Carson will be made to fetch you a chair and set you another place at the table. You'll see.'

It was almost certain that Adelina had guessed Angie's intentions. The White Witch knew she must strike now before Angie's power over her son grew any stronger. Did Mr Fox know too? He was aware of Angela's existence, of course, but in all the years she had played with Robbie, Angela doubted if Mr Fox had looked at her more than once or twice and even then without close attention. Children were to be seen and not heard in his book. A quick glance and a nod were the only acknowledgement she had ever received as far as she could remember.

Angela knew how much Mr Fox respected her father, Freddie, who had been head storeman from the day the hotel opened. His attitude to Freya was more mysterious. From the first, so the stories went, Mr Fox had taken a keen interest in her talent as a painter. He had even bought one of her landscapes for his picture collection in the gallery and commissioned a mural of plump auburn-haired mermaids like the sea maidens in Mr Arnold Böcklin's paintings for the lobby of the spa. For a while Freya taught watercolour classes on the terrace to artistically inclined female guests. Mr Fox would drop by her studio to admire a work in progress. But that all stopped years ago and Freya had not had a good word to say about Mr Fox or his wife since.

Angie hoped her mother would not come into the garden to make sure she had joined the party and find her still hiding here in the hedge. She was considering abandoning the plan altogether when she spotted Robbie sauntering across the lawn with his latest toy: a hunter's shooting stick, complete with a single-legged fold-up stool. He had been promised his first kangaroo hunt this autumn. *Spoilt little rich boy, not a care in the world!* The thought spilled out of her, unchecked.

Today she was angry with Robbie, and not just because he had not stood up to his mother about the birthday party. It was because this was the final proof that this summer he had changed. It had started with an unusual awkwardness the last time they had spoken, with Robbie fidgeting and avoiding her eyes the whole time. It continued with him finding any excuse to avoid her when he came to the hotel, which he did less and less, and ended with him deliberately ignoring her whistles and calls from the hedge and ducking away inside whenever she appeared.

What had changed?

It was not something she could ask her mother; over time Angie had come to realise how much Freya's view of the world diverged from reality. Angie also suspected her mother's praise of her cleverness and beauty had given her false hope. She loved and hated her mother for that. Certainly Freya's strangeness was well known. It was the reason the hotel staff took pity on her and Freddie. It was the reason Robbie rarely came to the cottage, even though he knew what it was like to have a mother everyone thought was mad. Her family was not normal, there was no doubt about that. Apart from Freya's regular outbursts of anger there were also her parents' frequent unexplained silences, their furtive glances, their covert and pained expressions of guilt. Angie noted them all. Urgent whispered conversations at night were impossible to understand though she strained to hear the muffled words through the bedroom wall. What were they hiding? For as long as Angie could remember, the atmosphere in the cottage was thick with secrets and her mother was the keeper of them all.

So Angie had to work out life's puzzles all by herself and come up with answers different from Freya's. What she had started to understand was that Robbie's friendship with Angie had been tolerated when he was a naughty little boy, but Robbie was now a young man, the only son of a respected businessman and lone heir to the Fox fortune. The innocent days of childhood were dwindling fast. No doubt Adelina had insisted that this childish friendship be brought to a natural end before more complicated adult feelings surfaced.

What hurt Angie most of all was how Robbie seemed to take this all in his stride. Maybe he understood the rules better than she did. Maybe he had always known their friendship was just another childhood toy to be put on the shelf when the time came. She had told herself she would never *love* Robbie, so why did this knowledge hurt her so much? It was partly because she felt so foolish for thinking she could ever have made him her husband. She was the daughter of the humble storeman and the crazy painter in the cottage. Girls like Angie Wood did not become Mrs Fox.

'Hey, you! Look what I've got!'

Angie stepped out onto the lawn and shouted, staring defiantly at Robbie as he ambled towards her, swinging his stick in lazy circles like a child's hoop. Startled for a moment, he came to a halt several yards from the hedge. With a flick of his hair, he looked back quickly over his shoulder to make sure his governess was not watching. But it seemed Miss Blunt was distracted today, possibly by her recently discovered interest in Mr de Witte, the new front office manager.

Robbie did not meet Angie's stare. It was what she was holding in her hand that caught his attention. Just as Angie had intended.

Her mother's anger on her behalf had given Angie the courage – and the excuse – to defy the White Witch for now and make an appearance at today's party. In fact, Angie had decided to go one step further. As she studied her own reflection in the bedroom mirror while her mother brushed and plaited her long black hair and buttoned her into her white linen dress, Angie knew what she must do. She feared she had only one more chance to win back Robbie's interest. He needed an irresistible reason to defy his parents.

'When did you get *that*?' asked Robbie. His eyes glistened and colour flushed his cheeks. He looked over his shoulder again and jabbed the sharp end of the shooting stick into the lawn, where it remained upright. Angie laughed and waggled the small object in her hand invitingly. She was teasing him. Robbie took a step forward like a sleepwalker. He licked his lips nervously.

'It's your birthday present, Robbie Fox,' she said. 'From me. Even though you couldn't be bothered to invite me to your party.'

'I'm sorry, Angie. I didn't . . . I couldn't . . .' His eyes flicked to hers for a moment and she thought she could detect a spark of real regret there. Or maybe it was just the hot, dry wind making Robbie's eyes water. He took another step towards her.

'Like to take a look?'

There was no doubt that Robbie very much wanted to take a look. The object in her hand was a secret that she and Robbie had discovered months ago. While Robbie had been the guide to adventures on the other side of the cottage hedge, she had repaid this debt with an adventure of her own. Treasures of a different kind were to be found on her side of the hedge: inside her mother's studio.

One day last spring, Freya had left the studio unlocked by accident when she went off on one of her sketching trips into the bush, and Angie had trespassed into this inner sanctum with her fellow adventurer. There, amid the chaos of half-finished canvases, dried-out paint tubes and jars of cloudy turpentine, they found Freya's collection of erotic French postcards.

They had both laughed at the photographs of nude women posing theatrically in exotic, usually oriental, settings. But Angie heard the quickening of Robbie's breath, saw how his fingers trembled a little as he held them. These cards excited him. Today she held one of the postcards in her hand: a curvaceous, broad-hipped, snake charmer wearing nothing but a necklace at her throat and bangles at her wrists.

Robbie took another glimpse over his shoulder towards the marquee and hotel. Without a word, he lunged towards his childhood friend.

She was ready for him and retreated a few feet to maintain the distance between them. 'Oh, no you don't, Robert Fox. You'll have to catch me first.'

Robbie's face, stuck in a kind of blissful torment and confusion, relaxed a little. He smiled. This was a game. Just like when they were children – but also very different. 'Alright then.'

Angie had always been the faster runner. Her legs were longer for a start. And Robbie suffered from asthma so he could only manage short bursts before struggling for breath.

Hitching her linen skirt to her knees, Angie turned and bolted down the stone steps from the hotel lawn to the lower terrace.

Out of the protection of the hedge, she could feel the full force of the wind, gusts slapping her face and clawing at her dress and hat. Robbie sweated in his dark morning coat and blue necktie, the perfect little gent; this birthday party marked his passage to adulthood, his parents were making no secret of that. His mouse-grey homburg was snatched off his head by the wind and bowled across the terrace, coming to rest against the stone balustrade. He let it go as he chased Angie down the second flight of steps to the cliff track below.

Angie hesitated for a moment at the bottom of the grassy slope that led to the cliff top. Which way should she go? The valley shimmered brightly before her. To her left was Sunbath Road, leading to the hotel's flying fox, a steel pulley and overhead cable that hauled fresh produce up the cliff face three times a day from Mr Fox's farm in the valley. To her right was the cliff-top bush track to Sensation Point. She turned right.

Later Angie would agonise over that single moment: how her whole life might have been different if she had chosen the other path. Or had destiny already decided how this day would end?

Fine dust was kicked up by her shoes as she ran along the bare, rocky path. To her left was the glorious view of the valley that tourists flocked from far and wide to see: grey-green forested ridges, sheer cliff faces, banded and mottled in orange, yellow and purple-grey, all filtered through a smoke-blue haze. When she was younger these fissured precipices made Angie think of ancient ruins, fashioned by long-dead giants out of massive, crudely cut blocks. Now scarred and weathered, these blocks were tumbling slowly back into the quarry from which they had once been dragged.

When the creaking of branches and thrashing of leaves in the canopy overhead quietened for a moment, she could hear Robbie scrambling along the track behind her. She glanced back to see him making his way around the silver-white pylon of a Blue Mountains ash, tripping over its ragged skirt of bark. His black trousers and morning coat were covered in a film of chalky dust and his face was glossy with sweat. She could hear him beginning to wheeze.

'Come on, Angie! Please!'

For one fleeting instant, she pitied him. But then she remembered how easily he had let go of their friendship, their seven years of secrets and memories. Why had he betrayed her like that? What prizes had Mr and Mrs Fox dangled in front of Robbie to make him forget her? What picture of misery had they painted for him if he chose her for his future? Or was it his own feelings he was most afraid of?

She let Robbie catch his breath a little and then she took off again. Dodging under a sandstone overhang as she came around the next bend in the track, she saw Sensation Point less than a hundred yards away. When she could hear nothing but the sound of the wind in the trees, she wondered, with a brief twinge of panic, if her pursuer had given up and turned back. Then she heard Robbie wail miserably, 'Angie! Angie! Wait!'

She knew what she was doing. She wanted to punish him for his betrayal. But she wanted to forgive him too. To take him in her arms and let him discover a new sweetness between them. The warmth of his chest pressed against hers. Her heart beating fiercely next to his. The taste of his lips, of her lips on his.

What would that be like?

She leaned against the warm wall of the cliff face and waited. A parrot's call tinkled bell-like above her in the fork of a gum tree. They would have their first romantic kiss here, at Sensation Point. The valley she loved so well would be the silent witness to their vows of love. It was her valley and her mother's valley and her grandfather's long before the Foxes came. It had a hypnotic power that had captured Mr Fox's soul and emboldened him to gamble against all the odds on an absurd dream. And the valley had repaid his daring a thousandfold. Maybe it would do the same for her.

Robbie saw her as he came round the corner, stooping so as not to bang his head on the overhang. He slowed now, realising that Angie was waiting for him. There was even a trace of his usual carefree, arrogant saunter as he came closer. As if he had chosen to have a stroll in the bush rather than engage in a desperate pursuit. His outfit was caked in dust, his hair and face damp with sweat. He wheezed a little but did not seem to be in any distress.

She smiled at him. But he was not smiling back.

'Where is it?' His eyes blazed and there was a definite note of urgency in his voice, maybe even anger. This was not the way the game was meant to be played, thought Angie. Or was it? The intensity of Robbie's gaze alarmed her.

'Robbie . . . ?'

She was trying to read the mood in his dark brown eyes, but the meaning of his gaze eluded her. She could hear her own voice pleading with him. It was not meant to sound like an apology, more a surrendering, a softening, inviting him closer. She hoped he would understand.

'I said where is it?!' Robbie was definitely angry now.

Angie let the postcard she had hidden up her sleeve slide into her hand.

He lunged at her and grabbed her wrist roughly.

'Robbie, please don't . . .'

'Give it to me.'

His voice was demanding, petulant. Angie felt her resentment rise like a surge of blood behind her eyes. Robbie's face was close to hers. She could see the blond downy hair on his upper lip, the lushness of his long lashes, the pink moisture of his mouth. He had grown into a handsome man like his father.

Leaning against him, she pressed her mouth against his and realised with a shock that she was the one who desired, who yearned, who loved. Robbie was only interested in the girl on the postcard. Not her. In that instant she saw a different Robbie, a tricky, lying, impatient Robbie who, like his father, got everything he wanted no matter what it took.

What happened next was hard for her to recall.

Did she push him away? She was not sure. She felt the card fall from her hand, felt his fingers reaching for it. Then they were both buffeted by a blast of hot air. The giant tree behind them groaned like the mast of a ship in a high gale, its branches grinding against each other in agony.

Robbie turned away from her in time to see the postcard flicked by the wind over his head. He did a strange little twist and leap, trying to catch it, and landed awkwardly, jamming his foot against the thick root of the gum tree.

And then he fell.

'Angie?' His first cry was a confused question, rising shrilly to pure terror. 'Angie!'

She watched his body tumble over the tree root and pitch forward through a gap in the scrub on the other side of the path. His foot dislodged a clod of earth that rolled away into the void. The struggle was brief. Robbie's arms flailed wildly, searching in vain for a firm handhold. She heard a soft grunt as he crashed through a wattle bush on the cliff edge. And then he was gone.

Angie heard her own scream and the shrieks of a flock of startled cockatoos as if in response. Below, the valley rippled like the waves of a cruel ocean that had swallowed up the only son and heir of Mr Adam Fox.

CHAPTER 2

Lisa

Meadow Springs, April 2013

Lisa stood in a kind of prayerful silence for at least five minutes. Her hands were numbed by the cold as they clutched the slick metal railing of the chain-link fence. Out of the sea of white mist she could hear the delicate chimes of bellbirds pinging in the distance and, much closer, the screech of yellow-tailed black cockatoos, invisible but unmistakeable, as they launched themselves into the cotton-wool-filled valley below. A steady drip-drip-dripping of water pattered mournfully on the leaves of the huge gum near the cliff edge. Behind her, the wail of a train horn and the high-pitched keening of its wheels added to the unnerving atmosphere.

Sensation Point. She sighed and a patch of mist escaped her mouth, mingling with the larger mist all around her.

She could feel melancholy seeping into her soul as stealthily as the clamminess of the mist through her anorak and jumper. She hugged herself for warmth but also for comfort.

The local history librarian at Springwood had told her on the phone that a marble plaque had been set into the sandstone to mark the tragic spot but it had been removed some time after the First World War. Now all Lisa could find was a ghostly rectangle of less weathered rock punctuated by the rust marks of four bolts. She had found a photo of the original plaque online. It read: *In Memory of Robert James Fox, beloved son of Adam and Adelina, who was taken up to the embrace of God on 14th January, 1914.* She smiled sadly at the brave metaphor of ascending – in complete denial and contradiction of the boy's fatal fall.

Lisa secured her Nikon to the railing with a flexible octopus-grip tripod and waited. As a young girl growing up in Katoomba, she had read about the Blue Mountains' most famous photographer, Harry Phillips. Leaving his wife in charge of his commercial studio in Katoomba, Harry would spend days at a time trying to capture the evanescent, dramatic beauty of clouds and mist over the valleys with a passion that bordered on religious fervour. According to village folklore, the sight of a heavy mist rising out of the Jamison would prompt the locals to declare 'Harry's happy!'

The mountains were a breeding ground for eccentrics and Harry was no exception. He was most famous for his photo *War Clouds*, taken in March 1914, in which he claimed a sinister black cloud formation, backlit by sun and shaped like a double-headed eagle, was a portent of the coming war with Germany and Austria-Hungary. Despite such nonsense, Lisa admired Phillips: for his craft, his work ethic, his prodigious output, his willingness to experiment and his gift for marketing himself. It took a single-minded vision to make a living as a professional photographer. A kind of madness, really. She should know.

This morning the surface of the mist crested like sea spray, flung up into the air in slow motion, and then drifted in ragged scraps of cloud above the ridge line. Satisfied with the composition, she shot off twenty exposures at different *f* stops and checked her watch. Her meeting was in ten minutes. It was time for her to return to the hotel.

Was it because she knew what had happened here that made the place feel so sad? she wondered as she repacked and zipped up her camera bag. Or was it something else, some intangible but real reminder of loss that lingered here at this cliff edge and touched people's souls?

As a photographer she understood the appeal of ruins. She was fascinated with the bittersweet triumph of nature and time over every human effort to control them both, moss and root and earth overwhelming brick and iron and glass. She was drawn to abandoned places and loved the lurid colours and riotous growth of verdigris, rust and mould. She also knew the power of a telling detail: a broken cup, a crippled chair, a lifeless glove. Lisa understood all this and sought it out in her art photography. But she rejected the idea of such places having 'spirit' or 'memory'. That was getting far too close to the idea of ghosts. She had stopped believing in ghosts when she was six.

So why *did* she feel so stirred up? Lisa asked herself as she trudged back along the track. It was not that hard to understand really. She was connected to this place by family history. The memories and stories of her mother, Monika, and grandmother, Laura. As Lisa turned the bend, ducking under the sandstone overhang, she saw the hulk of the Palace loom out of the mist above her. This was Monika's place, her childhood playground, her home away from home. If he had lived, Robert James Fox would have been Monika's older half-brother: Lisa's uncle.

The hotel was there at the very start of Monika's story. She was born there by accident. Adam Fox and his heavily pregnant second wife, Laura, were staying at the hotel for a weekend during the summer of 1930 while renovations were being completed on their new house in the nearby township of Leura. Three weeks before she was due, Monika decided it was time to enter the world. It would remain her way for most of her life: always in a hurry. As if there was never enough time to do everything she had to do.

Now, time really was running out for Monika Fox with the onset of Alzheimer's and, more recently, a stroke. Lisa had visited her mother at the Ritz nursing home in Leura earlier that morning. The rehab nurse had said encouraging words about Monika's progress but, in her heart, Lisa knew that her mother's story had entered its final chapter.

It was not easy for her to accept that this tiny birdlike creature, with her darting pale blue eyes and restless, bony hands, was the same woman who had ruled her life with an iron will for so many years. Seeing her mother's aloof and unwavering authority crumble into this pitiful wreckage of anxiety and dependence gave Lisa no satisfaction, though no one who knew her history could have blamed her if it did. Instead, being forced to watch her mother's decline was like witnessing the demolition of a magnificent cathedral. It was heartbreaking.

In her time Monika Fox had been celebrated as one of Australia's most gifted children's writers. Her Kitty Koala books had won the hearts of thousands of fanatically loyal young readers as well as praise from publishers, book councils, critics and librarians. For forty years she enjoyed a successful partnership with the illustrator Eric Blakeson, who'd brought her family of blundering, comic marsupials to life 'with irresistible charm, wit and unkempt fur' as one reviewer phrased it.

As fashions in children's literature changed, Monika's reputation remained that of an elder stateswoman whose readers were now parents and grandparents themselves. Their fond childhood memories kept her backlist in print and on library shelves, but it had been many years since she had produced a new title. The truth was that her Australian publisher had long ago been swallowed up by a global behemoth and her agent had retired from the game. Monika's time seemed to have passed.

By her late sixties, Monika didn't want to write another Kitty Koala book despite talk of a possible animated movie. She worked for six years instead on a manuscript entitled 'The Castle of Ice'. It was the story of an unhappy princess living in a castle carved from solid ice who escapes to the forest where she becomes the servant of a gifted witch. Publishers rejected this surreal, dark fairytale in an Australian setting, saying it was not the kind of book people expected from the famous Monika Fox. She didn't write another word after that, though she continued to 'make notes', a writer's habit of a lifetime that never deserted her.

While generations of Australian children felt a familial closeness to the vivacious red-headed woman on the back of their favourite copy of *Kitty Goes to Town* or *Kitty's Big Mistake,* Lisa knew her own mother largely as an imperious, remote figure. This was an irony that Lisa grasped from an early age.

Locked away in her study and her bubble of celebrity, Monika dedicated herself to these countless *other* children who in turn showered her with adoring letters, drawings and handmade offerings. Their flattery and affection contrasted starkly with the irritating demands of her own flesh and blood. As a smart, handsome first-born, Tom was an object of pride for his ambitious mother – at least for a while. But Monika's daughter was a different story.

Lisa was an unexpected and unwelcome change-of-life baby who spent most of her early years in the care of nannies. In the company of these crisp, professional women and her often moody older brother, Lisa would have most of her childhood to learn how to survive with little more than sporadic attention from her mother. Except, that is, in the matter of manners and grooming. Here, Monika Fox proved to be an old-fashioned martinet. As part of the famous author's public profile, her two offspring were wheeled out at promotional events with fixed smiles and brutally brushed and plaited hair as embodiments of doting progeny. Her 'biggest fans'. Despite this hypocrisy, Lisa could not give up entirely on the notion that, in her own obscure, unexpressed way, Monika really did love her.

So where were all those adoring children now? thought Lisa a tad bitterly, soothing Monika's forehead as she drifted in and out of a mid-morning nap. Lisa had brought the usual box of Monika's favourite handmade chocolates from the village: an eye-popping array of pralines, truffles and clusters. Monika had always had a weakness for 'the finer things in life', as she put it. Given her substantial inheritance from Adam Fox, the child support from her ex-husband and the healthy income from her best-selling books, she had always had the means to indulge this 'weakness', even as a single mother.

While Monika dozed, Lisa slipped the silk ribbon off the box and snuck one of the almond pralines into her own mouth. The chances were her mother would misremember how many she had eaten. Lisa felt a blush of shame at this childish act of deception. And then felt angry with herself for feeling ashamed.

By the window a vase of stock – a birthday bouquet from an admirer – was browning at the edges. Before the stroke, Monika had been lured from her room at the Ritz every now and then to be a monumental presence at a local writers' festival or book launch, but it had been at least eighteen months since her last public appearance. The dying flowers were the only acknowledgement that anyone apart from Lisa knew or cared about the existence of Monika Fox.

Why am *I here?* Lisa asked herself. It was a question that continued to preoccupy her but remained unanswered. Her brother Tom had left Sydney as soon as he finished his science degree and started his own life – a public service career and a family – in Canberra. He dutifully sent Christmas and birthday cards but rarely visited. Monika took even less interest – if that was possible – in her two grandchildren, Oliver and Sasha, than she had in her own children.

As for her own father, Michael, Lisa had not heard from him since he walked out of their lives two weeks before her ninth birthday, leaving his children alone with the famous author behind the locked study door. It was as if he had been killed in a car accident – like her poor uncle Alan – or lost at sea, fates Lisa had childishly imagined for him as preferable to his cold-blooded vanishing act.

Lisa had memories of Michael as a loving father when she was little. But his corporate legal career had enforced longer and longer periods of absenteeism from family life over the years. Hastily purchased souvenirs from Tokyo and LA airports were handed over as tokens of appeasement on his return from business trips. When Monika discovered Michael's year-long affair with a female colleague, the collapse of their marriage was no less noisy and heated for the fact of their largely separate lives. Nights of slammed doors, hurled objects and shouting were followed by their father's swift overnight departure followed by a legal battle to untangle assets and decide the fate of the children. Their father made no claims for custody. His relocation overseas for work meant the court decided they should stay with Monika. Her ready agreement to this arrangement was underwritten by a generous alimony scheme that paid for a live-in nanny who performed the general administrative and pastoral duties of a parent.

So what *was* it that kept Lisa here at her mother's side? Was it the absurd hope that she would be rewarded with some sign of maternal love, no matter how fleeting? As pathetic as that seemed, Lisa had to admit that it was probably true; that she was still that little girl standing outside her mother's study door longing for admittance.

Monika's eyes fluttered open and she stared vacantly at the fair-haired woman seated by her bed. She was momentarily bewildered, her voice a touch slurred as an after-effect of the stroke. 'Lisa?'

'It's okay, Mum. I'm here.'

Lisa wrapped her hand around Monika's frail fingers to reassure her of her protective presence. The tension in Monika's face subsided at this touch and the sound of Lisa's voice but her eyes still darted about questioningly.

'When is Tom coming?' she asked.

'Soon, Mum, soon.' Lisa had given up explaining to Monika that her son hadn't visited for two years and was unlikely to do so any time soon. Monika also asked for her own father, Adam Fox, who was even less likely to visit as he had passed away in 1957. She never asked to see her mother. Or her ex-husband.

For short periods each day, Monika's mind wandered freely, unconstrained by any sense of the present or past. She would conduct one-sided conversations with the long dead – her older sister, Lottie, her younger brother, Alan, and her father, Adam – which would sometimes end in bursts of angry confusion or weeping. Lisa did her best to calm Monika after these episodes and had even become used to them, but one such occasion had stuck in her mind more vividly than the others.

It was a morning about three weeks earlier, and they had been sitting in rattan chairs on the balcony of the Ritz on a cool, sunny autumn afternoon enjoying a cup of tea. Monika was making notes, as she liked to do most days in the dog-eared black notebook that she carried with her everywhere and kept locked in her bedside cabinet. She stopped writing, turned her pale, watery eyes on her daughter and said something completely unexpected.

'Whatever happened to Angie, poor Angie? Whatever happened to her?'

The words came out in a lilting rhythm like the refrain of a song. At first Lisa assumed that's exactly what it was: a snatch of some old show tune or love ballad that had bobbed up to the surface. But there was an urgency and emotion behind the question that seemed at odds with the singsong tone.

'What did you say, Mum?'

Her mother repeated the refrain word for word, her eyes widening with dismay as if she was hearing it again for the first time in an age.

'Who's Angie?' Lisa asked.

Monika replied in a strange, distracted voice, dredging a memory from a well deep in her subconscious. 'The girl who broke Adam Fox's heart.'

Lisa was astonished by the range of emotions that played across her mother's face as she spoke these words: a flush of surprise, even wonder, at stumbling on this long-forgotten fragment of knowledge, but also an aching tone of regret. It was a powerful memory, obviously, but to Lisa it made no sense at all. Who on earth was Angie?

'Broke Adam Fox's heart, she did.' Monika was not looking at Lisa. She was focused inwards, remembering.

'Who, Mum? Who broke Grandpa's heart?'

A tear ran down Monika's left cheek. 'Angie, poor Angie, whatever happened to her?' she sang quietly to herself as she stared into the fog of her past.

'Who's Angie?' she repeated, but Monika would say no more.

Even so, Lisa raised the name again on her next two visits. There was no response. Monika either refused to answer or had genuinely misplaced it in her disordered memories. But Lisa did not forget the name nor the description: 'Angie' niggled at her, haunted her. *The girl who broke Adam Fox's heart.*

Lisa's grandfather had a reputation for liking women. The endless parade of glamorous female guests at his hotel had certainly offered plenty of opportunities for flirtation. Adam Fox was, by all accounts, a charismatic man who was very attractive to the fairer sex. Gossips said that he and Laura, his second wife, had begun an affair while he was still married to Adelina.

Lisa never met her grandfather but she'd heard many stories of his taste for extravagance and risk. He also loved fun. Her favourite photo of him, archived in a musty album in her grandmother's house, was taken at a formal dinner at the Palace in 1924. It was the Annual Staff Ball, a topsy-turvy celebration where rules were broken in the name of merry-making. In the photo Adam wore a woman's silk evening gown and sported an absurdly huge floral hat on his head. He smiled broadly, one arm wrapped around Laura's waist as he brandished a champagne bottle to pour a glass for his gardener, Stanley Hicks.

So who, apart from his two wives, had ever had the power to break the old man's heart? After the death of her son, Robbie, the already frail Adelina had descended into a prolonged battle with insanity which finally won the day in the winter of 1921, when she sought peace by taking her own life. Surely that had broken Adam's heart?

And then there was Lisa's grandmother, the startlingly beautiful Laura, who Fox fell in love with that same year and married the following spring. This marriage so soon after Adelina's death and to a woman less than half Fox's age was a scandal that set tongues wagging and heads shaking gravely. It was the kind of risky, rule-breaking venture that made Adam Fox's unconventional heart race with excitement.

Laura became the bright star at the centre of the hotel's second golden age in the 1920s, when the Palace became a glittering hub of celebrity and fashion. But even that great romance, sustained by wealth and a shared wildness of spirit and imagination, had eventually lost its fire. This was the tragedy that cast a shadow over Monika's childhood: her parents' estrangement, her mother's unpredictable moods and violent scenes. Was this not enough to break Adam Fox's heart all over again?

So who was *Angie*?

And then, one evening, as Lisa sat in the silence of the bungalow and flicked through her old photo albums, a memory came floating unexpectedly to the surface of her mind: something her grandmother had once said to her.

Lisa had not spent much time with Laura. She was a forbidding if alluring presence on the few occasions they had met at her beautiful flat in Mosman. The place was a treasure trove of luxury, art and exotica. Large landscape paintings hung on every wall and stunning silk rugs were spread on the floors. Grandma Laura spoiled Lisa and Tom with offerings of sweets and amused them with her frightening collection of curiosities: a shrunken head from Papua, a stuffed rattlesnake from Arizona and several witchdoctor masks from the Congo.

'Your grandad brought these back from his travels,' she told them. Sometimes she would bring out an old photo album and flick through the pages, telling stories of Adam Fox and the Palace. Their father would join them on the couch, as eager to hear this history as they were. Monika would storm into the kitchen to pour herself another drink, calling out, 'Nobody is interested in all those old fairytales, Mother!'

Monika did not encourage these meetings and tried to keep them to a minimum. After her divorce from Michael (during which Laura had provided plenty of unsolicited and unwelcome advice), Monika and the children saw less and less of her mother, their contact dwindling down to birthday and

Christmas cards and the odd phonecall. But Lisa never forgot those nights of storytelling at the flat in Mosman and, out of the blue, had insisted on inviting Grandma Laura to her twenty-first birthday. To her surprise, Monika relented.

It was a memorable night. Dressed all in white to match her long white plaited hair, Laura was a commanding figure, the very image of a grand matriarch. Downing glass after glass of French champagne, she had clapped loudly and enthusiastically as her granddaughter danced. Later, her grandmother had taken Lisa aside and presented her with a small velvet-lined box. 'You remind me so much of myself when I was your age. This is for you, Lisa. To wear next to your heart.' Inside was an exquisite brooch: a silver mermaid with emerald hair set against a lapis lazuli wave. It was breathtaking. 'My mother gave this to me,' whispered Laura, 'to remind me to always keep listening to the mermaids singing.'

Lisa knew the line from T.S. Eliot's 'The Love Song of J. Alfred Prufrock'. She hugged her grandmother fiercely. She sensed that this private moment was precious, too soon to vanish like a bubble on the stream. 'Can I ask you something, Grandma? I hope you don't find it – you know – too personal.'

Laura's eyebrows shot up in surprise but she was smiling. 'Try me.'

'Were you and Grandpa Fox in love – at the end?' she asked impulsively. It was a dangerous and absurd question, but she had to know the truth. Her own mother said little enough about the past but what she did say painted a bleak picture of her parents' marriage.

Laura stared at Lisa for what seemed an eternity. Lisa feared she had offended her. 'You want to know the truth?' she said finally.

'Yes, Grandma.'

'Always,' she said at last. 'Despite everything. We loved each other always.'

Laura closed her eyes for a moment. She then looked up at Lisa intently, placing a cool finger against her granddaughter's cheek. 'Forgive your mother a little if you can, Lisa. She suffered more than the others.' And then she said, so softly it was as if she did not care if anyone heard her words, 'It was Angie who broke all our hearts, poor girl.'

This strange scene and these words came back to Lisa with sudden force as she leafed through the photo albums on her couch. She got up and went to her room where she rummaged around and finally found the small velvet box shoved to the back of a dresser drawer. She took the mermaid brooch out of its velvet lining and examined it under the lamp on her bedside table. It was a thing of great beauty but also mystery. A memento. A clue.

'It was Angie who broke all our hearts, poor girl.'

That was the night Lisa decided that she must find out about Angie. She was the secret at the heart of her family that cast a long shadow over her grandmother's and mother's lives. It was why Lisa was here now, on the track from Sensation Point, making her way towards the Palace, where she had an appointment with a Mr Luke Davis, the professional historian hired to research the hotel's past for its new owners.

She tramped up the grassy slope towards the terrace. The crumbling salmon-pink battlements and patched domed roof rose out of the mist.

'The locals call it the Palace of Tears,' Luke had said on the phone.

As she climbed the terrace steps and saw a man waving to her in the distance, it dawned on Lisa that she was carrying a burden of sadness for three generations of her family. Maybe finding Angie would be a chance for her to find peace as well.

CHAPTER 3

Freya
Meadow Springs, September 1904

On this particular bright, calm, early-spring morning, Freya sat on her front veranda watching Angie in the garden at the bottom of the stairs. Her dark-haired angel was practising walking. She wobbled on her chubby legs and clutched without success at a spray of blackboy grass before sitting down suddenly with a look of comic indignation. Freya smiled.

Thankfully it seemed that the peak of the winter winds had passed. All through August Freya had lain awake beside the snoring bulk of her husband, Freddie, and listened to the gum branches thrashing the cottage's tin roof with their leaf-whips. Over and over she rehearsed the nightmare of a giant gum torn from its moorings and crashing onto their cottage, killing them in their sleep. Every night Freya lay awake, convinced that it was only her sleepless vigil that kept this catastrophe at bay.

There had been no wind at all last night and Angie had slept without waking once. Her mood seemed much sunnier this morning. So did Freya's for that matter. She took a sip of tea from her enamel mug and enjoyed the play of sunlight through slender, curving gum leaves. Maybe she would do some painting today.

So much had changed in the last few years but this view barely changed at all. The blue smoky haze over the valley, the orange and purple of the cliff faces on either side, the silvery-green canopy of the gum forest flashing in the wind along the ridges. This view was a comforting constant in Freya's life, a still point where she could anchor her mind when everything else was in flux. She liked to recall the sight of her father, sitting in his fold-up canvas chair, down at the bottom of the garden under the paltry shade of the tallest gum. He would sit there for hours in his dirty canvas hat, watching the sun creep across the valley, shadows shifting like pools of dark blue water, dabbing at his easel with small, precise strokes of his brush. White-haired, hoary-bearded, his eyesight starting to dim, Wolfgang made an imperious figure on his canvas throne, surveying his kingdom of kookaburras and cockatoos.

Her eyes closed for a moment, the warmth of the morning sun bathing her face so that she felt something akin to bliss. Unbidden into this peaceful hiatus swam another image: *his* face, those restless brown eyes and slick of sandy hair, a spattering of freckles on the bridge of his nose. How she ached to hold him in her arms just once more. She knew this love was forbidden now, must be kept hidden. Promises had been made, negotiated in the best interests of all involved. A very civilised settlement, a gentlemen's agreement, never to be mentioned again, a secret buried.

Her good husband, the broad-shouldered and solid Freddie, had come to her rescue in her time of isolation and heartbreak. She would always be in his debt, she knew, though Freddie did not see it that way and refused to speak of it. Other men might have held this secret over her as leverage, always there to be used in anger or cold-blooded manipulation. Not Freddie. He was not that kind of man. He truly loved her and, in a deep sense that was neither trivial nor cynical, Freya loved him back.

But the ache did not go away. How could it? Every now and then, just over the other side of her garden hedge when she least expected it, was the living, breathing reminder of that powerful, insoluble love that she had sacrificed. This sacrifice was all part of Freya's strategy of survival. The discipline that Freya showed in this was something she had learned from her father.

A kookaburra's cackle broke the moment of stillness. Her father had told Freya about the first time he heard one of those raucous outbursts as a young man, less than two weeks off the boat from Germany. In panic, the red-headed artist had bolted from his tent in the goldfields of Ballarat one morning, brandishing a knife. '*Mein Gott! Wo ist der Wahnsinnige?*' he had shouted, convinced that he was about to confront an escaped lunatic. Freya loved that story.

Freya's eyes fluttered open. Silhouetted against the morning light was a familiar figure. She felt the shock of recognition crackle against the nape of her neck and at her temples. Why did he insist on doing this, after everything they had negotiated? It was a sweet torment seeing him so close. She hated and forgave him at the same time, knowing how hard he found it to stay away.

Adam Fox was wearing his usual blond-straw Panama and carrying that same gnarled ivory-handled walking stick she had seen him with the first time he came into her garden six years ago. Out of courtesy and neighbourliness, Fox had come to tell the painter and his daughter about his purchase of the adjacent allotments of land and his plan to refurbish and extend the old Belmont Hotel. A two-storeyed Queen Anne-style brick confection, constructed opposite the railway line in 1892, this red-and-white gingerbread hotel of multiple cone-roofed towers and fancy fretwork gables was well screened from the cottage but had still brought more human and horse traffic to the once quiet escarpment. The von Gettners had grumbled about the intrusion but eventually accepted that they had to share their valley views with others.

Wolfgang and Freya had reluctantly invited the charismatic young man into their cottage for a mug of tea. Here, he had dispelled their initial aloofness by commenting intelligently on Wolfgang's watercolours, several of which were hung about the modest parlour. Fox confessed to being a keen art collector himself and an admirer of Romanticism in particular.

Freya had watched her father struggle with the decision as to whether to reveal his true identity. He had met many men like Fox – urbane, well-dressed, rich and with a dilettantish predilection for fine art. They had once been his champions and sponsors, the Melbourne business barons and their dynastic heirs, all silk-hatted peacocks strutting their wealth and good taste at auctions and gallery shows. But where were they now that he was poor and out of fashion? Fickle, preening, soulless bloodsuckers. It was they who had started buying up the canvases of the younger painters, Fred and Tom and Arthur – not because they appreciated their vision but because their works were favoured with prizes and critical attention and therefore ripened in value. It was those same men who had persuaded Wolfgang to sink his fortune into land and borrow against his assets. The collapse of the land boom saw his investments evaporate followed by the forced sale of his property to cover debts.

Wolfgang sent his two daughters, Freya and Eveline, away to a friend in Sydney so they would be spared the agony of the public auction of all the family's worldly goods and the mansion in the Yarra Valley. He was only thankful that his wife was not alive to endure this final humiliation. At least the ruined artist managed to hang on to his tiny cottage at Meadow Vale, as the township was called until Adam Fox prevailed upon New South Wales Railways to officially rename it 'Meadow Springs' in 1900. This four-roomed retreat in the bush became his hiding place from the world, where Freya joined him to share his seclusion. Her older sister, Eveline, had fallen in love with a newspaper journalist and settled into a flat in Cremorne.

Wolfgang listened to the young man with the walking stick praising his watercolours and said nothing. Later, Freya wondered if Adam already knew exactly who her father was and had been strategic in his seemingly guileless admiration. The previous year she had resorted to teaching art classes in the local village to raise a little extra money and had disclosed the family name to attract attention. Gossip spread fast in small townships.

The smooth young man explained his vision with a passion that even the weary painter and his protective daughter recognised as authentic. Fox described the beautiful hotel he wanted to build, modelled on the luxurious spas of France, Switzerland and Germany. It would be a place of calm and elegance where guests would come to heal both their bodies and souls with contemplation of the view and treatments from the local spring waters. It would feature the most modern technology available in the world, including a telephone system so that each guest would be able to make a call from their room and a German steam generator that would supply electrical power to the township. It would also boast the finest artworks from Europe and Australia, reflecting Fox's deep respect for cultural heritage: sculptures, frescos, murals, tapestries, ceramics and rich furnishings, as well as a gallery devoted solely to the display of paintings. He planned to spend more on these artworks than he had so far spent acquiring the land.

He then made an offer of three thousand pounds for Wolfgang's land and cottage. Freya's intake of breath was audible; a sum like that would ease their financial situation for a considerable time.

The young man explained: 'I have purchased several allotments further along the escarpment closer to Blackheath where I plan to build cottages. I would be more than happy to rent you one of these or sell you a block for a most reasonable sum.'

Wolfgang closed his eyes for a moment, his brow creased in thought. He opened them again and studied his visitor. 'Mr Fox, you strike me as a very sincere and determined young man. I have always thought Australia had the potential to be as fertile a cradle of artistic beauty and refinement as anywhere on earth. And so I sincerely wish you all the best for your venture. But I am afraid that my land and cottage are not for sale. I have my own reasons, just as compelling as your own, for loving this piece of the world. And I have no intention of giving it up.'

'I understand,' replied Fox. 'So I can safely assume that if I were to increase my offer to, say, four thousand pounds, and include the tenancy of a cottage rent-free for five years, this would not change your mind?'

'I'm afraid not.' Wolfgang's tone remained unwaveringly civil and warm, almost one of sincere regret that he could not accommodate Fox's request.

'So be it.' Fox then explained he would plant a tall hedge at his own expense around their land to protect their privacy during construction and for when the new hotel commenced operation. 'I wish to remain a good neighbour and, at the risk of presumption, even a friend to your family over time.'

'I have no doubt we will become firm friends, Mr Fox. Please feel free to join us for tea whenever you have the time to spare.'

Regrettably Wolfgang only met the passionate entrepreneur on three more occasions, during one of which Fox coyly asked if he would be allowed to buy one of his small watercolours.

The German master demurred. 'I seem to be always saying "no" to you, Adam,' he said with a regretful smile. 'It is unfortunate, as I have grown to like you. But the fact is I have developed a strong distaste for the buying and selling of art. Let me give it some thought. When your *Traumschloss* is finished, Herr Fox, maybe I will give something to you to put in your gallery.'

Fox never got his watercolour. Wolfgang died of pneumonia the following winter, one of the coldest on record with a fall of snow so deep that a path had to be cleared to the cottage for the undertaker and his boy to collect the old man's body.

Eveline and her husband visited as often as they could but the next year proved the hardest and loneliest of Freya's life. Looking back, she understood how, in her state of grieving isolation, she had let her guard down so that this charming and endlessly considerate man stole his way, little by little, into her affections.

He paid regular visits to the building site of the hotel and always found an excuse to drop by the cottage to check that the workmen were not disturbing her. Sometimes he had an artistic matter on which he sought her opinion or a problem he wanted to air in her presence. Sometimes he came bearing small tokens of his appreciation for her help. He was never accompanied by his young wife, Adelina, who preferred to stay in Sydney or in the family's country house in Meadow Springs.

The first time they kissed was in Freya's studio, where she was showing him a new painting she was working on. Almost idly, he leaned towards her and tucked a strand of unruly copper hair behind her ear. His hand lingered there and traced a line tenderly to her cheek. She sighed, almost groaned, surprised at the depth of her response to this unexpected touch, and rested her head in his open hand. He drew closer and kissed her exposed neck. Without a word spoken, they fell into a frenzied exchange of kisses, hands clutching and caressing with unbridled urgency.

Their affair lasted all through the building and opening of the Palace and its first giddy, golden year of parties and balls. It was, for the most part, conducted discreetly behind the giant hedge that Fox's gardeners had planted around the von Gettner cottage. Adam even helped Freya design a garden for her cottage which she insisted should be planted with native shrubs and flowers. Freya joked that she was a fairytale princess, a Sleeping Beauty, trapped behind an enchanted barrier and in thrall to the lord of the castle next door.

Fox opened the Palace on 4 July 1900 in the middle of a winter snowstorm. His guests were all motored up into the mountains from the railway station at Penrith in a fleet of closed-in, heated charabancs provided with woollen blankets and flasks of hot chocolate and rum. They arrived in excellent spirits to be greeted by an honour guard of bagpipers along the driveway and the dazzling spectacle of the immense Edwardian hotel covered in a layer of snow, perfect and pure as white marzipan icing on a cake. Freya watched all this from the far side of her hedge as Fox stood in the grand doorway welcoming each guest personally, his pale, marble-limbed wife at his side.

Guests gasped at the sight of the imposing edifice illuminated in a blaze of electric lights and were astonished to find that each guestroom boasted a telephone on the wall linked to the Sydney exchange and able to make a trunk call to anywhere in the world. More exotic and novel delights awaited them. Under the elegant barrel-vaulted ceiling of the grand dining room with its Art Nouveau frieze and Corinthian columns, a team of Chinese waiters in gorgeous silk jackets served up a seven-course banquet while two Turkish boys in embroidered vests and white fezzes poured steaming aromatic coffee into glasses from swan-necked copper pots. It was a masterful piece of theatre.

It seemed in those first heady years that nothing could dampen the zeal of Adam Fox, master showman and hotelier. The failure of his hired geologist to locate the local spring on the escarpment momentarily threatened to unwind Fox's whole vision for his health retreat until he found an exporter willing to ship him barrels of mineral water from Germany at a reasonable price.

The elegantly curved dome of the casino, specially designed and prefabricated in a factory in Chicago, ran into endless delays and escalating costs, but Fox negotiated a good price for the stock and improvements on the six-hundred-acre farm he purchased in the valley that would provide fresh produce every day for his hotel. He managed all these problems with his characteristic optimism and calm.

He handpicked all his staff, including Freddie Wood, local mechanic and all-round handyman, as his head storeman. Given odd jobs over at the von Gettner cottage, Freddie became a laconic friendly presence in Freya's garden, making observations about the weather and the state of the garden and hotel over short tea breaks. Then, one day, he addressed her in impeccable German. '*Heute ist ein schöner Tag, Frau von Gettner.*' He blushed to the roots of his sandy-brown hair. It was obvious he had not intended to give away his secret.

'*Sind Sie Deutsch?*' asked Freya, her eyes widening.

He nodded and looked at her sheepishly, crumpling his hat in his big hands.

She laughed out loud and gently touched his shoulder. 'Freddie! Why did you not tell me before?'

In an agony of hand-wringing, Freddie confessed to being intimidated by her father's reputation and aristocratic mien. Freddie was from Saarbrucken, capital of the coal and iron district of Saarland. The son of a coalminer who had emigrated to New South Wales forty years earlier, he had grown up in Cessnock and worked as a farm labourer before settling in Meadow Vale. He had been raised speaking German and

English and was indistinguishable from most sun-browned Aussie men of few words. By way of explaining the gap between himself and the von Gettners, he concluded: 'I am a simple man. I work with my hands.'

Freya held up a paintbrush from the studio. 'So do I, Freddie.'

Freya felt even more comfortable than ever having this quiet, sturdy man around. They still spoke little but more often now in their native German just as she and her father had done. She liked to wander over to his machine sheds to borrow gardening tools and watch the subtle dance of his fingers as they fiddled with the intricacies of a lawnmower motor or the rewiring of a damaged fence line.

When the nausea and vomiting started, Freya knew her world was about to change forever. The announcement of her pregnancy to Adam Fox came like a thunderclap out of a blue sky on a summer's day. She knew that 'arrangements' would have to be made, a 'solution' found to this 'problem'. There was never any question of Adam deserting his young wife or allowing his reputation to be compromised in any way. Freya did not make any demands; they had both been careless. But she refused to slip quietly away somewhere and leave her father's property. The cottage and this valley were the centre of her life.

Freddie approached his employer before he even breathed a word of his plans to Freya. His offer was approved and so Freddie Wood proposed marriage. Freya accepted.

She believed in survival at all costs. She had seen her father walk away from the wreckage of his life and survive. She would follow his example. Sacrifices had to be made. This way she kept her father's cottage and her old life but with a husband and handyman. She desperately needed the money and help maintaining the cottage. That was what she told herself, at least.

Sickly, frail Adelina had her suspicions and finally confronted her husband. He did not lie to her and they came to an understanding. Freya assumed that Adelina still held the purse strings to the fortune on which Adam had built his hotel. She exacted certain promises from her husband, insisted on certain rules. And Adam was a master of managing things, striking deals, making people see his point of view. After a difficult period of readjustment, life settled back down to a semblance of normality.

Now here he stood on this calm early-spring morning, patting Angie on the head, chucking her under the chin, a little self-consciously as he knew Freya was watching him. She had not seen him for months and certainly never here, alone, in her garden.

'What is it, Adam? What do you want?'

'I have an idea for the spa. I want you to paint me a mural.'

Freya gave a short hard bark of laughter. 'You are impossible. Adelina will not tolerate having me anywhere near you or that hotel.'

A sly smile spread slowly across Adam's face. 'It's not her I'm afraid of.'

'I think it's a terrible idea.'

'But you still want to do it, don't you?'

Adam was like a child in many ways. When he wanted something, he wanted it greedily, unreasonably, passionately and would hear no arguments to the contrary. It was one of his more charming qualities but, if Freya were completely honest, it was also what made Adam Fox frightening. Like a spoilt boy, he would lose his temper without warning if he didn't get his way. She had witnessed this on more than one occasion, including a time when he had smashed a chair to pieces in her studio and left a bruise on her wrist. He had replaced the chair and begged forgiveness for the way he had held her against the wall. She was ashamed to remember that the violent display had thrilled her at the time because he had shown her how the white heat of his love for her conflicted with his duty to Adelina and his cold-blooded calculations of social disgrace. But it also left her worrying how far Adam Fox would go to protect himself and everything he had built.

They were not so different, Freya and Adam. Fox's father was a poor Irish immigrant, one of the thousands who had come to Victoria to try their luck on the goldfields and one of the few who had then found their nugget of good fortune in commerce. After studying painting at the Arts Academy in Dusseldorf with fellow student Arnold Böcklin and then travelling around the art capitals of Europe, her own father had jumped on a boat to Australia to seek gold at Ballarat. Gold had eluded him for a whole wretched year on the fields; instead he had painted small sketches of his fellow Diggers and come to the attention of some wealthy pastoralists who commissioned paintings of their vast holdings, the beginnings of his illustrious career. As children of immigrants who had climbed the slippery ladder to wealth and respectability, both Freya and Adam knew what was at stake if they put a foot wrong.

Except that Freya had a much higher opinion of her father's calling than Adam's. Art trumped retail. She teased Adam about this and it upset him, because he knew it was true. The other difference, of course, was that Freya knew what it was like to fall from the exalted heights of society whereas Adam could only imagine – and fear – that fall.

'Your father would understand,' said Adam now. 'A commercial proposition. Nothing wrong with that is there?' He shifted restlessly and the veranda creaked under his weight. He was only twenty-nine, barely seven years her senior, but he was starting to grow a belly under his white linen waistcoat. Too much of his private chef's cooking and too many expensive bottles of whisky and champagne, no doubt; the occupational hazard of the rich. He had always taken pride in his fitness and had been the best advertisement for the Palace as a health retreat.

'You're getting fat!' Freya was not smiling.

Adam ignored her insult. 'We have a real rajah staying at the Palace. An Indian king, can you believe it? The Rajah of Pudukkottai. Molly has been paying him a lot of attention as he's a pretty well-turned out chap in a dinner suit. Muntz has gone to ridiculous lengths to impress him: curried kangaroo and barramundi kedgeree, that kind of nonsense. We're having entertainment on the terrace at six if the weather stays nice and the wind doesn't get up. Why not come and join us?'

Freya glared at him. When they had been in the deepest throes of their affair, Adam had risked inviting her to parties at the hotel when his wife stayed in town. There were lots of parties in those heady, early days. It was his secret risky pleasure: to show off his lover even though no one among his guests or friends officially knew of their liaison. He had purchased her a stunning mint-green beaded gown that set off her copper hair and blue eyes to perfection. Adam would introduce her as Frau von Gettner, daughter of the famous painter and a talented artist in her own right. 'I have one of her works in my collection in the gallery – a beautiful vista of Mount Wilson.'

She was grateful for his appreciation of her talent as well as the commissions she received from some of the hotel guests. And she loved the parties. They gave her a chance to experience once again the world of sophistication she had admired and expected to inherit as a young girl: the world she had lost when her mother died suddenly and her father's fortune evaporated overnight. At the Palace, an interesting crowd of regulars either motored up for the weekend or were long-term residents of the hotel, renting rooms in a separate wing, simply called the Apartments. Molly Fink, whose cultured family had fallen on hard times and moved into the Palace, was snaring the heart of an Indian king with her golden hair, perfect oval, ivory face and pert pomegranate lips. Quiet, handsome, muscular swimmer Freddie Lane, one of Adam's closest companions, had become an instant national hero as the only Australian to win a gold medal at the 1900 Paris Olympics. And charming American actor and master of comic impressions Hugh Ward, a star with J.C. Williamson's in Sydney, was in the middle of a spectacular world tour, winning plaudits in London.

Freya enjoyed this lively company and the sense of a world beyond this windy cliff top. Much as she treasured the quiet of the cottage for her painting, she definitely missed the talk of theatre, art and politics, the latest plays and exhibitions in London, Paris, and New York. One day, she would see these cities for herself. But with the pregnancy, the confinement, the marriage to Freddie, the shameful secret hidden behind the hedge, all this had ended. Under the new rules, the new reality, the parties and world of the hotel and beyond were closed to her.

Until now. 'What is the meaning of this, Adam?' she demanded.

'The meaning of what?' Adam pouted.

'Don't play games with me. You know exactly what I mean. I thought we had an arrangement. To keep the peace.'

Adam sat down in the chair next to her. They lapsed into silence for a moment as they both watched baby Angie make another courageous attempt at walking. Small hands floated on the air and pudgy feet pounded the grass as the excited toddler took two, three, four steps in a rush before her knees buckled again and she plumped back down in the grass. She clapped her hands to applaud her own cleverness, checking her mother had been watching.

'Well done, my sweetheart!' cheered Freya, raising her mug of tea in salute. She turned again to Adam, her question still hanging between them.

'Well . . . ?'

'Oh, Freya, if you only knew . . .' Adam groaned. His hand wandered from the arm of the chair and came to rest on hers. She pulled away.

'If *you* only knew, Adam,' she hissed at him, 'what this costs me. Every day. I have agreed to everything you asked, made every sacrifice, and asked nothing of you – except that I be left alone with Angie and Freddie. Is that too much?'

'But Freya . . .' His dark eyes misted, his voice grew husky. A twinge of pain crumpled his handsome face for a moment.

'What?' She spat the word out, blood throbbing at her temples. She knew what he wanted to say. That he loved her. That he wished the whole situation could be different. That he should have chosen her over Adelina. That he wanted to turn back the clock. Something like that. But he had had his chance and he had traded this love for his marriage, his wealth, his reputation, his hotel. 'It's too late, Adam. We both know that.'

Adam stared at her for a long time, his right hand white-knuckled on his walking stick, but she refused to meet his gaze. Angie had crawled towards the cottage steps and was now making an attempt to climb them. Freya rose from her chair, leaving her empty tea mug on the veranda boards, and scooped the baby up in her arms, kissing her cheeks and cooing in her face.

'Forget this evening,' he said finally. 'But I want you to meet me at the spa in half an hour to talk about the mural. You need the money and I am willing to pay you. I'll send one of the house girls over to look after the baby.' With that, he got up and walked away through the garden, without stopping once to look back.

The Hydropathic Establishment at the Palace was the undisputed domain of Herr Doctor Gustav von Liebermeister and his team of assistants and nurses. The doctor was a well-respected expert in hydropathy who had worked at health resorts in Switzerland and Germany. He been lured to Australia by Adam's vision of a state-of-the-art spa on which the hotelier promised to spare no expense. Adam kept his promise, giving Liebermeister licence to fit out his facility with the most modern equipment available.

The labyrinth of rooms included two Turkish baths; a packing room with twelve beds; three rooms with hot and cold baths (from sitz baths and Hubbard tubs to spinal, foot and head baths for shallow, plunge, douche, wave and common morning sponge baths); two shower rooms (needle and rose sprays, and the latest Leiters tubes); two poultice and bandage rooms for local applications (such as stupes, fomentations and rubefacients); an electrotherapy room with galvanic and electro-vapour baths; a gym fully equipped with standing bicycles and weights; a water-cure fountain and bar; and a large well-appointed rest room with steamer chairs and potted palms. The money and space had run out, however, for Fox to include a *salle de gagarisme* (a gargling room) like the one at Vichy. The good doctor claimed he could cure, or at least mitigate the symptoms of, an astonishing array of common diseases affecting every major system and organ of the body, extending to mental dysfunctions and disorders including alcoholism and drug addiction. His clinic was open to everyone from severely afflicted patients with chronic and debilitating conditions – the sufferers from gout and dropsy and lupus – to guests who felt they just needed a rejuvenating 'tune-up'.

Freya stood in the reception area, waiting for Adam. She had never trespassed in this sacred space with its stern priestesses in starched white aprons and caps and its hushed atmosphere of earnest whisperings and whimperings. The moss-green tiled walls and bare concrete floors with their water gutters and drains also gave the rooms the echoing reverberation of a church.

Freya could hear the steady trickle of a fountain in the adjoining room and could not resist the temptation to peek inside. This was the water-cure bar, dominated by a monumental ceramic fountain. A faint sulphuric smell filled the room. Freddie had told Freya that the steel containers in which the German mineral water was stored gave the water such a pungent odour and taste that, in Freddie's opinion, it was undrinkable. Dr Liebermeister insisted that the appalling taste only confirmed the water's powerful medicinal qualities.

He was able to use his intimidating personality to persuade guests that they must take a swig of the stuff before every meal.

'*Willkommen*, Frau von Gettner.'

Freya turned to see Dr Liebermeister with his usual tight little smile and stiff-backed stance. At Adam's insistence, Liebermeister had examined her during her first few weeks of pregnancy and administered several tonics in the cottage before she was sent away to Victoria, far from prying eyes.

Freya had only met the doctor twice socially, and then only briefly, as he did not make a habit of spending time with his employer or the hotel guests outside official hours, no doubt to maintain an air of professional aloofness. This was no great loss, as he disapproved of alcohol and had only one topic of conversation, which consisted of sermonising about the scientific principles of hydropathy and its benefits.

'Good afternoon, Herr Doctor. You are looking well as always.'

The lenses of Liebermeister's round glasses flashed like a pair of bright shillings in the overhead electric light, momentarily obscuring his eyes.

'Thank you, Frau von Gettner. I understand that you are here to add a much-needed touch of beauty to our clinical surroundings. I think this will prove a great boon to both our guests and staff.'

'You are too kind, Herr Doctor.' Freya could not quite put her finger on why she felt so uncomfortable in the presence of this man except that she felt naked under his unblinking gaze. And there was that small, tight smile, as if he knew some secret about you that you did not want known.

'Sorry, I'm late.'

Given the unpleasantness of their meeting at the cottage, Freya was surprised at how relieved she felt to see Adam.

He touched her lightly on the arm by way of greeting and apology. 'Let's take a look around.'

'If I may be excused, Herr Fox, I have some patients to attend to.' The white-bearded doctor nodded his head in a formal salute and turned smartly on his heel, leaving Adam and Freya alone.

Adam was brisk and businesslike at first, and then increasingly warm and enthusiastic as he explained what he had in mind for Freya to paint: a large mural of mermaids – plump and gorgeous like Herr Böcklin's – in the lobby and rest room, and smaller panels of sea maidens swimming up the walls in the water-cure bar, gym and reception area. They walked side by side, nodding politely at the nurses and patients, many of whom were barely conscious as they lay on beds wrapped in wet sheets or clothed in cotton gowns, being soaked from overhead pipes or hand sprays.

Freya tried hard to disguise the war of emotions in her heart. She looked sideways at Adam as he illustrated what he wanted with a play of his hands, his handsome face a study in sweet earnestness. She had always loved him best when he was like this, unguarded and uncalculating. Every now and then he brushed the loose fringe of sandy hair out of his eyes as he talked, a gesture so familiar it triggered a rush of memory in Freya that made her dizzy as moments of intense intimacy – lips, hands, seeking, exploring, taking – flooded her mind.

How easily she could submit to Adam's intemperate passion again. Her body craved him, every secret place of her. But it was not just about their love anymore. Everything had changed. Adam had made his choice. And remembering that, she felt afresh the heat of her anger and sense of betrayal that Adam had sacrificed her. Money and respectability had trumped art and love. The unfairness of it drove her into a kind of frenzy: to think that her family had once enjoyed the wealth and position that would have made Adam's choice so different.

And then she saw *her*.

As they passed through one of the bath rooms, Freya glimpsed a familiar face in the distance. It was Adelina. She lay floating in a large green tub, her cotton gown billowing in the dark water that bore her up, her face a bloodless, almost corpse-like white. She had her eyes closed and her head tilted back in the repose of sleep, cushioned it seemed on a pillow tied to the rim of the tub. Her arms, enclosed in water-swollen sleeves, were spread open in an attitude of total surrender, her wrists turned out, palms up. She was Ophelia, half-submerged in the flower-strewn stream, suspended in a dreamlike trance moments before drowning. Dr Liebermeister stood beside her as a nurse drew a canvas cover over the tub as if to encase Adelina in her watery coffin.

Freya gasped, her hand flying to her mouth. Liebermeister looked up and his glasses flashed again, those two menacing discs catching the light. He spoke to the nurse, who rushed to pull a curtain across the strange scene.

For a moment, Freya was too frightened to look at Adam. Her heart was racing and she had to steady her breath. What had she just witnessed? Her rational mind tried to reassure her it was some well-meaning medical procedure, but there was something about Adelina's utter helplessness, the deathly pallor of her face, the water lapping at her chin, threatening to close over her, that disturbed Freya deeply.

She had hardened her heart against Adelina for good reason. The White Witch had triumphantly snatched away one of the greatest joys of Freya's life. She would never be able to forgive her for that. But to see Adelina like this, so powerless and exposed, caught Freya off guard. For one rare, brief moment, her heart was pierced with pity for this other woman. Despite the disparity in their situations, Freya and Adelina had one thing in common: the vulnerability of their womanhood. Even with her inheritance, the truth was that whatever status and protection Adelina enjoyed as Mrs Fox depended wholly on her husband and the state of their marriage. To underpin that marriage, she had given Adam her fortune. To rescue that marriage, she had endured his unfaithfulness. With his eager consent, she surrendered herself to the tender mercies of Dr Liebermeister. Freya and Adelina both knew that beneath the true bonds of love, duty and affection between men and women there often lurked something else.

Fear.

Freya saw and understood all of this in a passing moment of insight but her empathy with Adelina stopped well short of forgiveness and would soon be forgotten.

She looked into Adam's face. What she saw took her breath away: a storm of humiliation, grief and anger that left no doubt about Adam's sincerity. Mr Fox desperately wanted to help his wife.

As she turned to leave, Freya prayed that she would never be in need of such help.

CHAPTER 4

Lisa

Meadow Springs, April 2013

'So I have my work cut out for me,' said Luke Davis. 'I wish someone had taken the trouble to interview your mother about her life here years ago. You know, before . . .' The historian coughed apologetically.

Lisa had already explained to Luke in their first telephone conversation why an interview with her mother would be unlikely to produce any reliable stories. 'Not that she ever wanted to talk that much about the past, to be honest.'

Lisa was surprised to discover that Luke Davis was younger than her, if only by a few years. When she had first contacted the hotel's new owners about their 'historian', she had expected someone much older: a white-haired, bespectacled fellow in a cardigan and bow tie. Luke *did* wear glasses and *did* have old-fashioned dress sense – a corduroy jacket and wool twill trousers for heaven's sakes – but he carried it off with a touch of hipster irony signalled by his chunky, black-framed spectacles and the leather satchel in which he carried his laptop. He had a handsome, slightly careworn face, olive-skinned and featuring a generous mouth, intelligent blue eyes and short dark hair.

Luke had been overjoyed when she rang. 'What great timing! You were next on my list.' He was clearly excited to have the interest and cooperation of a member of the Fox family for his official history.

Luke described the hotel's steady decline as they did the grand tour, avoiding several badly damaged rooms sealed off by plastic tape and wooden barriers. They stood inside the casino with its velvet-curtained theatre stage, Corinthian columns and distinctive dome. Luke explained that 'casino' was the old-fashioned name for a music and dance hall rather than a gambling saloon. 'Nobody ever gambled here,' he said. 'Gambolled, perhaps. Waltzed, foxtrotted, charlestoned, cake-walked. But never wagered a penny.' The room had resounded to the music of many decades and even played host to famous opera singers. Now a musty, broken shell of its former self, the casino was silent except for the fluttering of birds high above them, no doubt protecting a nest.

Lisa's heart was heavy. There was no nice way of tarting up the truth: the fact was that the 'old lady', as Grandma Laura used to call the hotel, was in a sorry state. The Palace had lost its lustre under the previous owners and business had continued to slump despite a major refurbishment. Five years ago, they shut down the property, searching in vain to find a buyer to recoup their investment. The Palace fell into disrepair, abandoned since the day the front doors were last closed.

Lisa's Nikon still hung around her neck. She had been taking photos of the hotel interiors as they wandered the echoing corridors and rooms. In the gallery, she stopped to catch a wedge of light slanting sideways through the filthy cracked windows onto the golden drapes, thick with a fur of dust, hanging limply from scalloped canopies overhead. In this sepulchral gloom, the walls were an accidental mosaic of squares and rectangles where paintings had once hung.

Luke showed her a storeroom full of antique objects that had been rescued from the hotel so far, hiding behind walls and closed doors or under floorboards: shelves of odds and ends all tagged and awaiting closer inspection. Tennis racquets in screwed wooden frames, a rosy-cheeked china doll, a stack of old records and a gramophone horn, a steamer trunk with a luggage tag from the SS *Saratoga*. Most eerie of all was a dark green rust-ringed steel tub with a rotting canvas cover and rubber pillow. 'We found it behind a partition in the hydropathic clinic,' explained Luke. 'A continuous bath I believe it was called. A patient would spend hours, even days, immersed in warm water to cure depression, that sort of thing.'

Each empty room held some mute testament to frozen time: a martini glass, rimed with dust, sitting on the Art Deco cocktail bar; a broken-heeled woman's shoe lying in the corner of the casino under the peeling fresco and cobwebbed chandelier; a shabby umbrella with no handle leaning inside the open case of a silenced grandfather clock in the billiard room.

Lisa concentrated on each shot for the right balance of composition and mood, trying to capture a sense of suspended time in isolated, quirky details and the interplay of past glamour and present ruin. She tried to shut out the smell of mouse droppings and mildew and the sound of wings in the rafters and scrabbling behind the wainscoting. She tried to not think about how her grandfather would have felt to see his magnificent hotel reduced to this shambles. A knot of grief tightened in her chest when she let her mind wander in that direction.

As they entered the conservatory, a long, plaster-ceilinged room with panoramic views of the valley, Lisa experienced a flashback. She saw herself at age six, sitting up at a white-damasked table next to a big picture window, eating vanilla ice-cream out of a monogrammed china bowl. It was her birthday and she was the special guest of Uncle Alan who, like his ageing but elegant hotel, had an air of seedy grandeur and old-fashioned stuffiness about him. She had loved that visit to the Palace as a little girl even as she was puzzled by its ambience of moth-eaten decay.

This memory came back with a rush of emotion so strong that it took her off guard. It was enough to make her reconsider her decision to dig up the past. Her only consolation was to hear how the new owners planned to restore the property to its former glory with the help of heritage architects. And Luke. He was equally determined to restore the hotel's past using whatever resources he could find. He already had scans of documents and photos on his laptop which he had brought to show Lisa. He was keen to make her an ally in his hunt for whatever other scraps of the past could be saved.

'I wish I'd taken more of an interest when I was younger,' confessed Lisa as they walked out the front doors and onto the portico. 'Monika refused to set foot in the place once she'd met my father and left home for good. I only came here a few times when I was little. Of course, Grandpa was dead long before I was born, and my aunt and uncle both died before I was twelve. By the time I wanted to know more, it was too late. I wish I could be more help to you.'

'Well, maybe you can. Do you think your mother might have anything stored away? Any family papers or photos?'

'I can check,' said Lisa. 'She has a basement full of stuff that no one has really been through for years as far as I know.'

They crunched their way up the gravel driveway, the mist clearing a little now as sunshine struggled through the low cloud cover.

Lisa stopped near the giant hedge on the western side of the hotel grounds. 'Can I ask you a silly question?'

'Please. Those are the best kind.'

'Have you come across the name "Angie" at all in your research?'

'Angie, Angie.' Luke flipped open his laptop and began searching. 'There's nothing coming up. Do you know anything about her? Was she a staff member?'

'I don't know anything really. It's just that . . .' Lisa hesitated.

Suddenly she felt self-conscious, even guilty. As if she was about to betray a confidence.

'What is it?' Luke prompted her gently.

Lisa sighed. There was no point in being coy if she was going to peel back the layers of family history. 'Well, it's just that Monika mentioned an Angie the other day. She said something about her breaking my grandfather's heart, which makes no sense to me at all from the little I know.'

Luke looked thoughtful. 'Sounds unlikely to be a staff member, though I suppose we shouldn't discount anything. Most of the staff stayed with the hotel for many years. I have a copy of a letter here from Mr Fox commending his cook to a new employer. It's quite touching how much he values the man's loyalty; he seems deeply upset to be letting him go. Maybe that's what your mother meant by "heartbroken".'

Lisa did not think that fitted the force of the emotion with which her mother and grandmother had spoken of Angie.

'And then, of course, there is the possibility she was a guest.' Luke coughed politely.

'Yes, I know, I know.' Lisa smiled. 'Grandpa was no saint. There were always rumours about his eye for the ladies.' She had heard quite a few stories of Adam Fox's legendary charm and his attraction to his famous female guests, from American burlesque actress May Yohé – a striking beauty of Algonquin Indian descent who had scandalised British society by marrying Lord Francis Hope and helping him fritter away his fortune, including the infamous Hope Diamond – to 'Sweet Nell' Stewart, acclaimed Australian songbird and star actress of

Drury Lane who had performed at the opening of the nation's first parliament in Melbourne. Mr Fox had apparently charmed Nell into giving an impromptu concert in the casino for the hotel's guests. 'I agree it's possible, but it still doesn't feel right.' Lisa had a strong sense that Angie was more than an affair or passing fascination; according to her grandmother, she had broken *all* their hearts. She had to be someone intimately involved in the family's fate. 'Who else was close to the family apart from the staff, do you know?'

'Well, it's hard to say. His first wife, Adelina, was a notorious recluse, rarely seen in public. She became even more isolated after the death of her son, as you probably know. His second wife, Laura, was very active in the local community with charities and what have you, but very little seems to be known about her family background. Adam, of course, had friends and business colleagues in Sydney and entertained them up here in the mountains at the hotel. He enjoyed company. Especially parties.'

'So he did.' Lisa smiled. Adam Fox and the Palace were famous for parties.

A yellow-tailed black cockatoo soared over the hotel's dome and landed in the fork of a huge gum tree on the far side of the hedge. Out of habit Lisa raised her camera and focused for a shot. Through the zoom lens she saw a dark-green door set into the hedge further down the gravel driveway as it swept towards the terrace.

'Where does that go?' she asked, pointing over Luke's shoulder.

'Oh, I almost forgot. The cottage. Do you want to take a look? It became part of the hotel after the Great War. We haven't decided what to do with it yet.'

There was something about the wooden gate tucked into the giant hedge that tickled Lisa's curiosity. Was it childhood memories of reading *The Secret Garden*, the fascination of a portal into a forbidden realm? Or was it something else stirring in her memory that drew her to this almost hidden entrance?

'Sure. If you can spare the time.'

The gate's hinges were badly rusted and it took several determined shoves from Luke to open it, twisting the iron-looped handle in his fist to lift the latch.

On the other side was what must have once been a well-ordered oasis of flowerbeds, topiary shrubs, arbours and lattices: a formal European-style garden but with the odd, disruptive presence of towering gums here and there, along with their litter of shredded bark and massive, earth-splitting roots. The result presented a strange juxtaposition of picturesque cottage garden and unruly bush; five or more years of neglect had seen bush gain the upper hand, swallowing up all the paths and beds in a sea of native grasses and thick wattle and bottlebrush. The huge tangled photinia hedge surrounded it on three sides but left the cliff-facing side open to a view of the valley, still sunk deep in mist.

The cottage itself was in a sad state, its tin roof heavily rusted, its deep wooden verandas riddled with termite damage and sagging with rotten floorboards.

'Careful,' cautioned Luke as Lisa mounted the two steps to look through the cracked windows at the front. It was only a small building, not more than three or four rooms at the most, Lisa guessed, but it had an irresistible charm: this quintessentially Australian bush cottage perched next to the overblown mock European folly of a hotel. Lisa found herself smiling, wondering how it had managed to survive all these years in the shadow of Adam Fox's fortress.

'So who lived here?' she asked.

'Well, for many years, it was part of the hotel. It was a small teahouse or kiosk serving food for a short while, and then a kind of exclusive private villa that guests could book separately. Quite something with that view.'

'Yes, I can imagine. And presumably the garden was in better shape then.'

'Before that it belonged to . . . I have a copy of the original title deed, believe it or not.' Luke found the relevant document on his laptop. 'Wolfgang von Gettner. See, here.'

He pointed to the screen and Lisa looked at the fancy signature at the bottom of the deed. 'I know that name,' she said.

'He was a nineteenth-century landscape painter.'

'Yes, of course.' Lisa's mind was immediately crowded with images of deep canyons, purple and gold in the coppery glow of a sunset, of roiling bluish cloud banks tinged with pink against pale lemon skies, of tiny figures in wind-blown hats and walking coats atop rocky outcrops, dwarfed by the expanse of a snow-capped mountain range or a river-carved, forested valley. She had studied the German Romantic-inspired landscapes of

Wolfgang von Gettner in her art history classes at university, and had even seen some of his works up close: large, iconic gilt-framed canvases hung in the National Gallery of Victoria in Melbourne and the National Gallery in Canberra.

'*He* lived here?'

'Yes. He bought the property in 1878, as you can see. And we know he died here in 1899. His wife had predeceased him in Melbourne in 1890.' Luke was glancing down at his laptop again but he seemed to know this historical background fluently. Lisa tried not to smile at the use of the word 'predeceased'.

'So why did he move *here*? He had lived in Victoria his whole life.'

'True, but his brilliant career there was coming to an end by 1881. That year he resigned from his position as Master of the School of Painting at the National Gallery of Victoria. His vision of the landscape was going out of fashion and young students like Frederick McCubbin, Tom Roberts and other painters from the Heidelberg School were painting the bush in a newer, more popular style. And then, to make matters worse, he lost nearly all his investments in the crash of 1891.'

'Poor man.'

'It must have been terrible. He had a reputation for being very proud.' He stared out at the misty valley, his face clouded with thought. 'He'd been one of Melbourne's wealthiest and most respected citizens, but all he managed to salvage from his bankruptcy was this cottage he'd bought for the odd painting trip to the Blue Mountains. This became his refuge from a world that had rejected him. He must have loved this valley; he painted it many times, mostly in small watercolours. Several of them still survive. There are stories of a last great oil painting of this view but it's never been found.'

'So he died here alone?'

Lisa tried to imagine the crusty old German, once the grand master in oils, sitting out here in his cottage garden making modest watercolours of this beautiful valley.

'No.' Luke snapped out of his reverie. 'He had two daughters, Eveline and Freya. We know Eveline married an Australian named Marsh and lived in Sydney for some years. Freya lived here with him.' He pulled up another image on his laptop. 'Here's an announcement in the local newspaper from April 1897 offering painting classes at a church hall in Katoomba with a Miss Freya von Gettner. Her father might have decided to retreat from the world but his daughter could not afford to be so proud. One of the exigencies of a rapid demotion in socioeconomic status, I'm afraid.'

Lisa laughed. 'Well, as long as you promise not to use any phrases like that, I think you've got a best-seller on your hands,' she teased before she realised what she was doing.

'Sorry, professional hazard.' Luke grinned. He didn't mind being teased, it seemed.

To be honest, Lisa was impressed. Luke seemed undaunted by the task of re-creating the hotel's past from the smallest clues. His enthusiasm was infectious; she wanted to help him – and she was keen to know more about her family's history.

She glanced at her watch. She had a meeting at her agency in Sydney with a client later that day. 'Well, I'd better not keep you any longer. I'll give you a ring when I've had a look through the basement. Fingers crossed something will turn up.'

'Thank you, I appreciate that.' Luke extended his hand and she shook it. 'And I'll keep an eye out for any mention of an Angie.'

Lisa slung her camera back in her zippered bag and headed back towards the green door in the hedge. She had just about reached the door, when she heard Luke calling after her.

She turned. 'Yes?'

'I don't know if you'd be interested, but I'm having a cup of tea with a Rosemary Cuff next Saturday, up at Mount Wilson. She's the great-niece of Mrs Wells, the original housekeeper here before the Great War. Mrs Cuff says she has quite a few letters written by her great-aunt. Would you like to join us? I'm sure she'd be thrilled to meet one of the Fox family. Maybe she could even shed some light on Angie?'

Lisa gave it a moment's thought. 'Yes, that would be wonderful. Thank you.' She then remembered Luke's ancient Toyota parked outside the hotel on her arrival. 'I'm happy to take us both out there if you like. It's been ages since I got out that way for a drive. Text me the time and I'll pick you up from here if that's convenient.'

'Thanks, that would be great.'

Returning to her car, Lisa heard the clarion blast of a freight train passing through Meadow Springs. The mist over the valley had lifted. All traces of the melancholy that had seeped into her soul down at Sensation Point were now gone, replaced by a kind of giddy excitement she hadn't felt in years; here, poised on the edge of something new and unknown, she felt it drawing her forward.

CHAPTER 5

Lisa
Mount Wilson, April 2013

Lisa sat on an ancient weathered bench which sprouted pale-green wisps of lichen. The sycamore towering overhead had a canopy of golden yellow and brown but many of its leaves had already dropped. They littered the lawn in front of her like a pile of desiccated scrolls. She picked up several of these crackly leaves, each one larger than the palm of her hand, and crumpled them slowly into flakes with a sense of contentment that was hard to beat.

She remembered jumping into a heap of autumn leaves that her father had just raked up and kicking the heap apart with a squeal of defiant pleasure. Dad would chide her with a playful prod of his rake or, if he was feeling particularly energetic, chase her round the big garden at Beecroft, chanting: 'Lisa, Lisa, gonna squeeze her, roll her out like a big fat pizza.' A memory from the good times.

That part of her life seemed so far away now it was hard to believe it was even real. She normally hated dwelling on the past because it confronted her so starkly with the present. Lisa would turn thirty-eight in two months' time. Her last serious relationship had come to an end over four years ago. She realised recently that she was spending far too much of her time alone, but her life as a freelance photographer meant she was often on the road for work, which made dating difficult. She had no day-to-day work colleagues as such, though she did catch up with other photographers for social drinks and networking now and then. On her worst days, she told herself that was the only reason she had become her mother's carer: for the company, unrewarding as it was.

Her life felt frozen and mysterious to her in other ways too. She had just spent eight months preparing a portfolio which she'd submitted to a well-respected art gallery director in Sydney in the hope of mounting an exhibition. Two weeks ago, the director had called her. She appreciated how much time he spent on the phone with her and how thoughtful he was in his reasons for rejection. 'The work is technically faultless, Lisa, and in some cases truly excellent. But the problem is I don't know what to think or feel when I look at the body of work as a whole. There's something missing: a story, an overall idea. I think you need to be bolder. To decide what you believe and not be afraid to express it in your work.'

After shedding some tears of dismay, Lisa decided that the director was right. It was time to be bolder. It was time to stop running away from the truth of her life and herself, no matter how confronting or absurd that might be.

She feared the truth. In dark moments, Lisa struggled with an almost superstitious belief that the women in her family were cursed. Was she mad to even contemplate such a thing? There was no denying that they made unhappy wives and bad mothers: Adelina's suicide following her son's death; Laura's turbulent marriage, which had embittered Monika's childhood; and Monika, in turn, losing her marriage and withdrawing her love from Tom and Lisa.

What chance did Lisa have? She had been told that, as an unwanted child, she had never learned what was reasonable to ask for emotionally, always scared of being either too needy or too detached. She was still the little girl at the locked study door, desperate for her mother's attention but finally deciding that she expected too much.

This curse was the burden carried by three generations of Fox women: a psychological inheritance of failure handed down from mother to daughter. It was time for that chain to be broken. Lisa wanted to know what had happened to her mother in order to understand and, if possible, forgive. It was the only way Lisa would be free. It was why she was here today. To put the family curse to rest.

Lisa took her camera out of its bag and took several shots of the church near where she sat while she waited for Luke, who had popped into the bakery next door to pick up something sweet – a ritualistic threshold gift, he explained in his dry amusing manner – for the afternoon tea they had scheduled with Rosemary Cuff.

The drive west from the Blue Mountains had been shorter than Lisa remembered. Once they turned off the main highway, there were few cars on the quiet, winding back roads. She remembered the views to the distant bluffs of the mountains and the expanses of undulating hay-brown farmland before climbing into the lusher foothills around Mount Wilson. She loved this retreat into deeper seclusion and calm. It was a photographers' mecca too, especially in autumn and spring, when flocks of shutterbugs came to walk in the cool, moist air of its rainforests or revel in its lavish heritage gardens. Velvety moss-clad drystone walls, the backlit tracery of tree ferns, fragile tapestries of fallen leaves, the hypnotic underwater light below avenues of plane trees and beeches – all these photographic treasures waited to be plundered.

Every time Lisa drove out here and saw the tall trees in the distance, picked out in startling oranges, yellows or golds against the uniform drab blue-green of the bush, she thought of her grandfather. Adam Fox was just like the pioneer horticulturists who had felt compelled to transplant these cool-climate exotics to the Australian countryside. It had once been fashionable to sneer at this colonial mindset, but Lisa believed that botanic and heritage gardens had their place in the bush, as did exotic hotels that mimicked the luxuries of Europe.

She was intrigued to learn from Luke – in one of the gathering tide of emails in her inbox over the last week – that Freya von Gettner's cottage garden was unconventional for its time: it had been planted with natives. He had found a grainy photo taken in 1911 that clearly showed beds of banksia, acacia, hakea and clumps of xanthorrhoea under stands of Blue Mountains ash, scribbly gum, coachwood and casuarina. Several of Freya's surviving botanical sketches, still in the hotel's collection, showed her eye for the jewel-like beauty of grevilleas, boronias, geebungs and wattles. Later photos of the garden, when the cottage was part of the hotel grounds, revealed the natives were all replaced with azaleas and rhododendrons.

'I hope she likes chocolate cake.' It was Luke, bearing a white carton in both hands as he approached the bench beneath the sycamore.

They climbed back in the Honda and followed Rosemary Cuff's directions to her house.

Rosemary Cuff was not what Lisa had expected. Knowing that head housekeepers usually came with reputations for discipline and stern high-mindedness as they struggled to impose order on the physical and moral chaos bubbling away behind a hotel's closed doors, she had imagined a prim, forbidding woman with her hair in a tight bun. Why Mrs Cuff should be anything like her great-aunt made no sense on reflection, but Lisa still smiled to herself when she and Luke were greeted at the door of 'Toadhall' by a cheery, thin, nut-brown woman with long, flowing steel-grey hair, wearing a Balinese-print chemise over cheesecloth pants.

'Come in, come in. I've got some chai brewing on the stove.' Rosemary beckoned them into her tinkling, polished cave of a cottage bedecked with dream-catchers, ceramic chimes, and mobiles of glass and crystal. 'Oh, aren't you thoughtful!' she crooned as she took the white box from Luke and ushered him and Lisa to an old divan draped in a faded sarong. 'I won't have any, dear, as I'm allergic to gluten, but let me cut you both a slice.'

The room smelled of vanilla and something pleasantly spicy. Smoke wafted from a candle on a sideboard among a huddle of ceramic burners, carved animals, sea shells and a gorgeous brass Buddhist handbell. Lisa made herself comfy on the divan and ran her hands through the fur of the large ginger tom curled up asleep on a cushion next to her.

'What's his name?'

'Darwin. I know I really shouldn't have a cat out here in the bush, but he's so old now and stiff in the legs he couldn't harm a bird if his life depended on it.'

Once settled round the low coffee table with their chai and cake, Lisa and Luke were joined by their hostess, bearing a box stuffed to the brim with manila folders. Luke had obviously communicated with Rosemary at some length as she seemed well-prepared for this visit and quite businesslike.

'Before we begin, I hope you don't mind me saying this,' said Rosemary, clutching Lisa by the hand warmly and bestowing on her a beatific smile, 'but it is very exciting to have Adam

Fox's granddaughter sitting right here in my cottage. Your grandad is quite the legend in our family.'

'Well . . . thank you. It's nice to be here.' Lisa decided she liked Rosemary.

Rosemary turned her attention to the box. 'I've been doing some digging of my own. Don't worry, I've made some copies for you, Luke.' She took out a manila folder and handed it to the historian. He thanked her, sliding out the contents, clearly impatient to take a look.

'It's mostly letters from Daphne to her brother Eddie in Geelong,' explained Rosemary, 'She was a keen letter-writer, as you can see. She wrote to him at least once a month for the whole time she was at the Palace, right up to when she left in 1921. Thankfully my grandfather saved most of them.'

'Why did she leave?' asked Lisa, adding, 'If you don't mind my asking.'

'No secrets here,' said Rosemary. 'We must shine the historian's light unblinkingly into dark places. She left because she was unhappy. At least that's what she writes to Eddie. It was a terrible year at the Palace in many ways. Lots of things went wrong – the worst being the suicide of Adam Fox's first wife.'

'Yes, I've heard about poor Adelina.' Lisa felt a pang of guilt when she spoke the woman's name. This part of her grandfather's story made her feel very uncomfortable. She had always hoped the reason for Adelina's despair was grief for the loss of her son rather than Adam's affair with Laura. Whatever the truth, there was an undeniable whiff of shame about the haste with which Laura had supplanted Adelina in Fox's affections.

'Yes, yes. Very sad affair. Daphne seems to think she never did really recover from Robert's death. And she wasn't that strong to start with.'

'These are wonderful,' said Luke, looking up from the folder that he had been leafing through. 'She talks about the dismissal of the German staff in 1916 because of fears they were "disloyal and dangerous". I didn't know about this.'

'Oh yes, I'm afraid she does not cover herself in glory there,' said Rosemary. 'I suspect anti-German feeling was running high at the time. She was a dry old stick, Daphne, pretty narrow-minded in many ways. Admired your grandfather immensely, of course, but makes it clear that she thought he was far too soft on his staff.'

Lisa was interested, of course, in any light that the housekeeper's letters could throw on the past, but she was most curious to know if they made any mention of 'Angie'.

Luke must have picked up on Lisa's impatience. 'Rosemary, do you remember that I asked you about an Angie? Did you find any reference to her?'

'Ah, yes. I certainly did.' Rosemary became quite excited as she shuffled through letters and pulled one out marked with a pink sticky tab. Lisa felt a tingle at the back of her own neck.

'I think this is who you mean,' said Rosemary, finding the right page. 'Listen to this from 2 February 1914. May I?' They nodded, and she read the letter out loud.

Dear Eddie,

I am sorry for the long gap in our correspondence but these last weeks have been among the most intolerable in living memory. It is hard even now for me to write this letter as we are all here in the deepest shock and mourning. As I put pen to paper, I still find it impossible to believe what I am about to tell you.

Over two weeks ago, young Master Robert fell to his death from Sensation Point on the track near the hotel. I think you know the spot well as we have walked there several times on your visits and it is a favourite lookout for our guests. As if the tragedy could be any worse, this fatal event took place on Master Robert's thirteenth birthday with all his family and friends gathered to celebrate. My spirit is sorely tested even now to relate the terrible scenes I witnessed that day.

It is almost beyond the power of words to describe Mrs Fox's anguish at the news of her son's fate. How pitifully she clung to the hope that her beloved boy might have, by some miracle, survived the fall. How desperately she beseeched God to preserve her sweet child, offering herself up in his place. We all wept bitterly that day but none more so and with a purer heart than Adelina Fox. Her suffering was beyond all endurance.

I cannot do justice to the courage with which Adam Fox led the search party into the valley below. For four hours I attended Mrs Fox as we waited in an agony of anticipation for the searchers to return. I never thought I would live to see a sight so heart-wrenching as that of Mr Fox carrying the broken body of Master Robert from the cliff top. The utter despair that had taken possession of that man's face is a sight I shall never banish from my mind.

There was, of course, worse to come: Adelina Fox's cries of distress on beholding her dead boy. 'This is all my fault!' she wailed, cradling her son's pale face in her hands and wetting his cheeks with her tears. Oh, wretched motherhood that must bear such grief! Mrs Fox cried up an ocean of tears that day and it took Dr Liebermeister's expert ministrations to finally calm her.

Rosemary Cuff's eyes misted a little and her voice grew husky. 'Poor woman,' she whispered, clearing her throat before reading on.

At that point there was a dramatic new development. A man came forward claiming to have witnessed Robert Fox's final moments, insisting that he saw a young girl push the boy to his death. He identified the girl in question as none other than Angela Wood, only daughter of the head storeman Frederick and his wife Freya Wood from the neighbouring cottage.

Angie, as she is better known, had been a summer playmate of Master Robert's for some years, though it was clear their friendship had come to an end as no one at the hotel had seen her since last summer. Robert had not invited her to the birthday party that day either, a fact of which I was painfully aware as Frederick Wood had come to see me about this awkward matter earlier in the week.

The witness – a bushwalker approaching from the western end of the track – claims he saw Robert and the girl struggling at the cliff edge before he was pushed. Confronted by her father, the hysterical girl denied this accusation vehemently and returned to the cottage for further questioning by the Katoomba police officers.

Thankfully most of the party guests had long departed and were therefore not present to witness the abominable scene that followed. Mr and Mrs Wood were summoned by Mr Fox to seek an explanation for what had happened. I have expressed my private suspicions and concerns about Mrs Freya Wood, nee von Gettner, in my letters before this occasion, you might remember. She is an artist and one of that breed of young bohemian women who seem to think they live outside the normal moral rules and conventions of society, whether from some delusion of superiority or divine dispensation I cannot say. But I have noted before that her influence on Mr Fox has been, in my opinion, a pernicious and corrupting one.

My doubts about her state of mind were confirmed by the most appalling confrontation on this day in which she wept and screamed at poor Mr Fox. 'This is the price that we pay for our lies!' I heard her say. Mr Wood had to physically restrain his wife and escort her forcefully from the hotel.

At Mrs Fox's insistence, Robert's governess Miss Jane Blunt has been dismissed without any references despite years of loyal service. This is punishment of course for what Mrs Fox sees as her failure of vigilance to protect Master Robert. I do feel sorry for the poor woman. Don't misunderstand me when

I say that Robert was a charming young man but he was also headstrong like his father and not an easy child to discipline at the best of times. While I sympathise deeply with Mrs Fox's grief and rage, I do not believe the governess was remiss in her duties and therefore should not have borne such a heavy burden of blame for this tragic event.

Though there will be a coroner's inquiry, Mr Fox has made it clear that he believes the Wood girl did nothing out of malice aforethought and he will not be seeking any retribution through the law for his son's death. However the wretched girl is now banished from the hotel grounds, as the mere sight of her is a provocation and disturbance to the Foxes' peace of mind in their grieving. While we respect Mr Fox's decision in this affair, it remains a matter of firm belief among the staff that this callous and selfish girl, whether out of childish jealousy or foolish negligence, by accident or by design, was responsible for the death of poor Master Robert.

Lisa sat there, stunned. She could still smell the vanilla and spice candle and the fragrant milky steam from the cups of chai. She could hear the sound of the wind in the trees outside, the chink-chink of parrots and the purring of the tomcat dozing next to her. But it was as if the present-day world had ceased spinning for a moment and the horror and pity of that awful day long ago flowed through a gap in time and worked their power on her. Tears trickled down her cheeks.

Without knowing all the facts, the motives and circumstances, and even at this great distance, Lisa still felt an overpowering surge of compassion for all those involved. Because she suspected that this day had been a turning point in the lives of nearly every one of them. And in the lives of many others to come after them.

'*It was Angie who broke all our hearts, poor girl*,' her grandmother had said to Lisa. Well, that much was clear from this letter. Adam Fox's heart for one. Was he ever able to be a truly carefree, loving father again? Monika's refrain ran through Lisa's head. '*Whatever happened to Angie, poor Angie? Whatever happened to her?*' How did her own mother know about this girl? What had Laura told her?

Rosemary patted Lisa's hand and poured her another cup of tea. 'I'm sorry, Lisa.'

Lisa shook her head. While appreciative of Rosemary's sympathy, she was eager to know the truth, however painful, and anxious to learn more. 'Thank you, I'm fine. Do we know what happened to Angie? You know, I mean, after that?'

'I think we do – a little anyway,' said Rosemary, fishing through the letters again and finding a second pink tab. 'Here it is. Dated October 1916.' Rosemary coughed apologetically. 'This is not a pleasant letter either, I'm afraid. My great-aunt was not the most forgiving person in the world. And, well, times were different, I suppose you would have to say.'

She found the relevant passage and read aloud:

At last, dear Eddie, I can report that a kind of justice has finally been served. As I told you, two of the German staff were dismissed a month ago thanks to the lobbying of Mr

Hawthorne and myself. Our patriotic duty done, two military district officers took Frederick Wood and Chef Muntz away for internment in the Concentration Camp at Holsworthy.

Three days ago, I found out that Freya Wood and her daughter have elected to move to Liverpool to be nearer to the camp and Frederick. This morning, they vacated the cottage with all their goods in a motor van. Mr Hawthorne informed me that Mr Fox has arranged to pay the moving costs and gave Mrs Wood a considerable sum towards the rental of a house. God forgive the soft-hearted man.

Lisa stared at Luke in mute astonishment.

'This is all news to me,' said Luke, looking just as surprised as she felt. 'We have some more research to do.'

Rosemary read excerpts from several more letters and Luke showed her some photos on his laptop. Mrs Wells certainly made an imposing figure in the two photos in which she made an appearance: a tall, long-necked woman with a stern triangular face framed by dark hair, which was severely restrained by combs, Lisa noted, not a bun.

Lisa kissed Rosemary Cuff on the cheek as she left. 'Thank you for sharing your great-aunt's letters,' she said.

'It was a pleasure, my dear. I only hope they help you find whatever it is that you're looking for.' She squeezed Lisa's shoulder.

As she headed back to the car, Lisa stopped to take photos of Rosemary's garden. With the sky rapidly darkening under a bank of thunderheads, a strong storm light illuminated the autumnal trees in front of them; it made every surface glow with an inner radiance and rendered every detail startlingly clear.

This burning clarity was beautiful. But, try as she might, Lisa could not dismiss an unsettling conviction that such brightness was a sign of a great disturbance to come.

CHAPTER 6

Angie
Meadow Springs, January 1914–November 1915

It was all her fault. Robbie's death. The war. Her father being taken away to a prisoner-of-war camp. People throwing stones at their windows. And now this: her mother's decision to leave the cottage and move in with Auntie Eveline so they could be nearer to her father. Such were Angie's thoughts as she lay, curled up in a ball of misery, inside her hedge, waiting for the removalist van to come and take them away.

She had told the police the truth about that terrible day with Robbie. They wrote it all down and took it to court for a coronial inquest. Whatever that other man, the bushwalker, said was a lie. She might have pushed Robbie away from her but she did not push him over the cliff. The coroner's court dismissed the man's testimony as unreliable as he was standing 'at a considerable distance from the two children with foliage obscuring his line of sight'. The cause of death was determined as accidental and the hotel was made to build a fence along that section of the track to prevent any such tragedy ever happening again.

Even so, there were many days after that when she felt as if she *was* to blame. Over and over, the 'what if' questions nagged at her. What if she had never stolen the postcard? What if she had given it to him on the lawn? What if she had turned the other way and run to the flying fox instead of along the narrower path to Sensation Point? What if she had not been so foolish as to fall in love with Robert Fox?

Freya and Freddie had been angry with her for the theft of the postcard, but they were unable to find the words to chastise her for what happened at the cliff. What could they possibly say that would encompass the awfulness of Robbie's death? Maybe their reticence was also because they both knew, in their hearts, that her mother had played no small part in encouraging Angie's resentment towards the party and, even before that, her friendship with Robbie.

To be honest, Angie was used to Freya's anger and would have preferred it. Her mother had retreated into silence for days on end, a white-faced, shrunken silence in which tears leaked from her eyes and she moaned like an animal in pain.

Looking back, Angie wondered if Freya knew then just how terrible the consequences of Robbie's death would be, how the whole world would turn against Angie and her family, and their simple life at the cottage would be torn apart.

Her father also seemed bowed down, crushed under the weight of the disapproval he felt directed at him by his colleagues at the hotel. It seemed to be the way of the world that when something bad happened, someone had to be blamed. If not Angie, then it would be her father, accused of being too soft-hearted and lenient with Angie, for letting her mother encourage her to think she was better than she was.

There was one surprise none of them anticipated: a letter from the governess, Miss Blunt. While the full force of Adelina's rage was focused on Angie and her parents, Miss Blunt had taken some of that heat for ignoring her charge that day, despite the fact he was a young man perfectly capable of looking after himself. She lost her job, of course, and was given no references despite her years of service. Her letter was short but kind: 'Please tell Angie that she is not to blame for what happened and that she must forgive herself.'

Mr Fox did not come back to the hotel for another six months. There were even rumours that he would sell the Palace and walk away from this painful reminder of his son's death, either out of his own grief or at the insistence of his distraught wife. The rumours proved to be false but they caused such distress among Freddie's colleagues that, again, the poor man bore the burden of their hostile stares and icy demeanour.

Freddie's boys – Ben, Wally, Jacko and Dave – stayed ferociously loyal to their boss, communicating their sympathy without any formal declarations but with determined cheerfulness and hard work.

Of course, Angie knew she was not really to blame for the war, though it came so soon after Robbie's death that sometimes the two things were merged in her mind. The war was the fault of the Kaiser and Germany, according to the newspapers. At first Freya refused to take any interest in 'this lunacy' and insisted Angie ignore it too. But with his usual gentle insistence, Freddie persuaded Freya to let Angie read the papers and ask questions if she wanted to. 'She's bright, Freya, and she wants to know.' Angie *did* want to know, even though she could not imagine for a moment how this great drama thousands of miles away could possibly affect their lives in Meadow Springs. It would not take long for her to find out.

On 10 August 1914, only six days after Britain had declared war, Dr Liebermeister and Chef Muntz reported to the police station in Katoomba. They had both kept their German citizenship and so, as subjects of the Kaiser, they were required to fill in yellow registration forms as 'enemy aliens'. As well as providing all their personal details, declaring any firearms and agreeing to report to the police station once a month, they promised to 'neither directly or indirectly take any action in any way that was prejudicial to the safety of the British Empire during the war'.

'How many guests of the Palace do I have to poison with my undercooked salmon before it's considered "prejudicial to the safety of the British Empire"?' joked Chef Muntz grimly later that week when Freddie came by with blocks of ice from the freezing works. The storeman shrugged. He noticed that Muntz had been careful to share his joke in German in case any of the kitchen staff overheard.

The same day the cook and the doctor registered as enemy aliens, the newspapers announced recruitment offices were opening all over the country to raise the twenty thousand soldiers Australia's prime minister had pledged to Britain. The war came a little closer to Meadow Springs when Freddie's two youngest boys, Jacko and Ben, went down to Penrith to sign up for the First Division of the Australian Imperial Force. Freddie went down as well, watching over them in a protective fatherly fashion as the only way he could express his grief at letting them go.

'Don't worry, Freddie,' Jacko told him with his cock-eyed grin. 'You'll have to work a bit harder until Christmas and then we'll be back to help you out next year.'

'Yeah, well, I reckon I'll get a lot more done without having to chase after you two clowns the whole time,' Freddie laughed, though his heart wasn't in it. 'Just as long as you promise to keep away from those bloody bullets!' When Jack and Ben finished their training, their battalion was scheduled to embark for Egypt.

Angie liked Ben and Jacko. They had been in the search party that collected Robbie's body from the valley but they never looked at her unkindly or said a bad word. She was banished from the hotel and its grounds, so she hardly ever saw anyone from the staff, but every now and then Freddie's boys greeted her with a wave if they spotted her in the distance in the cottage garden or on the way to school. Now Ben and Jacko were gone and she could tell their absence haunted her father, who had only just managed to hang on to Wally and Dave as they were not fit enough to join up.

One evening shortly afterwards, Angie had her head bent over her homework in her tiny bedroom when she overheard her parents talking in the kind of earnest whispers she knew from long experience meant upset and trouble. Angie crept to the bedroom door and put her eye up to the crack of light.

'What if they decide we are not loyal?' she heard Freya saying. Her mother had handed Freddie his supper and was pointing at the copy of *The Mirror* lying open on the table. 'It says that Britain has already started locking up their Germans and we should do the same.'

Freddie took a sip of the broth. He reminded his wife that *The Mirror* was one of the nastiest of the Hun-hating papers with its cartoons of ape-like soldiers in pickelhaubes, menacing nuns with bayonets and machine-guns.

'It makes no sense to do it here,' Freddie reassured her. 'Of course, they had to lock up the crews from German merchant marine and naval ships, that sort of thing, as they can't go home. And I read that some German plantation owners and their families have been brought out here from New Guinea and Fiji. But why would they lock up us Germans already living here? Except for some German nationals like Muntz, we are mostly Australian citizens like you or naturalised British subjects like me. We've sworn an oath to King and country. And anyway, what could we possibly do to help the Kaiser, all the way over here?'

Freddie's reasoning made good sense to Angie but did not seem to reassure Freya.

Only a few weeks later, Freddie was enjoying his usual Friday-night lager up at the Gardner's Inn in Blackheath with Wally and Dave. They listened to Tom Coffee telling the publican a story he had heard from Sydney.

'This bloke tells me that the Waverley Political Labour League have adopted – and these are their exact words – "a pledge to abstain from the drinking of Resch's Ale for the duration of the war".'

The bar erupted in a roar of laughter.

'Won't let a drop of the nasty Hun beer stain their dainty lips!' shouted Tom as he took his handle of the precious amber from the outraged publican and raised it by way of a toast. 'Bunch of bloody crackpots, if you ask me! It's the best piss in town! Drink up, boys!'

Freddie cheered, as did all the men at the bar, and raised his glass in solidarity with his fellow Australians. He told Freya and Angie the story when he got home to cheer them up and reassure them that, in the Blue Mountains at least, nobody took this kind of anti-German nonsense seriously.

Freddie knew that this pledge was a protest against the big brewery in Sydney founded by German immigrant Edmund Resch. He had seen the old man's photo in *The Mirror*: a dapper white-bearded gent who had lived in Australia for over fifty years. Herr Resch had handed the business over to his two Australian-born sons and, in a very public effort to prove his patriotism, promised to make-up to full pay the wages of all his staff serving with the AIF. But Edmund's generosity did not save him. *The Mirror* kept up a determined campaign to have him arrested and, soon after, Freddie read how Edmund, aged seventy-one, was taken from his harbourside mansion on Darling Point and sent to the internment camp at Holsworthy, in the bush near Liverpool.

Despite fewer bookings from overseas guests, life at the hotel continued much as normal. With some of his previous vigour and zeal for publicity returning, Adam Fox drew up plans for a large civic dinner at the hotel in December to raise money for the war effort and boost community morale. The mayor and the federal member of parliament were to be the guests of honour. There was a rumour that renowned English contralto Clara Butt, currently on tour in Australia, would make a guest appearance to perform 'Land of Hope and Glory', the rousing patriotic song that Sir Edward Elgar had composed especially for her powerful voice. Anticipation was at fever pitch in the upper Blue Mountains and everyone at the Palace, including Freddie, was kept busy sprucing up the hotel for the big day.

A week before Christmas, Freddie was working in the garden when he saw two army officers from 41st (Blue Mountains) Infantry arrive with their driver and march into the lobby, where they were greeted by Mr Hawthorne. It seemed they had an appointment to see the general manager and Mr Fox.

Freddie did not mean to eavesdrop on the conversation in the GM's office, but it was hard not to overhear the angry, raised voices. Fox stormed out shortly afterwards and Freddie caught the words 'speak to my solicitor'.

Mr Hawthorne explained the whole thing to Freddie the following day. The two officers had come to inform them that under the War Precautions Act the Palace was ordered to cease all trade with any businesses in Germany or any German-owned companies in Australia. This trade included the Hydropathy Establishment's importation of mineral spring water, shipped every two months from Baden-Baden.

As it happened, Fox had already sourced an alternative supplier. The costs of shipping and insurance from Europe had become prohibitively expensive as German U-boats targeted merchant shipping. The previous year a small brewery in the nearby town of Lithgow had begun bottling spring water as a medicinal tonic and Fox was happy to give the locals his business. Freddie now stacked up the barrels of Lithgow mineral water in the basement where the German mineral water barrels had once been stored. Even so, Fox resented this kind of interference in his affairs. He sought legal advice and was told there was nothing he could do: the War Precautions Act conferred extraordinary powers on the government that could not be challenged.

In the New Year, the newspapers continued to bombard their readers with grisly tales of German atrocities in Belgium and France. Over breakfast Angie would read out the headlines from the *Sydney Morning Herald* and ask her father which bits interested him the most. She knew he wanted to hear any news he could about Jacko and Ben's battalion training in Egypt.

From April 1915 the papers were full of reports of the Australians fighting and dying on a peninsula called Gallipoli. Angie read out loud the eyewitness account by the war correspondent Mr Bean of the first day of the ANZAC attack. Australians stormed 'tier after tier of cliffs and mountains apparently as impregnable as Govett's Leap' and occupied enemy trenches 'like a section of the Blue Mountains, full of winding gullies'. Freddie listened solemnly as he ate his boiled eggs. Angie also read out the lists of men killed in action. She and Freddie said nothing to each other, sharing in silence their dread of finding a familiar name.

One day in early May, as Freddie was working down at the sheds, he saw Chef Muntz at the back door of the kitchen beckoning urgently. 'Come, come,' he said in a loud whisper, trying not to attract attention from any of the other staff. It was mid-afternoon and most of the kitchen hands were on a short break following the lunch service. When Freddie stepped inside the warm kitchen, to his surprise he found Dr Liebermeister standing by a bench, looking exceptionally agitated and grim.

'Coffee?' the chef asked.

Freddie nodded. 'Yes, thank you.'

What was this all about? Such a gathering was highly unusual. Freddie and his two colleagues had never had much reason to speak to each other in the past. The hydropathist was clearly the social superior of the cook and the handyman, and the chef regarded his own station loftier than Freddie's. Their relations were always polite, civil, formal. So why the sudden outburst of hospitality?

'Have you seen today's paper?' asked the doctor, clutching that morning's edition of the *Herald*.

In the rush for school, Angie had not had time to share the daily news with her father. Freddie shook his head.

The doctor held up the headline. It read: LUSITANIA TORPEDOED OFF IRISH COAST.

The doctor read out the story. A German U-boat had sunk a British luxury cruise liner off the coast of Ireland. Nearly twelve hundred lives had been lost, provoking outrage around the world. The German government had not improved matters by declaring a public holiday to celebrate the sinking and trying to claim that the ship was carrying munitions.

'People are very angry, as you can imagine,' the doctor told his colleagues. He had been on the phone that morning to a medical colleague in Sydney who described how German shopkeepers in the city had had their windows smashed when the morning papers hit the newsstands.

Muntz nodded. 'My brother Hans heard about a worker at the local biscuit factory in Alexandria who was beaten unconscious – just because his name was German!' He then told them about the Anti-German League, a fast-growing patriotic association with over thirty branches across New South Wales, including one in Penrith. 'Trouble has been brewing up here for some time,' Muntz continued. He was a paid-up member of the golf club in Blackheath. Until recently, one of his regular golfing partners had been a German fellow named Alfred Marx who ran a real estate agency in Katoomba. A business competitor who had signed up with the AIF wrote an angry letter from his training camp in Liverpool to the local newspaper asking 'why this German should be allowed to trade while other Australian real estate agents were away fighting' and demanding that he be interned.

'It turns out others shared this opinion,' Muntz told them. 'Last week the police decided they had received enough reports of "suspicious" and "disloyal" behaviour to have Marx arrested and sent down by train to Holsworthy. His business is now boarded up and the golf club has cancelled his membership.'

Dr Liebermeister was particularly aggrieved by his own shabby treatment as a registered doctor. Two months earlier, the professional body for Australian physicians had cancelled the membership of all German-born doctors.

'It is only a matter of time before they arrest us all,' hissed the doctor, his glasses flashing in the bright lights of the kitchen. I hear there are literally thousands of internees held in this prison camp in Liverpool. And they lock people up there without a proper trial or any kind of legal defence. It is a disgrace.'

'We live in difficult times,' said Muntz philosophically, handing his countrymen fresh cups of coffee. 'I know Mr Fox will do everything in his power to protect us, but it is clear that anyone German is being watched – even Australians with German backgrounds like you, Freddie, and Freya. I know that the police do their own surveillance, but they also listen to what other people have to report. Neighbours, co-workers, friends. So be careful who you talk to and what you say.'

The three men sipped their coffee in silence for a few minutes. They agreed to keep their ears out for any nasty rumours and to meet again in a week or so. Freddie thanked them both for their trust and, with a heavy heart, went back to work.

Angie saw the change in her father. He became distant and distracted, and when he was tired, his right hand shook ever so slightly. He gripped the arm of his wicker chair out on the cottage veranda to hide the tremors but Angie saw and noted every little thing. But if Freddie seemed weakened by the family's isolation, Freya had become possessed with a fanatical, almost manic energy. She spent every hour from dawn to dusk in her studio, working with the curtains drawn and the door shut tight. On the one occasion that Angie had ventured inside with a message from her father imploring her to come and have a bite of lunch, Freya had angrily dismissed her.

'How many times do I have to remind you to knock?' her mother shouted, as she hastily shut the door in her daughter's face. In the brief moment that the door was ajar, Angie had glimpsed a large canvas: an oil painting as far as she could tell, but not in her mother's usual style.

What was her mother doing in there day after day? Freya of all people, who hungered for daily walks in the bush, shut up in her hot, dark studio all day long? Whatever it was, Angie knew better than to ask. And she noticed that her mother returned to the cottage every night exhausted but also calmed by her long hours of work, which was something to be grateful for, at least.

Her parents were not the only ones to suffer. Angie had already endured a whispering campaign at her school when Robbie died, not to mention the nasty notes in her school bag and elbows in her ribs at assembly. To her credit, the headmistress, Mrs McMahon, had put an end to that round of torment. Addressing the whole school, she made it clear that Angie was not in any way to blame for the death of Robert Fox and that no more bullying would be tolerated. But the hostility had only gone underground and was now fuelled by anti-German hatred. Freya and Freddie had never made a secret of her background and so Angie too was now tainted by the family's Germanness. Micky Shales, the eldest son of the butcher in Katoomba, had formed an anti-German gang at school who chanted 'Hun, Hun, Hun' under their breath when teachers were out of earshot. And whenever Angie's class discussed the progress of the war, she felt the eyes of her classmates burning into the back of her neck.

She did have one protector though: Simon Rushworth. A year above her at school, Simon made a habit of escorting Angie between the railway station and the school without ever formally acknowledging this was what he was doing. He was a tall, stocky, red-headed boy with big hands and broad shoulders. His father had been killed in a horse accident on their farm out at Hartley and his mother struggled to raise three sons alone. Simon now lived with an aunt at Mount Victoria. Shy, gentle and softly spoken, he reminded Angie of Freddie.

'Hun! Hun! Hun!' chanted Micky Shales and his gang one afternoon behind the toilet block after school as Angie came around the corner to use the bubbler. They were so busy flicking spitballs and hurling insults they failed to notice Simon coming up behind them. It took no time at all for Micky Shales to learn the power of Simon's headlock and right hook as did several other bullies who limped away with split lips, aching jaws and sore shins.

'Thank you.' Angie stood on tiptoe and bestowed a small kiss on her protector's cheek. Simon blushed and a confused smile spread across his usually solemn face. Little did Angie know that with this one act, she had sealed a bond of enduring loyalty for years to come.

But the cowardly torments continued. A week later, Angie found a letter in her school desk. It called her a 'murdrer just like the Kaizar' and 'a Hun-loving traytor' who had killed Robbie Fox so he would not be able to fight against 'her Hun frends'. The crude handwriting was accompanied by an equally crude drawing of a girl with long dark hair, hanged on a gibbet with the words 'YORE DEAD'. The letter made Angie feel sick and afraid but she decided, for her father's sake, to keep it secret. She hurried home to the privacy of her garden, an island of peace and safety in a sea of hatred, where she could hide in her hedge, away from the hostile gaze of the world.

In November a great assembly of men on foot and horseback, dressed in blue dungarees with white canvas hats, arrived at the Explorer's Tree in Katoomba bearing a banner reading: FIRST STOP BERLIN. These were the patriots of the Coo-ee March that had set out the previous month from Gilgandra, a town further west, and were marching all the way to Sydney, gathering fresh young recruits along the way to help 'the boys at the Dardanelles'.

Freddie went down to Katoomba to watch the speeches and the flag-waving, keen to ensure his neighbours and colleagues could see how loyally he supported the war effort. Welcomed by the mayor, Mr James, the marchers raised their battle-cry of 'coo-ee' and headed into the main street of Katoomba for a civic dinner at the California guesthouse and a recruiting rally on the street afterwards. One of Freddie's boys, Wally Garner, was among the twenty-one recruits who signed up that day. A bale of hand-knitted woollen socks was presented on behalf of the ladies of the Katoomba Red Cross Comforts Fund and the mayor's wife, who had personally knitted ten pairs.

Later that night, Angie lay in bed listening to her parents arguing in the next room. Freddie had started it all by talking about volunteering for the AIF. Freya begged him to put such a stupid idea out of his head. 'I cannot believe you are talking like this! You want to abandon me and Angie? To prove what? That you are willing to die for this country so they will believe you do not love the Kaiser?'

'I want to do it to protect you both, don't you understand? If I join up, how can they accuse us of being unpatriotic? I will get paid a wage so you won't go hungry, and when I come home with my rifle and my slouch hat, no one will be able to look me in the eye and say I am not a bloody Australian!' This was followed by a soft, low sound Angie had never heard before. It took her some time to realise it was her father crying. There was no more talking after that.

Angie folded her hands and prayed for God to watch over her father and mother and make sure that Freddie did not have to go and die in the war.

CHAPTER 7

Lisa
Katoomba, May 2013

Lisa had opened a door on her family's past and there was no turning back. Over the next few days, the Palace's eager historian continued to send Lisa a string of emails beginning with: 'Dear Lisa, I hope you don't mind me sending you this but I thought it may be of some interest . . .' and 'Dear Lisa, Please ignore this email if you are too busy but it struck me that . . .' She was taken by Luke's strategic charm and considerateness. She was sure that this gently assertive but unthreatening approach got him through many more doors, backwards, than would any direct assault. Lisa had discovered that a similar self-effacing adaptability was the mark of a good photographer; to put her subjects at their ease, she adopted whatever social camouflage was needed to become invisible.

The most surprising email of all was one Luke forwarded from a man in Germany. Lisa had given Luke a selection of the best shots she had taken on her visit to the Palace to post on the hotel's website as a 'thank you' for his time. Her only condition was a copyright acknowledgement. Luke then talked her into a short profile revealing the fact she was the granddaughter of Adam Fox. 'It will make a nice touch,' he insisted. She reluctantly agreed.

The email was from an Ulrich Kraft in Stuttgart. He said that he had been doing some research into his family's past and found Lisa's photos and profile on the Palace website. 'I am planning a trip to Australia in June,' he wrote, 'and have some material you may find interesting. I have reason to believe we may be related. I hope you do not find this communication intrusive and might share my interest in learning more about the past. With sincerest thanks, Ulrich Kraft.'

A relative in Germany? Was that possible? Monika had never mentioned any branch of the family there. But then she had said so little about her family. Intrigued, Lisa replied directly to Ulrich's email.

Dear Ulrich,

Yes, I am happy to meet up with you when you come in June. As it happens, I have just started to take an interest in my family history and welcome any information you are willing to share. I am doing some research of my own but have also been in touch with Mr Luke Davis who is writing an official history of the hotel my family built. I will introduce you when you come out.

Cheers,

Lisa Fox

'Your grandfather did have a great interest in Germany and many things German, especially hydrotherapy and health,' Luke reminded her when she emailed him about Ulrich's message. 'We know he visited Matlock Bath in England quite a bit. But he also went to Baden-Baden as a young man with his own family and, as you know, hired a German therapist for the spa.'

That night she rang her brother, Tom, in Canberra. He sounded alarmed at first to hear from her. 'Gosh, I thought something had happened to Mum.'

'No, she's doing okay – considering,' said Lisa. 'She'd still like you to visit – if you can make time in your busy schedule, of course. Who knows how much longer her mind will hold out?'

Tom began making the usual excuses about his family and career commitments. She cut him off. They'd had this conversation already on more than one occasion and she had no interest in repeating it. 'Look, it's really up to you what you want to do about Mum. She's *not* the reason I rang.'

There was a pause on the end of the phone. Lisa could hear her niece and nephew in the background, the usual resisting-going-to-bed rumpus. She heard Tom's wife, Natalie, call out, 'Can you ring her back? I could use a hand.'

'I know it's not a good time,' Lisa said apologetically. 'I just wanted to ask you something.'

'What is it, sis?' Tom's voice softened a little, losing its defensive edge.

'Do you remember Mum ever mentioning relatives in Germany?'

There was another pause as he appeared to be considering the question. 'No. No, I don't think so. I'm sure I'd remember something like that. Why?'

'It's a bit weird, but I've had an email from a guy in Stuttgart who thinks we could be related.'

'How strange. What did he say?'

'Not a lot. Just that he had done some research and had documents he wanted to show me. He's coming out to Australia in June and we're going to meet up.'

Tom put on his concerned-older-brother voice. 'Hey, be careful, sis. It could be one of those internet fishing expeditions . . .'

Lisa smiled. While he had been a moody bugger most of her childhood, she still cherished the times when Tom had stood up for her – mostly to their mother.

'Thanks for caring, but I think I'm smart enough not to fall for that. He's not from Nigeria or Ukraine, you know. Anyway, I'll make sure Luke comes with me.'

She realised she had dropped some bait in the water with that slip. Tom and Natalie were tirelessly inquisitive about the status of Lisa's love life – out of loyalty and concern, of course – and always sensitive to the merest hints in that direction.

'Who's Luke?' said Tom, trying to sound neutral.

'He's a historian who's researching the Palace. He showed

me around last week. It's a terrible mess but the new owners are going to spend a bundle fixing it up – properly this time.'

'What's this all about, Lisa?' Tom sounded worried. 'Are you okay?'

Lisa hesitated. The simple answer was 'no'. But then what? 'Mum's losing all her memories. And the thing is . . . I want to know more about my past, Tom, to find out where I come from – before it's too late.'

There was a short silence on the other end, broken by high-pitched squealing from another room and Natalie calling, 'Tom!'

'When are you coming to Canberra again, sis? It's been at least eight months. The kids miss their aunty. You know you're always welcome here.'

'Thanks. I know. You'd better go. Give me a call when you get a minute.'

'Okay, will do. Take care of yourself. Talk soon. Bye.'

Lisa hung up. She had told Ulrich that she was doing her own research. And she had just confessed to her brother that she was in a race against time to find out about her past. So why had she not lifted a finger in the last week to look in her mother's basement as she had promised Luke? What was she afraid of?

When she'd moved Monika into the nursing home two years earlier, Lisa had been stumped about what to do with the bungalow. For the longest time, she resisted the idea of moving in despite the fact it was much more spacious than her own cramped flat in Sydney. It seemed like an admission of defeat to come back to the maternal home in Katoomba after all these years, a pathetic retreat from her independent life in the city. Even though she flatly rejected the notion of ghosts, she knew the house would be filled with bittersweet memories. And some plain bitter.

During a long professional dry patch last year when she'd struggled to pay the bills and had even taken on commissions for weddings – oh, the teeth-gritting required to get through those extravagant displays of so-called love – Lisa had finally surrendered to her fate and moved into her mother's empty house.

Before Monika's mind began to fail, she had been approached quite a few times by a researcher at the University of Western Sydney to sort out her archives. The woman harboured the secret hope that she might be the one to curate a major retrospective exhibition or, even better, establish a permanent Monika Fox collection at the university. Monika had not been cooperative, however, refusing to become 'a living corpse whose tomb is raided before I am even in my shroud'.

None of this was an excuse, however, to avoid looking in the basement. So Lisa put on some old track pants and a grungy top and found the key to the blue door at the rear of the house. It was sticky but opened after a determined tug. She was relieved to find the electric light on the stairs had not blown and she did not have to descend in the dark or go back to the kitchen for a torch.

Given Monika's seeming indifference to her standing with posterity, Lisa was amused to discover that, once she pushed past the jumbled barrier of broken furniture and old newspapers, the basement was surprisingly well-ordered. The 'living corpse' had made quite a fist of preparing her tomb for the grave robbers to plunder. Archive boxes of draft manuscripts and official paperwork were clearly labelled and stacked on shelves. Photo albums were sealed in bubble wrap and posters furled inside cardboard tubes. Kitty Koala dolls and soft toys of all sizes sat arm in arm, their beady glass eyes staring into the dark, waiting to be reborn as museum artefacts.

Lisa turned on the naked bulb overhead and sat on an old trunk in its bright circle of light for hours, opening boxes and leafing through papers. Most of it was related to her mother's professional writing life, of course: proofs from her publisher, contracts, letters and receipts from her agent, sketches and letters from her illustrator, Eric, albums of photos from launches and festivals and visits to schools and libraries. Thousands of beaming faces, adoring eyes and eager hands thrusting forward copies of Monika's books for her to autograph.

Not a single photo of Michael, Lisa and Tom.

Lisa's eyes had begun to water from the dust and electric glare of the bulb. She was about to retire upstairs when she looked down and noticed that the trunk she was sitting on was secured with a brass padlock not much smaller than her fist.

Why on earth had her mother padlocked this trunk? Everything else in the room was easy to access. It did not make any sense except to suggest that Monika had something to hide.

Lisa recognised that what she was about to do was a kind of theft. As long as she could remember, Monika had been reluctant to talk about her past other than to drop hints that it was a place of pain and disappointment she had no wish to revisit. For many years Michael had tried to persuade her to show the kids around the family's famous hotel but Monika refused even to do that. Lisa's visit as a six-year-old guest of Uncle Alan's had been a singular exception to celebrate her birthday. Her mother had not joined them on that occasion.

Monika had firmly shut the lid on that part of her life and no one could ever persuade her to lift it. But Lisa was convinced that no writer could completely abandon their past. There had to be traces of her mother's childhood buried here somewhere, she was sure of it. What girl of that generation, who would later grow up to become a writer, had not kept a diary, for example?

All Lisa had to do was justify the act of theft she was about to commit. How could it harm Monika now, she told herself, for her daughter to know the truth of her past? In fact, it could give Lisa some insight into Monika's experiences as a child. How could this be a bad thing?

The hunt for the key took several more hours and tested Lisa's resolve to its limits. It was close to midnight before she stumbled on a set of small keys on a ring in among dusty jars of nails and boxes of brass garden-hose attachments in the garage. Exhausted but excited, Lisa sat on the floor of the basement trying key after key, her hands dirty and sweaty with the effort of searching the house.

What if none of these fitted and the key was missing? What if, in one of her early Alzheimer episodes of forgetfulness, Monika had thrown it away? She had done equally neglectful things, misplacing bills, letting pots boil dry and the bath overflow. Lisa tried to remember if there were any tools in the garage that would help her break this padlock if she had to, but nothing came to mind.

The more she fumbled unsuccessfully, the more anxious she became that her search would be fruitless. Or worse still, a voice inside her head warned, it would reveal a family secret that rewrote the past and changed everything she understood about her mother, her life and herself. Lisa put the last key in the lock and hesitated: maybe it would be better if she stopped now, walked away.

The key turned and she heard the padlock click open. She grabbed the handle and pulled back the heavy lid. A stale, musty odour rose from the depths of the paper-lined trunk and she saw a nest of silverfish scatter in the sudden light.

There was no going back now.

She pulled out a black plastic bag and untied the knot. Inside were two photo albums, bound in Moroccan leather, their black pages separated by sheets of tissue-thin paper chewed into delicate filmy lace.

Lisa sat on the floor, her back against the wall, and began turning the pages. Photos hung precariously from corners whose gummed backs had long since lost their stickiness. Spidery handwriting captioned each photo: *Christmas 1936. Frankie, Joan, Adam and Laura play doubles. Lotz, Monz and baby Alan have tea. Monz with Captain Pogo.*

Lisa gasped and tears sprang into her eyes. The little girl in the sunhat, standing on one leg next to a black cocker spaniel, was her mother. *Monz.* The girl squinted into the sunshine with a cheeky grin. Lisa kept turning the pages. She did not recognise the house. It was a two-storey mansion with deep verandas top and bottom, Victorian-era ironwork and high arched windows looking out over a tennis court and tree-bordered lawn, rolled to perfection. It must be the Jersey Avenue house in Leura, she thought. There were lots of photos of children's tea parties on the lawn and verandas with dolls and bears, dressings-up in Laura's old shoes and hats, chasing Captain Pogo with a bow and arrow, the usual childhood games and antics.

Lisa smiled at a photo of her grandfather, a fit, stylish man in his forties, wearing a neat rabbit-fur trilby and a dark pinstriped suit, and posing proudly in front of a shiny new white whale of a car in the driveway of the Palace. Adam Fox's love of cars was legendary; some said he even learned to drive behind the wheel of the first car imported into the country. According to Grandma Laura, Adam's craving for speed and the freedom of the open road never left him. Even in his late sixties, Adam enjoyed nothing more than hurtling down the Victoria Pass and roaring westwards along the highway to Bathurst. 'That's where poor Alan got the speed bug,' Laura said, shaking her head.

Lisa studied the photo. She knew very little about vintage cars but loved this one's low sleek profile with its extravagant curving mudguards, long running boards, thrusting rocket-nosed radiator grille and fat, white-walled tyres. It was helpfully captioned: *Foxy and the Hudson 8.*

There was no doubt about her grandad's good looks. His eyes were hidden in the shadow of the hat's brim but Lisa could see his broad face with its sharp chin and well-defined jaw, his sun-bronzed cheeks and that compelling grin, as if he had just thought of an excellent joke. He stood with his arms loosely folded and feet planted wide, the stance of a man who faced the world with a brazen, undented confidence, fearing nothing and prepared to take on anything. Lisa wished she had met him.

She looked more closely at the photos of her grandmother, of which there were only a few. Even so, there was no doubt that Laura was the society queen, the focal point of those handful of snapshots, laughing or smiling, arms outspread, enclosing her male and female friends in her generous embrace. She wore extravagant evening gowns with mink fur wraps and diamond brooches. Even in these small faded pictures it was easy to tell she was exceptionally beautiful: jet-black, glossy hair framing an aristocratic face with heavy-lidded eyes.

In one particular photo which caught Laura in a more unguarded, pensive mood, Lisa was struck by how much her grandmother resembled Garbo: that same intense, smouldering gaze and air of enigmatic melancholy. The family story was that Laura had once had ambitions to be a movie actress and even had a small part in a film by the famous Australian director Raymond Longford before she met Adam and settled for the life of wife, mother and high society beauty.

And Monika?

'Monz' seemed happy enough, all copper curls and pigtails, wonky teeth and freckles, rambling through a privileged childhood of handcrafted doll's houses, cowboys and Indians on the lawn, pushing Captain Pogo dressed as a pirate down the hill in a wicker pram, hugging her older sister, Lottie, on a tartan picnic rug, crowning baby brother Alan with a coronet of daisy chains. There were a handful of photos of the whole family together in front of the Palace or panoramas of lighthouses and churches; not surprisingly, adults and children seemed to lead largely separate lives.

Lisa continued to flick through the album: tennis matches, croquet tournaments, Christmas parties, birthday parties, fancy-dress parties, expeditions in the Hudson to beaches and parks and lookouts around Sydney and down the south coast. All this was what Lisa had expected of a wealthy Australian family's life between the wars. What was unexpected was how good the photos were: nicely composed, well-lit and in focus, capturing people in a natural, spontaneous way rather than as if they were facing a firing squad.

And then there were the photos of things that Lisa had not anticipated. A photo of her mother, aged five, with her sister, Lottie, both in full riding outfits, looking very comfortable astride two pretty chestnut ponies: *Jimmy and Bob, Megalong Farm, 1935.* The three children cavorting demonically around an Empire Night bonfire piled high with broken packing cases and old car tyres. Grandma Laura, in a fur-lined hood, squinting into a beautiful silver and black camera as she photographed the sheer face of a glacier in Canada. *Mount Edith Cavell, June 1936.*

Lisa looked more closely. Amazing. The camera she was holding was a brand-new Kine Exacta, the world's first 35mm film SLR manufactured in Dresden, the capital of camera engineering. It was a sure bet that Adam Fox had purchased this state-of-the-art German camera for his wife on one of his overseas trips. Flipping back through the album, it dawned on Lisa that the reason there were so few photos of Laura was obvious. *She* was the family photographer. And a good one to boot. Lisa felt a strange mix of elation and sadness at this discovery – too late – that she shared a passion for photography with her own grandmother.

The most startling photo of all was one of her mother as a small girl with a gun. She was taking aim at the sky, the stock of the rifle expertly tucked against her shoulder with her head cocked and one eye squinting, while, out of focus in the background, a clay-pigeon trap flung its saucer-shaped target into the air. Her mother with a gun? Lisa was flabbergasted. She had never imagined such a thing. With a sharp pang of remorse, she realised she knew next to nothing about her mother's past.

Lisa took a deep breath, stood up and stretched.

My God, what time was it? The light through the small window behind her head had paled to a pre-dawn blue-grey. She had been sitting here, lost in these albums and her mother's childhood, for hours.

As if to cover up her theft, Lisa decided to put the albums back in the trunk and close the lid, though no one had access to this basement apart from herself. As she did so, her eye was caught by the corner of something brightly coloured tucked away at the bottom of the trunk: a bundle of notebooks with red, marbled covers, bound together with string. Each one was labelled with stickers on which appeared neatly hand-printed dates: *January–June 1940.*

This, she knew immediately, was the prize.

She leaned down and scooped out the diaries carefully, almost tenderly, hoping they had survived the ravages of silverfish and time. Her hands began to shake. Was she sure this was what she wanted? Who knew what they would reveal? Secrets were as explosive as the undetonated hand grenades one heard about, hidden for decades under a hedge in an English country lane, waiting for some curious schoolboy to poke them with a stick.

Lisa decided it was a risk she was willing to take.

CHAPTER 8

Angie
Meadow Springs, December 1915–June 1916

The day before Christmas, Auntie Eveline and her husband, John, arrived, staying at an inn just up the road in Blackheath. In what had been a gloomy year, it was a rare patch of sunlight. Angie noticed how much Freya's mood lightened in the presence of her sister; she seemed younger, sunnier, more carefree. They sat on the cottage veranda with their mugs of tea, laughing at shared memories of their parents, singing snatches of lullabies and songs from their childhoods, telling stories of the grand balls and parties before their mother died. It had been a long time since Angie had seen her mother smile. Her father also seemed happier, less agitated, partly because he, too, could see the change in Freya.

On Christmas Eve, after a light dinner of bockwurst and roast potatoes, Aunty Eveline treated everyone to a concert in the cottage garden. Freddie had hung paper lanterns in the trees and they rocked gently on the breeze. Eveline possessed a bright lyrical soprano voice and delighted her small audience of John, Freya, Freddie and Angie with traditional German carols followed by airs from Mozart's *Magic Flute* and Lehar's *Merry Widow.*

'I wonder what the neighbours will think?' mused Freddie at this unapologetic performance of songs by German and Austro-Hungarian composers whose music, in more civilised days, had been recognised as a gift to the whole world.

'Tonight, my dear Frederick, I don't care what anyone thinks!' laughed Freya, dancing around her husband and kissing him repeatedly.

John and Eveline had come bearing extraordinary news. Eveline was pregnant with their first child. And John was enlisting for the Fifth Division, AIF, which was being formed in Egypt in February next year. Freya's joy at hearing about her sister's pregnancy was quickly overshadowed by the shock of learning that John was going away. Freya struggled to hide these mixed feelings but Angie saw the clashing emotions in her mother. Angie also noticed how conscientiously Eveline tried to reassure her sister that she had plenty of support from friends in Sydney. 'If you visited whenever you could, I would be grateful,' she told Freya. The sisters hugged, and cried with happiness, and hugged again.

The following day the family enjoyed a Christmas dinner of roast goose, red cabbage and more roast potatoes, followed by wedges of Dresdner Stollen. This fruitcake had been made for them by Chef Muntz from his hometown's historic recipe as a discreet gesture of solidarity with his German colleague. They all sat out on the cottage veranda afterwards, digesting. The women sipped cherry brandy while the men downed brown bottles of Resch's from the crate Mr Fox had given Freddie as a gift.

John related some of the stories he had been hearing from fellow journalists about the targeting of Germans, especially troublemakers like union leaders or professional men with a public profile. The Hun-hating newspaper *The Mirror* had published a list of the names and addresses of 'prominent' German-Australian citizens who should be locked up. The wave of surveillance and arrests continued unabated.

'Don't get me wrong, I believe in the cause. Why else would I be joining up? But here at home, the military have been given the authority to interfere in everything,' said John, sipping his beer with his heels propped up on the veranda railing and looking gravely at Freddie and the two women. Angie listened keenly.

He told them about letters being opened at the General Post Office, newspaper editors being told what they could print, and Germans being sacked from all public-service positions. 'They have yet to catch one proven saboteur or spy, but the net is cast wider all the time. The Minister of Defence now has the power to intern "disloyal natural-born subjects of enemy descent" and "persons of hostile origin or association".'

'What does *that* mean?' asked Freddie.

John took another swig of beer. 'That means just about anyone they don't like.'

The following year, 1916, brought worse news. Freddie still insisted that Angie read him the headlines over breakfast every morning, despite the irritation it caused Freya, who dismissed the whole business as 'madness'. The Gallipoli campaign had turned into a bloody stalemate which ended with all ANZAC troops pulling out in December 1915. When the news of this undignified withdrawal reached Australia in January, another spate of violent anti-German riots, brawls and assaults broke out in Sydney and Melbourne.

The secret coffee klatsch at the Palace had started meeting late at night to avoid attracting suspicion from their colleagues. These meetings grew even more feverish and paranoid when in April Australian troops began to arrive in France. They would soon be facing German bullets and bombs, a prospect that would surely intensify hatred for the enemy back home.

Freddie was stunned when Muntz announced one night that Councillor Johannes Berghofer had been voted off the local council. Johannes was a well-liked tavern owner, and one of the most respected public figures in the Blue Mountains. He had discovered a safe route for motor cars down the steep western slopes which had been named Berghofer's Pass in his honour.

His son, George, was serving with the AIF. Everyone had thought that Johannes, though German-born, was untouchable.

'So that's the thanks you get for years of devoted service. Would you believe they're even taking his name off the pass!' said Muntz. 'The world has gone crazy.'

Then, in May, the government broadened the legal meaning of 'enemy alien' to include naturalised residents and 'any Australian natural-born subject whose father or grandfather was a subject of a country at war with the King'.

'We are no longer citizens in our own country!' declared Freya in tears the day the notices arrived in the mail for her and Freddie to register. 'How I've prayed that it would not come to this.'

Angie was at school that morning when her parents went down to Katoomba police station to fill in their yellow 'enemy alien' registration forms. But she felt the profound change of mood in the cottage when she got home that night. Terror sat like a black dog at the back door, baring its teeth.

'Don't worry yourself, my angel,' Freddie told his daughter as he kissed her on the forehead that night. 'We've done nothing wrong, so there's no need to worry.'

She wanted to believe him, her big strong father who had always protected her, but in the instant before he turned out the lights she saw fear in his eyes.

Two weeks later, Angie had just arrived home from school and was in her favourite hiding place in the hedge when she saw an unfamiliar car pull up in the driveway of the Palace. Senior Constable Malcolm Robertson from the Katoomba police stepped out with a red-capped military officer and was greeted on the front steps by Mr Hawthorne. The trio then walked across the lawn in the direction of the hedge so Angie could hear them distinctly. The thin-lipped man introduced himself as Captain Woodcock from the Intelligence Section of the Second Military District and explained the purpose of his visit to the general manager.

'We have been reliably informed that a Mr Frederick Octavius Wood who works here at the hotel might have access to firearms or weapons. He is of hostile origin and frequently associates with other German nationals on your staff.'

Angie heard Mr Hawthorne call Benedict. 'Where's Freddie, do you know?'

'Down at the sheds last time I saw him,' the fat waiter replied.

'Ask him to join us, would you?' Hawthorne commanded.

Angie's heart thumped painfully in her chest with fear and pity for her father. She wanted to warn Freddie of this coming danger but realised with a jolt of anguish that there was nothing she could really do to help him.

Freddie looked stunned when confronted by the policeman and the army officer, accompanied by Mr Hawthorne, but he showed not the slightest sign of resistance. He was courteous and cooperative as these men inspected the outhouses, where they found the usual array of tools needed for heavy work and repairs around a hotel. These included several axes for chopping wood and clearing the bush.

'I am afraid these will have to be stored separately under

lock and key and not made available to Mr Wood,' said Captain Woodcock, refusing to make eye contact with the storeman.

Angie saw her father gulp for air and pump his hands, half-forming them into fists and struggling to repress his rage. He lowered his head to stare silently at his shoes in an effort to hide the hot flush of shame that suffused his face.

'Do you have any firearms in the hotel?' the captain asked the general manager.

Hawthorne confirmed there was a gun room inside the hotel for guests to hire guns or store their own firearms for game hunting and clay-pigeon shooting.

'I think, to be on the safe side, the gun room should be locked at all times and the interior of the hotel should be out of bounds to Mr Wood, restricting his access to guests as much as possible,' Woodcock decided, making notes in a small black book he had fished out of his jacket pocket. 'Mr Wood will be required to report to Senior Constable Robertson at Katoomba police station weekly and I will be checking with you, sir, that he has not breached any of our agreed conditions of his continuing employment here. He will also agree not to have any further private conferences with the other German nationals on staff.'

My God, thought Angie, who on staff had been spying on her father so closely and reporting all this to the police?

The final indignity was the requirement that Freddie surrender all his keys to Mr Hawthorne. 'In future you will collect a key as needed by sending one of your staff up to the manager's office,' said Woodcock. 'You will also be accompanied at all times by another member of staff when you enter any of the private areas of the hotel and particularly when you handle the barrels of spring water for the clinic.'

Angie saw her father flinch as each instruction struck him like the lash of a whip. Unable to bear this scene of humiliation any longer, she slipped from the hedge and ran back to the cottage, devoutly wishing she had never seen her father suffer so.

She barely recognised Freddie as he lurched into the cottage later that night, muttering curses and reeking of alcohol.

Freya barked at Angie to go to bed. Soon after, the light in her parents' room went out and she heard her mother singing softly in the dark, just as she had when Angie was small:

'Wie ist die Welt so stille,
Und in der Dämmrung Hülle
So traulich und so hold!
Als eine stille Kammer,
Wo ihr des Tages Jammer
Verschlafen und vergessen sollt.'

How still is the world
In twilight furled
So intimate and sweet
Like a quiet room
Where our daily gloom
Fades and is forgotten in sleep.

Little by little, Freddie's moans gave way to deep snores.

CHAPTER 9

Angie
Meadow Springs, July–September 1916

Freddie went back to work and Angie to school and Freya returned to her painting. They were determined to continue their lives as if nothing had changed but in their hearts they all knew that a storm was gathering strength over the horizon. The air in the cottage and the hotel grounds and the schoolhouse hissed with its deadly charge. It would strike the Wood family with full force in mid-September but it would claim its first victim weeks earlier.

In the first week of July, Eveline wrote to her sister to say she had received a letter from John stationed with the 59th Battalion, 15th Brigade, somewhere behind the lines in France. John complained in a jocular way about his uncomfortable new steel Brodie helmet as well as the cold and the mud but otherwise reported, 'I am in excellent spirits and keen to join the fight with my brothers-in-arms. Please send my good wishes to Freya, Freddie and Angie. Tell them how proud I am to be here and how much I look forward to seeing them again.'

On 28 July Australian newspapers included in their reports a short British military communiqué: 'Yesterday evening, south of Armentières, we carried out some important raids on a front of two miles, in which Australian troops took part. About 140 German prisoners were captured.'

These 'important raids' were conducted by troops of the Australian Fifth Division, newly arrived in France, on the Sugarloaf salient near the small village of Fromelles. As the men of the 59th and 60th battalions waited on the fire step, they did not know that the artillery bombardment laid down to prepare for their attack had made no impact on the enemy's concrete bunker overlooking the battlefield. They advanced across no-man's-land in four waves, five minutes apart, to be cut down in a lattice of German machine-gun fire. Eyewitnesses later described 'hundreds . . . mown down in the flicker of an eyelid, like great rows of teeth knocked from a comb'. Over five and a half thousand Australians were killed or wounded that night.

In mid-August the official death notices began to arrive in Australia.

The phone at the Palace rang just before dinner time and a woman on the other end begged Mr de Witte, the front office manager, to fetch Freya Wood from the cottage next door. Moved by the tears of his caller, de Witte sent one of his staff to the cottage and he returned with Freya, who looked wan and anxious.

The caller was Eveline. She had just received a telegram to say that Private John Rupert Marsh had been killed in action 'somewhere in France'. Their baby was due in two weeks' time. Freya broke down and wept, right there in the front lobby of the Palace, as guests stopped and gawked.

Hearing the sound of a woman sobbing, Mrs Wells emerged from Mr Hawthorne's office where they were conducting a meeting.

'Why is this woman using the hotel's telephone and causing a disturbance?' she demanded of the front office manager.

Mr de Witte began to explain as fast as he could. 'The circumstances were unusual, Mrs Wells. There has been a death in the family and I thought—'

But the housekeeper cut him off. 'Get her out of here!' she commanded in a low, angry voice.

Freya whispered to her sister, 'I have to go, my darling. But I will come to you soon. Very soon.'

Her hands were shaking so badly, she could barely put down the receiver. As she looked up at the scowling housekeeper, she caught sight of an enamel badge pinned to Mrs Wells' blouse. It showed two flags crossed, a Union Jack and an Australian Red Ensign, encircled by the words 'Anti-German League'. Freya's temples began to throb, blood surging with rage as she realised it must have been Mrs Wells who had reported her husband to the police and the military.

Mr Hawthorne came out of his office and stood behind Mrs Wells as the housekeeper raised her hand to point at Freya. 'I *said* get this woman out of here!'

Before anyone had time to move, Freya took a step towards the housekeeper and spat in her face. She heard the shriek of dismay and the gasps of horror all around her. But she did not look back as she marched out the front door of the Palace and headed towards the distant lights of the cottage.

As she waited for her train to school the following day, Angie stared at the recruiting poster on the wall of the railway station at Meadow Springs. It was one of Mr Norman Lindsay's best efforts. A firing squad of spike-helmeted German soldiers aimed their rifles at a young Australian farmer, his back pressed against a corrugated-iron water tank just like the one behind her cottage. His mouth was bloodied and his chest exposed to their deadly muzzles through his ripped shirt. Behind him, his mother had fallen to her knees, begging the German officer in charge to spare her son, but it was too late: he had already given the order and one of his men struck the woman down with the butt of his rifle. The farmer's father, with his long beard and grey hair, lay dead on the ground, a trail of blood oozing from a bullet hole in his head. Flames engulfed the farm as more enemy soldiers violently restrained the family's daughter. WILL YOU FIGHT NOW OR WAIT FOR THIS? the poster demanded.

Angie sighed. Did anyone really believe the Kaiser's soldiers would invade Australia? She knew exactly what this kind of nonsense was meant to do: make everyone feel as if they were in mortal danger from the dreaded Hun. It was what boys like Micky Shales and women like Mrs Wells needed to believe in order to feel they were part of this great drama, even though it was all happening thousands of miles away. And it was probably also because they felt guilty about their sons, fathers, brothers and uncles facing death far away when all they could do was send puddings in tins and knit socks. If they couldn't shoot German soldiers on the battlefield, they could at least do their bit by rooting out 'the enemy within', the only Germans they could hate face to face.

The following evening, Angie was to feel the full heat of that hatred.

It was coming on to dusk, the valley sunk into purple shadow and the first star visible low on the horizon. Freddie was outside having his customary smoko and Angie was doing her homework at the kitchen table. Freya was not there; she had caught the train to Sydney two days earlier to help Eveline with the birth of her child.

Angie was roused from her reading by the sound of shouting from next door. She came out onto the veranda and saw her father had already risen from his wicker chair and was listening to the commotion on the other side of the hedge, voices raised in a frightening chorus of triumph and aggression.

'Can you hear what they're saying?' Angie asked.

Freddie shook his head. 'Not really.'

But the steely expression on her father's face indicated otherwise, as did the note of urgency in his voice. 'I'll go take a look. Back inside, missy. Right now!'

Angie obeyed her father and retreated behind the flyscreen door as he stubbed out his cigarette and headed into the garden. She could make out some of the words, more distinct in the cacophony next door: 'Death to the Hun bitch!' 'Let her burn!' She smelled smoke and saw the first flicker of flames making a halo of light against the darkening sky. Her stomach cramped with terror. Up until now, she had dismissed the possibility of violence against her family as fantasy, despite the horrible letter in her desk at school, the threats from Micky Shales and his gang, and the stories of attacks on Germans in Sydney. She refused to believe that anyone she knew here in Meadow Springs would actually do them any harm. But the hammering of her heart and the knot in her chest told her in a way more forceful than words that she was wrong.

She stepped out onto the veranda again and looked for her father in the thickening gloom, praying he wouldn't reveal himself to the mob. The flames were crackling loudly now and sparks danced into the night air.

Angie crept out into the garden and found her usual vantage point, hidden in the heart of the hedge, from where she could watch the scene unfolding on the lawn beyond. A group of forty or so people, mostly men but including the unmistakeable figure of Mrs Wells with her stiff-backed carriage and tightly coiffed hair, stood in a circle with the light of a blazing fire illuminating their angry faces. The group erupted into rowdy cheers and cries of 'Burn! Burn!' and 'Kill the bitch!' as they punched their fists into the air.

The object of their rage was a burning piano. Even from this distance, Angie recognised the Bechstein from the casino, the glossy black grand piano with a polished plate that read: *In gratitude to the Palace staff – Baroness Bertha Krupp von Bohlen und Halbach, December 1908.*

Without warning, a sob broke from Angie's throat at the memory of herself and Robbie hiding in the storage area behind the stage in the casino, so close to the palm court orchestra she could read these words. The memory was so vivid it was as if her skin recalled the warmth and weight of Robbie's body next to hers as they lay squeezed together in the dusty darkness and her eyes drank in all the forbidden wonders of that evening. Tears streamed down her cheeks. She cried with an overwhelming sense of loss for the past: for a time when she and Robbie were just friends, and her father was happy and loved by his boys, and a rich German woman could show her gratitude to the Palace with a beautiful and generous gift.

The Bechstein had been hacked at with an axe. It must have also been doused with petrol; Angie could smell the acrid stink of it in the air. The piano's glossy hide peeled away in black scrolls and the heat caused the piano strings to warp and snap so the whole unnerving spectacle was accompanied by an eerie music of high-pitched shrieks, explosions and loud groans. As if to mock the piano in its death throes, the Katoomba Anti-German League members had propped the lid open and arranged sheet music on its stand. The pages of the burning sheet music were turned as if by invisible fingers; they curled up, floated into the air in a brief waltz of glowing scraps, dissipating as embers. The crowd's whoops and cries grew louder and louder as the flames roared higher.

Then Angie's heart skipped a beat. She heard someone shout, 'There he is!'

She watched in disbelief as Freddie walked slowly towards the mob and stood before them, silhouetted against the fire. There was a moment of unnerving silence except for the crackling of the flames and the ghostly music of the dying piano. Then the voices began again: 'Spy!' 'Saboteur!' 'Your girl killed Master Robbie!' 'You've been poisoning the spring water!'

'Shame on you!' she heard her father bellow at them, his voice loud in the crisp night air. The mob fell silent again. Freddie continued: 'We are not your enemies! We are your neighbours. We have lived and worked with you for years. How can you say these lies?'

Angie heard small stones flying through the air. Someone must have scooped up a handful of gravel from the driveway. Her father's back was still turned to her but she saw him flinch as the stones struck him on the temple. She wanted to cry out 'Stop!' and run to his aid, but her limbs had melted like candle wax and her throat clamped shut. She was in the grip of pure icy terror, her whole body convulsed with the shock of it, her heart enormous in her chest.

Another voice called out, one she recognised. It was Benedict, chubby Benedict who had chased balloons across the lawn on Robbie's birthday.

'Your Hun friends have killed Jacko. Did you know that? Jacko's dead!'

Angie saw Freddie stagger under this blow. His shoulders slumped and she heard a sound unlike anything she had heard before, a high, keening wail, escape her father's lips. Jacko had been the youngest of his 'boys', and his favourite.

Freddie stood, head hanging down, arms lifeless. More stones came pinging through the air and cut Freddie's face but he barely moved. The crowd began to advance, fists raised, some clutching kerosene lamps and torches, angry voices chanting: 'Murderer! Hun-lover! You killed Jacko!'

Without warning, the stillness of the night sky was split by the thunderclap of a rifle blast. The mob startled and froze, its chant dying away. A new voice rang out, an unmistakeable voice of authority. 'STOP THAT RIGHT NOW!'

Angie saw a figure on the terrace walking briskly towards the crowd. It was carrying a gun which still smoked from the discharge. The figure walked into the firelight and she knew at once it was Mr Fox.

'How dare you! How *dare* you!' Fox raged at the astonished crowd. He came a step closer but did not lower the gun. 'This is a disgrace! Look at yourselves! What have you become? A kangaroo court? A rabble? Believe me, I share your grief and anger at this war, which is why I agreed to sacrifice this piano, donated by an armaments manufacturer whose guns now rain down death on our boys. But I will not stand by and watch a gross act of cowardice. I will *not*!' His voice was steady and clear. 'Any of my employees still on this lawn in the next five minutes will be dismissed instantly. The rest of you can answer to this.' He levelled the rifle at the crowd. 'Now get off my property!'

The mob dispersed quickly. Fox waited until they had all gone before approaching Freddie and saying in a calm but commanding voice, 'Go home, Freddie. We'll talk in the morning.'

And with that, he turned and walked back to his hotel.

The following morning, there was a knock on the cottage door. Freddie opened it to find Mr Fox, immaculate in a silk necktie and dove-grey suit, standing with his walking stick in his right hand. 'I hope I am not too early. For a Saturday.'

Freddie and Mr Fox sat and had tea in the kitchen. Angie had been sent to her room but listened at the keyhole to the lowered voices. She heard her father express his thanks to Mr Fox for intervening the previous night. 'I don't know what would've happened if you hadn't arrived,' Freddie said. 'I feared for Angie and for the cottage.'

'This war has changed people and not for the better.' Fox sighed. There was a long pause. 'Please listen to me, Freddie. I have something very difficult to say. You are one of my longest-serving, most loyal members of staff. I hired you myself. But, under the circumstances, I have to let you go. I'm sorry but my hands are tied.'

The storeman said nothing.

'The fact is most of the staff of the Palace have threatened to go on strike if I keep any Germans on my payroll,' Mr Fox explained. 'Wells and Hawthorne came to see me with their demands a week ago. I said I would consider my position.'

Angie listened in disbelief.

'I could sack them all of course but I think that would destroy the hotel.' Mr Fox coughed apologetically, perhaps aware that this might not be Freddie's main concern right now. 'But I have another problem. The military intelligence officers have identified you and your family as a public threat, especially after Freya's confrontation with Mrs Wells. The local branch of the Anti-German League wrote to the federal member, the mayor and the district commander. It's ridiculous I know but . . .'

Mr Fox sighed again then continued, 'I'm not going to lie to you, Freddie. I'm letting Muntz go as well, but I'm going to try to keep Dr Liebermeister. Without the doctor, I will be forced to close the clinic. I may not succeed in keeping him but I have to show I am willing to cooperate with the authorities. I tell you these things because I believe you deserve the truth. But the fact is your future is now out of my hands. I have been informed that the military are going to arrest you as soon as they have a warrant. I'm deeply sorry, Freddie. But, to be honest, I think you'll be safer in an internment camp until this has all blown over. I hear the camps are well-run and properly guarded. And I promise there will be a job for you here when this war ends and everyone comes to their senses. Sooner rather than later, I hope.'

There was another silence.

Mr Fox finally went on, 'In the meantime I want you to persuade Freya to rent a house near the camp so she can visit you regularly. The government will pay her an allowance for food and other necessities while you are interned but I will help her with the rent. I think last night proved it is no longer safe here for her or your daughter. I will make sure no harm comes to this cottage in your absence.'

Angie heard her father clear his throat. His voice was hoarse as he said, 'Thank you, sir. You have always been kind to our family.'

Mr Fox and Freddie spoke for a while longer, mostly about practical matters, such as where Mr Fox would find another storeman, before Angie heard the flyscreen door of the cottage close behind them as the two men left for the hotel. She came out from her room. The smell of Adam Fox's hair oil lingered in the air. Angie stood at the front door of the cottage for what seemed an eternity, watching the parrots clowning about in the trees.

The following morning, two soldiers arrived early with a warrant to arrest Freddie Wood as 'a dangerous person of hostile origin and association'. They carried rifles with fixed bayonets and behaved as if Freddie might attack them at any minute. Freddie explained that his wife was returning by train from Sydney that evening and he wished to say goodbye to her. Also, who would look after his daughter until then? The lieutenant leered at Angie. 'She looks old enough to look after herself to me.' He refused to come back later and the two officers stood guard outside Freddie's bedroom to keep an eye on him as he packed a few belongings in a canvas bag and wrote a short note.

'You won't need much,' the lieutenant said. 'Holsworthy has all the modern luxuries a prisoner-of-war needs.'

Angie thought her heart would break as she hugged her father goodbye. Freddie held on to her tightly until the lieutenant gave him a nudge with his rifle butt.

'Come on, grandad, we have a train to catch.'

Freddie kissed his daughter one last time. 'Promise me you'll be brave. And look after your mother. I'll write to you every day and see you soon.'

The second officer picked up Freddie's bag and slung it over his shoulder while the lieutenant took out a set of handcuffs and ordered Freddie to put his hands behind his back.

'Why is *this* necessary?' Freddie protested.

'It's military procedure, grandad. Get used to it,' the lieutenant said as he clicked on the bracelets.

Angie tried not to cry when they marched Freddie out the front gate and bundled him into a waiting truck. She recognised a familiar face in the dark interior where several men sat in despair and shock. It was Chef Muntz, his chin unshaved, his eyes glazed; she had never seen this proud, fastidious man in such a state. He did not look in her direction; his attention was focused far away.

Angie stood on the roadside and watched her father's pale face as it receded into the distance. She turned to go back into the garden and saw a figure standing in the portico of the hotel, dressed all in white.

It was Adelina Fox.

CHAPTER 10

Angie
Meadow Springs, September–October 1916

Angie waited on the cottage steps all day. There was still the smell of burning wood from where the Bechstein had been immolated and the memories of that night played in her mind like some lurid silent movie. Again and again, she saw Fox step into the firelight just in time to stop the mob. To stop it doing what? Killing her father? Burning down the cottage? Was any of this possible?

She looked at the tranquil garden. The white bell-like tubes of beard-heath perfumed the air with their light scent. The underbrush was speckled with bright yellow 'bacon and egg' pea flowers and pale pink orchids. Sunlight flickered through curtains of she-oak needles as they stirred in the breeze. Following their ragged aerial ballet, butterflies coupled on sunny rocks. The bush rustled with the swift dashes of copper skinks chasing each other through the grass.

Angie lost all sense of time. Hours seemed to pass as she watched a handsome satin bowerbird in his glossy midnight blue-black plumage do his courtly dance for the green female he had lured into his bower of twigs and reeds. He hopped back and forth, flicking his wings and using his bill to pick up and flaunt the finest items from his collection of blue treasures: glass beads, a shirt button, flower petals, a pencil stub, even specks of cobalt pigment he had purloined from her mother's studio. But all his efforts came to nothing. Unimpressed by his display, the female left the bower and took wing.

Angie would turn thirteen in a few weeks, the same age as Robbie when he died. She wondered if she would ever find someone to love and cherish her. Her quiet protector at school, Simon, was sweet and chivalrous and she was grateful for his reassuring presence, but she couldn't reward his devotion to her in the way he would have probably liked. She had squeezed his hand a couple of times and bestowed a single chaste kiss on his cheek when he beat up Micky Shales, but he was a simple farm boy from Hartley and Angie still yearned for a gallant knight in a well-cut suit and necktie. She wanted a gentleman of quality and standing to swear an oath of love to her and make her his rich wife. Like Adelina Fox. That childish fantasy seemed more remote than ever, given the way her life was about be ripped apart. She might have to settle for a kindly protector like Simon. Much as Angie loved her father, Freddie, she could see that her clever and cosmopolitan mother had made a similar hard choice.

She ate a light lunch, leaving two eggs, three rashers of bacon and the heel of a loaf of bread for a simple supper with her mother. As dusk descended and the garden grew dark and chilly, she felt intensely lonely. Listening to the melancholy music of the currawongs – their throaty gargled notes swooping through the gum branches overhead as the shadows lenghened – Angie was struck with a sudden dizzying fear that she might never see this beautiful garden ever again. She had promised her father she would be brave – for his and her mother's sake – but she was still in shock at how quickly her familiar world had been snatched away.

The moment that Angie dreaded would soon be upon her. How would her mother bear the cruelty of Freddie's sudden absence, the lost opportunity to say goodbye?

Freya arrived from the railway station as the moon rose, bright and full, over the valley. Angie was curled up on the wicker chair on the veranda, wrapped in a woollen shawl, half dozing. The night's vast silence was interrupted only by the cackle of tree frogs and violin-saw of crickets in the distance

'They've taken him already, haven't they?' Freya was dry-eyed, her voice dull and hard.

Angie woke from her half-slumber and ran to her mother. Freya took her in her arms and hugged her, stiffly and reluct-antly at first but then with a fierceness that Angie had never felt before. They both wept, great sobs racking their chests, clutching at each other like two survivors of a shipwreck washed up on a deserted shore.

They spoke little that night and the following day, too deep in shock to say much more than small words of reassurance, love and comfort. The following night, as Freya prepared supper, Angie asked her mother what she planned to do. 'I heard Mr Fox tell Papa that he would help us rent a house near the camp.'

Freya dismissed the idea with a laugh. 'I'm not falling for that.'

This was the same man, she reminded her daughter, who had persuaded the New South Wales government to change the name of the town and managed to sell foul-tasting imported water as an expensive curative elixir. He had sponsored a national Olympics hero, donated magnanimously to local charities and council works, supported the campaigns of councillors and MPs and pledged large sums towards war loans. He had powerful and influential friends in Melbourne and Sydney.

'He could have done more to protect your father, but he chose not to,' she told Angie as she served up their supper. 'He had to show off his patriotism to fanatics like Mrs Wells to keep the staff and the local community on side. At least he was honest about the fact he traded Freddie and Chef Muntz to keep the doctor. Don't you see, Angie? He sacrificed your father to save his hotel. That's what he saved!'

Freya was working herself into a rage. The last two years had stamped deeper worry lines on her mother's face and added silver strands to her hairline but she still had the fiery energy of a much younger woman; Angie wished Freddie was here to mollify Freya as only he knew how. It was exhausting – and, at a time like this, frightening – to see her mother's anger consume her so utterly.

'You don't know him like I do!' cried Freya, her eyes ablaze. 'Men like Adam Fox are not knights in shining armour. They are cold and calculating men of business. They only ever do something if it benefits them!'

Angie had had enough. 'Of course *I* don't know anything. How could I? All my life, you've made sure I never knew what was going on!' She retreated to her bedroom and slammed the door.

'Only to protect you. Don't you understand?' shouted Freya.

'And hasn't that turned out well!' Angie shot back.

'Come here and eat your supper!' Freya grabbed the door handle and was about to wrench it open, when, as if on cue, they both heard the crashing of glass.

Angie screamed as shards and splinters rained onto her bed and bookcase. She saw a rock about the size of her fist on the floor. It had a sheet of paper wrapped around it, tied with string. It was a miracle it had not hit her.

Angie flung the bedroom door open and fell into her mother's arms, weeping.

'Oh my God! Why do they hate us so much? I'm so scared.'

There was a second explosion of glass in the parlour followed by a third in her parents' bedroom at the back of the cottage. Now both Angie and Freya screamed in terror.

Mother and daughter huddled under the table where Freya had just laid supper, their hands covering their faces in case more glass came flying into the room.

In the dark outside they could hear voices calling to each other, laughing and yelling, and the sound of boots on the road, growing more distant. There were at least two, maybe three or more, young men, guessed Angie. Was it Micky Shales and the boys from school? Or was it someone else entirely?

She knew better than to ask her mother to call the police. It was people like Senior Constable Robertson who had helped get their father locked up in the first place.

They brought the three projectiles into the parlour and laid them on the table gingerly as if they were live shells. All three – two rocks and a half-brick – were wrapped in paper, secured with string. Freya reluctantly spread out the notes and read them. 'YOU HUNS MURDERED ROBBIE FOX AND ALL OUR YOUNG MEN.' 'GO BACK TO GERMANY AND YOUR BELOVED KAISER.' 'THIS IS A WARNING – GET OUT BEFORE IT IS TOO LATE.'

The two women did not sleep a wink that night.

Adam Fox appeared in the garden the following afternoon.

Freya was in the parlour, going over some bills. Angie had just got home from school and was in her bedroom doing homework. She told her mother how Simon punched Micky Shales in the nose for tormenting her about Freddie being locked up 'as a dirty Hun spy'. It was obvious that the entire village knew their shameful secret.

Fox saw the broken windows, patched with old tarpaulins, as he approached the cottage. 'I see you've had some visitors,' he said as Freya came out onto the veranda.

'A couple of local louts showing off,' said Freya breezily. 'Nothing we can't handle.'

'Can I come in for a cup of tea?' Fox leaned on his walking stick. 'I have something I want to discuss.'

Except for the visit following the night of the burning piano, Adam Fox had not set foot on the cottage side of the hedge since the day of Robbie's death. It was as if the cottage and Freya and her daughter no longer existed, banished from his mind as phantasms of a sweeter, more innocent past that had transmogrified into a source of unending pain. Fox's world now finished at the high hedge; everything beyond it was veiled in shadow. This was the mental barrier Fox had managed to erect for his own sanity and it took an effort of will to keep it intact.

Freya understood exactly what he had done and why. She also knew that he could never forgive the injury done to him. The pain and anger would always be there, anaesthetised for a while so he could survive the loss of his son, but present nonetheless. One day it would resurface and Freya and Angie and Freddie would be punished for what Adam Fox believed they had done to him. She was sure that day had come now. Here he was, in broad daylight, as dapper as usual with his cane and his impeccable manners, asking to come in for a cup of tea. Freya had not forgotten what she had learned from the scene she had witnessed all those years ago in the hydrotherapy clinic: to beware of Adam Fox most of all when he wanted to help you.

'What is it you want to discuss?' she asked.

'Your future,' he answered simply.

Freya thought about how everything had turned out better for Adam than he could have hoped for: the war, the anti-German hysteria, the scapegoating of families like the Woods. He had already got rid of Freddie. Now it was Freya and Angie's turn. Freya must keep her wits about her. She was better off knowing his intentions than letting him plot against her behind his hedge, she reasoned. She invited him in.

'I assume you know about my proposal to help you rent a house?' he asked as Freya set a mug of tea before him.

'Yes.'

'And . . . ?'

'We will be staying here for now. But I appreciate the offer.' Freya was careful to remain diplomatic and appear suitably grateful.

Adam clucked his tongue against the roof of his mouth disapprovingly and closed his eyes for a moment – almost a wince – as if Freya's decision caused him physical distress.

'Freya, please. Don't be stubborn. Let me help you. It's not safe for you here anymore. It starts with burning a piano and rocks through the windows and ends where? I cannot stand by and watch you get hurt. Or worse. You must leave.'

Freya leaned forward. 'And who will look after this cottage when I am gone?' Her voice was shaking but she tried to keep it calm. 'Will you, Adam?'

Adam shifted uneasily in his seat. He did not like the tone of accusation in this question. But he chose to ignore it. 'Well, yes. That would be the most sensible idea. Please God the war will be over soon and this hysteria will come to an end. Then you and Freddie can move back in and life will return to normal.' Adam looked a little self-conscious about his choice of word, given that life had hardly been 'normal' at Meadow Springs since the death of his son.

'Do you think that is what will happen?' Freya asked a little too brightly.

'Well, yes, of course. Don't you?'

She shrugged. 'Who knows? Life is very unpredictable.'

Adam put down his mug of tea. 'Look, Freya, I know what this property, this cottage, means to you. It is your inheritance that you want to protect and pass on. It is also your connection to your father. To your past. It is part of who you are. I understand that.'

Freya was caught off guard by this change of tack. She had almost forgotten just how clever Adam was, how subtle and disarming he could be. She had revealed herself to him long ago and he had kept those precious intimate truths up his sleeve like a magician.

Adam took Freya's silence as agreement.

'So I assume you would do anything to keep this cottage safe. As you say, life is unpredictable. And we live in very strange times. I have heard that many "enemy aliens" have had their businesses wound up, their assets sold off and their properties confiscated and placed in the hands of the Public Trustee. The government has extraordinary powers, as I have found to my cost. They can and will do anything.'

Freya listened. What trap was he laying for her? she wondered.

'There may be a way to protect the cottage. As a registered enemy alien you are forbidden to buy or sell any property. Instead, I can have my solicitors draw up an agreement by which you transfer the land title into my name for a sum of money. It is not strictly a sale as the money is kept in a trust account for a period of time – say, three years – and earns interest. You get income from that interest to support you. At the end of three years, the property reverts to you and the capital sum in the account reverts to me. In other words, I hold the land in trust for you and no one can touch it.'

Adam sat back, hands folded. His cards were on the table.

Freya stared at him. 'Why?' she asked.

'What do you mean "why"?' Adam sounded hurt.

'Why do you want to do this?' she insisted.

'Isn't it obvious?'

They were on thin ice now. Freya felt the dangerous urge to make Adam explain himself. She knew this would enrage him as he could not afford to be honest. He would be forced to lie: to say that he still loved her and wanted to help her, that he forgave them both for what they had done to Robbie, that the past could be healed. But she and Adam both knew that wasn't true. The past could never be healed. It could only be buried under a growing mound of secrets and untruths.

'I will consider it,' Freya said. 'Thank you.'

She saw Adam's fist close around the arm of the chair, the tightening in his jaw, the familiar toss of his sandy hair in irritation. At least she now knew what he wanted: the cottage. Was this his plan all along? To finally take over the entire cliff top and to erase completely any painful memories of his neighbours? In a way, she could hardly blame him. And the circumstances were perfect. He had Freya at his mercy.

'This is not charity, Freya.' His hand strayed from his tea mug and picked up one of the bills on the table. He held it between his fingers. 'With Freddie interned, you will receive a small allowance from the government. It is a pittance. Ten shillings a week for you and two shillings and sixpence for your daughter. It will barely cover food. What will you do about new shoes, school fees, extras? If you become destitute, the government may even take Angie away too.'

Freya's face burned. No doubt Adam knew Angie was listening from the other room. He wanted her to hear this, to pressure her mother into being responsible.

'I *said* I would think about it,' Freya repeated. 'In the meantime, I have a proposition for you.'

Adam sat up, unable to disguise his surprise.

'Come with me. I have something I want to show you. In the studio.'

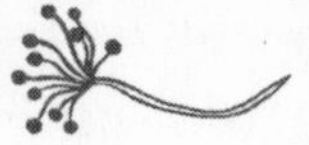

They both stood and looked at the oil painting. Freya had pulled it out from its hiding place at the back of the dusty, dark room and removed the layers of burlap and oilskin fabric that encased it. Adam stood there flabbergasted, the wind knocked out of him. He had never seen anything so magnificent in all his life.

It was a landscape of the valley behind them: a breathtaking vision that transformed the view Adam knew so well into an epiphany. He felt tears prick at his eyes and his heart swell in his chest. There was no mistaking what this was: the last major work of Wolfgang von Gettner.

There had been rumours of a last work in oils but Freya had denied all knowledge of it when Adam had asked her about it years ago. She confessed now that she had lied. Her father had finished the work in the last six months of his life. It was his final gift to his artist daughter.

Adam extended his hand tremulously and touched the canvas as if to reassure himself this was not a mirage that would melt away in front of his eyes. He then half kneeled as if in genuflection before the painting to inspect it more closely. Freya smirked to see the art collector's gaze fixated on her father's signature.

'Yes, it really is his,' she said.

Whatever pleasure this painting gave Adam aesthetically was embellished by the added satisfaction of knowing its market value would be considerable. While von Gettner's work had declined in value towards the end of his career, eclipsed by the popularity of the Heidelberg School, there had been a reappraisal since then by academics and curators – and, most importantly of all, by the market. In June 1914 a panorama of Mount Kosciuszko and the Victorian Alps had changed hands at auction at Sotheby's in Melbourne for over two thousand pounds. Too late to be of any help to the artist himself or his family, Freya had noted bitterly when she heard the news. Adam could not help but imagine the excitement that the discovery of a 'lost' von Gettner would create, especially once the war was over and anti-German sentiment had died down. Hung in the gallery at the Palace, it would become an object of fascination and pilgrimage. And it would likely prove an exceptional investment.

Adam knew exactly what Freya was doing: negotiating her survival on her own terms. She knew how greatly he admired her father's work and she knew the circumstances that made this painting especially valuable. The purchase of a rare painting was not an act of charity and preserved Freya's defiant but fragile dignity. She stood there, staring at him, her eyes glistening with triumph, just waiting for him to make her an offer.

'You cannot sell this to me,' said Adam.

'I cannot afford the luxury of sentimentality,' replied Freya. 'My father was a practical man. He would understand.'

'I still think it would upset him,' observed Adam coolly. 'He made it pretty clear he had washed his hands of us money-grubbing collectors. But that is not what I meant. As a registered enemy alien, you are not allowed to buy or sell property of any significant value.'

'So let's do it some other way,' said Freya, not so easily put off as that. 'Like you proposed with the cottage.'

She watched as he made his calculations. His gaze was drawn irresistibly to the canvas, his eyes lit up by a fervent craving for this thing of great beauty. It reminded Freya sadly of what she had once loved in Adam, that impetuous passion that would not be denied, that uncompromising lust that had been directed, for a short while, at her. She saw the struggle between his desire to take over her land and his desire for this painting: he was trying to work out if there was some way he could have both.

'Very well,' said Adam. 'I will have an agreement notarised that settles on a sum of money I will pay you in instalments for *borrowing* your painting rather than buying it. In other words, a fixed-period loan. This should get us around the legal issues. We will sign and date the agreement but keep the existence of the painting itself secret until the war is over. I will keep the work hidden and safe until then. In the meantime, you will receive regular "rental" payments in cash for the loan of the work with a guaranteed option for me to buy it as soon as you are legally able to sell. We will each keep a record of these down payments. Does that sound fair?'

Freya thought about this for a moment. 'I think that could work,' she said. 'So tell me, Herr Fox, how much are you willing to pay me for my father's last painting?'

Adam looked at her for a long time, as if trying to penetrate beneath Freya's crisp demeanour. Had any feelings survived from their golden time together? How could he possibly tell? He was not even sure of his own feelings about Freya anymore.

'I will let you know,' he said politely, and doffed his hat before stepping out of the studio and disappearing into the garden.

Within days Freya had agreed on a generous offer from Adam. The document was signed and delivered with a brown paper bag of banknotes to the cottage in exchange for the painting, rewrapped in its burlap and oilskin, and stored in the basement of the Palace for its public unveiling in a much-anticipated time of peace.

Mother and daughter tested their courage to its limits as they carried on with the normal routines of their life in an unrecognisable, hostile world. More stones were flung at the cottage, their milk bottles smashed, their front fence set alight. Hate mail arrived for Freya two or three times a week, its language more virulent and threatening with each passing day. She hid and burned these vile letters for fear of the nightmares they would cause Angie. But those nightmares were unavoidable.

Two weeks went by and Angie was sent home from school with a note from the headmistress. Her usual brave protector Simon had been absent with the flu. Four students she barely knew had held her down in the laneway behind the school grounds and hacked at her hair with scissors. They had also written on her forehead in ink the words 'HUN SPY'. Her screams had been stifled with rags stuffed in her mouth. The headmistress said in her note that she could no longer guarantee Angie's safety and 'in the light of recent events and strong public sentiment' she had no choice but to expel Angie from her school as a 'disruptive element'.

Freya had raged at this injustice but even her righteous anger no longer seemed inexhaustible. Angie's spirit could have been broken in so many ways but it was the horror of finding the bloody and broken corpses of three birds, including the handsome satin bowerbird who had kept her company that lonely day in the garden, that finally undid her. Their small bodies were pinned to the boards of the veranda with a note that simply stated 'YOU'RE NEXT'. Angie could not stop shaking and crying for hours.

Freya received a letter from Eveline the following day. Even a war widow and her newborn were not immune from suspicion. She had been outed by the local Anti-German League and her letter detailed the many casual and calculated insults and injuries she had suffered at the hands of neighbours, tradesmen and her landlord. A rent increase meant she would have to leave their Cremorne flat, sell most of their furniture and other belongings, and seek accommodation elsewhere.

As a prisoner-of-war, Freddie was only allowed one heavily censored three-hundred-word letter once a week to his family.

Freya could read between the lines of his stoic reassurances that he was 'among friends' and 'well looked after'. It was obvious he was wretchedly unhappy and missed his family desperately. She and Angie had attempted one trip to Liverpool but the camp commander had changed the visiting hours that Sunday without warning and, after more than four hours of train travel in the sweltering heat, they had been turned away.

Amid these days of terror and bitterness, one letter arrived that kept the flame of their faith in human kindness sputtering. It was from Robbie Fox's former governess, Miss Jane Blunt, who was now a Sunday school teacher in Lawson. In her letter she expressed her sympathies for Mrs Wood and her daughter with a passionate indignation that Freya found touching:

I am shocked and saddened by the news I hear of your situation: your husband's dismissal and internment and your ongoing torment at the hands of cowards. You have been treated shabbily and I detect the overbearing hand of **a certain person** *in much of this. Please remember that you have a friend who is willing to help you in any way possible.*

But one lone voice of support was not enough to change Freya's mind. She announced her decision one evening as she sat opposite her daughter, who was sunken into a silent fit of depression and had not touched her supper.

'We have no choice, Angie. We must move away. We will share a house with Eveline and Greta. Your father needs to see us as well. It is the right thing to do.'

16 October 1916

The sky is the colour of tin. It will rain this evening but she will not be here to see it. From her usual hiding place, she watches a distant rain veil, watering the valley from the grey keel of a cloud bank as it steams majestically towards her cliff top. The golden light fades rapidly from the bluffs all around her and the wind-tossed gum trees lose their sunlit sparkle and groan and hiss, waving their tortured limbs in protest. Cockatoos scream at the coming storm and dive for cover. The hedge rattles and shudders in the rising wind and the rain begins its manic tattoo but she will not budge until she hears the first crack of thunder.

Rain is a fitting farewell. It mirrors her own tears, which flow for hours as she sits, curled in a tight ball of misery, inside her hedge and thinks about the gradual crumbling of her cherished world since the day Robbie died.

She hears Freya calling. The van is packed. She looks back one last time at the Palace, its dome and battlements so familiar against the darkening sky, and wonders if she will ever lay eyes on them again.

She runs through the garden. The rain is here. It is time to go.

CHAPTER 11

Monika
The Ritz, Leura, May 2013

Lashed by the wind, raindrops continued to strike the window pane in Monika's room, making their unpredictable patterns on the glass. It was freezing outside and the staff had cranked up the oil heaters in the corridors to pump out a soup of hot air that made the windows fog and everyone feel drowsy.

Even so, Monika was having an exceptionally good day today. She sat upright in her armchair, smiling and attentive, with a box of handmade chocolates and a cup of Earl Grey at her elbow and played Scrabble, her favourite game, with Lisa. Neither the ravages of Alzheimer's nor the stroke had touched Monika's mastery of Scrabble. She was a clever tactical player with a vast vocabulary that meant she could lay out infuriatingly short obscure words in high-scoring patterns;

Lisa nearly always lost, even when she was blessed with the ten-point Z and Q tiles.

They played in a companionable near-silence for over an hour, interrupted every now and then by a mischievous chuckle from Monika or some playful baiting from Lisa. '*Boffo*? What's that? You made that up!'

'No, I didn't. It's used in reviews. Of films and plays. It means a knock-out success, a box-office hit. A boffo.'

Lisa had her laptop open and checked the Oxford. Monika was right of course: origin 1940s.

B on the double-letter-score, O, F, a second F and the final O on the triple-word-score finishing off HELL to make HELLO. A total of forty-eight points. Monika clapped her hands with glee. 'Boffo!' she exclaimed, and her eyes twinkled at Lisa.

There was definitely something of Monika's former sharpness, her arch humour and hauteur, alive in her today. Lisa smiled. Inside she struggled with her usual mixed feelings about her mother but she was still gratified her company brought Monika some small degree of happiness. A morning like this was something to be treasured, wasn't it? How many more like these were left to them?

Lisa had continued to work on deciphering the childish handwriting in her mother's diaries and its anarchic, freewheeling style of notation in pencil. She had scanned most of the pages from the first three volumes and two of the photo albums onto her laptop. Luke kept in touch with messages about the latest ex-staff member or guest who had surrendered some precious photo or memento for the hotel's growing archive.

Every now and then he would ask how her reading of the diary was progressing. She knew how much he wanted access but Lisa felt a strong sense of protectiveness that she could not fully explain, though she suspected it was probably some misplaced expression of loyalty to her mother. She promised she would share them with him very soon.

It was Lisa who suggested Luke meet her for coffee in Katoomba. She had decided to hand over the 1930s photo album for copying. There was nothing there to hide and she knew how excited he would be.

Luke was ecstatic when he saw it, turning the pages of the album reverently. His eyes seemed to feast on every little detail, as he nodded and murmured, 'Ah, yes, I thought that was when they extended the garden beds' or 'Well, that *is* unusual.'

The conversation inevitably came round to the diaries from which Lisa was making notes and marking up pages she thought Luke would find interesting.

'Those damn diaries,' said Lisa. 'They're driving me mad. In a good way, I guess. Pages of the most pedestrian stuff: roller-skating and dances and cake-making. And then, out of the blue, amazing things I never imagined.'

'Such as . . . ?' asked Luke, arching his eyebrows in an exaggeratedly prying manner. Lisa laughed. She couldn't help herself.

'Such as my mother spending half her childhood in the scrub, building cubby houses and playing Bushies and Bobbies with Lottie and Alan. And trapping and shooting rabbits! Turns out she was some kind of Aussie Annie Oakley. She got her first lady's rifle when she was only seven and was taught how to use it by her father. She ended up quite a crack shot, apparently. Even won ribbons at the Lithgow Show.'

Lisa warmed to her storytelling as she saw how much these details delighted Luke. Was there anyone else – even her brother – who would greet these discoveries with the same enthusiasm and wonder that she felt?

'An Aussie Annie Oakley. I like that.'

'It gets better. One time, she and Lottie got caught clay-pigeon shooting with their parents' gramophone record collection out on the tennis court. The old man went berserk!'

It was an image to conjure with: a flock of 78s spinning like giant black discuses overhead and then exploding in mid-air in a shower of shellac. Bing, Billie, Benny, Fats, Art, the Count and the Duke, Judy and Frank, all blasted to smithereens. Such savage vandalism, so shocking and liberating.

'Priceless!' laughed Luke.

'And how's this?' said Lisa, leaning closer for dramatic effect. 'When she was only seven, Monika got lost in the bush. They had to send search parties out to find her. She survived out there for nearly two days in the middle of summer. The story even made the local paper. I can't believe she never told us any of this.'

'I'll have to check the newspaper and police files for that one.' Luke made a note.

Lisa was in her stride now. 'There was one entry a few nights ago that really caught my attention. April 1936. A young girl visited Laura for about eight days in Leura. Spatzi, they called her. German for sparrow. "Spatzi, a good friend of Mama's all the way from Germany, stayed the whole week. Very pretty, lots of fun." She and Laura played tennis, went on walks, took in the sights. Adam was away on business at the time. The whole visit had this air of secrecy about it. Monika seemed to know instinctively not to tell her father. Very strange. I wonder if Spatzi could be the link to Ulrich? I'm so tempted to ask Mum.'

'So why don't you?' asked Luke.

Lisa looked at him directly. She felt she could trust Luke – or sincerely hoped she could – as she did not want to take this journey totally alone. Even so, there was a moment of hesitation before she replied. Luke looked back at her with a sympathetic half-smile but did not jump to fill the silence.

'The truth is, Luke, I'm afraid.'

'Afraid? Of what?'

'That I might uncover something terrible.' Lisa's voice had dropped to a whisper. 'It's all very well for me to go digging around in Monika's past. But what if she has turned her back on it for a very good reason? What if I end up hurting her all over again? Am I being selfish, Luke?'

'I don't really know the answer to that,' he said. 'But I think you'll know what to do when the time comes.'

It was as good an answer as she could reasonably expect.

Two nights ago she had started reading Monika's entries for the end of 1941.

The Palace had survived the Depression by lowering its full board to two pounds, eighteen and sixpence a week. It remained heavily booked throughout the toughest years as many families closed up their houses in Sydney and came up to live more cheaply in rooms at the hotel. It also remained a favourite honeymoon destination and its menu was still one of the most popular west of Sydney, with mains of roast baron of beef with horseradish cream, baked saddle of spring lamb in mint sauce, roast larded fillet of veal with lemon seasoning and roast suckling pig, all with lashings of savoury rice, mashed swedes, French beans and Saratoga chips. Chantilly wine trifle, apple pie and cognac sauce pudding were favourite desserts.

The family moved to Mosman in September 1938, leaving the mountains and Monika's tomboy childhood behind her, despite frequent return visits on weekends. The girls missed the bush a little at first, but the Foxes soon took to their new beach and city life in Mosman. Adam even bought a new car and *The Seagull*, a small yacht for harbour racing. Lottie and Monika were enrolled at Queenwood School for Girls, not far from their home.

It soon became clear to Lisa as she read her mother's diary that the carefree days of Monika's childhood in the mountains – the endless parties and games, the freedom and wildness of the bush – were beginning to vanish. Like Australia itself, forced to face the crisis it had long feared, eleven-year-old Monika would watch the untroubled, privileged life she knew begin, bit by bit, to fade.

Since it had started, the war had seemed a remote drama to Monika Fox, mostly stories on the radio about Herr Hitler and Mr Churchill and the Blitz. When Prime Minister Menzies announced cutting the petrol ration to only one thousand miles a year, Monz thought father would 'blow a gasket' as he stormed around, yelling, 'Bloody hell! This will kill the Palace stone dead. No one'll be able to drive to the mountains. *And* we'll have to cancel all our day trips for guests out to Jenolan.'

Papa liked nothing better than to drive the family up to the Jersey Avenue house in Leura on the weekend in the Hudson so he could get in a round of golf at Leura or Blackheath and keep an eye on the Palace. Monz and Lottie liked to play croquet on the lawn and hide-and-seek on the verandas and in the hedges and feed Captain Pogo's meat scraps to the kookaburras. Bowing to the inevitable, Fox had installed one of those big ugly charcoal gas producers on the back of the Hudson and cut back his visits to about once a month. Sacrifices of wartime and all that.

Business had begun to pick up slowly at the Palace when the war began as more and more young men hastily tied the knot on enlisting. On one of Papa's trips to the hotel, Monz and Lottie saw five Diggers in their slouch hats loitering in the drive. They were on their honeymoons, waiting for their young brides to fix their hair and make-up and join them for a sightseeing tour to Echo Point and the Three Sisters.

'I was a bit surprised by their loping and larking about, smoking cigarettes and cracking jokes,' Monz noted haughtily in her diary. 'It was not how I imagined real soldiers to behave.'

When the government took 'hotels and restaurants' off the List of Reserved Occupations later that year, five of the Palace staff joined up, including the general manager Mr Merewether's son Roger. Monz was amazed. 'Roger is such a drongo. He can hardly tie his shoelaces much less fire a gun. God help Australia if we're going to need boofheads like Roger to save us.' Monz loved to collect juicy words like 'drongo' and 'boofhead' for her diary, words that would shock her parents if they knew.

Everything changed three weeks before Christmas 1941, when the two girls were called into the living room after school. Mama and Papa looked very solemn.

'What is it?' Monz asked nervously, wondering if Captain Pogo had dug up Mama's pearl earring that she and Lottie had buried as treasure in a box in the rose bed last spring. Instead they were told to be very quiet and gathered around the AWA walnut cabinet to listen to the new prime minister, Mr Curtin, announce in his broad flat voice: '*Men and women of Australia. We are at war with Japan.*'

Monz wrote that night under the bedsheet with her torch: 'Tonight Mama and Papa looked the unhappiest I have ever seen. They told us not to worry but said that this was one of the most important days in Australia's history. I hope we are all going to be safe and that Papa does not have to fight in the war.'

Monika's parents had good reason to look grim. Within days there was a call up for more recruits, the petrol ration was cut again, the Christmas vacations were shortened and holiday train services cancelled. The Palace began refunding bookings. Business looked doomed. Adam slept badly, pacing his study at night, smoking cigars out on the balcony and watching the lights on the harbour. Laura observed his anguish, soothing it as best she could but unable to make it go away.

And then a miracle happened. In the weeks following the attack on Pearl Harbor, the Blue Mountains woke up to find it had become a refuge for thousands of people fleeing Sydney. 'Invasion panic' took grip like a bout of flu. All the guesthouses, hotels and cottages were booked solid. Mr Merewether at the Palace was laughing when he rang Adam.

'The phone's been ringing off the hook all week, sir. I've raised the rack rate twice but the calls keep coming. Rents and house prices have gone crazy from Katoomba all the way out to Bathurst. People are paying up to eight pounds a week for rooms and five guineas a week for a cottage, can you believe it? I've seen houses for sale up here for one thousand four hundred pounds, cash on the nail.'

That morning Monz and Lottie were playing a game of Beetle in the front room while their mother was flipping through the *Women's Weekly* picking out a dress for a luncheon with her Mosman crowd the following week.

Papa bowled in and announced at the top of his voice, 'Guess what? The Palace is booked solid until the New Year. And I just got a *twelve*-month lease on one of our cottages in Blackheath!' Adam hugged and kissed his wife with the air of a man who had been given a stay of execution.

The atmosphere of triumph was infectious and the children cheered and clapped and were scooped up in their father's embrace.

'Let's take *The Seagull* out for a sail,' Adam suggested. 'What do you say? A beach picnic somewhere. And we'll take a few special treats to celebrate.' He winked at Laura. 'Special treats' usually meant pastries, lollies and ice-cream for the children and a gourmet hamper and bottle of French bubbly for the parents. A fresh breeze had just sprung up and the sky over Sydney Harbour was a cloudless delft blue. It was perfect sailing weather.

The next few weeks Papa was the happiest Monz had seen him for some time. The Blue Mountains continued to attract a steady stream of new residents and the Palace thrived. Adam scoffed at the angry letters in the papers lambasting these 'bomb dodgers' whose wealth bought them a way out of danger ahead of others. The nastiest of these letters targeted refugees from Europe, particularly German Jews, as the worst offenders. 'War always brings out the worst in people,' Adam said over his morning coffee. 'It was the same in the Great War.'

He and Laura also read in the papers about the attacks on Italians and Germans living in Australia. Shop windows smashed, assaults, boycotts. New South Wales Premier Mr Mair called for the government in Canberra to intern all 'enemy aliens'. Camps had been opened in Hay, Cowra and Holsworthy and Japanese civilians would soon be joining the German and Italian families already interned there.

'I can't believe it's happening again!' cried Laura, crumpling the pages of newsprint in her fists. 'Haven't we learned anything?'

'What's the matter, Mama?' asked Monika, alarmed at her mother's distress. The girls were about to head out the front door to school. Pogo raced up and down the back veranda, barking.

Laura tried to calm herself but her chest heaved with sobs.

'What is it, sweetie?' Adam asked, taking her in his arms and stroking her hair. He had not seen Laura cry like this before.

'I don't know. I'm sorry. It just seems so cruel,' said Laura.

Adam paled a little at that. He turned to the two girls. 'It's alright, my darlings. Mama will be fine. Now, hurry along. You mustn't be late for class.'

Singapore fell to the Japanese the following February and there was an air raid on Darwin four days later. Panic was in the air like lightning over dry scrub.

Papa told us today that Mr Merewether got a telegram from the Red Cross saying that Roger is now a P.O.W. (that means a prisoner-of-war). He is one of 15,000 poor Aussie soldiers captured by the Japs in Singapore. He's in a place called Changi. I hope he'll be alright. He doesn't deserve to die even if he is a drongo.

In the window of Tooheys' newsagents, Monz and Lottie saw a big poster pasted on the glass. 'Bloody hell!' Lottie grimaced at the giant Japanese soldier striding across the globe, the Rising Sun at his back and iron-heeled boot planted on Australia.

HE'S COMING SOUTH, trumpeted the poster. IT'S FIGHT, WORK OR PERISH.

'I hope we never meet one of those marching up Middle Head Road,' said Monz.

That night she sat with her torch under her blankets, her bedroom lights off and curtains drawn as Sydney prepared for war, writing in her diary and giving herself nightmares with her drawings of Jap planes dropping bombs and waves of buck-toothed soldiers advancing with bayonets dripping blood. Mosman was submerged in the murk of a 'brown-out' every night with windows papered up or covered with blackout drapes, streetlights hooded and car headlights masked.

As Christmas approached, the girls watched sweaty men with picks and shovels dig slit trenches in Memory Park and Rawson Oval and in the grounds of Queenwood School. When Laura took Monz and Lottie and Alan down on Sunday for a swim they found that the older gentlemen of the Volunteer Defence Corps – the Retreads as they nicknamed themselves – had strung up coils of barbed wire the full length of Balmoral Beach. 'It's all very well to stop the Japs but how are we meant to have a dip?' moaned Laura, tramping back up the street in the heat with her three children trailing behind, whining.

The start of school was delayed for two weeks while the government ordered more trenches to be dug and hoped the drought would last so they would not fill up with rain. Monz and Lottie spent their afternoons on the balcony of their house watching the ARP wardens blowing their whistles and conducting air-raid exercises down at the pavilion with ladders, buckets, hoses and fake bombs made out of cardboard. They could also hear the whooshes and blasts of mortars and anti-aircraft guns up on Middle Head. The city held its breath and waited for the enemy to come. It did not have long to wait.

Sunday 31st May 1942

Lottie and I woke up around 11.00. The windows were rattling and the whole house shaking from top to bottom. We could hear booming sounds like cannons being fired. Were they bombs? Was this the invasion? But there had been no air-raid sirens or planes screaming overhead. Were all the ARP wardens and the Retreads already dead and the Japs swarming up Balmoral Beach to kill us in our beds?

We ran next door where we huddled with Mama. I could tell she was afraid too. But she kept saying how everything would be alright. Captain Pogo was barking his head off and poor Alan began to blub. Papa was downstairs on the phone talking to Lionel, his friend who lives over in Lavender Bay. He shouted up the stairs: 'All the ships near Garden Island have blacked out their lights. There's some kind of hunt going on. Enemy submarines, they say.'

After a while, the night calmed down and there were no more loud noises. Mama and Papa let us bring in a mattress and blankets and sleep on the floor in their room. Alan fell asleep after a while but I don't think anyone else slept a wink all night.

I kept listening for more explosions. Could this attack be just the start? When would the bombers come and destroy Sydney just like they had Darwin? I could see Papa staring out the window until the sun came up. He didn't say anything but I saw him take his hunting rifle out of its case in the study and check if it was loaded. If it came to that, I am a crack shot myself and wasn't going to let Papa fight alone.

There were more loud booms for hours the next morning, really close by. The whole house shook terribly. I have never been so scared in my whole life but I refused to cry. And part of me was a bit excited too.

Adam came home with the following evening's special edition of *The Sun* headlined SYDNEY'S WILD NIGHT OF EXCITEMENT. The Foxes sat down to hear him read the whole story aloud after dinner. Three Japanese midget submarines had slipped through the Heads and attempted to torpedo the USS *Chicago*, sinking a moored ferry which was serving as a floating barracks instead. Houses were shaken by concussion waves from depth charges dropped in Sydney Harbour by the navy. Late-night ferry passengers had been scared out of their wits by bursts of machine-gun fire and the sight of red tracer pom-poms and searchlights sweeping the dark waters. The hunt for subs lasted all night long and the persistent booms that morning were an attack by depth charges on the last submarine, stranded in nearby Taylors Bay.

A week later one of the 'mother' submarines, which had launched the midget subs, bombarded the Eastern Suburbs. Only one shell detonated and miraculously there were no fatalities. But Sydneysiders knew nobody was safe anymore.

'They can call us "bomb dodgers" if they like, but that's it!' Adam said the next day as he looked at the photos in the *Sydney Morning Herald* of damaged houses in Woollahra and a crowd of boys gathered around a crater in front of a corner store in Bondi. 'We're moving camp to Leura for a while. At least until the real threat blows over. I need to keep an eye on the hotel and . . . well, I think it's for the best.'

Mama seemed perfectly happy to move back up to their big weekender in Jersey Avenue, but Monz and Lottie hated the whole idea. They desperately missed their new friends at Queenwood and dreaded having to start another high school.

'We all have to make sacrifices,' announced Papa. Monz and Lottie's misery deepened when, on their first day at Katoomba High, they discovered they were among five hundred extra students enrolling, all children of families who had relocated from Sydney.

'The whole place is so bodgy!' Monz complained to her diary.

The principal, Mr Bentley, has called in teachers from all over the place to help out – the blind, the lame and the incredibly ancient. They're even holding classes in the corridors and the outdoor lunch shed. Our maths master Mr Greenwood is some poor bomb-happy chap from the Great War. He tries to keep order by shouting and threatening to cane everybody but his hands tremble and the boys make fun of him. It's a total shambles.

Monz and Lottie's suffering was mercifully short-lived. A letter arrived a few weeks later from Miss Rennie, the head of Queenwood, informing Mr and Mrs Fox that, because so many parents had moved away, she had arranged for her co-principal, Miss Medway, to evacuate with a group of students to Glenleigh, near Penrith, at the foot of the mountains. Other private schools were doing the same. The junior boys from Sydney Church of England Grammar School had already moved to Mount Victoria while the girls were accommodated at the grand Chateau Napier guesthouse on the hill overlooking Leura. Mona and Lottie would have to catch a train an hour each way every day to Glenleigh but Monz rejoiced: 'I will be reunited with Shirley and Valerie and Antonia and escape this purgatory!'

Monz tried to fit back into her old life in Leura but it was not easy. Leura was a pretty little town, especially in autumn, but the freezing cold waters of Katoomba Baths were no substitute for a swim at Balmoral. And the bush that had once been her playground no longer called to Monika the way it had when she was little. She had changed.

It was not just the fault of the mountains. Despite the cinematic distractions offered by the Embassy and the Savoy in

Katoomba, the dreariness of the war crept like a numbing fog into every minute of Monika's days. Into her lunchtimes in the school hall making camouflage nets with rough hessian and rope. In the shortages of everything from tinned tomatoes to sugar and, worst of all, no hot-water bottles! In the deafening roar that woke her and Lottie every morning before dark as the trains carried workers to the Small Arms Factory at Lithgow further west.

Two anti-aircraft batteries guarded the Lithgow factory against air attack. Every time a plane rumbled over the mountains, necks craned and eyes squinted skywards. As a senior girl guide, Lottie had put her hand up to train for the Volunteer Air Observers Corps as a plane-spotter. She didn't get a special uniform but she did get a splendid badge with a golden eagle. Every Wednesday after school and on weekends, she reported for duty at Wentworth Falls. She was insufferably proud.

Their brother, Alan, like all small boys who spent hours each day playing outside, learned rhymes to memorise the shape and names of aircraft, friend and foe.

Four engines hurl the tapered wings
Across the topmost skies,
Its turrets guard the bombs it brings
When Flying Fortress flies!

Over and over, Alan and Lottie would practise these rhymes together after school until Monz wanted to scream and tear her plaits out.

It seemed as if everyone except Monz had war fever. Even her mother, the glamorous society queen, had decided it was time to 'do her bit'. Laura Fox had played a part on Red Cross and Comfort Fund committees, but in May she went one step further. She enlisted with the Red Cross Voluntary Aid Detachment looking after TB patients at the Bodington Sanatorium in Wentworth Falls for four shifts a week. At her induction parade she stood to attention with her fellow nurses in her short-sleeved VAD dress and soft wide-brimmed hat. 'Mama always looks like one of those Hollywood stars in the magazines,' Monika wrote in her diary. 'Today she looked like a cross between the Virgin Mary and a lady lawns bowler.'

While her sister kept watch for Zeros screaming over the Grose Valley and her brother collected scrap metal in a billycart as a member of the local Ginger Meggs Salvage Corps, Monz's only escape from all this wartime dullness was lying on the rug in front of the AWA listening to her favourite radio program, *The Argonauts Club*. No matter how tedious each day, each night promised the rousing chorus of the rowing song and 'adventuring to yet uncharted shores'. The budding writer sent in dozens of poems and stories which were judged to be so outstanding they earned their author enough points for an *Order of the Dragon's Tooth* certificate as well as book prizes displayed proudly in her bedroom. Laura and Adam sometimes joined Monika when one of her compositions was being broadcast and they made an appreciative audience with cries of 'Bravo!' and 'Boffo!' and loud applause. 'She'll make us proud one day, that girl!' Adam predicted.

As it turned out the Japs did not invade Australia that year to make Monz's life a misery. Instead that job was left to Mr Curtin and his well-named Minister for War Organisation, Mr Dedman, with their religious zeal for a new kind of wartime drabness called Austerity. In the middle of the year everyone was issued with ration books for clothing, which meant no more lovely evening gowns or hats and gloves or smart suits or summer dresses or swimming costumes. Everything had to be patched and darned and homemade. Monz and Lottie were no longer expected to wear a new school uniform and made do with threadbare blouses and skirts instead. Father was reduced to wearing his old suits, shiny at the cuffs and elbows, and he put the Hudson up on blocks in the garage. The Palace struggled again as prices were fixed for meals and fine dining was cut back to two courses. Austerity ruled supreme.

Adam and Laura and Lottie and Alan seemed to take all this in good spirits, but Monz pined for the sparkling warm waters of her harbour and her sunny, comfy life back in Mosman. It did not look as if they would be returning there any time soon. Father had let out the house to a family of Hungarian refugees who were prepared to pay good money on a long lease.

Here she was, twelve years old, a prisoner in her darned lumpy jumpers and prickly wool stockings, locked up like a nun with not a male in sight under the age of fifty except telegram boys delivering tragic news on their bicycles or bunches of brats not much older than Alan collecting scrap metal and rubber for the war. No dances, no parties, no fun.

'Everyone is making sacrifices, Monika,' Laura lectured whenever Monz looked glum or complained. 'And privileged families like ours must be seen to be doing their bit like everyone else. Never underestimate other people's capacity for envy, you mark my words.'

'Visiting hours are over, I'm afraid.'

As Lisa packed up the Scrabble board, she studied Monika out of the corner of her eye. It was all so disconcerting, learning about the inner world of her mother as a twelve-year-old, privy to her intimate hopes and fears for the future, only to come to the Ritz every Tuesday and Friday to see this same life staggering to its conclusion. It was like reading the opening and final chapters of a story at the same time. It made her feel traitorous and yet also tremble with a feeling she had never imagined she would feel for her mother: compassion.

Monika had won Scrabble again of course and was very pleased with herself as the nurse served her lunch.

'See you, Mum,' said Lisa as she headed for the door.

Monika, preoccupied, did not reply. 'Boffo!' she said under her breath, a small smile playing on her lips at the sound of this word she had dredged up from so long ago. 'Boffo!'

CHAPTER 12

Angie
Liverpool, October 1916–May 1918

If Freya and Angie had any notions that Liverpool was an escape from the intrusive and belligerent atmosphere of Meadow Springs, they were soon dispelled. In accordance with the War Precautions (Aliens Registration) Regulations, Freya had filled out Form E – 'Notice of Change of Abode' – in triplicate at Katoomba police station and presented her certificate of registration to the aliens registration officer.

Within two days of their move to Liverpool, she had presented herself again, as required by law, to the registrations officer at the police station there. He inspected her papers, asked her several questions about her family, her business, her intended movements and if she had changed her name.

He then recorded her address. 'How old is your daughter?' the ruddy-faced man asked as she turned to leave.

'She has just turned thirteen.'

'Well, don't forget that when she turns eighteen she will have to be registered as an alien herself.' The man smiled unpleasantly through tobacco-stained teeth.

'Let us pray the war is well and truly over by then,' said Freya, keeping her face as composed as she could manage. 'For all our sakes.'

Angie could tell her mother was fuming as they trudged back up George Street past Liverpool's town hall. The petty official had reminded Freya as she left that she must report to him fortnightly and that failure to do so could result in a fine of a hundred pounds or a six-month prison sentence.

Liverpool was much bigger than Meadow Springs but it still felt like a country town, with its broad main streets surrounded by the hot scrubby plains of south-west Sydney. It was also a military town. On the other side of the Georges River lay the largest training camp in New South Wales, preparing thousands of volunteers for the Australian Imperial Force. Originally rows of bell-shaped white tents, the camp was now virtually a town in itself, with barracks, stables, latrines, cookhouses and a hospital. From the weatherboard cottage on Rose Street that Freya, Angie, Eveline and baby Greta rented, the crack of rifle fire could be heard distinctly from the range across the river. Other smaller training camps were close by in Casula and Warwick Farm, all only a few miles from the sprawling German Concentration Camp in Holsworthy.

There were at least six other German families renting cottages on Rose Street; all of them had relocated to Liverpool for the same reasons as Freya and Angie. Not surprisingly they kept a low profile but cautiously welcomed the newcomers. Mrs Eyl – whose husband was a doctor interned at Holsworthy – and her daughter Astrid invited them over for pastries and coffee.

The Eyls were a cultured Jewish family, interested in the arts and politics, who had migrated to Australia from Leipzig twenty years earlier. Their daughter had been born in Double Bay in Sydney where Dr Eyl had his rooms. Mrs Eyl was deeply flattered to have the daughters of the great Wolfang von Gettner in her house and proudly displayed their collection of lithographs and paintings from Germany. While they loved the visual arts, the family's talent lay in music.

'My daughter takes after my husband as a fine violinist. You must come and hear her play sometime,' said Mrs Eyl. Eveline revealed her passion for singing and they promised to perform a concert. Both Eveline and Freya decided they liked Mrs Eyl a great deal; it felt good to have a neighbour who was so sympathetic for a change.

Before they left, Mrs Eyl gently warned them about their first visit to the German Concentration Camp – the GCC as it was called – at Holsworthy. 'It can be a bit of a shock at first.'

It *was* a shock. The camp was so big, so spread out, stretching as far as the eye could see. From the vantage point of the visitors' compound, which was no more than a grassless paddock, Angie stared in amazement at the long parallel rows of wooden huts separated by narrow 'streets', once grass but long since trampled to dirt. Washing hung on improvised lines and men in white canvas giggle hats shuffled back and forth or collected in small knots.

From a distance, the camp had the busy, almost grotesquely festive atmosphere of an outdoor marketplace, though it shimmered in the blisteringly hot sun with barely a gum tree in sight. Everything was coated in a thick layer of yellow dust, and everywhere you looked there stood a uniformed soldier with a slouch hat and a rifle with fixed bayonet sloped at his shoulder. Another group stood guard over a machine-gun on a tall watchtower to the south. Fence posts and stone boundary markers were all whitewashed and every view ended in a high, triple-layered wall of barbed wire.

Freddie was thinner than Angie or Freya could ever recall seeing him. He had made an effort to shave and comb his hair but he still appeared grizzled and shabby, and was obviously ashamed of his canvas fatigues with 'POW' stamped on the back. Angie struggled very hard not to cry that first time. Tears brimmed at the corners of her father's eyes, too, as he pushed his hands through the barbed-wire fence between them and gripped hers.

'I've missed you, Papa,' she whispered.

'What about the cottage?' he asked Freya on that first visit.

'It will be fine. I'm sure Fox will look after it for us until we can return,' she reassured her husband, who knew more than anyone the sacrifice she had made in leaving her father's bush kingdom behind.

They tried to visit Freddie every fortnight for the two hours allotted on a Sunday afternoon, despite the obtrusive presence of the guards who patrolled the narrow passage between families and internees. Sometimes they were defeated by weather and train timetables and sickness. They brought Freddie comfort packages: soaps, Mrs Eyl's *schnecken* and *rugelach* and, when they could afford it, books.

He never complained once. He never told them how the guards tore apart all their care packages to check for illicit weapons or coded messages and sometimes just to steal things, as they had with his luggage that first day. He never told them about his sleepless nights, his fears of the criminal thugs and the drunken, corrupt guards, the daily taunting and swearing, the bitter cold, the rats and the swarms of blowflies and mosquitoes, the rotten food, the stench of the latrines, the queues for the cold showers. Worst of all, though, was the soul-destroying boredom. There were no lights in the huts so he read by the light of the moon: anything to take his mind off the tedium of endless repeated days. 'Barbed Wire Disease' they called it: depression, apathy, loss of hope.

The war would end soon. This was the only prayer that sustained them. And the belief that, when the war ended, life would return to normal.

Angie's life was boring too but she could never say so. Her circumstances were not nearly as harsh as her father's, so she had to bear it all in stoic silence. She knew she would get it in the neck from Freya if she didn't.

She missed Meadow Springs. She tried hard to hang on to her memories of the valley, the hedge and the Palace, but day by day they grew blurrier. Their rented cottage in Rose Street offered a meaner, more pinched view of the world. It looked over a small backyard boxed in by a gap-toothed, weathered grey fence with a lantana bush straggling along the back of the block. Beyond this, Angie could see the roofs and brick chimneys of neighbouring houses and the sparse forest of electricity poles. Instead of the chinking of parrots and carolling of magpies, all she could hear was the sullen cussing of crows perched in threes and fours along the electricity lines.

Freya decided there was no point in risking exposure to persecution again at the local high school, so she kept Angie at home and took her education into her own hands with daily lessons in painting, art history and German. Angie was impressed by how much her mother knew. She even enjoyed the art classes, though she knew she could never meet her mother's exacting standards. Too poor to buy oils, canvas and brushes, they stuck to life drawing with pencils and charcoal.

Everyone tried their best to get along that first summer but the atmosphere in the cramped weatherboard cottage grew tense when Greta cried all night in the appalling heat and Angie, Eveline and Freya sweated and tossed in their beds. Their only escape was when they would take Greta down to the river in the pram. Here they enjoyed the cool evening breezes, and the sight of the willows dipping their long leaves in the water and galahs coming down for a drink at the river's edge. The two sisters and their children would sit and watch until the sun touched the horizon and the first star appeared in the evening sky and then hurry home to a simple supper.

To Angie's delight, Astrid Eyl was encouraged by her mother to join Freya's lessons as she too was avoiding the local high school. Angie thought this was an excellent development as Freya had to modify her habitual strictness. What she lacked in academic brilliance, Astrid more than made up for in her genius for music. Angie never ceased to be astonished at how her friend's air of awkwardness and misery evaporated when she tucked her violin beneath her jaw, closed her eyes and raised her bow. By some mysterious process, the music changed this melancholy plain-faced girl into a graceful angelic creature transported to a state of bliss. The concerts she gave at the house in Rose Street would become Angie's best memories of that time.

The landlord, Mr Hughes, hiked the rent on the cottage twice during 1917, thanks to growing demand from German families for accommodation in Liverpool as the population of the GCC climbed towards six thousand. Freya and Eveline were just grateful that Mr Hughes was happy to exploit them and not evict them, as had happened to several other families nearby. They were also thankful when every month a courier arrived with a brown paper bag of banknotes as part of Freya's secret agreement with Adam Fox. Eveline's widow's pension and Freya's allowance as an internee's wife were barely enough to cover the essentials.

And then, abruptly, the payments stopped.

'"I regret to inform you that your agreement with Mr Fox has been rendered null and void as of today."'

The words rang out as loud and alarming as a gunshot. Angie had switched off her reading light, tucked her copy of *The Songs of a Sentimental Bloke* under her pillow and turned her face to the wall in the dark narrow space of the sleep-out. The louvred door behind her was closed but even so she could not mistake the panicked rage in Freya's voice as she read aloud to her sister the contents of a letter from Adam Fox's solicitor. Her voice was shaking.

Given your past confidential and close relations, my client naturally took on trust your representations to him as to the authenticity of the work which is the subject of your agreement with him. The work in question is currently stored for safekeeping and my client's intention is to keep it from public view until the war has ended. It is as a result of a private viewing of the work by a close and trusted friend of Mr Fox, who also happens to be expert in art history, that doubts were initially raised about the work's pedigree.

Further examination by suitably qualified persons reinforced the view that this painting is a forgery. Mr Fox does not impute any malicious motives to you in this matter but regrets to inform you that he cannot justify any further down payments on a work that has little to no market value and would only bring discredit to your father's reputation.

As an act that he hopes will be understood as one of generosity and good faith, he proposes not to reclaim any monies paid to date. In recognition of your straitened financial circumstances, he also renews his original proposal to you of a transfer of land title by way of a trust arrangement for a period of three years. He hastens to point out that such an arrangement will secure the property from attempts to have it transferred to the Public Trustee as the confiscated property of a registered enemy alien.

In anticipation of your speediest response.

Arthur J Pullen, Solicitor.

'Liar!' shouted Freya. 'The painting is real, I swear it is! You see how he threatens us while pretending to be our friend and protector? He has us at his mercy and will steal our land if it is the last thing he does. Monster!'

Angie lay in the dark, not daring to move. Even though she was now fourteen, moments like these made her feel as vulnerable as a little girl. She thought her heart would break to hear her mother's distress. Freya's outburst had woken Greta, of course, and it felt as if the baby's wailing expressed Angie's own anxiety.

'*Beruhige dich, liebe Schwester!*' urged Eveline, trying to quieten her distraught sister as best she could. Eveline understood Freya well – her changeable moods, her violent tempers – and could often find ways to console and comfort her. But tonight Freya was beyond such help.

'It's all a trick, don't you see? He is *so* clever! He set this trap and I have walked right into it. We cannot afford lawyers to do our dirty work for us. He has all the power and we have none.'

As Angie listened to her mother's rant, a memory swam back to her through the dark waters of that sombre year following Robbie's death. While her father was staggering under the blows of public disapproval at the hotel, her mother had retreated into a sustained burst of painting in her studio. The memory that struggled up to the surface was a glimpse through the studio door of a large oil painting: a landscape of purple and gold cliffs and silver-green forest.

In the darkness of her bedroom, Angie opened her eyes in a moment of terror. Dear God, was it possible that Freya had lost her mind? Had she in fact planned to deceive Mr Fox with a fake Wolfgang von Gettner for a sum of money and then been found out? Was she so lost in delusion that she now imagined that this fake she had created was in fact real and railed against its discovery? It was too horrible a possibility to contemplate.

The following morning, Angie did not say a word. Freya postponed their lessons and for several days did nothing but sit quietly in the front room. Sometimes she sat alone. Sometimes she sat in companionable silence with Eveline as her sister breastfed Greta or rocked her in her bassinet. After a week of thinking the matter over, she replied to Fox's solicitor. She also wrote a personal letter to Adam Fox himself.

The following month Angie saw Freya give Eveline enough cash to pay for Greta's visit to the doctor and medication for her whooping cough. She assumed that her mother and Mr Fox had reached an agreement. Angie was tempted to ask her mother point blank about the cottage, but when she looked at Freya's pale face, the worry lines imprinted ever deeper across her forehead and the ever-thickening silver hairs at her brow, she decided it could wait.

Astrid and Angie called themselves the 'Rose Street internees', imprisoned under their mothers' joint protection. Their only joy was in each other's company. Left alone in Mrs Eyl's front parlour one long rainy winter's afternoon, they dug out an old board game from the linen cupboard. Courtship and Marriage it was called, the colourful board lavishly illustrated with wedding bells and romantic vignettes of Edwardian couples enjoying picnics and jaunts in their vintage motors. 'Come on, let's play!' said Angie. 'It looks hilarious!'

They soon discovered that the game was altogether designed from a male suitor's point of view. From square one – *Introduction* – each hopeful bachelor threw a die to proceed along a curving, wedding-bell-shaped path. Players advanced by turns across the many stepping stones of courtship: from *Picnic*, *Motor Ride*, *All Smooth with Family*, *Parents Charmed* and *Croquet Party* to *Proposal*, *Fancy-dress Ball* and *Engagement*, finally landing on *Happy Wedding* and matrimonial bliss. Pitfalls along this knotty path included *Flirtation*, *Offend Parents*, *Rival*, *Jealousy*, *Short of Money* and *Jilted*.

They played for a while, putting on mock gentlemanly voices and making silly expostulations such as 'Egad, that's just too damned bad!' or 'Oh I say, poor show, old chap!' Astrid and Angie fell about giggling and shushing each other in case Mrs Eyl came in and discovered they were making fun of a favourite girlhood game.

Angie won the first round and Astrid's mood changed.

'Shame they didn't include a square for *German, Dirt Poor and Despised*,' she said gloomily as she munched on one of her mother's pastries.

Angie gave her a hug. 'Now, come on, don't be like that. We won't be trapped like this forever. And guess what? Aunty Eveline told me a new family have moved in on Reilly Street. And they have a son!'

Angie related how Aunty Eveline, while pegging out the washing in the backyard, had surreptitiously let Angie know about Oskar Krause. Eveline had met him last Friday on her way to the clinic with Greta. 'We spoke briefly. He seemed a very polite young man. Fifteen years old. Going to Liverpool Boys High School. His father is a political journalist. Interned, of course.'

'And . . . ?' Angie prompted.

'And what?' said Eveline with a teasing smile.

'What does he *look* like?'

Oskar Krause was tall for his age, golden-haired, dark-eyed

and had lightly tanned muscled arms. In short, he was handsome. Angie was determined to find a way for them to 'accidentally' meet.

'Well, that takes care of you then,' said Astrid moodily. 'It was nice being your friend. Come by and visit whenever you can spare the time.'

Angie thumped Astrid with one of Mrs Eyl's hand-embroidered cushions. 'Don't be such a ninny! We haven't even met him yet. And anyway, *our* friendship comes first.'

Astrid smiled a little but she still looked unconvinced. 'Have you ever been in love?' she asked.

The question took Angie completely off guard. Tears pricked at the corner of her eyes. She had not thought about Robbie for such a long time. Should she tell Astrid? The temptation to unburden herself of her secret past was great. It would either strengthen their bond or destroy it. She decided to take the risk and unfolded the history of her childhood friend and his death in detail.

Astrid was lost for words, not something that happened very often. 'It's a story worthy of a Wagnerian opera,' she said at last. 'You are such an *interesting* person, Angie Wood. Which is probably why I like you so much.'

Oskar *was* handsome. And tall. Allowed out for a short excursion to the post office to mail a parcel for Mrs Eyl, Angie and

Astrid encountered him one Monday morning as he was leaving the house for school. Much to Astrid's dismay, Angie hailed him in German: '*Wo gehen Sie, Mein Herr?*'

Oskar spun around, a scowl of alarm on his face, and rushed towards the two girls. 'For heaven's sake, not so loud! Are you crazy? What if the neighbours hear?'

Angie apologised. 'It got your attention, though. Can we walk with you? We live over in Rose Street. No more German, I promise.'

By a stroke of good fortune, a local publican had commissioned a painting from Freya for his hotel. She insisted on being paid in cash – and not beer as he originally proposed – and so she was kept busy, using the wash shed out the back as her makeshift studio. Aunty Eveline asked that Angie and Astrid keep her company on her afternoon walks to the park with Greta now the spring weather was here and Freya welcomed the solitude to work. Thus did Angie's aunt conspire with the two girls to meet up once or twice a week with Oskar for twenty minutes or so at the park on his way home from school.

'If mother ever finds out . . .' Angie had objected at first when Eveline put the idea to her with a wink.

'Then I shall remind her of what she was like at your age. And anyway, it's all an innocent lark. I am your chaperone and Oskar is a true gentleman.'

The two girls and the tall boy walked and talked under the trees. They tossed sticks into the river and cracked jokes. Oskar was talented at boxing and showed how he had dealt with the Hun-baiting bullies at school. Encouraged by both her new friends, Astrid even smuggled her violin out of the house and gave a short concert by the willows. Galahs shrieked and whistled in the distance as the violin swooped and sang. Oskar did cartwheels in appreciation of the performance.

It soon became obvious that Oskar liked Angie and Astrid – and especially Angie. The painter's daughter and the journalist's son coyly exchanged notes in which they expressed their appreciation of each other. Angie could feel her pulse race whenever the golden-haired young man came near. His face sweetened her dreams. She had sworn never to let herself feel this way again, but she couldn't help it. She had already begun to let her guard down. Maybe it was time to let Robbie go finally and put all that pain behind her.

The moment of truth came one magical spring afternoon. The air was soft and the lemon fluff of wattle blossom floated on the breeze. Oskar and Angie found themselves alone in the park, hidden briefly from Astrid and Eveline. They had their backs pressed against the smooth bark of a willow tree.

Their conversation had dropped away to a long silence. Angie looked up at him. Oskar's dark brown eyes had narrowed to a gaze of intense seriousness and his brows were knitted. She nodded as if in answer to an unsaid question and Oskar leaned closer and kissed her tenderly, if a little awkwardly, on the lips. Angie felt her heart bolt and a feeling of bliss and possibility unlike anything she had ever known flowed through her whole body.

'Angie? Oskar? Where are you?'

They both heard Astrid's sulky cry. It sounded as if they were kids playing hide-and-seek and she was put out that they had stayed hidden so long. They grinned at each other, and Oskar squeezed Angie's hand tightly before they emerged from behind the tree.

After a month, Eveline decided that they should introduce Oskar to Freya. 'We can't keep him a secret forever. Better to tell the truth now than be found out later!' She was right of course and they broke the news to Angie's mother that she wanted to invite a boy over to tea. 'He's a fine young fellow,' attested Eveline.

Freya took the news well when it was explained how they had met at the park one day. 'Well, I guess it can't do any harm. His father is a journalist, you say?'

Oskar came with excellent family credentials. His father had been a writer for a left-wing workers' paper – which was why he had been interned – and his great-aunt had been active in the Australian suffragette movement. An invitation was sent to him and his mother to come for tea.

Oskar and Mrs Sascha Krause duly came, as did Astrid and Mrs Eyl. Eveline and Freya prepared a *Bienenstich* or 'bee-sting' cake for the occasion. Even Mrs Eyl was impressed. While the adults shared their stories of suffering, Angie, Astrid and Oskar exchanged meaningful looks. It was strange to have their secret friendship out in the open like this but it was also a welcome relief. How good it felt to have friends, thought Angie. Friendship provided a refuge against the hostility and cold indifference of the world. She had felt so terribly alone in

Meadow Springs. Now, though she missed her garden and her view of the valley, the friendship of Astrid and Oskar was a marvellous compensation for her forced exile in the hot bleak wasteland of Liverpool.

Later, tea and cake was followed by a concert in the front parlour. Accompanied by Eveline on piano, Astrid performed Brahms' *Violin Concerto in D Major*, its beauty eclipsing for the moment the ugliness of the world at large. Surrounded by friends and family, Angie studied each face transported by the sublime music and felt her heart swell with hope and love for them all.

Eveline came into the cottage trembling, her face as white as a sheet. It was Anzac Day, 25 April 1918. News of the great German spring offensive on the Western Front was everywhere, the Kaiser's last desperate throw of the dice.

That evening Eveline opened the letterbox and found dog excrement mixed with broken glass and a piece of paper that simply said 'BOCHE SHIT-EATERS'. The two sisters hugged each other and prayed that the nightmare would not begin again. They did not tell Angie.

How was this fair? They were two poor women living with a young girl and a baby. What harm had they ever done anyone? They were always courteous to people they met on the street when they took Greta for a walk in her pram. They paid their bills at the butcher's and the grocer's and the doctor's like everyone else. They had even used some of their meagre savings for a War Loan subscription and Eveline's husband had died fighting for Australia. They were Australian citizens. They were patriots. They did not deserve to be treated this way.

As she walked home from her violin lesson with Mr Weiss the following day, Astrid was confronted by a wild-eyed man who spat at her and yelled, 'Boche bitch!' He snatched at the violin case and it slipped from Astrid's grasp and crashed to the footpath. The instrument was badly damaged and would cost money they did not have to be repaired. Angie tried to comfort her afterwards but Astrid was heartbroken. 'I just don't understand it. I don't know what *we* have done wrong.'

They found their neighbours' pet schnauzer, Suzie, dead, poisoned, in the back lane a day later. Then the vile letters began to arrive under the front doors of every German family on Rose Street. Stones were thrown through windows. Buckets of blood were splashed across fences. Graffiti screamed: HUN SCUM GO HOME.

Freya did not bother Freddie with any of these troubles. Even as she privately worried about her husband's worsening state of mind, she was forced to make excuses for their less-frequent visits to the camp. The truth was that she and Angie had become afraid to catch the train from Liverpool to Holsworthy. And with good reason.

It was a Sunday afternoon in mid-May. Angie kept looking over her shoulder, convinced that the woman in the raincoat a few yards behind them had been shadowing Angie and her mother as they walked from Rose Street to the train station. She kept telling herself she must be imagining things; the unpleasant events and sleepless nights of the last few weeks had them all spooked. Even so, on the railway platform, Angie sensed the figure of the woman draw closer.

Then, without warning, the stranger lunged at Freya, screaming at the top of her voice: 'Murderer! Murderer! You killed my brother at Polygon Wood!'

A murmur of dismay went through the crowd of soldiers from the Liverpool camp who were waiting to go on leave to Sydney. The stationmaster rushed forward, followed closely by three men in uniform.

'Whoa! Hang on there! Take it easy!' Angie noticed how solicitous these men were towards her mother as they did their best to restrain and calm her attacker.

'Don't you understand?' the deranged women cried at the soldiers as they pinned her arms. 'These are the Kaiser's whores. They gave birth to the monsters who murdered poor Angus. Such a sweet boy. Just like you. How can you let these demons walk free?'

Angie was afraid now. This woman's revelation about Angie and Freya being German and her appeal to the brotherhood of soldiers would no doubt tip this confrontation in her favour. Angie expected every soldier on the platform to turn on them.

'Please, miss, we understand how you feel, we really do,' reasoned the shortest of the three privates, a blond-haired young man with sad eyes, 'but I'm sure these ladies do not mean you any harm. Our fight is with the Hun. Over there, not here.'

Angie studied the young soldier's face. He was not that much older than her. Something about his freckled nose and dark eyes reminded her of Robbie. And his lick of blond hair made her think of Oskar. She was deeply touched by his words. *I'm sure these ladies do not mean you any harm.* He put the case in their defence so simply and sincerely. He seemed an honourable man, no less a soldier trained to kill but not an unthinking brute either.

But the reaction that surprised her the most was her own when she looked at the face of their attacker. Realising she had not won over these men, the woman hung her head in defeat. When she looked up again, Angie could see the woman's face had crumpled from an expression of outrage to one of total anguish. With the hardness melted away, she looked much younger, possibly no older than twenty or so.

What tore at Angie was her expression of utter bewilderment. With that look, Angie felt a bright sliver of insight enter her heart. She suddenly understood that this attack was the only act of public grief this woman was allowed. Widows were expected to bear their suffering with quiet dignity: they could shed tears but could never give voice to their lust for vengeance. Who else could this wretched woman blame for her brother's death? Who else could she punish? She was a frail woman, powerless to act and without the soldier's sanction to kill. No wonder she seemed lost.

The closest person Angie had ever had to a brother was Robbie. And now she loved Oskar with a fierce tenderness. When she thought about how helpless she would feel in this woman's place, there came into her heart an unfamiliar feeling: compassion.

She looked around at the soldiers on the platform. None of these feelings or insights relieved her anxiety or reduced the danger of her situation. The freckle-faced soldier also looked over his shoulder at the crowd of men who were growing restive.

'Need any help, madam?' a corporal demanded in a voice steely with suspicion. Angie saw hope rekindle in the woman's eyes.

'Let's go,' Angie whispered urgently, grabbing Freya's arm. She knew her mother would want to make a scene, call the police, have the woman arrested. Mercifully, however, she seemed frozen, paralysed.

'I really think you should leave – now,' the young soldier implored.

Angie seized her mother's hand and hissed at her, 'Come on!'

The note of alarm in her daughter's voice woke Freya from her trance. Without looking back, mother and daughter mounted the stairs from the train station to the footbridge and walked quickly home.

CHAPTER 13

Lisa

Katoomba, May 2013

It was so cold, you could taste it in the air. Everyone talked confidently of snow. Lisa had spent the morning at the Ritz again: another round of Scrabble, her mother triumphant, celebrating with chocolates.

Lisa met Luke for coffee in Katoomba that afternoon. He had texted her the night before asking if she had time for a quick catch-up. He had something he wanted to show her, he said, and it would be more interesting in person.

They were gradually becoming friends, and had even shared a little personal history. Luke had grown up in the mountains, the only son of a local high school teacher and a council officer, both born overseas in Cyprus. Luke truly loved the Blue Mountains and had taken an interest in its history at

Winmalee High and then as an undergraduate at UWS, joining the Blackheath Historical Society when he was only twenty-four. He was now in his mid-thirties, and was finishing his PhD at the University of Western Sydney. One of his supervisors had made introductions to the right people for this job as official historian with the Palace redevelopment.

'How's the diary going?' he asked over their first cappuccino. They were both wrapped in heavy winter coats and scarves which they unfurled as the fug of the crowded cafe warmed their hands and faces.

She knew how much he wanted access to her mother's diaries and did not resent his persistence. Even though Monika had given Lisa power of attorney over her property at the insistence of her doctors and solicitor, Lisa was still struggling with the ethical dilemma of giving Luke carte blanche – especially on days when Monika seemed so present and mentally sharp.

She was just beginning to realise, too, what the digging-up of family secrets would actually mean for her. She would be forced to confront her own past: her childhood, her parents' failed marriage, her loneliness. Would she ever feel able to hand over the diaries and expose her own pain to the world?

She studied the earnest, olive-skinned face of the man opposite as he tapped away on the keyboard of his laptop. She had made a commitment to unpeel this history without fear and wondered what had changed. Did she feel she would somehow be exposed if this journey of discovery brought up terrible, shameful secrets? Was it because, little by little, she'd begun to care about Luke's opinion of her? She realised that she had slipped into the silence of her own thoughts. Luke was looking at her curiously.

'Have you talked to your mother about any of this yet?'

'No, not yet. Although . . .' She decided to share one little secret. 'I did something a bit sneaky this morning. I thought it was alright to test Monika's memory. She was having a good day, seemed clearer, stronger, if you know what I mean. We played Scrabble and she beat me as usual. As I was packing up I put down some tiles just to see how she would react.'

Luke smiled. 'Interesting idea. And?'

'I spelled out SPATZI, the name of the girl who had visited in 1936 – Laura's friend from Germany.'

'Yes, I remember. What happened?'

'She went very quiet, distant, as if I was no longer there. I assumed she was trying to recall a memory. And then it came. A look of such terrible sadness. I felt so bad. But I thought I should seize the chance. "What is it, Mum?" I said. "What do you remember?"

'And she said, "It wasn't her fault." And then she began to cry. Just a few tears. So I tried again. I felt like a torturer. "Who? Laura?" But she just shook her head and said, "It wasn't her fault. Not at all." Then she shut down. I felt as if I had spoiled our nice morning together. And for what? More mysteries.' Lisa sighed.

Luke fumbled with his cup awkwardly. She could tell he wanted to say something comforting or reassuring but didn't feel it was appropriate. 'Maybe Ulrich will be able to shed some light on this Spatzi. Has he been in touch again?'

'Yes.' Lisa welcomed the change of tack. 'He's very excited about meeting up and seeing the hotel. He's making his travel plans right now. Apparently he's a keen rock climber and is hoping to do some climbing while he's here. Sounds an interesting guy.'

Luke smiled and cleared his throat. 'Well, I have something to show you I hope you find interesting. I followed up some details from the housekeeper's letters – about Angie's father, Frederick. Remember how Mrs Wells said he was interned at the German Concentration Camp at Holsworthy?' He pulled out an ever-fattening sheaf of clippings and photocopies. 'Well, the files on Holsworthy internment camp are not extensive but there are some interesting items in the archive. Including this.'

He extracted a photocopy from the file. 'A letter dated May 1919, six months after the end of the war. It's from a group of internees at Holsworthy to the Minister of Defence complaining about the conditions of their internment and demanding some justice. And you'll see at the bottom of the letter the signatories include a Mr Frederick Octavius Wood of Meadow Springs, New South Wales.'

He handed her the letter and she read with growing horror about the conditions under which these so-called 'enemy aliens' – most of whom were actually Australian-born or naturalised citizens – were held.

'We regret to inform the Minister that the barracks in which we are forced to exist are inferior to the housing usually provided for domestic cattle.' The letter described cramped, primitive huts with no proper bedding or furniture, open to rain and wind in winter, over-run with vermin and choked with dust in summer. The internees complained of woefully inadequate food and medical care, the provision of only forty-two cold showers for six thousand men, the torment by bored, vengeful guards who bayonet pricked them or fired shots into the camp at random.

All this and the mental strain of 'Barbed Wire Disease' these men endured with remarkable resilience, organising their own communal life with bakeries and butchers, cafes and restaurants, sporting and cultural clubs, even a theatre. But what chafed most of all was the injustice of their confinement. She read:

That we unfortunate citizens should be interned for no other reason than that we happen to be of German descent or have German names seems inconceivable in an advanced democracy like Australia. It is to be wondered if all Australians who are descended from other than purely English ancestry are liable for such treatment in any future war.

When Lisa had finished, she sat there mute, one hand cupped to her mouth.

Luke looked up. 'Quite a letter, eh? You have to wonder how many Australians have any idea this went on. Locking people up with no formal charges.'

Lisa shook her head. 'I'm shocked.'

'There were camps in every state – and three in New South Wales – holding nearly seven thousand internees all up. Four and a half thousand of these were resident in Australia before the war started. It's strange that Holsworthy, where the majority of these Australian citizens were sent, was by far the harshest.'

'Did the government do anything to improve their conditions after this letter? Was there an inquiry after the war, at least?'

'No, it appears not,' said Luke. 'In fact, things got much worse.'

'Worse? What do you mean?'

'Well, when the war ended, it made sense that enemy subjects such as German naval crews and Germans sent from other colonies be sent home. But the public mood against what were now called "ex-enemy aliens" – Australian-born and naturalised German-Australians – remained hostile. These men were not going to be allowed to go back to their normal lives before the war. Far from it. Instead, there was a huge orchestrated campaign pressuring the government to have all internees *deported*.'

'Deported?' Lisa was stunned, confused, 'You mean . . .'

'Put on ships and sent to Germany,' Luke said, his face flushing with anger. 'I know, it's hard to believe. But the government did just that. They adopted a policy of compulsory deportation for all internees. And their families, too, unless their wives were British subjects before their marriage or their children were born here. Then they could choose whether to go with their husbands or stay behind.'

It appeared to Lisa that Luke's normal enthusiasm for the detective work of history had changed into something else: a deeply felt indignation at this forgotten crime.

'There was an appeals tribunal but it was a farce. Out of more than a thousand appeals only three hundred and six were upheld. The whole policy was cruel and punitive. In all, over six thousand internees and their families were sent to Germany. Many of them did not speak a word of German and had no connections there, and most of them had never set foot outside Australia. Mind you, given the hostility and uncertain future they faced in Australia, Germany might have looked like a better choice at the time. But it's still a shameful chapter in our history. Some have even called it an ethnic purge.'

Lisa felt tears sting her eyes. Why did this move her so? How was she connected to this story? She didn't really know, despite her conviction that the fate of Angie, the girl from the cottage, was in some way intimately bound up with that of her grandmother and mother.

'I'm sorry, Lisa, I didn't mean to . . .'

Luke grabbed her left hand, still holding the letter on the table between them, and patted it. Then, seeming to realise what he had done, he quickly withdrew his hand and began to type again on his laptop.

Lisa couldn't decide if it was better to ignore what had just happened or acknowledge it. She was about to say something when he asked her a question instead.

'Do you want to see him?'

'Who?'

'Angie's father. Freddie Wood.'

She nodded. He turned his laptop around and she saw a black-and-white photo on the screen. It showed a man in his early fifties, his face lined but impassive, trying not to give away any emotion to the official photographer. On closer examination, a crease in his broad forehead just above his tired, deep-set eyes betrayed the ghost of a scowl. In the bottom third of the photo was a piece of white card with the numbers 5538 printed on it, which he held in his hand.

'He looks – how can I put it? – wounded,' said Lisa, feeling strangely calm as she contemplated the photo. It was as if, at last, there was something tangible, knowable about the mysterious Angie. 'Do we know what happened to him?'

'Yes,' said Luke, checking his notes. 'He was deported on 3 June 1920 on the SS *Maine* bound for Bremen. I haven't been able to find any further records of his whereabouts after that. I'd have to look into the German archives.'

'And his family?'

'I checked the shipping lists for that year,' Luke said. 'Two passengers, a Miss A. Wood and Mrs F. Wood, embarked three months later on the MV *Koenig*. Legally they could have stayed in Australia, but it appears they chose to go with Freddie.'

Lisa exhaled. So that was it. The story of Angie and her fateful role in the Fox family drama. The answer to Monika's singsong riddle: *Whatever happened to Angie, poor Angie? Whatever happened to her?* She had played her part and exited the stage to disappear into the chaos of a defeated Germany.

Lisa felt a pang of sadness at saying goodbye to this mysterious girl. Part of her did not want to let her go so quickly and easily: a niggling doubt lingered in her mind that this was, in fact, the end. But she had no reason to doubt Luke's findings.

The historian had his head down, still checking his notes, possibly avoiding her gaze.

'Luke?'

He looked up again. Lisa smiled at him warmly and placed a hand over his.

'Thank you.'

CHAPTER 14

Angie
Liverpool, November 1918–January 1920

On the Monday that the war ended, the streets of Liverpool were filled with loud soldiers, cheering, laughing, howling with a kind of hysterical glee, many of them just off the trains from Sydney where jubilation reigned. The tension had been building for days.

The newspapers had prematurely announced the signing of an armistice the previous Friday and Sydney came to a virtual standstill as thousands poured out of offices, shops and warehouses, yelling, waving flags, banging kerosene tins and blowing hooters. Armistice Day itself repeated these scenes of exultation as waves of people surged through the streets of every capital city and town and hamlet, an ocean of happy humanity, singing, whistling, shouting, hugging, dancing.

On the Wednesday of that same week, a big crowd turned out on the streets of Liverpool to watch a parade led by the mayor, the commander of the training camps and the troops of the Light Horse battalions. The Liverpool civic band played martial airs, hymns and patriotic songs while banners were held aloft of famous Australian battle names and the single word: PEACE.

Freya and Eveline had debated whether they should risk showing their faces. 'You of all people have a right to be there,' insisted Freya. 'John laid down his life so this day would come.' It was a persuasive argument. The only catch was that Eveline refused to attend without Freya and Angie. So in the end, all three women – with little toddler Greta riding on Angie's back – joined the celebrations. Angie was reassured by the presence of so many police officers; surely they wouldn't allow any trouble to spoil the jubilant mood. Surely the public appetite for revenge had been sated by the resounding military victory.

Angie scanned the crowd, hoping to spot Astrid or Oskar. They had not seen each other for weeks as Oskar had to study for exams and Astrid was trying to catch up on lessons with her newly repaired violin. Angie missed them both.

Amid the whooping mass of people, she saw a wounded soldier standing silently at the roadside. He was surrounded by a knot of his mates, all shouting. Noticeable for his crutches and the trouser leg pinned to where his left leg had been amputated at the knee, the soldier was also conspicuous for another reason: the expressionless mask of his face, a startling blank among all these cheering men.

When she had heard the news of the armistice, Angie's heart had soared at the prospect of a new life for her and her family, as if they would finally wake from a long nightmare. But now she wondered how many others there were like this lone soldier in the crowd, already staring into the vertiginous uncertainty of their future and contemplating what this war had cost them. She knew the war's end would bring little comfort to her father and the other internees at Holsworthy for some time. A two-line report in the morning paper had stated that 'no German internees would be released until the results of negotiations at the Paris Peace Conference are known', and who knew how long that would take?

Freya and Angie visited Freddie the following Sunday. They came bearing their care packages now almost as offerings to assuage their guilt that they were free while he still wasted away behind barbed wire.

Angie hated to see how Freddie's habitual calm and good cheer had deserted him as he was swallowed up by depression. It was like watching a man drown slowly. He did his best to hide the fact his hands shook, but he could not hide the thinning of his hair and his weight loss, so he joked about them instead.

'They called me grandad when they brought me here,' he chuckled bitterly. 'Looks like they were right after all.'

Freya tried her best to be cheerful during their visits with

Freddie. When he fell silent or became sullen, she would chide him gently, lowering her voice so the guards couldn't hear. 'Come on, Freddie, we're not going to let these bastards win, are we? Hang on, my love. This will all be over soon.' After every visit, however, Freya came away muttering, 'We must get him out of there – before it's too late.'

Far from fading away, hatred against enemy aliens was reaching fever pitch. Freya read the endless letters to the papers and reports of resolutions at meetings of the British Medical Association and Returned Soldiers' and Patriotic Citizens' leagues. They all called for the mass deportation of internees, Australian-born or otherwise.

The women of Rose Street refused to believe the government would seriously consider such a possibility. Even so, they wrote letters, pleading to be reunited with their husbands and resume their lives as good and loyal citizens who had never broken any laws. But then, out of the blue, a letter arrived from the Department of Defence. It informed every internee's wife in New South Wales that deportation was indeed possible and that, if her husband was deported, she and their children would have to accompany him. That was unless she was a British subject before the marriage; then she had the right to remain in Australia as did any of her Australian-born children if they chose to do so. Those who were being 'repatriated' were allowed to take five cubic feet of luggage per person and no more than fifty pounds in cash.

The same day Freddie was notified in a one-line telegram that his naturalisation had been revoked and he was on the official deportee list. He would be assigned a ship and departure date in due course. He told Freya and Angie this news on their next visit to the camp. He appeared resigned to his fate. 'So, it is decided.'

He lowered his voice to a whisper. 'I don't want you to come with me to Germany. Some of the naval officers here have been getting letters. It's chaos over there. With the Kaiser gone, there's violence everywhere, revolution brewing on the streets. And it's not your home. Go back to the cottage. Talk to Mr Fox. He is a good man. He will look after you.'

Freya bit her lip. She was sorely tempted to tell him how that 'good man' had cheated her over her father's painting, how she had been forced in desperation to sign over her land title to him in an agreement she knew he never intended to honour. His lawyer would find ways to make sure she never returned to her cottage. It was her punishment and Angie's for what had happened to Robbie and all the pain they had caused Adam and Adelina.

'We will talk about this more next time,' said Freya.

They both knew what lay behind Freddie's words. His concerns about their future in Germany were justified. But there was history behind this too. Freddie knew it was Fox she had loved in the beginning and it was Fox she would always love. Freddie was a broken man, an outcast, and no use to her now. It was time for Fox to step in and protect her. He had a duty to do so.

But Freddie didn't know Fox like she did – and he underestimated his wife. She wrote to the Aliens Board and to the minister, begging for her husband's release, but for weeks on end she heard nothing. Still, she was determined. She would not abandon Freddie, the man who had never abandoned her.

The first three deaths from pneumonic flu in Liverpool were reported that April. The disease had been carried by returning soldiers coming off troopships in Melbourne and crossing the border from Victoria into New South Wales. It had then swept through Sydney, suburb by suburb, and started picking off country towns in New South Wales one by one. It moved with a stealth and rapidity that reminded Angie of a bushfire. Each day the papers reported new outbreaks. These were small at first, no more than tiny spot fires here and there, and the papers tried to reassure readers that the disease had peaked. But the fire storm of infection was just starting to build to its full strength.

It was all very well for the government to urge people to stay calm, thought Angie, but it was hard to pretend everything was under control when Liverpool had turned into a ghost town. Under the new quarantine regulations, schools, libraries, theatres, public halls and picture theatres had closed. Unlike most people, Angie didn't grumble about the gauze mask she was forced to wear by law out on the street; it helped her feel anonymous and safe from the hostile stares of strangers.

The death toll climbed quickly in May and June. By July it was over four thousand in New South Wales and the epidemic showed no signs of slowing. The state borders were closed and guarded by troops. Angie and Freya lined up twice a week to take a deep whiff of zinc sulphate in the public inhaling chamber. The smell was disgusting and there was no proof it worked but Freya was not prepared to take any chances, especially with baby Greta in the house.

Angie sat in the front parlour and stared out the window. If she'd thought life was hard before, it was unbearable now. She waited for the Red Cross workers on their 'S.O.S' patrols as they drove down each street seeking out families in need of help. They would pass by her window in their knee-length white gowns, long white gloves, white caps, veils, masks and goggles like a cavalcade of ghosts. She listened out for the tinkling of their handbells as they laid out trays of hot food on the front paths and doorsteps of infected houses, each one signposted with a white or yellow flag. These had blossomed, one by one, like flowers of death, along Rose Street. The disease, which could kill within forty-eight hours, mostly took fit young men and pregnant women. Angie of course worried about Oskar, whose recent letter confessing his passionate love for her remained tucked under her pillow, heavily creased from repeated rereading. How ironic it would be if, just as their romance bloomed, her lover would be struck down by illness. Fate seem to favour such cruel timing, she thought.

Only that afternoon she had discovered to her horror that not everyone she loved would be spared this illness. She'd been carrying home rations of bread, fruit and buckets of warm soup covered with a towel from the town hall – all the bakeries and shops were closed – when she had seen the dreaded flag fluttering outside 36 Rose Street. She had knocked at the door which was answered by Mrs Eyl.

She was shaking from head to toe when she arrived home to tell the news, her chest heaving with sobs. 'I saw a flag out at number thirty-six. It's Astrid! Mrs Eyl said she's been sick since yesterday. She wouldn't let me in to see her.'

'You spoke to Mrs Eyl?' Freya demanded. 'At her front door – even though the flag was out?'

'Astrid's my best friend!' shouted Angie. 'I just wanted to know if she was alright.'

Freya was furious. 'This is not just about what you want. What about Greta? What about Eveline? Did you think about them? That's it: you are not to leave this house again. I'll go for the rations myself.'

Freya continued to rant as Angie trembled before her in a silent rage. She couldn't believe Freya could be so hard and unfeeling. All Angie had done was show loyalty to a friend. For years Angie had endured her mother's intemperate moods and rages. She loved her mother, but recently Angie was becoming more and more convinced that Freya's mind was unhinged. It was all too much, too much to bear!

Over the last few months, Angie had begun forming a plan of escape. She would turn seventeen this year and she was sick of being treated like a child. It was time for her to start her own life. If by some stroke of madness – for anything was possible in her mother's deluded world – Freya decided not to go to Germany with Freddie, then perhaps that was a sign for Angie. She would accompany Freddie instead. She would ask Oskar to go with her. Together, they would find a way to survive. They would build a new life.

Without Freya.

Two days later, Freya fell ill.

It began with a shiver and a chill accompanied by an intense headache. When Freya woke up that morning, her eyes were watering and the pains in the small of her back radiated throughout her body, making her feel tender all over. There was no doubt that it was the flu. Freya summoned Angie to her bedside and told her to go to Mrs Menzel's to fetch some aspirin; she always had a supply handy.

The following day, the sneezing and coughing began. Her nose ran and her throat burned. The skin all over her body was hot and dry and took on a strange blue tinge. Most alarming of all, Freya grew weak and dispirited, barely speaking a word and then only in a hoarse, quiet voice. This was so unlike her mother that Angie began to feel truly afraid.

There were no public beds available at the hospital so Angie got one of the S.O.S patrols to call a nurse to the house. The nurse advised keeping Freya isolated in the sleep-out with only Angie to attend to her care. She was instructed to keep her mother well-wrapped in blankets. She must not be allowed near draughts or cold air to avoid the complication of pneumonia.

It was also vital that Angie keep an eye out for any signs of delirium, which was a very serious symptom. Angie had to keep a face mask on the whole time, and change her clothes and wash her hands regularly. The nurse or one of the other volunteers would come by at night to see how she was doing.

Angie had to make sure that whenever her mother sneezed, coughed or spat it must be into clean rags, which had to be collected and burned straight away with kerosene in the big steel bin out in the backyard. Eveline sat on her bed and cut up some of their old clothes to make a heap of such rags. Forbidden any physical contact with Angie, her aunt left these scraps outside her closed bedroom door. 'Don't lose hope, Angie, my love,' she said as her niece collected them.

Angie's constant round of nursing duties was a welcome distraction from the grief and panic that threatened to overwhelm her. She had never seen her mother as vulnerable as this. It shook her to her core. Whatever resentments she harboured against Freya, she realised now how much she had always relied on her mother's righteous anger to protect her from the cruelties of the world.

On the third day, the vomiting began. Angie held her mother's head tenderly as she coughed up streams of frothy white sputum stained with blood into the nests of rags by the bedside. Freya's silver-flecked copper hair clung damply to her skull. Angie cried as she felt her mother's body convulse with each bout of retching. In that small, darkened room, with its odours of sweat and sick and the stink of burning zinc sulphate, Angie and her mother had swapped roles. The daughter was now the anxious, attentive mother while Freya was the frightened, helpless child.

When she wasn't in the sickroom, Angie sat in the half-light of the front parlour and stared out the window, listening to her mother's moans and weeping. Aunty Eveline whispered soothing words to Angie through the keyhole of her closed door whenever Greta was napping. She slipped letters under the door too, full of kind, reassuring words, praising Angie for being so brave and devoted.

One morning Angie stopped in front of the mirror in the hallway. She was not in the habit of studying herself for very long in its surface except to adjust the sleeve of a dress or the angle of a hat before leaving the house. But today she paused a moment longer, struck by the startling pallor of her own face. Suffering had sculpted her features with a refined, even ethereal, quality that many would call beautiful. But the thought that arose in Angie on seeing her own pale reflection was how much life had changed her, inside and out, these last few years. Where was the girl who had left Meadow Springs? Vanished. This new Angie was so much taller and her figure and face more womanly, but it was in the outward expression of her soul she saw the greatest change. Thirteen-year-old Angie had been sad but still hopeful that she would one day resume her old life. The woman in the glass now was an altogether altered creature, burdened with the knowledge of life's disappointments.

Angie thought she had cried out all her tears the first two days of her mother's illness. With those tears she had reproached herself bitterly for exposing her mother to the flu. She knew she was to blame. She had gone to the Eyls' house without thinking. But her self-recrimination was not over and there were plenty more tears to come. Angie told herself she was also being punished for wanting to abandon Freya. She had imagined a new life without her mother. Now fate would deliver just such a life. With an appalling certainty, Angie knew it would be her fault if her mother died.

Four days later, the flu lifted. Her mother's temperature dropped, the sweats disappeared and the vomiting stopped. Freya rested for another week in bed and felt weak and tired for weeks after that. But she had survived.

Angie cried yet again, but this time with relief and joy as she held her mother tightly in her arms. 'I will never let you go,' she whispered. Eveline was overjoyed at her sister's recovery and relieved to be released from the back room. The white flag was taken down from the front porch.

The next day, there was a knock at the door. It was Oskar. His face was pale as milk and his eyes rimmed red. He had come to tell Angie the terrible news: Astrid had not survived. She'd died after only two days of illness.

Angie was still nursing her own mother when the cart came down Rose Street, ringing its mournful bell, to collect Astrid's corpse. Angie was still locked away inside the white-flagged cottage when the funeral procession passed on its way to the synagogue for Astrid's burial.

Mrs Eyl burned all her daughter's clothes and her violin. She told Oskar that when her husband was released from Holsworthy they would return to Germany. They hoped they would be safer there than in Australia.

Angie and Oskar hugged awkwardly and he left. Their love seemed tainted now, almost a betrayal. Angie cried for her dead friend. But she confessed to no one her gratitude that God had chosen to take Astrid rather than Freya or Freddie or Oskar.

Two weeks later Oskar called around again to tell them that his father was being deported to Germany at the end of the month. Oskar and his mother would be joining him.

Angie was lost for words. She had opened her heart once more, and once more the object of that love had been snatched away.

Oskar could not look her squarely in the face as he delivered his news. His voice trembled. As he left, he kissed her on the left cheek right there in the parlour in front of Freya and Aunty Eveline, and tucked a small note into her hand.

It read: '*Wo gehen Sie, mein Herr? Weit von meiner Liebe.*' Where are you going, sir? Far from the girl I love.

In January 1920, a letter finally arrived from the Aliens Board. Freya read it in the privacy of her bedroom. She waited until Eveline and Greta had gone out for their daily excursion to the park and then summoned Angie into the front parlour, sat her down and read her the contents of the letter out loud.

Without stating any specific reasons, the letter rejected the appeal against repatriation that had been lodged on behalf of Frederick Octavius Wood. He remained on the government's official list of deportees. On 3 June he would embark on the S.S *Maine* from Darling Harbour bound for the German port of Bremen. He would be allowed to take some luggage and a small sum of money but would surrender his Australian passport. Furthermore, the camp at Holsworthy was still locked down and all visiting rights were suspended. It was possible they might not see Freddie again before he embarked.

Angie broke down and wept. Freya held her daughter in her arms, rocking her like she had when Angie was small and frightened, stroking her long black hair and crooning in her ear, 'My poor little *liebchen*.'

When Angie's sobs finally subsided, her mother soothed her brow with her warm hands. 'Please don't be heartbroken, my angel girl. There is still hope. Listen.'

Freya had another letter to share with Angie. It was from Karl von Gettner, Freya's paternal cousin in Dusseldorf, the son of Uncle Horst and nephew of Freya's own father, Wolfgang. Assuming the worst, Freya had written months ago to Karl at the printing works in Dusseldorf which had been in the von Gettner family for over a hundred years. Her letter had explained their terrible situation in Australia.

Karl was an honourable man, a pillar of the community and devoted father. Now in his early sixties, he still worked every day at his beloved printing house with the support of the eldest of his three sons, Franz. Shocked to hear Freya's news, this good-hearted patriarch had replied that he and his family would do everything they could to save the Australian branch of the von Gettner tree.

'Freddie will go to Dusseldorf,' explained Freya. 'Karl and his family will look after him.'

Angie felt her breathing steady. How could she ever have doubted her mother? Freya always knew the right thing to do.

'As you know, our government has kindly agreed to pay our passage to Germany to join him when we choose to do so,' Freya continued. A grim smile made plain her sarcasm. 'Which we will do as soon as we've taken care of everything here.'

A wave of relief flooded through Angie: her father would be taken care of and they would see him again. Then it struck her . . .

'What about the cottage?'

The question burst from Angie's lips before she could stop herself. She had refrained from raising this subject ever since the letter had come from Adam Fox's solicitor nearly two years ago, though it had continued to torment her all that time.

To Angie's surprise, Freya did not scowl at her. Instead, a smile spread across her face and she kissed her daughter on the forehead. 'Ah, my sweet. You miss that place as much as I do. I do not blame you.' She sighed deeply and cupped her daughter's face in her hands. 'There are things I must tell you,' she said. 'Painful things that I have kept hidden for far too long. But no more!'

Freya was now looking steadily into her daughter's eyes. 'As you are learning, my love, the world is a deeply unfair place. Good men like Freddie suffer while cruel men like Adam Fox prosper. It is hard to see God's plan in any of this. Except that He has given me a second chance. A chance to make things right.'

A monumental stillness had descended on the house. Dust motes floated slowly in the molten morning light. Angie knew she would never forget this slice of time. Every mundane detail of this room was engraved on her memory: the worn chairs, the threadbare rug, Aunty Eveline's Delft china dog on the mantel, and above the fireplace Freya's delicate pencil and watercolour sketch of a pink callistemon.

'To think I might have died and left you . . .' Freya's voice cracked a little. 'Listen to me. I must tell you the truth now. We are being punished. Punished unfairly by Adam and Adelina for what happened to Robbie all those years ago. That is the real reason why Adam sacked your father. Why he pressured us to leave. Why, despite my efforts to stop him, he has forced me to sell our cottage. He told me that all he wanted was to hold it in trust, that the agreement we had was only temporary. To help us, he said. He lied.

'The agreement expired this month and Saul, my father's lawyer, sent Adam a letter to reclaim our title. It arrived too late. Adam's solicitor sprang his trap. A sub-clause in the agreement meant I had no choice but to sell the cottage and land to Adam. To be honest, I was not in the least surprised. It has been Adam's intention all along to have that land. My father would not sell it to him so he picked on me instead. Never forget: what Adam Fox wants, he gets. And above all, he wanted everything to be perfect. After Robbie's death, my living in that cottage with you and Freddie spoiled Adam's perfect life. Which is why, in the end, we had to go.'

Her voice quavered at this point but did not become shrill. 'I even sold Adam my father's last painting in order to avoid signing this poisonous agreement to give up my land. The painting was a gift to me and should never have been sold. But even *that* was not enough for him. He lied about it being a forgery and stopped his payments. But he never gave it back. His greed is endless. He is, in every way, a thief and liar.'

Angie did not blink at this story, even though she harboured her own private doubts. She was tempted for a fleeting moment to confess she had caught a glimpse of the 'other' von Gettner landscape painting in her mother's studio back home. But now was not the time.

'Adam Fox seems determined to take away everything my father has left me. In the end, I had no choice but to sign away the cottage; I desperately needed his money to keep going. But I have worked out a way to get it back.'

Angie searched her mother's face. There was an unnerving calmness in the way she talked about all this, with no sign of anger or even agitation. It was as if she had run through these calculations over and over again and was merely reciting them.

'I know what you are thinking, Angie,' said Freya.

'You do?' she whispered.

'You are afraid I have lost my mind.'

Her face must have given her away. Angie dropped her eyes in shame.

'Listen, I do not blame you. In order to survive, I have been forced to do things and agree to things that look like madness. I may still have to do such things. But I am determined to win whatever the cost. I will get our cottage back. *Our* cottage, Angie. *Ours*. Given to us by my father.'

She smiled sadly. 'Do you wonder why I am so afraid of Adam Fox?'

'Maybe I understand a little better now,' Angie said.

'You will understand even more when I tell you the whole truth, my poor Angie.'

The room stilled. It was as if it had taken a deep breath and all the outside sounds – the birds, the distant hum and rattle of trains and traffic, the murmur of voices on the street – had been swallowed up in its bubble of silence.

'There is a secret that Adam Fox and I have kept all these years . . .'

Freya closed her eyes, unable to look directly at her daughter as she unburdened herself of her life's secret shame.

'That secret is that Robbie was *our* son. *My* son. Your brother.'

Angie stared at her mother, uncomprehending at first. Her mind scrambled through a wild assortment of memories, each one a flash of her and Robbie – in the cottage garden, on the hotel lawn, in the hedge. She tried to recall the faces of her parents and of Adam Fox back then. How had they all kept this secret from her?

Freya was thinking too, but her memory was of a spring morning in 1904 when Angie was a toddler learning to walk among the blackboy grasses while her mother basked in the sunlight on the cottage veranda. Into this peaceful scene swam another image: his face, those restless brown eyes and lick of sandy hair, a spattering of freckles on the bridge of his nose. How she ached to hold him in her arms just once more. She knew this love was forbidden now, must be kept hidden. Promises had been made, negotiated in the best interests of all involved. A very civilised settlement, a gentlemen's agreement, a secret buried.

Her son, Robbie! Her little boy that she had given away. Oh the pity of it!

Freya began to tell her story. 'When my father died I was all alone. And Adam Fox came into my life. He saw my soul and my talent and my beauty so clearly. And he craved them so passionately I could not, I did not, resist. I loved him and he loved me. One day you will understand what I mean, my darling.

'For nearly two years we were like this, behind Adelina's back. We lived in a fool's paradise, thinking we would never be found out. Such happy fools we were. And then it all came crashing down. When I fell pregnant, I knew I had few choices, none of them good. I was at the mercy of Adam Fox – and his wife. It was his idea to make it look like the baby was Adelina's. It was obvious to Adam by then that she was never going to bear him a child; she was so fragile in mind and body. And I did not want to leave my home.

'So arrangements were made. To save the marriage. To give Adam an heir and Adelina a child. To allow me to stay in my cottage where I could watch as my son was raised to wealth and position even if he could not have my name. All this as long as I agreed never to tell him the truth.

'In the end it was simple. Adelina announced her pregnancy and was sent away to a private clinic in the Dandenongs. At around the same time, as far as my neighbours and the town gossips were concerned, I fell sick and went to stay with a relative in country Victoria. In fact, I was hidden away on a farm belonging to Adelina's youngest aunt, a kind and sensible woman. When the time came, I went to the clinic, gave birth and surrendered my baby boy to his new parents. They named him Robbie and returned to Meadow Springs in triumph with their son. I stayed with Adelina's aunt for another six weeks, then returned fully recovered from my long illness.

'That was a very hard time. I was disowned by Adam, despised by Adelina. I had made this terrible pact with the devil and did not know what the future held. My son had been taken away and given to a woman who seemed incapable of loving anyone. Then Freddie proposed to me and we married soon afterwards. I admit the marriage was a refuge from my distress and loneliness. But I grew to love your father ever more truly as the years went on and I understood what a fine man he was.

'So that I could cope with my loss it was suggested I should fall pregnant again as soon as possible. Your arrival was meant to help ease my grief over Robbie. I fell in love with you all for yourself, of course, and not as a replacement for my lost son. And the joy you brought to my life did heal my wounded heart.

'As you grew up I was keen for you to have your half-brother as a playmate. Why should you miss out just because you were not Adam's child? So I encouraged your friendship every summer when they stayed at the hotel. Adelina hated that. She had settled for the compromise of having me – her husband's ex-lover – living next door to the hotel, though it chafed her like an iron collar. But your closeness to Robbie – that was too much! Now I look back . . . well, maybe she was right.'

Tears were now streaming freely down Angie's face. 'My God. This means I – I killed – I killed my . . .'

'No!' Freya barked, her face dark with rage. 'You did no such thing. You were not to blame for what happened, Angie. We lied to you and Robbie. And we paid a terrible price for that lie. Your feelings for him – even your jealousy – that was perfectly natural. As was his love for you. Neither of you knew the truth. And that was our fault. What we did was monstrous. I am so sorry, Angie. I can only hope that one day you may be able to forgive me. Though I do not deserve it, I know that.'

Angie was sobbing uncontrollably now. Her mother let her cry until her eyes were red and dry. Her grief encompassed many losses: her brother's death, thoughts of what might have been, and all the lonely days she had endured without him.

This rewriting of history cast everything in a new light. Angie realised she had barely known her mother. Like so many children, she had been in the easy habit of blaming her parents for everything. Knowing now of her mother's suffering and the impossible choices she had been forced to make, she could not condemn her so quickly. What would she have done differently in the same circumstances?

She couldn't even blame Freya for falling in love with Adam in the first place. Angie had tasted such love with Oskar. She still ached for his touch, his face, his voice even now. She could not find it in her heart to judge her mother harshly for that. But, oh, the terrible, terrible cost!

'We cannot let Adam Fox hurt us anymore,' said Freya. 'We will get back our land and our cottage no matter what it takes.'

And so Freya laid out her plans for their future and Angie listened to her carefully.

PART 2

Adelina

CHAPTER 15

Adelina

Meadow Springs, January 1921

Everyone at the Palace was excited that Saturday but none more so than Adelina Fox.

It was not like her to spend more than a day or two at the hotel if she could help it, usually for her long treatments with Dr Liebermeister. In Adelina's mind the Palace symbolised Adam's infidelity and the failure of her marriage. She even told herself in her more desperate moments that he had loved this hotel long before her; that the Palace was, in fact, the pretext for their marriage, as her inheritance had largely financed its construction to the tune of one hundred and twenty thousand pounds.

It pained her to admit that this folly inspired more passion in her husband than she ever had. He loved nothing more than to hold parties at the hotel with his loud and clever friends paying court to him, a spectacle that both intimidated and disgusted her. And then there was Adam's affair with the woman next door and its ultimate disastrous consequence – that looked, in retrospect, like a punishment both for Adam's weak-willed betrayal and her own weak-willed compliance. Adelina had many reasons to hate the Palace but her son's death eclipsed them all.

Mr Hawthorne and Mr Carson were surprised when Mr Fox requested a room for his wife and a place reserved for her at dinner on Saturday night.

'To what do we owe this rare honour, sir?' Mr Hawthorne had asked, careful not to sound disrespectful or prying.

'My wife's curiosity,' replied Adam Fox with an enigmatic smile.

The truth was that Adelina had insisted on being included in Adam's inner circle for dinner. Her reason was straightforward. The Palace was playing host that week to one of the most famous men of the British Empire: the celebrated and prolific author Sir Arthur Conan Doyle, whose brilliant detective Sherlock Holmes was a favourite of millions of readers worldwide and had made his creator a fortune.

But Adelina's interest in meeting Sir Arthur was not literary; it was spiritual. The famous writer was currently on a lecture tour around Australia to spread the word about what he called the 'great philosophy' of Spiritualism; this had become his 'highest purpose' to which he had devoted the remainder of his life. Travelling with his wife and three children, Conan Doyle had been in Australia since the previous September giving public talks to packed halls and theatres in Perth, Melbourne and Sydney. He had decided on a sojourn in the beautiful Blue Mountains and booked a week's stay for his family at the Palace.

'You know, Sir Arthur lost his son *and* his brother, both to the Spanish flu,' Adelina informed her husband over breakfast on the morning that Adam told her about Sir Arthur's forthcoming visit. She was perusing the *Sydney Morning Herald*, which ran regular reports on the famous author's visit. 'His first wife died of tuberculosis. And he received news of his mother's death just before last Christmas while still on tour here. Dear me, he's certainly drunk his fill of grief! No wonder he understands the consolation that Spiritualism offers.'

Adelina had first heard about Spiritualism back in 1914, less than a month after Robbie's death. Mrs Wells, the head housekeeper at the Palace, who was in every way an apparently sensible woman, immune to whimsy, had approached Adelina on the terrace one day after her therapy session with Dr Liebermeister.

'I'm sorry to disturb you, Mrs Fox,' said the white-haired housekeeper, bending down to where Adelina lay stretched out in a sun chair, wrapped in a thick cotton gown.

'No, that's fine, Mrs Wells.' Adelina nodded in greeting. 'How are you?'

Mrs Wells clutched in her hands a magazine, *Harbinger of Light*. 'I have something here that may bring you, I hope, some small degree of comfort,' she said earnestly. 'Please feel free to keep it as long as you want. And, if you find it to be of any interest, I am happy to answer your questions.'

Adelina was touched. 'Thank you. Thank you so much.'

Over the next few days, Adelina read the psychic magazine from cover to cover, and on her next visit to the Palace sought out Mrs Wells.

'Have you ever been to a séance?' she asked.

Mrs Wells had been to many séances. She told Adelina about the remarkable Mrs Foster Turner. Mrs Wells had recently attended a public meeting with the famous Australian medium at the Little Theatre in Castlereagh Street in Sydney. Under the guidance of the spirit of Mr W.T. Stead – the well-known English pressman and avowed Spiritualist who had drowned on the *Titanic* – Mrs Foster Turner had prophesied the war to come. In her deep, rich voice, she had proclaimed: 'I want to warn you that before this year, 1914, has run its course, Europe will be deluged in blood. Millions of precious lives will be slaughtered, but Britain will emerge victorious.'

By the end of the year, it appeared that the medium's prognostication was at least partly right. Adelina was intrigued. Finding an excuse to visit an old school friend in Sydney, she secretly met up with Mrs Wells and together they attended one of Mrs Foster Turner's public meetings in the city. Here, for the first time, Adelina saw messages delivered from the spirits of the departed. The experience changed her.

In the privacy of her grief nearly a year after Robbie's death, Adelina had found nothing to heal the gaping wound of his loss. Even the thought that her son had been spared the horrors of the bloodbath in Europe that now threatened to consume a generation of young men gave her no consolation. 'Have you found peace, my love?' she asked in her prayers, haunted by the idea that having died so suddenly and so young his spirit might not have found its resting place. She longed to hear his voice, but she also feared that her maternal grief questioned God's will and her impulse towards Spiritualism contradicted her Christian faith.

Adelina struggled with the temptation to consult a medium for a private séance. Her husband and Dr Liebermeister thought it ill-advised. Not only did they have serious doubts about the credibility of séances, they were concerned at the harm they might do to Adelina in her weakened mental state. The therapist continued to administer regular bath treatments to help Mrs Fox with her melancholia. He did not want to risk having all his good work undone.

Adelina understood why Adam was protective. In the wake of the terrible toll of the Great War and the Spanish flu, millions of people had found comfort in Spiritualism's promise of communion with, in Sir Arthur Conan Doyle's own words, 'the sound of a vanished voice and the touch of a vanished hand'. For the same reason, mediums and believers had also been savagely attacked by sceptics as charlatans exploiting the grief of a generation.

Not surprisingly, Conan Doyle's Australian tour also attracted its share of hostility. 'Listen to this!' Adelina exclaimed as she read the *Herald*'s interview with Sir Arthur about his travels. '"I have been told that some Presbyterians actually prayed for my ship to sink before I arrived in Australia. This is akin to murder in my books if their rotten prayers had prevailed."'

'Quite right. That's just not cricket!' said Adam as he expertly dissected his morning kippers. He was surprised – and relieved – to see his wife so animated about their famous guest. It made a pleasant change. They had shared far too many breakfasts in silence these last few years.

'I say we hold a dinner party at the Palace in his honour,' suggested Adam. 'Give him a proper send-off before he sails home. What do you think?'

'I think it is a brilliant idea, my dear.' Adelina beamed at him.

Her heart raced with excitement. Sir Arthur's stay provided the opportunity she had dreamed of for the last seven years: the chance to attend a séance. Adam could hardly object if he was present. And there was the added reassurance of having one of the most respected spiritualists in the world in attendance.

On the first weekend of Sir Arthur's stay, Fox went over to the Palace to greet his distinguished guest. The hotelier tracked him down in the billiard room, where he was racking up.

'Fancy a game, Sir Arthur?' asked Fox, introducing himself. 'I hear you're quite the player. Rumour has it you were a semi-finalist in the British Amateur Billiards Championship a few years back, is that so?'

Sir Arthur laughed. The tall, thickset Scotsman, grown stout in his early sixties and with his luxuriant moustache turned snowy white, seized the hotel owner by the hand and clapped him on the shoulder. 'Well, this is indeed a pleasu*rrrr*e,' he rumbled in his distinctive Anglo-Celtic burr with its resonant consonants and clipped vowels. He had nothing but praise for the Palace. 'This is a little ea*rrrr*thly paradise you have here, Mr Fox – the most *rrrr*estful spot we have found in our wande*rrrr*ings.'

Over a friendly game of billiards – which Fox chivalrously lost – he invited Sir Arthur and Lady Doyle for a dinner later that week to be hosted in their honour. Sir Arthur was flattered and said he greatly looked forward to it.

Adam made plans for an intimate but impressive event. It wasn't every day one had a guest like Conan Doyle. He rang several members of his usual coterie whom he hoped would amuse the great man. They included Freddie Lane and Fanny Durack, both Olympic gold medallist swimmers, and Hugh Ward, the comic actor now turned managing director of J.C. Williamson's theatre company, and his clever musical wife, Grace. Fox knew that Mr Raymond Longford, Australia's most celebrated film director, was staying at the Carrington Hotel in Katoomba while scouting locations in the Blue Mountains for his next film, so he also invited Longford and his partner, the much-loved film star Miss Lottie Lyell. They both enthusiastically agreed.

As plans for the evening were made, Adelina seized her chance.

'Ask Sir Arthur to attend a séance after dinner,' she suggested. 'Your guests would find it fascinating. Mrs Wells knows a local medium in Springwood with an excellent reputation. We could hold it in the library. Sir Arthur would be deeply flattered to explain the whole thing to the company.'

Adelina had him snookered and she knew it. He might have his personal doubts about 'table-rappers' and 'spookists' but he could hardly question Sir Arthur's credibility or deny him an opportunity to show off. Even so, he made a half-hearted attempt to dissuade her. 'He's been travelling all over Australia giving lectures and going to séances! He probably just wants a quiet night . . .'

This was so patently untrue that Adam did not even bother to finish. Conan Doyle had the reputation of being a tireless public speaker and storyteller; his restless intellect furnished him with an opinion on every subject and he spoke ex tempore and at length with a disarming simple eloquence that few could rival. And when it came to the subject of spiritualism, Sir Arthur's passion was inexhaustible.

'Very well,' said Adam.

Adelina smiled and kissed him on the cheek. She had not felt this happy or enthusiastic about anything for as long as she could remember. She hoped that now, seven years almost to the week after Robbie's death, she would be able to find peace for both her son and herself.

Adam Fox studied his image in the mirror. He did not like to think of himself as a vain man but, at age forty-six, he was quietly pleased with what he saw. He was in good shape thanks to regular exercise and a sensible diet. In his early thirties he had resolved to banish his 'rich man's belly', an occupational hazard for hoteliers. He was looking forward to tonight's dinner party as a celebration. The Palace had survived some lean years during the Great War and was now thriving, not just restored to its pre-war prosperity but boasting a worldwide reputation as a haven for the rich and famous, including actors, politicians, opera singers and writers.

Adam dared to hope that his marriage, too, might have turned a corner. After the great rift in their lives, Adam and Adelina had retreated into their own private places of suffering. The bitter recriminations about Robbie's death raged for a long time but eventually died down. The marriage settled into a state of precarious truce. Even so, Adelina's grief-stricken face had remained a permanent accusation.

Adam had done what he could to make amends. Dr Liebermeister worked long and hard to maintain his wife's health and sanity despite her congenitally weak constitution. And most important of all, Adam had finally given in to Adelina's repeated tantrums and comatose silences and erased the painful reminder of his adultery and Robbie's death. He had driven the Woods out of their cottage next door and made it part of the hotel's grounds.

Still, Adam managed to salve his conscience by telling himself he had been protecting the Woods rather than taking advantage of their circumstances. It had certainly not been safe for them to stay in Meadow Springs in 1916 when anti-German feeling was running so high. Even at the end of the war, there was no evidence this hatred had died down. Following his secret dealings with Freya over the von Gettner painting, he had insisted she sign over her land title to him on payment of monies into a trust account which would support her and her child for three years. The agreement expired in early 1920 and Freya's family solicitor, Saul Mendel from Lithgow, had sent a letter asking for the return of the title.

It would have been the simplest thing to do so. But Adam had become used to the calm in his household since Freya left. His wife seemed to have partly forgiven him for the suffering he had subjected her to. Given the dreadful situation they had all found themselves in, he felt he had tried to deal fairly with Freya, only to be faced with her unremitting coldness and stubbornness. She had never shown any gratitude or sympathy. In truth, it was a relief to be rid of her and the ever-present shadow of his guilt. On making inquiries with the Intelligence Section, Second Military District, Fox learned that Freddie Wood had been deported and his wife and child would soon join him in Germany. Did they ever intend to return to Australia? Did they even have that choice? He didn't think it was likely.

With the phenomenal financial success of the Palace since its opening, Adam had been toying with plans to expand the hotel for some time. The property next door presented an ideal solution. Adam saw no reason why he shouldn't make use of the cottage and its gardens which had been abandoned for three years and could sit empty for who knew how many more. So he instructed his solicitor to invoke a sub-clause in the agreement with Freya that allowed for the automatic sale of the property for an agreed sum to Fox 'if the other party failed to notify of their intentions to renew or terminate the contract within twelve days of the date of expiry'. It was a low legal trick, he knew that. His solicitor's letter persuaded Freya to desist from any legal challenge to this sale with veiled references to the fact his client had chosen to keep silent about the matter of the painting. It also pointed out that Fox was paying above market price for a property that could easily be seized as an asset by the Public Trustee at any point and held until the government decided how to dispose of it. All the money in the trust account was now Freya's. It was a generous settlement. As an ex-enemy alien in exile and with few legal rights to protect her, Freya should look on this arrangement as a lucky break. He was not to blame for Freya's fate. He had not started the war or stirred up animosity against his neighbours. He had even stood up for them when the threat was greatest. He had done everything he could to help Freya under difficult circumstances and had taken care of any obligations he had to Freddie and Angie. Beyond that, he believed, he owed them nothing.

Of course, such feelings could never really be tidily filed away in a box. Shortly afterwards Adam had received a personal letter from Freya. After railing against him for his treachery, her letter changed its tone to that of a desperate plea. 'I cannot fight you. But you of all people, Adam, should know what that cottage means to me. If you have any shred of decency or tenderness left in your heart from when you once loved me, I beg you to find it now and undo this terrible wrong.'

Adam was reminded of a spring morning in the cottage garden many years before when he had come to confess his undying affection for Freya and beg her for forgiveness. He was tempted to reply echoing the words she had used that morning to silence and reject him: 'It's too late. You know that.' Instead, he had crumpled Freya's letter into a ball and thrown it into the fire.

Adelina was nervous about Saturday night. She rarely made an appearance at social gatherings and was anxious to make a good impression. Even though she was in her mid-forties she had remained relatively lissom compared to other women of her vintage – some would have said unnaturally thin and small-breasted – and she was not immune to womanly vanity. Her husband was rich and liked to buy her beautiful things. It seemed perverse for her to hide away when her wardrobe and jewellery would have driven most women mad with jealousy.

Adelina studied her pale oval face and angular body in her dressing-room mirror and was pleased at how they were flattered by the latest fashions. Her chestnut hair had been bobbed and Marcel-waved to show off her delicate ears and slender neck. She wore pearl drop earrings and a silk bandeau embroidered with tiny pearls like a tiara above her brow. The silver-beaded evening dress in deep purple silk, imported from Paris, had a daring diaphanous skirt sparkling with appliquéd paisley teardrops and peacock-feather eyes. She admired how her alabaster flesh showed off to perfection the art nouveau onyx, gold and jade necklace and the sinuous bracelets on her upper arms.

Adam came in to fetch her at seven. He looked very smart in his new custom-made midnight blue dinner jacket and white waistcoat with matching white bowtie. He was nervous too, she could tell by the way he fidgeted with his clothes and said he hoped that Sir Arthur and Lady Jean would not find his lack of full evening dress 'presumptuously modern'.

'I suspect Sir Arthur is very broad-minded in such matters,' she reassured him with a touch of good-natured teasing, 'If it's good enough for the Prince of Wales, I'm sure he can have no objections.'

Adam smiled. For a moment, he stopped fussing with his bowtie in the mirror and took in the full-length view of his wife. 'You look lovely, my dear.' He gently took her right hand in his and kissed it.

'Are you glad I'm coming tonight?' she asked, looking at his handsome face in the mirror. It was hard to hate Adam Fox when he looked so charming.

With startling clarity Adelina remembered how she had stood at her husband's side the night the Palace opened, welcoming their guests in the thick of a snowstorm nearly twenty years earlier. Her rightful place at his side had been taken from her by illness and infidelity, and later by tragedy and grief. But tonight she and Adam were united once more. The clock had been rewound.

Adam Fox felt his heart settle. Adelina looked radiant and calm. Tonight would be a triumph, an evening to look back on with pride. He had nothing to fear. 'Yes, Adelina, I am,' he whispered in her ear.

Adam noticed that Sir Arthur was in fine form. He abstained from alcohol throughout the evening but, as champagne, cocktails and wine flowed all around him, he remained the wittiest and most convivial of the guests, sipping his sodas with slices of lemon. He began by entertaining the company with stories about his recent travels, including his family's trip this last week in the Palace's charabanc out to the Jenolan Caves and his encounters with parrots, wombats and kangaroos. His son Denis had been thrilled to be photographed holding up a dead red-bellied black snake that one of the groundsmen had killed in the long grass on the south side of the hotel.

The prolific author, who had written weighty historical novels, stories of the supernatural, critically acclaimed stage plays, the Professor Challenger adventures (including the best-selling *The Lost World*), essays, memoirs and a six-volume history of the Great War, graciously answered the perennial questions about his hero Sherlock Holmes – 'that monstrous growth out of such a small seed,' he chuckled

– and insisted that he had no intention of writing another word about him.

'The curious thing is how many people around the world are perfectly convinced he is a living human being,' Sir Arthur told his rapt audience, 'I get letters addressed to him all the time. I've even had ladies *wrrrr*iting saying they would be glad to act as his housekeeper!' Laughter rippled around the table.

Mr Longford explained that he and his collaborator, Miss Lyell, were currently writing the screenplay for an ambitious new film; it was a murder thriller adapted from a novel and set in a luxury hotel, to be called *The Blue Mountains Mystery*. They intended to start filming later this year and were definitely interested in using the Palace as a location if Mr Fox was agreeable. Mr Fox warmly welcomed the idea.

Dinner was served in the grand dining room under the elegant half-barrel vaulted ceiling with its twin chandeliers. Mr Carson's boys outdid themselves with their polished choreography of flashing cutlery and juggling crockery. They served a banquet of alternating 'rich' and 'poor' dishes, mixing simple fare with gourmet delights, starting with a silver platter of oysters served on blini with Oscietra caviar. The second course of roast garlic and potato soup served en croute in their own baked pastry 'bowls' was accompanied by gin and champagne cocktails. As the third course of poached Scottish blue lobster with shaved black truffle arrived, the conversation had turned to sport, and Sir Arthur listened to Fanny Durack describe her record-breaking swim at the 1912 Stockholm Olympics.

'I am of course familiar with the aquatic prowess of Australians. Has not your lovely countrywoman, "the mermaid of the south", Miss Kellerman taught the whole world how to swim? I believe she has even written a book on the subject,' said Arthur, winning over his audience with his knowledge and appreciation of all things Australian.

The fourth course, planked squab with bacon and pink fir potatoes, was followed by a fifth of roasted rack of veal with golden brown sautéed cep mushrooms in a bordelaise sauce. The claret and champagne flowed as freely as the conversation, which had turned to theatre with lively exchanges between Hugh and Grace Ward and Sir Arthur about their favourite dramatists and leading actors.

Adam looked around the table and allowed himself a glow of satisfaction. This was the reason he had become a hotelier. Hotels brought interesting people together in unexpected ways, gave them a stage on which to perform. Like theatres, hotels were places of magic and danger, where different rules applied; they combined secrecy and discretion with public displays of extravagance and high emotion. They were indeed the perfect setting for dramas of all kinds: murders, romances, intrigues and new beginnings.

As he looked round at the smiling, animated faces of his guests, he tried to banish a vision of Freya from his mind: her braided copper hair and pale face, her sea-blue eyes and that beautiful mint-green gown he had bought her. How she would have loved a night like this. Where was she now? he wondered.

No, he must not let his thoughts dwell on the past and spoil the pleasures of the present.

Adelina spent the evening in a state of quivering attentiveness. It had been years since she had spent time among such people. It dawned on her now that her customary aloofness had simply been a reflection of her own anxiety; the truth was she had been intimidated by the witty, educated and accomplished people her husband had gathered around him. Who was she, Adelina Fox, compared to them? What had she ever achieved? But tonight was different. She did not feel estranged or patronised. She felt accepted. A keen reader of novels, including several of Sir Arthur's, Adelina ventured an opinion every now and then and was rewarded with a concurring nod or compliment from their distinguished guest. 'I believe you are quite right, Mrs Fox!' She flashed a smile at Adam whenever he glanced in her direction and she could see the relief and happiness in his face.

The sixth course of Welsh rarebit with grape chutney was followed by a spectacular dessert of opera cake with gold leaf and milk-and-honey ice-cream, which was greeted with a round of applause.

'Time to withdraw to the library,' announced Adam at the conclusion of the meal. The conversation had inevitably come round to the subject of Spiritualism. Freddie Lane had asked Sir Arthur if he had any spirit photos on him and the author was happy to oblige, fishing several out of his dinner jacket pocket to show the company.

Adelina leaned in to take a closer look. In each of the sepia prints men and women stared solemnly into the camera oblivious to the disembodied faces that floated above their heads or close by their shoulders. Each floating face was framed by a halo of light which Sir Arthur explained was the shining ectoplasm used by the invisible spirit to reveal itself. Adelina found these portraits unnerving. It was as if the living were in constant proximity to the spirits of the dead but chose perversely to ignore them.

In the library, Mrs Wells had set chairs around a large dark oak table and lowered the lights to a few candles flickering on the bureau. She entered the room with the medium: a short, grim-looking woman whose head was wrapped tightly in a silk shawl so that only her face was visible. The face itself was ageless, pale but unlined, with protuberant eyes that scanned the room restlessly. Adelina wondered if she had seen the woman somewhere before.

'Ladies and gentlemen, may I present Miss Glanville-Smith from the Spiritualist temple in Springwood,' announced Mrs Wells. 'She has been conducting séances as a sensitive in the district for the last five years and Mrs Fox asked that I should invite her here tonight for the enlightenment and interest of our distinguished guests. She has also brought with her Mr Upton, who has some experience as a spirit photographer.' A bowler-hatted gent in a velvet-cuffed coat bowed and proceeded to unfold a tripod and set it up in front of the table.

'Excellent,' murmured Sir Arthur.

'Interesting,' said Mr Longford.

'Please be seated,' the short woman directed in a light, young voice at odds with the severity of her expression. She herself took the chair at the head of the table. 'May I welcome you all here, believers and non-believers.

'I would like to extend an especially warm welcome to Sir Arthur Conan Doyle and Lady Doyle who have consecrated their lives to the spread of our glorious gospel, which contains more proof of the eternal love of God than any truth yet revealed to Man. I am honoured to have you present.'

Sir Arthur and his wife nodded in acknowledgement of this tribute. Miss Glanville-Smith cleared her throat and led the gathering in a hymn.

Shall we gather at the river,
where bright angel feet have trod,
with its crystal tide forever
flowing by the throne of God?
Soon we'll reach the shining river,
soon our pilgrimage will cease;
soon our happy hearts will quiver
with the melody of peace.

Adam looked across the table at his wife. Did he have any reason to be concerned? She looked happier and more at peace tonight than for as long as he could remember. What was she hoping for from this séance? He hardly dared guess.

When the hymn concluded, Miss Glanville-Smith placed both hands on the table, palms down. She had arranged several of her tools in front of her: a trumpet to magnify the voices of the spirits, a hinged slate on which they might chalk their messages, and sheets of paper and a pencil for automatic writing. Mediums had to be prepared for whatever method the spirits chose to communicate. Mrs Wells had been nominated as her 'control', able to assist with the tools and ready to intervene if the medium was in danger of slipping into a coma or choking. Two lengths of rope also lay on the table for no obvious reason. Mr Upton's camera had been mounted on its tripod and at Mrs Wells' signal the plate would be exposed by opening the lens.

Miss Glanville-Smith asked Mrs Wells to blindfold her and she then sat straight-backed in the chair, arms tensed, fingers spread flat and face tilted up as if basking in the manner of Dr Liebermeister's patients when they took 'sun baths' on the rooftop.

The company sat in the trembling glow of the candles in near silence for some time. Adam tried to avoid making eye contact with anyone else at the table in case he disturbed the ritual. He was decidedly a sceptic when it came to this business of talking with spirits but he did not want to offend his guests or upset his wife. He caught a glance from Freddie Lane, who was also struggling to take the whole thing seriously. Longford and Lyell appeared fascinated by the entire procedure while Hugh and Grace Ward had their heads bowed as if in prayer.

A low moan escaped the medium's lips. Her lips contorted into a grimace and then the moan resolved into a voice, small and childlike: 'Who seeks our friends?'

Mrs Wells leaned towards Mrs Fox. 'Rosie. Miss Glanville-Smith's spirit guide. She will help us. You must state your name clearly.'

Adelina was suddenly overcome with trepidation. This was the moment of truth. Was she really ready to talk with Robbie after all these years? What could he possibly tell her that would allay her guilt and soothe her agony? And what if he could not be found? Or, even worse, what if he refused to communicate at all? Her breathing grew shallow and rapid.

'Are you alright, my dear?' whispered Adam.

'She'll be fine, I assure you,' said Sir Arthur.

Adelina sucked in a lungful of air and nodded to indicate she was feeling calmer. 'Adelina Fox,' she stated loudly.

The medium gulped as if devouring the name whole and her nostrils flared with a deep inhalation of breath.

The small childish voice again. 'Whom do you seek?'

'My son.'

Adam heard the tremor in his wife's voice.

The medium gulped again, swallowing the words. Her head swivelled from side to side and even beneath the blindfold her eyelids could be seen to be twitching violently. A long slow hiss escaped the woman's lips but her head continued to swing back and forth for some minutes.

'No one answers,' came the small voice, almost churlishly.

Panic spasmed in Adelina's face and she cried out in great agitation, 'I wish to speak with Robbie. Robbie Fox.'

After a short repeat of the head-swinging, the medium's throat convulsed and her jaws distended in a ghastly silent scream. Out of her mouth a tube of glowing white jelly was excreted and snaked over her chin and down her blouse, breaking up into long shiny filaments that dissolved into the air like thick, creamy smoke. A murmur of horror spread around the table. Mr Upton stood by his camera.

'No need to be alarmed,' said Sir Arthur. 'It is merely the ectoplasmic fluid. The spirit is near.'

Adelina was trembling now and steadied her breathing by an act of will. Mrs Wells wiped Miss Glanville-Smith's mouth clean as if she was tending an infant. It was such a familiar domestic gesture in so strange a context it verged on the comical.

The medium's right hand clutched at the table. Mrs Wells realised what was happening and slipped the pencil into her grasp. Miss Smith did not look down. Her head was tilted so far back, all they could see was her silk-covered neck. Her hand jerked across the blank paper with a life of its own, animated but with a heavy reluctance like the wooden limbs of a string puppet. Mrs Wells read out each letter as it was formed.

'F-O-R-G . . .' There was a pause as the fingers hung limply.

'Forget?' Adelina whispered to no one in particular. She looked bewildered.

The hand resumed its writing: '. . . I-V-E,' intoned Mrs Wells. 'Forgive.'

Adelina's breath caught in her throat. The hand continued its jerky movements. 'H-E-R. Her.'

'Forgive her?' said Lady Doyle, looking around the table. 'Who?'

Adelina felt a fever begin to burn in her brow.

Adam tried to catch her attention but she seemed to be avoiding his eyes. 'Darling, maybe we should stop this,' he suggested gently.

'No,' she replied. If this was a message from Robbie, Adelina was determined to know the truth. Whom should she forgive? Freya or Angie? There was only one way she could be sure. She must know the reason.

'Why? Why should I forgive her, Robbie?' she demanded.

The medium's lips chewed on these words and swallowed them like a lump of bitter gristle. Miss Glanville-Smith sat bolt upright now. More jelly spewed from her mouth, glistening and smooth like a paste. Mr Upton opened the lens of the camera as the room filled with a golden miasma.

'He has something to show you, Addie,' said the girl's voice. She was using Robbie's pet name for his mother when he was small.

'It's really him,' whispered Adelina, her eyes shining with tears as she looked at Adam. 'It's Robbie.'

'Bind her,' said Mr Upton urgently. Mrs Wells seemed to know exactly what to do and seized the two lengths of rope lying on the table. She pinned Miss Glanville-Smith's arms to her side and bound them.

'Why is she doing that?' Fanny asked Sir Arthur.

'Miss Glanville-Smith is about to do an apport. She must sit very still so that she does not thrash about and accidentally injure herself or anyone else. And this way you can also see that she is not using her hands or arms in any way to manipulate objects.'

They all stared at the medium, who was now blindfolded, bound with ropes and as rigid as a board. She began to moan again, rocking from side to side as her cries grew louder and wilder until they climaxed in an inarticulate shout. The candles on the bureau dipped and their copper glow winked out for a second.

'My birthday present,' said Miss Glanville-Smith in a new voice, still young but deeper. A boy's voice.

Adelina gasped, her hand to her mouth.

From the ceiling there dropped a small object which landed on the table in front of the whole company. It was a rectangular piece of card, stained and dog-eared, and completely blank on the side facing them.

'Turn it over,' said Sir Arthur.

Adelina's breathing was laboured, her hands clenched. Adam reluctantly picked up the card and turned it over. It was a sepia photo of a young naked woman wearing only a necklace of clear crystals and bangles at her wrists. She sat on a beaded cushion, legs crossed delicately, but with her arms raised to show off her breasts. At her feet lay a basket from which a snake had risen, evidently mesmerised by the woman's beauty.

'Good God! It's one of those naughty French postcards from before the war!' exclaimed Sir Arthur.

Fanny Durack giggled. Longford shrugged. 'What does it mean?' he whispered.

Adelina trembled from head to toe. She was staring at her husband. All the blood had drained from his face. He looked haggard and old. He knew what this was. He had seen it before, she could tell. It was Freya's. It had to be. Had she given it to Robert? Was that what she must forgive?

'Forgive her,' repeated the boy's voice.

The blindfold, though securely tied to Miss Glanville-Smith's face, came loose and dropped into her lap. The medium's eyes rolled back like marbles and her mouth gaped, a raw, pink wound. The voice deepened again and sang a lilting chant:

In the valley, here I lie
Here I lie but am no liar
Before the snows come, two shall die
One by water, one by fire
Before the snows come, two shall live
But only if they can forgive.

As the last words died on the medium's lips, the candles blew out. The room was plunged into darkness. All the guests could hear in the yawning blackness was the sound of a woman's inconsolable sobbing.

Adelina Fox knew she must die because she could never forgive.

CHAPTER 16

Laura

Meadow Springs, June 1921

With a boyish mix of nerves and excitement, Adam could hardly wait to head over to the Palace that morning to meet the cast and crew of *The Blue Mountains Mystery.*

The cameraman, Arthur Higgins, and his assistant had begun setting up their Klieg lights and blackout drapes in the casino before sunrise. It was no surprise that word had spread among the guests that Australia's most celebrated director, Raymond Longford, and his partner, Lottie Lyell, the adored film star, were shooting scenes in the hotel for their latest film. Some fans were disappointed to learn that this time Lottie was remaining behind the camera as Longford's co-director. Even so, by mid-morning a large crowd had gathered near the entrances to the casino, held back by ropes strung across the thresholds. One of the crew, a tall stocky lad named Simon, had gained permission from the general manager to display placards on the walls.

NOTICE
All persons not in actual scene PLEASE keep away from FRONT OF THE CAMERA and OFF THE SET
by order of the Director

While those instructions were mostly for the benefit of the throng of curious onlookers, they were also a reminder to less experienced members of the cast. Adam Fox had read how Longford, with a string of box-office hits to his name – including *The Sentimental Bloke*, *Ginger Mick*, *On Our Selection* and, most recently, *Rudd's New Selection* – was praised for his 'natural' style of directing which 'captured the truth of Australian life and manners' and avoided the melodramatic stock gestures and expressions of most silent-movie acting. He achieved this in part by using not only experienced screen and theatre actors but also untrained non-actors, usually for smaller roles. He would pluck someone off the street because he liked their face.

Which is how Adam came to meet Laura.

Raymond and Lottie were in the billiard room making notes when Adam arrived at the hotel. They were sitting, heads close together, scripts in their laps, talking in low voices. They both looked tense and tired.

Adam had spoken with Longford and Lyell about their

film back in January on the memorable night of the Conan Doyle dinner so he had some idea of the pressure they were under. *The Blue Mountains Mystery* was a new kind of film for Longford: a high-society crime thriller set in a luxury hotel where a rich businessman is found dead and his wife suspected of the murder. Based on a popular novel, the story's main plot twist was that the dead man turned out to be an imposter, an underworld gangster who was holding the businessman hostage and blackmailing his wife.

The lead male was a good-looking veteran actor, John Faulkner, who usually played tough guys and villains like the German spy-ring leader in *Enemy Within*. His challenge in this film was to play the double role of suave rich gentleman and ruthless thug. Longford had cast Mrs Marjorie Osborne as the female lead. Marjorie was the cosmopolitan wife of a rich Queensland squatter. She was very helpful in the costume department, as she knew all about high-society fashion, but she had never acted in a film before and needed close direction.

The shoot had been going on since April. The crew and cast had been staying at the Carrington in Katoomba and were now occupying an entire floor of the Delmonte Wing of the Palace. This film had the biggest budget of any film Longford had ever directed, with a large cast and many outdoor locations all over the Blue Mountains as well as inside the beautiful Carrington Hotel and the Palace. For the next month or so they would be shooting scenes in and around the Palace as well as down in the valley. While his previous films had done well in Australia and Britain, Longford's producers, Dan and E.J. Carroll, had high hopes for this film in America. All in all, it was a monumental undertaking.

'I hope I'm not interrupting,' said Fox as he drew near.

Longford looked up and smiled broadly. He was a tall, thickset man, handsome in a world-weary way.

With her restless dark eyes, Lyell also looked up and acknowledged the hotelier with a curt nod. Adam noticed the translucency of her skin and heard the wet cough in her chest; according to gossip she had spent time last year in a clinic in the mountains recuperating from a bout of tuberculosis.

'No, not at all. Welcome. We were expecting you,' Longford said affably. 'Come and meet the actors and crew.'

Given the early-morning frost and plummeting temperatures outside, it was strangely hot and stuffy inside the casino. Every small detail of the grand room was illuminated startlingly in a blaze of brilliant white light that poured from six giant carbon arc lamps on tall stands. Adam could hear them crackling and sizzling as they radiated waves of intense heat.

Arthur Higgins was busy making final adjustments, tweaking a barn-door here and there on the lamps as he tiptoed over the riot of cables snaking across the casino floor. He doffed his cap in greeting at Mr Fox as he passed. 'One of the best cameramen in the business,' said Longford proudly.

This morning's scene was to be shot on the casino's stage, usually used for concerts and palm court orchestras. Today it had been dressed with a giant web of wires for a performance by dancers Fred Leslie and Ivy Shilling, darlings of Australian and

London variety theatre. Adam had first seen this duo perform their famous 'Spider's Web' routine in a revue at the Tivoli back in 1913. He dimly recalled the sensuous writhing and flutterings of Ivy, a long-legged beauty, dressed in multicoloured silks as a butterfly in a colossal web at the mercy of the predatory arachnid, Fred. It was all very artistic and titillating, as he remembered, but then so were most of the entertainments offered at the Tiv.

As Longford and Adam made their way through the crowd of onlookers, the hotelier saw a knot of people assembled in the middle of the ballroom. Some were already in full make-up and costume while others were still in their street clothes. They had been summoned from their dressing rooms upstairs especially to meet the owner of the Palace.

Adam immediately recognised John Faulkner, even with his shocking mask of white pancake and thick, blackened eyebrows. Standing next to Faulkner was a slender young woman, still in her overcoat. She had glossy black, shoulder-length hair, tied back from her forehead with a scarf. Her pale fine-boned face had an aristocratic air of boredom when in repose, but when she smiled, her eyes were animated with the most compelling warmth and intelligence Adam had ever seen. And those lips, so luscious and full, struck him as irresistibly ripe for kissing.

Adam was taken completely off guard by this vision of loveliness. He felt the axis of his everyday world tilt off-centre. Not since the first time he had laid eyes on Freya in her cottage all those years ago had he been so unexpectedly smitten. Before he could stop himself, he lunged forward.

'So you must be Miss Marjorie Osborne,' he declared, loud enough for the entire assembled cast to hear.

There was an awkward silence during which the young woman in the overcoat looked at him in alarm.

Longford coughed and hastened to the hotelier's aid as a flustered older woman stepped forward from among the knot of actors.

'Ah, no, actually, that is Laura, who is playing Mrs Osborne's *maid* – and *this*,' the film director said with great emphasis and a theatrical flourish, as if presenting a member of royalty, 'is Mrs Marjorie Osborne, our leading lady.'

'Oh. My sincerest apologies,' said Adam Fox as he realised his gaffe.

Mrs Osborne graciously laughed it off.

Fox shook hands with all the cast and crew, welcoming them to the Palace and leaving them in no doubt about his enthusiasm at having such luminaries on his premises. He was all charming smiles and attentive nods, but every now and then his eyes flicked in the direction of the 'maid'.

Finally, Longford glanced at his watch. 'You must excuse me. It's time we got to work.'

'Would it be alright if I stayed and watched the dance?' asked Adam.

Laura was standing with her back to him, talking to a fellow actress. He admired the way her hair moved under the light like the motion of dark water in a stream.

'We would be honoured, Mr Fox,' the director said diplomatically. 'Let's find you somewhere to sit.' Longford called over his runner, Simon, and told him to fetch a chair.

Lyell appeared at Longford's side with her pencil and script, making no secret of her impatience to get started. 'The pianist is ready. And Fred and Ivy are in costume, Raymond, and waiting in the wings.'

'Alright, everyone!' said Longford clapping his hands and assuming an air of command. 'Arthur, are you ready?

Higgins stood by his hand-cranked camera, a bulky black box topped with two film magazines, the whole contraption mounted on a heavy wooden-legged tripod. He leaned forward, squinting slightly as he rechecked his framing, then gave Longford the thumbs-up.

'Fred, Ivy, how about you?' Longford called in the direction of the stage. A male voice replied in the affirmative from the wings. 'Ready when you are, Mr Longford!'

'You know this routine inside out so I hardly need to give you directions. Let's go for a take, shall we? Mr West, if you please.' Longford nodded at the pianist and signalled to his cameraman. Higgins began cranking the long slender camera handle with a steady metallic whirring. A hush fell over the onlookers, both the guests of the hotel and the cast members who had never seen Leslie and Shilling perform. Among these, Adam noted, was Laura.

The piano began its high, silvery, meandering tune. Entering the stage on pointe like a ballerina, Ivy Shilling tiptoed cautiously at first as if aware of the dozens of curious eyes upon her. Her costume was tastefully erotic: a tight bustier emphasising her shapely bosom while its short gauzy skirt revealed the creamy perfection of her thighs. Midnight blue satin shoes matched lustrous stockings that stopped provocatively just above the knee. Long buttoned gloves encased her elegant arms, beneath which butterfly wings opened out in silken folds as iridescent and hypnotising as sunlight on oil. As the music spiralled upwards, Ivy danced with sensuous abandon, basking in her own magnificence and the warmth of an imaginary sun.

Adam glanced towards the group of actors close by in the half-darkness behind the lights. There *she* was. Laura. *Laura, Laura, Laura.* Adam was forty-six years old, a respected businessman at the height of his success and a husband about to celebrate his silver wedding anniversary. So how was it that, all of a sudden, he felt as giddy and helpless as a lovesick adolescent?

Ah there! Laura stole a quick look in his direction. Their eyes met. Adam smiled. She smiled back, a small, tentative smile, before turning her attention again to the stage, her chin tilted up at a slight angle. Bewitching.

With a menacing discord, the butterfly's spring dance stopped as she detected a malign presence nearby. With an unexpected crescendo from the piano, a pair of flash pots ignited, blinding the audience momentarily and spewing twin columns of smoke into the air. These geysers quickly mushroomed into two scattering clouds of grey into which beams of bright light were shone. The resulting effect was electrifying. With gleaming jewelled eyes and bristling, sticky legs, two giant spiders magically appeared and crawled up the furled golden drapes either side of the proscenium arch before disappearing into thin air. The audience gasped in horror.

Now the wires of the giant web glimmered menacingly as a sinister, lithe figure, clad in charcoal black top hat and tails, clambered down from the darkened upper reaches of the stage. Fred Leslie's dark eyes glittered and his moustache twitched as he leered at his victim.

The spider-man circled the butterfly, the music growing oilier and murkier as he beckoned her to join him in his seductive dance. She feigned aloofness at first and then made several half-hearted but futile attempts at escape, blocked at every turn by the agile leaps and pirouettes of the male. Strains of a classic tarantella quickened the tempo of these exertions as the seducer's dance grew ever more energetic and lustful, his jumps and kicks wilder and higher.

All pretence of indifference now abandoned, the butterfly's fluttering resistance grew more desperate before giving way, little by little, to her lover's power. Subtly mirroring her every movement, the spider-man enmeshed the butterfly in a languorous pas de deux, her body twitching and melting with passion as they merged in rhythmic unison. At last, she yielded. In swooning erotic submission, the butterfly surrendered and was entwined in her lover's arms. As the piano crashed towards its furious conclusion, the spider carried his recumbent victim up into the highest reaches of his web and hung her there: his bejewelled prize.

'Bravo! Bravo!' The audience broke into noisy applause as Fred and Ivy climbed down to take their bows. Adam saw

Longford and Lyell conferring with Higgins. 'Thank you, Fred. Ivy. That was wonderful! We'll take a short break and then go for a second take,' announced Longford.

The crowd began to disperse. Adam and Laura's eyes met again as she was jostled by her fellow actors, hurrying back upstairs to their dressing rooms. She held his gaze longer this time, her expression serious. She studied him for a long moment. And then turned away.

Adam was used to having women flirt playfully at parties, dropping perfumed cards into his jacket pockets, leaving pretty gloves on his chair at dinner or slipping pencilled notes under his champagne glass. But ever since his affair with Freya – and despite all the gossip to the contrary – Adam had strayed only a little from the path of virtue: a discreet kiss here, a nuzzle or fondle there; nothing compromising, nothing for which he could be seriously reproached. He was always the spider in these encounters – well-practised, masterful, in control. Only with Freya had he ever felt vulnerable, and then only momentarily. It was a kind of vertigo, terrifying and exciting.

And here it was again, that same feeling of pleasurable danger. He had not forgotten that sensation of standing on the brink of the unknown, of falling under the sway of another's mystery, of surrendering oneself. It was a feeling that threatened to obliterate him. The difference this time was that, with all the pain that had accumulated these past few years, obliteration seemed a welcome prospect.

He stood up, waving at Longford to signal his intention to leave and to convey his gratitude. Longford waved and smiled back, resuming his earnest conversation with his cameraman. Adam threaded his way through the crowd towards where he could still see Laura, her black hair shimmering under the overhead lights as she headed towards the stairs.

'Miss Laura,' he called, trying to keep his voice low but still attracting odd glances from her fellow actors. She stopped, allowing him to catch up to her.

'I just wanted to say sorry for being such an ass earlier,' said Adam, unable to think of a better excuse for chasing her and instantly regretting his use of the word 'ass'. 'I hope I didn't embarrass you –you know, in front of your colleagues.'

Dear God, what a stuffed-shirt he sounded.

Laura smiled and a small laugh slipped out from between those perfect lips. 'No, not really. No more so than right now!' she teased.

'Yes, right.' Adam realised they were both being stared at. 'So when are they shooting one of *your* scenes? If that's the right expression.'

He could tell Laura was flattered by his attention. Her eyes sparkled and her cheeks were faintly flushed but she held his gaze without any attempt at flirtation or evasiveness. 'I'm in a scene in the billiard room after lunch.'

'Well, I might drop by and take a look. If you have no objections.'

'It's your hotel, Mr Fox,' said Laura. 'I suspect you can do whatever you like!'

And with that, she hurried up the stairs before he could say another word.

CHAPTER 17

Lisa
Canberra, June 2013

A squad of eastern grey kangaroos stood about on the neatly trimmed lawns, chewing thoughtfully and scratching their ears with their forepaws. When Lisa walked to the Australian War Memorial that morning every blade of grass had been coated white with frost. By mid-afternoon, however, the frost was all gone and there was even a hint of warmth in the weak winter sun as she stood outside the AWM's research centre, munching a ham sandwich with the same thoughtful rhythm as the kangaroos nearby.

Her quest to discover the past was no longer an idle one. She had decided it was not fair to let Luke do all the legwork. The Palace history had many other aspects that needed his attention: interviews with staff members and guests, and weeks of research in local, state and national archives and libraries. The list was long and the days short. Luke's deadline to deliver a first draft was in August. His employers planned to publish a sumptuous small-run coffee-table book to coincide with the grand relaunch of the property later in the year.

Lisa made a commitment. For her, too, the clock was ticking. Monika's health ebbed and flowed, as did her mind. But overall, the tide was going out. If Lisa ever wanted to know the truth, there was only one person who would find it for her – which was why she had put her freelance work on hold for a week and come to Canberra. The Ritz promised to alert her if Monika became too distressed in her absence.

Of course, she paid a visit to Tom, Natalie, Sasha and Oliver. Their house in Watson was too small for her to stay unless she was prepared to settle for a sleeping bag on the couch, so she had booked a room at the Hotel Kurrajong in Barton, close to the old Parliament House and the National Library. The Palace and the Kurrajong had something in common. Ben Chifley had famously died of a heart attack at the Kurrajong in 1951 in the room he had occupied the whole time he was wartime prime minister. An ex-national leader had also died of a heart attack at the Palace. Sir Edmund Barton, Australia's first prime minister, had earned the nickname 'Toby Tosspot' for his love of drink and food, which finally caught up with him when his heart stopped in the shower at the hotel in 1920.

'History is boring,' Oliver confidently informed his aunt over hamburgers on her first evening at Tom's house.

'Why?' asked Lisa, trying to keep any tone of judgement out of her voice.

'It's all about dead people,' Oliver replied. 'That's what Daddy says.'

Tom blushed bright red and almost choked on his burger. 'Oliver!'

Lisa smiled. Tom was 'caught out rudely' as they used to say when they were kids.

'I didn't say that exactly,' corrected Tom. 'I just said history has its *place*.'

Lisa was familiar with this argument. As a professional scientist responsible for a substantial research program, Tom lined up like everybody else for crumbs from the government coffers. Sometimes, out of frustration, he had expressed unflattering views about his competition in the humanities. 'Wankers' pretty much covered it.

Not surprisingly, he and Lisa had gone over this well-trodden ground a few times until they had decided – as with so many subjects – to agree to disagree. Not that the sting of Tom's lack of interest in, and she suspected disdain for, Lisa's own work as a professional photographer ever really went away. Apart from the odd peremptory 'How's work going?' he never asked to see any of her photos.

'Well, Daddy is right. It is about dead people and it does have its place,' said Lisa, disguising her alarm that a seven-year-old could be so sure about such things. I guess it's the privilege of parents to brainwash their kids, she thought. Monika had done a half-arsed job with her and Tom. Except for their immense discipline, she realised. Maybe her absence behind the study door and her brilliant career had provided a role model after all. Lisa and Tom had never been afraid of hard work.

'So how is your digging up of dead people going?' Tom asked her later over their fourth glass of wine. Natalie had rushed off to the kids' room to deal with some crisis.

Lisa laughed. She told her brother a few stories from the diaries. Then, encouraged by what appeared to be genuine interest, she showed him photocopies she had made that day at the National Film and Sound Archives of publicity stills from *The Blue Mountains Mystery*, the Raymond Longford film partly shot at the Palace. There was Grandma Laura, so young and beautiful, in a maid's costume in the middle of the casino. She opened her laptop and flicked through some photos from the albums of Monz and her siblings, of Grandad and the Palace.

Seeing Lisa and Tom together, heads bowed over the laptop, Natalie made an excuse to withdraw to the kitchen. To Lisa's amazement, Tom was rapt. He stared for a long time at each photo and asked lots of questions. At one point she looked across and saw his eyes glistening. He had stopped speaking and she could tell he was in the grip of an unexpected wave of emotion.

'Are you okay?' she asked.

Tom shook his head. 'I – I didn't expect . . .'

'I know.' She placed her hand on her older brother's shoulder. 'I know nothing will really explain Mum to us. But I still want to try.'

Tom nodded and squeezed his sister's hand. 'Good on you, sis.'

Lisa finished her ham sandwich and shook the crumbs onto the grass where they instantly attracted interest from the kangaroos. Probably not meant to do that, she thought, or was that just parrots? She could not stop thinking about the unguarded moment she had shared with her brother the night before. It was obvious that Tom was as frightened to confront his feelings about the past as she was. She was delighted when he had asked her to keep him posted about her progress.

Back inside, another pile of files awaited her. She had spent five uninterrupted hours so far in her research booth for good reason: Monika's diary entries for 1942, which she had finished reading a week ago with the realisation that they opened a fresh field of investigation into the past.

Just when Monz thought life had hit rock bottom, fate delivered another blow. Even before the attack on Pearl Harbor, officials from National Emergency Services had visited the Palace and recommended it be listed for possible conversion into an emergency hospital. Seven months later officers from the US Army 118th General Hospital came up for an inspection tour. Monz had watched as her father put on his best suit and tie that day to impress the five American colonels whom he would personally escort around his pride and joy.

Adam Fox made no secret of the fact he liked Americans. While he had grown up revering the fruits of European and British culture, he had always admired the industry and genius of the New World. Like him, Americans were 'can do' people: ambitious, practical, no-nonsense. The casino dome of the Palace had been designed and prefabricated in Chicago, and the hotel itself had been opened on 4 July 1900.

One canny journalist for *The Bulletin* had noted that the Palace, built and opened on American Independence Day only six months before Australian Federation, was 'a brazen assertion of Antipodean pride, leaving the mother country in no doubt that Australians were members of a cultured and civilised society and the equals of any nation on earth.' It was the kind of gesture Americans would applaud.

The Palace had hosted the sailors and officers of the Great White Fleet during its historic visit to Sydney back in 1908, intended to send a signal to the rest of the world – but mostly to Japan – of the friendship between Australia and the USA. The hotel did the same again when the Fleet came back in 1925 and Fox even gave one of the sailors who jumped ship that year a job driving the hotel's bus to Jenolan Caves.

For all his talk of making sacrifices and his fondness for Americans, Adam Fox was still shocked when the order finally came from the US Army on 3 July 1942 formally requisitioning the Palace for use as a military hospital. The order gave Fox and his general manager, Mr Merewether, only ten days to vacate the premises, including all the guests, staff, furniture and fittings. It was a near impossible deadline.

Precious artworks were trucked out to the basement of the Savoy cinema in Katoomba and filing cabinets overflowing with paperwork were stashed in Fox's house in Leura. All the staff were laid off and much of the furniture was either sold or put into storage. Fox supervised the whole process like a doctor overseeing the terminal stages of a dying patient – with a focused and clinical detachment.

His daughter Monika could see the emotions at war in her father. It was obvious that part of him welcomed this opportunity to demonstrate his patriotism. Three months ago, he had taken up a commission as the colonel-in-chief of the local Volunteer Defence Corps regiment. He spent every Sunday afternoon down at his farm in the valley drilling his Retreads, rehearsing for guerrilla warfare and the demolition of bridges and rail lines when the Japs invaded the Blue Mountains.

But Monika could tell that another part of her father was already in mourning for the Palace. Nobody ever thought of Adam Fox as sentimental, so it came as a surprise when nearly every member of staff who had ever worked at the Palace – most of them locals living in and around Meadow Springs – received a phone call from him the week he was given the US Army papers. Two days before the advance party of American officers and doctors arrived to hoist the Stars and Stripes over the casino in a formal handover ceremony, Adam Fox gathered his extended family around him for a staff photo outside the front entrance of the hotel.

The day was brisk and overcast and they came dressed in their smartest overcoats and jackets, beaming with communal pride and jokey camaraderie. The whole gathering was tinged with the tender glow of nostalgia. There were hugs and handshakes and glasses of champagne all round to toast the health of 'the grand old lady'. Seated on the bottom step of the front stairs between Mr Fox and Mr Merewether, the receptionist Shirley Rice held up a placard for the photographer: THE PALACE – CLOSED FOR THE DURATION.

Adam was the only person in the photo not smiling. Despite the fixed grins all around him, the scene had an air of finality. The placard read like an epitaph.

During those ten days of closing, Monika watched her father's grief settle on him like an old overcoat. She could tell that he was haunted by the conviction that this was the hotel's death knell. Over the next two months, doctors and nurses arrived from Johns Hopkins University in Baltimore to set up the 118th General Hospital, its name affixed in big letters in place of the hotel's on the building's facade. Fox regarded this as an overly officious and ominously indelible act of effacement.

More changes were to come. Carpenters and plumbers made up an advance guard, repairing leaks and draughts and fixing drainage and heating, followed by gangs of workmen tearing up carpets, laying tiles and sanitising walls, ceilings and floors with buckets of whitewash and carbolic soap. Stripped of all their furnishings and fittings, every public area of the hotel was now converted into a sterile, sun-bleached ward, crammed with rows of narrow, iron hospital beds and echoing with the clatter of kidney dishes and bedpans. Barbed wire surrounded the entire hotel grounds, including the terrace and tennis courts; ambulances and stretcher-bearers replaced the buses, cars and tourists in the driveway; and military police stood guard at the stone entrance gates instead of stray village dogs.

Despite the naval battles of Coral Sea and Midway, victory in the Pacific was still a long way off as American casualties climbed steeply in the bloody battles for Guadalcanal. By September 1942, wounded Americans started arriving at the Palace in large numbers on special hospital trains, their carriages painted completely white, even the window panes, and marked with prominent red crosses. All week, these eerie white phantoms snaked their way up the mountains in the dark, clanking into Meadow Springs around midnight with their silent cargo of human suffering.

Monika decided that her father was no fun anymore. Where was the Adam Fox who always liked to joke around, play games, even turn a blind eye now and then to Monz and Lottie's shenanigans? Where was the Adam Fox whose idea of a good time was to throw a few bags in the back of the car and head out for a spontaneous adventure? Horse-riding with Monz and Lottie through a quiet stretch of bush up the valley. Or camping somewhere out west with the whole family. Or spending a day on the Hawkesbury fishing and diving off the back deck of *The Seagull.*

In the last few weeks, that Adam Fox had begun to change into someone they did not recognise. Short-tempered, silent, surly. He paced the rug in his study all day, unable to settle on any one project, chain-smoking and running his hands through his hair. Except for Sunday VDC drills, nothing held his interest: his rifles, his fishing tackle, his riding gear, his tennis racquets, his golf clubs, all lay idle.

Life did not improve as the year wore on. As if Monz needed any more evidence that Mr Curtin and Mr Dedman hated her personally, the government announced that this year's Austerity Christmas would be especially dull and joyless as all mention of Santa Claus and gift-giving was officially banned. Her father's growing ennui was beginning to infect them all, despite Laura's efforts to cheer them up with trips to the roller-skating rink and the movies at the Savoy and Embassy on Saturdays.

'I'm going to stay up at the cottage for a while,' Adam informed Laura over dinner one evening the following January. 'Just to keep an eye on things at the hotel.'

With battles raging in New Guinea, the hospital was now filled to capacity. While the patients were made to wear striped pyjamas and bright crimson dressing gowns all day long to keep them from going AWOL, this did not stop some hard cases stealing out of the hospital grounds at night and getting rotten in the pubs in Blackheath and Katoomba. Fox had heard alarming stories from the hotel's neighbours that groups of bored soldiers, mostly walking wounded, were using the statues in the garden for pistol practice and had killed most of his prize Angora goats.

The cottage next to the hotel had fallen out of use during the war but it needed only minor repairs to make it habitable. Besides, Adam added, the cottage was more convenient to the farm, where he had decided to increase VDC training to twice a week.

Monika saw a strange expression flit across her mother's face, a mix of pain and sympathy.

'It will only be for a little while,' Adam assured Laura. 'And you and the children can come up on weekends, if you like, and visit the farm. Take the horses out maybe.' He smiled but his voice lacked any enthusiasm.

Puzzled by this strange development, the girls both looked at their mother for an explanation but none was forthcoming. As if this was not disturbing enough, their father then dropped an even bigger bombshell. 'I have also decided it's not safe anymore for the girls to travel down to Glenleigh every day by train.'

Where was this all heading? Monz and Lottie exchanged looks of alarm and Laura appeared taken by surprise. Monz could tell from the way her father refused to look at them directly that what she was about to hear wasn't good.

'I've enrolled them both in Osborne Ladies' College up at Blackheath. They'll board there during the week. It has an excellent reputation and I'm sure they'll be perfectly happy there.' Adam raised his hand like a traffic cop to forestall their protests. 'And I will not hear one word of complaint or you will both be severely punished, do you understand?' His voice was so cold and hard it froze Monika's heart.

Their father was right about one thing. Osborne Ladies' College certainly came with a reputation. For lunacy. Converted from a big old rambling hotel on Paradise Hill, the college had lush grounds with sweeping views over the Kanimbla Valley, and boasted that since 1923 it had produced 'well-educated young ladies inculcated with habits of courtesy and refinement'. But the best-known fact about Osborne was that its eccentric headmistress, Miss Violet Gibbons, modelled every aspect of her institution on the British navy. The classrooms were named after British naval vessels, such as HMS *Sirius* and HMS *Revenge*, while Miss Gibbons' private quarters were HMS *Pelican*. In the main assembly room (HMS *Nelson*) Miss Gibbons, formally titled 'the Admiral', addressed her tender charges from a small stage she called 'the bridge'. The students wore naval-inspired uniforms of small-brimmed, beribboned straw hats, white blouses with broad collars and white-piped blazers, and progressed through the ranks each year of schooling from lowly midshipmen – 'middies' – to lieutenants and captains.

The college was Monika and Lottie's idea of hell. Living conditions were spartan: every room was freezing, the beds were musty and lumpy, and the food was inedible stodge. Over the last twenty years, the Admiral had perfected a stringent regime of lessons, chores and outdoor callisthenics in all weathers that fitted the two Fox girls about as comfortably as a straitjacket. The girls implored their father to reconsider his decision but he insisted that a little discipline and hardship would be good for them. 'Miss Gibbons is not cruel, just strict, and she takes girls' education seriously. One day you will thank me for sending you to Osborne.'

That day was a long way off. Monz recorded her conclusions in her diary: 'I hate this war. I hate this school. I hate everybody. Except Mrs Wickham, my English teacher, who thinks I have a bright future as a writer. She explained to me that suffering is essential if I hope to be a novelist of any note. I hope she is right. Otherwise, I cannot see the point of it at all.'

On Saturday, 13 March 1943, Monika and Lottie and their baby brother, Alan, were dropped off at the cottage with Adam as their mother was busy that day with her war work. Their father also had VDC training down in the valley that morning so he had called in Mrs Merewether, the wife of his erstwhile general manager, who lived nearby.

'I'll only be gone for three hours,' Fox told the babysitter as he straightened his Sam Brown belt in the mirror and adjusted his cap. Mrs M. had brought her fifteen-year-old daughter Maggie to keep Monika and Lottie company. 'Now, you three, be good for Mrs M. and when I get back, I'll take you all out for a treat at the Paragon.'

The girls cheered. Monz and Lottie had missed their father these last three months but had noticed that his pessimism and ennui had lifted a little. Work was progressing on a huge hospital complex at Herne Bay for the US Army and it looked as if the Palace would be handed back sometime later in the year. The government had also promised to compensate Fox for any damages and loss of income.

Undaunted by the demands of Austerity, Fox had recently bought a brand-new RCA Victor phonograph and installed it in the cottage. Thanks to a friendly US officer, he had also secured a stack of 78s with the latest hits by Jimmy Dorsey and Glenn Miller. Imitating dance moves they had seen in newsreels at the Embassy, the girls wiggled and bopped to 'Chattanooga

Choo-Choo' and 'I've Got a Gal in Kalamazoo'. The cottage was filled with the unusual sound of high-pitched laughter.

Monz felt carefree for the first time in a long while. With the strict routine and long hours of study at Osborne, as well as the unsettling arrangements in her family life, she barely remembered what fun felt like. She dared to let a small ray of optimism pierce the gloomy chambers of her heart. Maybe things were about to change for the better.

The music drifted through the open windows of the cottage and out into the sunny garden where a breeze gently swung the slender gum branches back and forth overhead, drumming on the old iron roof. Alan sat on the veranda playing with his toy Spitfire while Mrs M. flicked through a copy of *Smith's Weekly*, whistling along to the music. A flock of rosellas added their accompaniment of chirruping calls as they arrived in a flurry of red and purple wings, looking for seedlings in the tall native grasses that had all but overwhelmed the old rockery and flowerbeds.

'Keep an eye out for any snakes!' called Mrs M., raising her hand to shade her eyes from the sun for a moment as she watched the three girls chasing each other around the big blue mountain ashes and scribbly gums and shrieking like parrots.

'Can we go look at the view?' Maggie asked her mother. 'It's so beautiful. Especially on a day like today.'

Monz had to agree. The sky was a startling blue interrupted by the merest wisps of cloud. She hadn't been into this cottage garden in years and was surprised by how truly peaceful and pretty it was, even if the gazebo was falling down and the Japanese ornamental fountain was choked with weeds and moss.

Mrs M. looked doubtful at first but relented. 'Only as long as you don't go anywhere near the hospital perimeter, alright? I don't want anyone getting hurt or into trouble.'

'We promise, Mama!' shouted Maggie, and the trio ran off through the garden, whooping and singing 'Chattanooga Choo-Choo'.

When they came out under the casuarinas overlooking the valley, they could see the high barbed-wire fence that surrounded the hospital, hung with metal signs: ENTRY PROHIBITED – US ARMY PERSONNEL ONLY. They stood and looked at the view for a minute or two. Maggie cupped her hands and made a funnel-shaped tannoy of her mouth.

'Coo-ee!' she called, and the sound of her voice whipped around the bowl of the valley like a stone skipping across water.

Monz followed suit and laughed as a flock of yellow-tailed black cockatoos scattered in alarm from the canopy below. She felt as big as the sky, giddy as the wind. This place excited her, unnerved her, filled her with childhood memories of delight and terror. They had moved from Leura to Mosman when she was eight and in all the excitement and glamour of her new life there, she had shed her old skin, like a snake sloughing, leaving behind the tomboy who had spent days playing in the bush.

Down there in the valley, her father was practising killing Japs. He owned all this land up and down the escarpment as far as she could see: the hotel, the cottage, the maze of walks zigzagging back and forth across the cliff tops and beneath them, six hundred acres of farmland, including a racecourse, stockyards, a shooting box and a farmstead. And she, Monika Fox, would one day own this magnificent place herself.

'Hey, follow me. I've got something to show you!' Maggie flashed them a conspiratorial grin and ducked along one of the winding paths towards the giant hedge that separated the cottage garden from the old hotel grounds. Before either Monz or Lottie could object, they saw her disappear inside its dense leafy mass. She stuck her head back out again and waved at them. 'Come on, what are you waiting for?'

Monz shrugged and headed inside. Lottie hung back and called out, 'Hey, Monz, what are you doing? We'll get into all kinds of strife! Come back!'

When Monz showed no signs of returning, Lottie had no option but to follow. Pushing through the springy branches and glossy leaves, she soon found her sister and Maggie on their knees inside the hedge close to the fence line.

'Look what I found,' said Maggie with a sly smile. The barbed-wire fence ran flush all the way along the other side of the hedge; many of the hedge's branches were so entangled with the wire it was as if hedge and fence were becoming one – except where Maggie had found a hole. It was a crude semicircle snipped out with wire-cutters to provide access to the hospital grounds.

'This is where the guys sneak out at night when they get bored. And it's where we can sneak in.'

Lottie's face went as white as a sheet. 'We can't go in there. They have guns. It's forbidden.'

'Don't be such a baby!' teased Maggie. 'They're not going to eat you. They're really nice.'

'You mean you've been in here before?' asked Monz, torn between her sister's fear and Maggie's boldness. She felt bad for Lottie but she also felt her heart begin to race with excitement. Men with guns. Soldiers. Americans.

A memory surfaced briefly of her mother tucking them into bed one night, her lipstick smudged and her face a little blurry from one too many glasses of champagne. She was all dressed up for a party and she looked beautiful as always but her mouth betrayed a touch of sadness. 'Be careful, my darlings,' she murmured softly to them as if uttering bedtime prayers. 'Beware of men. They are dangerous.'

Maggie crouched down low and wriggled her way under the wire. Lottie began to tremble but Monz grabbed her hand and squeezed it hard. 'It'll be okay. Trust me.' And she dragged her timid older sister after her through the gap.

On the far side they were blinded for a moment in the sun. In the distance Monz could hear loud voices and rough laughter. There were figures moving about, up on the terrace, shouting. Soldiers. Jap-killers. Yanks.

Maggie scurried along the inside of the fence for a few yards and then stood up. Beside her Monz could now clearly see the men in their red dressing gowns, smoking in deckchairs in the sunshine. Maggie waved and called. One of the men waved back and gave a piercing whistle. 'Hey there, sweetheart!'

'Come and meet Larry,' Maggie said, smiling at Monika with an air of such supreme worldliness it made her feel hopelessly naive. 'He's from Chicago. His brother was a war hero who was killed at Pearl Harbor and got his face printed on a box of sweets. Larry'll show you. He might even give you some chewie, if you're really nice.'

Monz felt her pulse throb and the blood rush into her cheeks. Their father would be furious if he knew what they were about to do. Lottie shook her head violently but Monz chided her. 'Come on, silly. They're not allowed to hurt us. They're our friends.' Lottie looked as if she was about to cry. 'Just for a few minutes, alright?'

The three girls dashed up the slope to the terrace, crouching behind the Italian balustrade so as not to attract attention from anyone in the building. It was obvious that Maggie was a frequent visitor and knew her way about. When they arrived on the terrace, several men hailed her with big smiles and loud, twangy voices.

'Well, look who we have here!' exclaimed a short muscular man with a shaved, bandaged head, blowing blue smoke from his nostrils. 'What's buzzin', cousin? Who are these two pretty dolls – friends of yours?' The man had shocking pink lips like the inner flesh of some peeled fruit.

Lottie whispered urgently to her sister, 'We should go.'

'Now don'cha go looking so worried, toots,' said another patient, a taller man with his left arm in a sling and his right forearm covered in tattoos. 'Old chrome-dome here looks a helluva lot scarier than he is. Just a big pussycat ain't ya, Sarge?'

'Hi Larry,' Maggie purred at the short sergeant with the bandaged head who the Fox girls then realised must be her 'squeeze'. 'These are my two girlfriends, Monz and Lottie.'

'Well, it's a privilege and an honour, ma'am,' said Larry, rising from his deckchair and saluting them both with an exaggerated theatricality. Monz could not decide if he was mocking or sincere. 'Fancy a stick of Wrigley's?'

The other men chuckled in a manner not altogether pleasant as the soldier fished a packet of gum out of the pocket of his gown and waggled it at the two girls like a man offering a treat to a dog.

Monz felt light-headed. Her brain hummed with fear, excitement, curiosity. She breathed in the male odours of tobacco, sweat, aftershave and Lifebuoy soap. These creatures had the whitest teeth she had ever seen. They swaggered and rolled on the balls of their feet. Their biceps bulged impressively. Their big-knuckled hands had fired machine-guns and thrown grenades and thrust bayonets into the bellies and faces of Japs.

She took a step towards the grinning sergeant and accepted the stick of gum with a formal 'Thank you, sir'. A step closer and she was inside the cloud of blue smoke from his cigarette. He was as smooth as a bar of soap, no hairs on his arms or hands, and she could see every curve of muscle under his skin.

'You girls come over here to party?' said a man with an oily leer and pockmarked cheeks. 'We like to party, don't we, boys? It's kinda boring here all day.'

Maggie did not seem concerned by the fact that more and more men were joining them on the terrace, one or two hobbling on crutches, others trailing IV drips on mobile stands. She was too busy laughing at one of Larry's jokes and fiddling with her hair. She even took a drag on his Lucky Strike and blew smoke out of her nose. What a show-off. What would Mrs M. say if she could see this!

'You ever met a Yank before?' asked the leering man, flashing his white teeth at the two Fox girls. Monz shook her head. 'Well, we're not so different to your Diggers – 'cept we're better looking and better paid!'

'That's right!' laughed the man with the sling. 'And we're here to protect you, ain't we, Sarge? You Australian dolls have nothing to fear now the Yanks are here.'

Monz's face flushed. She might have been disappointed in the less-than-martial bearing of the Australian soldiers she had seen honeymooning at the Palace, but she was incensed by this kind of talk. Men she knew from Meadow Springs were fighting in New Guinea right now or languishing in Changi, like Maggie's brother Roger. For all his admiration of Americans, even her father snorted derisively whenever Jack Davey's song 'Mister Doughboy' came on the radio praising the 'Stars and Stripes' for helping save the 'Union Jack'.

Last year Monika had seen the newsreel *Kokoda Front Line!* at the Embassy. She had felt proud and moved by the images of Australian soldiers slogging up jungle tracks, still managing a smile and wave at the camera despite the exhaustion etched in their gaunt faces after weeks of combat.

'We don't need your protection, thank you,' said Monz fiercely, her face burning as she fumbled with the packet of gum, wondering how the bandaged soldier would react if she handed it back.

Maggie rolled her eyes and swore. 'Christ Almighty, Monz! There's no need to be so bloody rude!'

'Aw, now look what you've gone and done,' said Larry, wagging his finger at his fellow patient. 'Say you're sorry, fat-head, before I bust your lip!'

Monz could tell the soldiers were making fun of her. She hated them for it. It was not just her patriotism that made her angry. The real reason was that these men excited and frightened her at the same time. She felt dizzy in their presence. Her prissiness was a pathetic attempt to resist their spell. Lottie tugged at her hand impatiently. Monz was just about to retreat when she saw something over Larry's shoulder that rooted her to the spot.

At the far end of the terrace, near what had once been the hydrotherapy clinic, was a half-open door. Monz had a clear view of the stairwell inside leading to one of the wards. She could see a woman talking to a tall man in uniform, probably one of the medical officers from the hospital. He was handsome, that was obvious even from this distance. Broad brow, square shoulders, blue eyes and short, fair hair. The woman stood close to him and touched him on the arm in a manner that spoke of intimacy and ease. A slim, off-white rectangle of paper, probably an envelope, passed from her hand to his. She wore the sky-blue uniform of a VAD nurse and her laughter was as clear and throaty as the call of a currawong. Monika knew that laugh.

It was Laura.

Monz knew at once that something was dreadfully wrong. *Beware of men. They are dangerous.* That's what her mother had said. But she did not look afraid of this man. Quite the opposite.

Monz glanced back at Lottie and hoped that her sister was too distracted to notice. Her own throat had gone dry and she realised her greatest fear was that Papa could arrive at any moment and see his beautiful young wife laughing and smiling and touching this other man so intimately. An American.

That must not happen. It would be the end of her father. The end of their family. The end of everything.

'Thanks for the gum. We have to go now,' said Monz and began walking away quickly towards the hedge with Lottie in tow, ignoring Maggie's protests.

Monz wrote in her diary that night: 'I wish I could un-see what I saw. I tell myself there's nothing to worry about. But I know it isn't true. I will never tell a soul. Never. All I hope is that it is not already too late. But I have a bad feeling in my guts that a bomb has been dropped and is already speeding to its target.'

When Lisa had read that entry in her mother's diary a week ago she had felt her chest tighten with pity for the frightened, solemn thirteen-year-old whose world of happiness and safety was about to be turned upside down. It was a feeling Lisa knew all too well, the pain of powerlessness that could only be dealt with by imagining that you had some power. The power to keep a secret.

Before she left the Ritz that day, she had leaned over and kissed her mother gently on the forehead. Monika looked up in surprise, a little flustered. 'I'm sorry, Mum,' she whispered. 'For whatever happened.'

CHAPTER 18

Adelina
Meadow Springs, January–July 1921

Adelina had apologised to Adam for the way she had broken down the night of the Conan Doyle dinner. The famous author and his wife had been truly solicitous. Sir Arthur had even reassured both the Foxes that it was not uncommon for people to have strong reactions to such encounters. 'After all, communion with the other side is a profound and confronting experience.'

Playing the role of good host to the bitter end with remarkable self-restraint, Adam had thanked the spiritualist for her services and brought the evening to a rapid close. It pained him to think that this final scene, half tragedy and half farce, would eclipse his guests' recollections of the night, despite their effusive reassurances to the contrary.

Only Adam and Adelina knew the secret history behind the medium's cryptic message. Only they felt the painful reawakening of emotions that had been sealed off in dark chambers of their hearts for years. When his guests had departed and he and Adelina had withdrawn to their private rooms, Adam had hurled the erotic postcard into the fireplace and refused to discuss its 'meaning'.

'Meaning? There is no meaning! It's nothing more than a cheap magician's trick pulled by that ridiculous charlatan to frighten us,' fumed Adam, pacing in front of the fire. 'I tried to warn you, Adelina, but you insisted on having your own way. What did you expect to hear from "the other side"? Some fairytale ending about how Robbie is happy now? That all is forgiven and forgotten? As if life is ever that simple!'

Tears spilled from Adelina's eyes as her husband's anger built with the fury of an approaching storm.

'I knew it would end in disaster. I should never have let it go ahead. But never again, do you hear me? I forbid you and that busybody housekeeper to indulge in such dangerous nonsense ever again. Do I make myself perfectly clear? I have done everything you asked to make amends for the past. I loved our son, Adelina, just as much as you did. I miss him just as deeply. No one can say any differently. But Robbie is dead and gone. There is nothing we can do to change that now. I will not tolerate this maudlin obsession any longer. Let that be an end to it!'

How Adelina wished she could obey her husband and bury the past. But she simply could not. Over the next few weeks, she began sleepwalking again, a telltale sign that she was heading for a relapse of melancholia or, worse, an episode of hysteria. Dr Liebermeister deemed it wise to increase her treatments and so she spent two days of each week at the Hydrotherapy Establishment.

But none of the immersions and showers, tonics and massages, could expunge her conviction that a terrible fate awaited her. The evidence ran all the other way. For a start, there were the spirit photos that Mr Upton had taken the night of the séance. Mrs Wells had discreetly obtained copies and slipped them to Mrs Fox as asked. With its shock of sandy hair and its dark, sad eyes, there was no mistaking the handsome face floating in a halo of light close by Adelina's shoulder. Adam could say what he liked but here was the proof that her son had crossed the Great Chasm to deliver a message to his mother: a message she ignored at her peril.

Every night as she fell asleep, she saw the pornographic postcard tumbling through the air and heard Robbie's singsong voice in the darkness:

In the valley, here I lie
Here I lie but am no liar
Before the snows come, two shall die
One by water, one by fire
Before the snows come, two shall live
But only if they can forgive.

Ignorant of the exact circumstances of that horrid card, Adelina was certain of one thing: it was connected to Freya and Adam's adultery, the Original Sin that had blighted all their lives. 'My birthday present,' Robbie had announced as the card fluttered to the table. Adelina shuddered to think what it was intended to signify.

Had Robbie become sexually attracted to Angie, his own half-sister? Was that the 'present' she had promised him that fateful day, the abomination her poor boy had paid for with his own life? She had feared something of the sort might happen, which was why she had begged Adam to put a stop to their ongoing friendship. She knew nothing good could come of the elaborate falsehood they had all conspired in to deceive these innocents – but she had never imagined it could result in such evil.

Now Adelina was torn between fear of her husband's anger and fear of the spirit's message: two women would 'die' before the first snowfall if neither could forgive. This warning clearly pointed to herself. But who was the second woman?

Freya, surely. The last time she'd inquired as to the fate of Freya and her family Adam had informed her that they had been deported to Germany along with hundreds of other enemy aliens. He also told her that Freya had finally agreed to sell him the cottage and its land and reassured her there was no possibility of the Woods ever returning to live next door. When she heard this news, Adelina had thanked Adam with tears of gratitude and felt borne up by a great wave of relief. She had even dared hope that maybe, at long last, this dreadful, drawn-out chapter of their lives was over.

It looked as if exile was God's final punishment of the woman who had destroyed Adelina's marriage and happiness. There was no punishment too severe for the injury Freya had done her. Even the sacrifice of a child was barely enough. Adelina had settled for the promise of a newborn's love in exchange for the loss of her husband's. His love, she knew, remained hostage to Freya forever.

But even that did not satisfy Freya's greed. While she still held Adam in thrall, she had also wanted to steal away Robbie's love too. To turn him against her. 'White Witch' – that was the name Freya taught Angie to whisper whenever she appeared, mocking her ill health and ghostly appearance. Ah, the cruelty of that woman! And the recklessness! Was there nothing she would not stoop to?

It was true that they had all conspired in deceiving their children and were equally to blame for that lie. But Freya had gone one step further. She had encouraged Angie to grow close to her own half-brother! How could any mother with a conscience take such a risk? The fact she did this in defiance of Adelina's efforts to protect Robbie *and* Angie revealed just how monstrously selfish Freya really was.

Adelina saw her enemy's motives plainly enough, perverse as they were. Freya's overweening sense of entitlement as the daughter of a once-famous painter had so poisoned her mind that she had lost all perspective. She felt justified in doing whatever it took to restore her former status and esteem, no matter how illusory or second-hand: steal the love of another woman's rich husband, make a transaction of her newborn son, endanger her own daughter's soul. All of this so Freya's ambition could survive vicariously as she clung to her threadbare pride.

Adelina did not know how she could forgive such a venal creature. And yet this seemed to be exactly what her dead son demanded. Had her little boy come to her as a ministering angel to show the path to salvation? And if she could forgive Freya, then what act of atonement perforce would follow? Would an apology suffice or would it require a more material restitution: the return of their land and cottage?

Even more pressing was the question of whether the death promised in the message was metaphorical or real. It was this question that tormented her every night as she struggled to fall asleep. Adelina needed to know the truth. How else could she understand what was at stake? Was she literally fighting for her life?

The promise of finding out that truth was dangled before her nearly four months after the night of the séance. Mrs Wells had already been called into Mr Fox's office and given a stern warning not to raise the subject of spirits or séances with his wife ever again, on pain of dismissal. But the housekeeper was not that easily deterred in her bond of female fealty to Mrs Fox.

One bright morning in May, the head housekeeper found the patient sipping a cup of Dr Liebermeister's liquorice tea and taking in the warmth of the sun on the terrace after a vigorous wet-sheet rub-down. 'A word, Mrs Fox, if I may?'

'Yes, yes, of course, Mrs Wells. But keep an eye out, please,' replied Mrs Fox, aware that her husband had spoken to Liebermeister about Mrs Wells' 'unhealthy influence'.

Mrs Wells nodded conspiratorially. She leaned in close and whispered, '*He* has been seen.'

'You mean . . . ?'

'Yes, Robbie. Here, in the hotel.' Mrs Wells held up her fingers. 'Three times.'

Mrs Fox gasped and spilled tea on her cotton gown.

Wells glanced towards the glass doors of the clinic to make sure no one was watching, then placed her hand solicitously on Mrs Fox's shoulder. 'I swear it is true, my dear. He has come back to speak with you. It is a good sign. He understands your distress and wants to comfort you.'

Mrs Fox wished she could share in Mrs Wells' optimism. Instead she felt an anxious fluttering in her chest.

'Last Monday, two guests saw him in the billiard room and told the night manager. He was hiding behind the davenport the way he used to do, remember? The following night, one of the housemaids saw him running down a corridor, calling out your name.'

Mrs Fox drew a deep breath.

'Then yesterday, right on dusk, I saw him myself. As clear as I see you now. Standing on one leg, in the smoking lounge. "Please, Addie," he said.'

Adelina gasped at this final proof. 'What should I do?' she asked.

'I could arrange another session if you like. Miss Glanville-Smith would be more than happy to help. We can hold it somewhere quiet, out of the way.'

'I don't think so. If Adam ever found out . . .'

Wells was careful not to say a word against Mr Fox. 'Of course.' And then she had an idea. 'The other possibility is we could reserve you a room in the hotel overnight. You have such an early start each morning at the clinic. I'm sure Mr Fox and Dr Liebermeister would understand.'

So that was how it was settled. Every Tuesday and Wednesday night, Adelina stayed in a room in the Megalong Wing at the western end of the hotel so that she could begin her treatments early. Mr Fox agreed to the arrangement as Liebermeister resided in a cottage close by and could be summoned urgently if there were any problems. And, to be frank, given his wife's agitation and frequent episodes of sleepwalking, Adam welcomed a few nights' peace.

It was here at the Palace two weeks later, half an hour shy of midnight on a cold, autumn night as Adelina tossed beneath the sheets of her hotel bed, that she heard a light tapping at her door.

'Who is it?' she asked.

There was no reply. Two minutes later, the tapping recurred.

'Hello?' Adelina called out.

Silence.

Slipping on her silk dressing gown, she unlocked the door and peered through the crack into the dimly lit corridor.

It was empty. She was about to withdraw when she heard a voice at the far end of the passage: male, young, aching with sadness. 'Please, Addie. Please,' it whimpered. A flicker of pale-blue light cast a beam along the carpeted passageway and came from the same direction as the voice. 'Please, Addie. Please,' it repeated.

Adelina opened the door fully now and stepped into the corridor. Her heart was pounding hard in her chest but there was an undeniable sense of excitement and longing mingled with the adrenaline. To her right, she saw the blue light flicker like a candle flame guttering in a draught. Her ears buzzed and she could hear her own breathing, rapid and shallow, as she advanced towards this source of illumination.

'Is that you, Robbie?' she whispered.

The corridor turned at an angle, making a corner as the west wing joined the main building. Here, three squat white pillars supported a fancy Ionic capital and an archway. As Adelina crept forward, she could see that the blue light was coming from somewhere around the corner; from here she could only catch its blurred edge.

'Don't be frightened,' she said, trying to steady the quaver in her own voice. She took another step forward and the blue light flickered again. A few more feet and she would clear the corner and see it face on. She noticed a pungent, acrid smell in the corridor ahead of her and wondered if it was smoke from the fireplace in the lobby.

'Please, Addie. Please,' the voice pleaded.

Her hand holding her room key trembled and no act of will could steady it.

'Please, Addie.'

She took two more steps and rounded the corner. There stood Robbie enveloped in a blue haze, floating and rippling on the air. He wore an Argyle sweater and long pants and had his hands shoved in his pockets. He was leaning a little sideways and favouring his left leg like he always did. He stared at her solemnly with those familiar dark eyes. Adelina marvelled at how, from head to toe, her son appeared to shimmer inside a silvery blue aura and she could see right through him to the white pillars and the archway beyond.

'Please, Addie,' he mouthed again and held his arms out to her. 'Please forgive them. Please make it right.'

A sob broke from Adelina's lips and she rushed towards her phantom boy.

'Please make it right,' he said again. At that instant, Robbie winked out as abruptly as if the light of a lamp had been switched off. Adelina's empty embrace swept up nothing but an eddy of cold air.

'Oh Robbie, no, I beg you. Please don't go!' she cried, crumpling to the floor.

A door opened behind her and she heard concerned voices in the corridor. She must get up. If anyone found her in this state, her secret would be exposed and Adam would forbid her to come anywhere near the hotel. It was this thought – that she might never lay eyes on Robbie again – that gave her the strength to stand.

A young man in a dressing gown came around the corner. 'Are you alright, ma'am? I thought I heard someone call out.'

'So did I,' said Mrs Fox artfully. 'But I suspect it was just the wind from the valley. It can make the most uncanny noises.'

And with that, she returned to her room and locked the door.

Adelina knew better than to breathe a word of 'Robbie' or 'spirits' within earshot of her husband or doctor. But she had finally heeded her son's message. Winter was close. Time was running out. Since the séance, she had been paralysed by fear. Fear of looking foolish, fear of angering Adam, fear of offending God, fear of losing her mind, fear of facing her own guilt and hatred. It would take a supreme effort of will to find forgiveness in her heart and to act on it. Robbie's message was simple. Adelina could only absolve herself of guilt by an act of restitution, of genuine Christian charity. She must, in the words of her son, 'make it right'. There was only one course of action and it would take courage. She must change Adam's mind.

A week later, Adelina and Adam sat in their rosewood steamer chairs, taking a light supper out on the veranda of their house in Meadow Springs. It was a cool evening but not yet too cold. Adam Fox sipped a glass of sherry as he drank in the spectacle of the western sky, ablaze with orange and vermilion fire behind ramparts of dark purple cloud. Birds skittered and dived in the gathering dusk.

Adelina spoke. 'Adam,' she said in a low voice.

'Yes, dear?' Adam turned to his wife. It had been a gratifying but demanding day at the hotel and he was savouring this scene of poetic serenity. He hoped his reverie was not about to be broken.

'I know this will sound strange, but I have been thinking a great deal about the cottage recently,' said Adelina.

Adam looked at her with an expression of mild surprise. He took a deep gulp of his sherry. 'Is that so? And what have you been thinking?'

'Well, I wonder – I wonder if you shouldn't write to the Woods in Germany and see how they are faring.'

Adelina tried to keep her voice light and neutral so as not to alarm Adam unduly. Over the last few weeks, Adelina and Adam had seen little of each other and even then, when their paths did cross at supper or breakfast, Adelina had begun to feel like a ghost herself, barely present to her husband, whose attention always seemed focused elsewhere. The overwhelming sense of loneliness, even when in his company, was becoming unbearable. Adelina knew that this was all part of her punishment, the warning signs of her impending doom. At least this remark had arrested Adam's attention.

'Why on earth would I do that?' he asked, a note of irritation in his voice. What Adelina did not know was that Adam was well aware of how Freya was 'faring'. Freya was not about to allow him to forget.

In March 1920, Adam's solicitor had received correspondence from Freya's threatening to file a legal action in the district court to challenge the sale of the land and cottage. Repeated attempts were made to persuade Freya that her cause was doomed. It was pointed out that anti-German feeling was still rife in Australia and it was doubtful she would get a sympathetic hearing in any court. She was determined, however, to see justice done and instructed her lawyer to proceed. The case was finally heard in November. Freya's suit was dismissed with legal costs awarded against her. Adam offered to pay these as a last-ditch attempt to head off more mischief. Stiff-necked as usual, Freya refused the offer. Adam had decided it best to keep all this unpleasantness hidden from his wife so as not to stir up painful memories. All in vain, it seemed now.

The truth was that Adam had not yet finalised his plans for the land next door to the Palace, even though the way was now clear to do whatever he wished. If business continued to increase as smartly as it had in the last two years, he was tempted to add another wing to the hotel to take advantage of the cliff-top views. This would mean demolishing the cottage and its garden altogether.

In the meantime, he had put a door in the hedge, replanted the garden of natives with colourful beds of azalea, rhododendron, cherry blossom and camellia, and installed a small gazebo, several arbours, a rockery and a decorative fountain. This ornamental garden made the perfect retreat for guests to saunter in or enjoy a light lunch at the cottage itself, which had been refurbished as a kiosk.

'I know how much you want to leave the past alone,' said Adelina, 'but I ask that you hear me out for a moment. The truth is I am *afraid*, Adam.'

Adam frowned and made a dismissive noise in the back of his throat.

'No, please listen to me, darling. And don't be angry. I know how unreasonable I have been in the past and I am sorry for that, I truly am. I take full responsibility for everything that has happened. That is why I am the one who will be punished. For making you do bad things. Unjust things.'

'For heaven's sake, Adelina! This is not still about that ridiculous séance . . .'

'Forget the séance,' Adelina said. 'This is beyond any of that. This is about making amends. It is about redemption. How we will be judged. How *I* will be judged.'

'Adelina, I beg you, please don't—' Adam sighed and stopped mid-sentence. After a moment or two, he put down his glass with great deliberation and looked at his wife. This was *his* punishment: to have to listen to poor Adelina's ramblings. He must take his medicine like a man. The unexpected silence was filled only by the sawing rhythms of the crickets in the blue shadows of the garden. At last he spoke.

'So tell me. What exactly do you want me to write about to the Woods?'

She studied his face for a long time before she replied. She had rehearsed several approaches to this conversation and then decided to abandon them all in favour of the most direct: a quick blow instead of a thousand needling thrusts.

'I think we should give them back their cottage.'

Adam sat bolt upright, his eyes opened wide. What next came out of her husband's mouth was the cruellest sound Adelina had ever heard: a short sharp bark of bitter laughter. If he had slapped Adelina in the face, it would have been kinder. She whimpered at the blow. When Adam saw the effect of his outburst he swallowed his bitter rage and apologised. 'I am sorry, my dear, I did not mean to . . . but this – this sudden reversal of everything you have asked . . .' He took a deep breath. 'It is complete *madness*!'

Adelina tried to hold in her tears but her resolve crumbled. She was just a weak woman after all. Sobs were torn from her throat; sobs of grief and self-hatred. 'No, no, Adam, you have it all wrong. It was *madness* what I asked of you before. I was out of my mind with grief for Robbie. And anger. Against you, against Freya. For losing my little boy. I wanted to punish Freya and her daughter for what they'd done. But I see it clearly now – I must bear blame for that too.'

Adelina stood up, impelled by a sudden clarity of insight that she had to articulate before it vanished. 'What I did all those years ago, what I agreed to – that was the *madness*!' she shouted. 'Ripping a newborn babe, still wet from the womb, out of the arms of his natural mother. Yearning so insanely for that infant's love that I would deny his real mother that same love. Baptising that child as ours, a lie before God and humanity – and, worst of all, a lie to him who bore our name. All done knowingly against every law that is moral and natural and sacred, hoping that God would not punish us for our monstrous deceit and cruelty! Sweet God in Heaven, what *were* we thinking, Adam?'

Adam was struck dumb.

Adelina's tears came unchecked now and her voice did not quail as she pressed on. The sun's last fire was reflected in her eyes as the long shadows began to swallow up the garden and house. '*We* were the ones who acted wrongly, Adam. *We* committed the sin and *we* must make amends. It is not too late. Please, I beg you, write to the Woods and give them back what is rightly theirs. We must seek their forgiveness or we have no future. This is our last chance.'

Adam looked at her mutely. He was almost a silhouette now against the darkening sky, his face impossible to read in the dying light.

He was thinking. Adelina was right. They *had* wronged Freya and her family. *He*, Adam Fox, had wronged Freya, more than Adelina would ever know. With one call to his solicitor he could restore the cottage to the Woods. He could possibly even make representations on behalf of Freddie to have him brought home. He had the power to seek favours, bend rules. He could arrange such things.

But life is not a fairytale. What Adelina did not understand was that he had arranged things in the past – cruel, underhand things – in large part to protect her and to save their marriage. Did his wife not know herself at all? She would be consumed with despair all over again if Freya or her daughter came back into their lives.

It was all very well to feel guilt about the past but Adam had learned that the past cannot be changed. It was what he too had wanted so fervently that spring morning he had gone to Freya's garden all those years ago. And Freya had made it clear there was no turning back the clock.

'It is too late, Adelina. Too late for you and me,' he said. His voice trembled with deep emotion.

Adelina felt her soul swoon and her whole world begin to come adrift. 'Please, Adam, please,' she whispered in the darkness, echoing her own son's cry. She was begging her husband to save her life.

But Adam turned and disappeared into the house without another word.

It was a windy afternoon in mid-July. Bright arpeggios of birdsong could barely be heard over the churning surf that surged up out of the valley, rocking the great gums and soughing in the long grasses at the cliff edge. Overhead, king parrots chinked as they barrelled headlong into the wind like bolts of flame, each with their scarlet head and breast and brilliant flashes of aqua under dark-green wings. Explosive gusts shook the arthritic branches of a nearby banksia. Here, a wattle bird held on grimly to dip her beak into its bristling flowers, bobbing about like a rack of fat orange candles upright among the serrated glossy-green leaves.

Adelina could count on the fingers of one hand the number of times she had ventured along this track in the entire time the Palace had existed. The bush held no fascination for her and offered nothing in the way of spiritual nourishment. Knowing how much these flowers and plants had appealed to Freya – Adam still kept several of her botanical drawings in his office – only reinforced Adelina's determined indifference to their beauty. Even now, she wondered why she had come to this fateful spot which she had sworn never to lay eyes on. This cursed place.

Sensation Point. A timber and wire-mesh fence skirted the largest gum and continued for about ten yards along the narrow path on either side. It had been erected within weeks of Robbie's fatal fall, as had a marble plaque bolted into the cliff face. *'In Memory of Robert James Fox, beloved son of Adam and Adelina, who was taken up to the embrace of God on 14th January, 1914'.* A lie immortalised in marble.

The plaque was not there at this very moment. As instructed by Mr Fox, Gregory, who had replaced Freddie as head storeman, had removed it to give it a thorough clean. Rainwater had pooled inside the bolt holes and caused tears of rust to stain the memorial marble. The heavy slab now lay on the terrace near Gregory's shed awaiting his tender mercies.

Adelina looked at the blank rectangle on the sandstone behind her. She wondered if Adam would have preferred to leave it like this. 'I will not tolerate this maudlin obsession any longer. Let that be an end to it!' Adam had a gift for 'moving on', as people liked to say about suffering. 'Time to move on!' they insisted. 'Life must go on!'

Adam was preoccupied with the future. In two days he would preside over the grand opening of his new art gallery at the western end of the Palace. He had shown Adelina the architectural blueprints and artist impressions late last year. It was a worthy temple for his fine-art collection: high barrel-vaulted ceilings, elegant Art Nouveau chandeliers, maroon walls with a frieze of stylised waratahs, and plush golden drapes with silken ropes and canopies over arched windows. With his usual flair for publicity, Adam promised something dramatic for the launch of this new addition to the Palace: the unveiling of a major new acquisition for his collection. In the meantime, Adam and Adelina had not spoken in the two weeks since her outburst at their home. She barely saw him; Adam was so busy with preparations for the gallery opening, he worked until late in his office, even taking his meals there.

The Palace itself had never been busier either. Every morning the driveway was a colourful congestion of motor cars: Packards, Vauxhalls, Rolls-Royces and usually some Australian Six tourers from either Mr Bartlett or Mr Rolfe's hire car company dropping off passengers for a quick gawk at the hotel before heading out to Little Hartley and Jenolan Caves. Mr Longford and Miss Lyell continued to film around the hotel, attracting crowds of curious onlookers and creating even more confusion, despite the best efforts of the runner Simon to cordon off the film crew.

Less than ten minutes' walk from the Palace, Sensation Point seemed a universe away from all this feverish human activity. As the winds from the valley tore at bush and bird alike and arcane shadows flickered across the mute rocks, Adelina thought how odd it was that such contrasting worlds sat side by side. Down here at Sensation Point, the primitive, impenetrable strangeness of the bush, with its timeless cycles of life and death, presented a face of supreme indifference to the fervid, petty human dramas taking place up at the Palace.

Adelina knew that people like Freya felt enlarged by their encounters with nature. Adelina could not understand this at all. Standing here, looking across the windswept valley that had taken her son, she felt diminished.

The bush frightened Adelina. The hot-blooded scurrying and fluttering of small animals, the brief glory and rapid withering of its bush flowers, the savage, immutable crags of ancient sandstone, all these whispered in Adelina's ear: *You are merely dust blown on the wind, flesh eaten by the worms, bones whitening in the dirt. You spring up like the grass and are cut down.*

Adam had sacked Mrs Wells the day before, giving her to the end of the week to pack her bags and go. Someone had told him about the housekeeper giving Adelina the spirit photos and spreading rumours of a 'ghost child' in the hotel. Never before in the history of the Palace had the staff witnessed a scene to match this one. The angry voices from the general manager's office could be heard all the way across the lobby to the west wing and the casino. Fox remonstrated at the top of his voice while a distraught Mr Hawthorne tried to mediate.

It was an ugly scene and one that rattled the hotel staff to their core. Whatever their opinion of Mrs Wells, everyone knew she had served the Palace for over eighteen years. And now she was gone. Just like that. Unable to face Mrs Fox directly, the housekeeper left her a note which had been delivered to Adelina that morning.

Dear Mrs Fox,

Please excuse my presumption in writing to you in this intimate fashion. As you will have learned by now, your husband has decided to terminate my employment exactly as he said he would for my 'meddling' in his 'family matters'. He gave me fair warning and I disobeyed him. So be it. I have served him loyally for many years and will not now say a word against a man whose finer qualities I have always admired.

I have decided to leave immediately and have my belongings sent on to my brother's house in Geelong, where I will be living until I gain another position. It is not good for the hotel or the morale of the staff for me to linger any longer.

I hope you understand that it is because I did not wish to distress you by making a scene at the hotel that I am writing you this short note rather than addressing you personally before I departed. In other circumstances I would have made the most of such a farewell as I have valued our friendship with, I hope you will excuse my frankness, a great deal of genuine respect and affection on my part.

I just wanted to reassure you that I regret none of what has happened in connection with this situation and am glad to have played some small part in looking after your spiritual welfare. I sincerely hope you find some measure of peace and happiness in the future. You richly deserve it. Miss Glanville-Smith can be contacted on the number below if you feel the need of her services.

With affection,
Daphne Emily Wells

Adelina was astonished. Adam had not even given her a chance to defend Mrs Wells.

And now Adelina was all alone.

Dr Liebermeister was no ally. He worked for her husband. She had grown used to his clinical manner and aloof formality. He administered to her body with intimate knowledge and unassailable expertise but nothing resembling empathy or warmth. She conceded that his intentions were honourable even if his treatments – as far as her mind was concerned – were ultimately ineffectual. For some years, the continuous baths had managed to pull Adelina back from the abyss of depression, at least for short periods. But that safety net had become increasingly unpredictable. Adelina had at last faced the truth that her worst demons were probably beyond Dr Liebermeister's curative powers to banish.

Adelina had received Mrs Wells' letter just before her therapy session at the spa. Her treatment finished at four o'clock and she began walking back to her room. Little did she suspect that the cruel legacy of this day was far from over. One final blow remained to complete Adelina's isolation and seal her fate.

As she passed through the lobby she had a clear view through the picture windows where the curtains had been pulled back on this overcast wintry day to reveal a silver-white sky of endless clouds. She saw her husband out on the terrace with the film crew. The actors were taking a short break while Higgins reset his camera and Longford and Lyell conferred.

Adam was talking to a young woman. She was dressed in an unflattering Edwardian maid's costume: a short-sleeved, high-waisted black dress, white lacy cap and stiff white apron, thick black stockings and ugly, sensible shoes. She was still wearing her thick unnatural film make-up in shades of white and grey.

Nevertheless, it was plain to see that the girl was a great beauty: high cheekbones, perfect teeth, full lips, sky-blue eyes and glossy shoulder-length hair. Adam smoked a cigarette, sitting with his back to the view while the young woman leaned her elbows on the marble balustrade, looking up at him. Their body language – the intimate way they tilted towards each other, their eyes locked in an unbroken gaze – was easy to read.

They were in love.

Destiny is a cruel mistress. There it was: the final proof that Adelina could not escape her punishment. She was once again 'the white witch' as she had been all those years ago: the queen of ice, the living corpse, invisible, forgotten, unloved, beyond redemption. She was not even worthy now of Adam's deceit and secrecy as she had been in the past. His new infidelity was on display for all at the Palace to see – including her.

Adelina was left in no doubt that she no longer mattered to her husband.

The gum tree above her groaned in the wind and its boughs rubbed against each other, creaking in protest. These were the sights and sounds that Robbie must have heard just before he died, thought Adelina. Was he frightened as he fell? Did he think of her or his father? Did he die quickly or did he linger in pain? She had turned these unanswered questions over and over in her mind.

She walked back along the fence line and stood at the edge of the track, close to the low overhang of rock on the bend. The shadows of the trees stretched out now like fallen giants and the silver cloud-choked sky blushed pink and blue.

But the beauty of the coming sunset was lost on Adelina. Though the fur-lined hood of her cloak was tied securely, the wind slapped her face and punched her ears, buffeting her body so violently she had to brace her knees to keep it from pushing her backwards. She was so thin that Adelina imagined the wind snapping her fragile joints like twigs.

'A sad old chook ready for the chop,' her grandad would have said. She shuffled closer to the chalky edge and leaned towards the valley. She could feel the pull of vertigo like a magnet willing her forward. She wished she had the courage to let go.

One, two steps. Just go.

For Adelina knew for certain now that the woman she could never really forgive was herself.

CHAPTER 19

Adam
Meadow Springs, July 1921

Laura looked up with tears in her eyes. Adam was astonished at the force of her feeling. Her irises sparkled for a brief moment from the droplets that trembled on her lashes before they spilled over and streaked down each cheek.

'Is it really *his*?' she asked, her voice hoarse with emotion.

'Yes. It really is.'

In the freshly painted interior of the Palace's new gallery, Adam and Laura stood before the focal point of his entire collection, hung in an alcove all to itself: *The Valley*, the last-known oil painting of Wolfgang von Gettner. It was a panorama of the same valley that could be seen from the Palace's windows and the cottage garden next door, Adam explained, and a fitting climax to the long and distinguished career of a great artist.

'It is remarkable, isn't it?' said Adam, with something akin to lust lighting up his face as he contemplated the masterpiece. 'Subtle and grand. Intimate and epic.'

'It *is* beautiful,' whispered Laura. Her face was suffused with a blend of ecstasy and sadness. She was no doubt moved by the sublimity of the painting itself, but also touched by the story Adam had told her of its creation by a neglected master at the end of his artistic life.

The 'lost' von Gettner was, of course, the dramatic surprise at the centre of Adam Fox's grand gallery opening. The invitations had all been sent months ago and some of Australia's most prominent artists had promised to attend. They included the celebrated landscape and war artist Arthur Streeton, who had been a student of von Gettner's when he was Master of the School of Painting at the National Gallery of Victoria. The invitation did not reveal the secret identity of the painting that was to be unveiled but had alluded to 'a discovery that will electrify the art world'.

'I met Wolfgang several times before he died,' said Adam, resting his hand gently on the nape of Laura's neck, her skin cool to his touch. 'I remember asking him once if I could have one of his works. "When your *Traumschloss* is finished, Herr Fox," he said, "I will give you something to put in your gallery." And here it is.'

Adam knew this was a simplified version of the truth, but the last thing he wanted was to talk about all *that* complicated history. To his mind Laura was a fresh start, a clean slate, a second chance at happiness. He knew he would be judged harshly for this affair but Adam prided himself on the fact he did not lack courage. He was used to standing against the tide of public opinion. He had ignored ridicule and scepticism when he built 'Fox's Folly', stared down gossip and disapprobation when he introduced his lover Freya to his society friends, and withstood paranoia and anger for protecting 'his Germans' during the war for as long as he could.

And the fact was he no longer felt any guilt. True, he felt pity for his wife and a deep sadness that the long, affectionate companionship which was all that survived of their marriage was now dead. He had done everything in his power to help Adelina to be happy but to no avail. He was not completely blameless for the current state of affairs, he knew that, and he would never abandon Adelina, but he could not see why he should sacrifice his own wellbeing to her deluded and wilful misery. *Carpe diem*, that was his creed. Life was too short for senseless self-sacrifice.

Adam leaned down to kiss Laura tenderly in the soft crook beneath her right ear. She smelled so good, her silky skin's perfume an intoxicating melange of lavender and salt. To his surprise he felt the muscles jump in her neck and she pulled away. 'Is everything alright?' asked Adam.

'Yes, yes,' the young woman murmured impatiently and retreated a step or two. She caressed the marble head of a young faun on a nearby plinth and looked at Adam from underneath her black fringe. 'Just remember, Mr Fox, I am not part of your official collection. Not yet. Too much handling will spoil the merchandise.'

Her teeth flashed white in a sardonic smile and she drifted even further off among his assembly of artworks.

Adam was perplexed. He thought of himself as someone who respected an independent spirit in a woman. He certainly never wanted some wretched, cowed creature to worship him. Or so he told himself. But Laura was moody in a different way to the other women he had known. It was not so much that she blew hot and cold – he was used to that, even expected it – but that her entire manner was strangely detached. There were moments, certainly, when she expressed strong emotions and responded to his touch with genuine passion. But it was intimacy she shunned, revealing little of herself while still taking pleasure in Adam's attention. In many ways this suited Adam Fox. Weighed down with the sorrows and regrets of middle age, he was happy to bury his past and content to live in an oblivious eternal present. Even so, Laura puzzled him.

Maybe this coolness, this diffidence, was characteristic of the 'new woman' everyone was talking about, thought Adam, to whom the old rules did not apply and for whom everything was an adventure. She smoked, she drank, she voted and spoke her mind, she was the equal of any man and did not need his approval. In that way, Laura reminded him of Freya. Twenty years earlier such a woman had been looked on with distrust, even fear. Now she was valorised. How the times had changed.

Adelina's outburst about the Woods two weeks ago had taken him by surprise, but the truth was Freya was never far from his mind. Adelina was tormented by the ghost of her son because she had 'unfinished business' with him. That was what Mrs Wells had argued when she defended her meddling in Mrs Fox's welfare. Perhaps she was right. It seemed that Freya was Adam's ghost. She would haunt him to the end of his days. Unfinished business.

Three weeks ago, Adam had received another letter from Freya, postmarked Dusseldorf. It threatened to expose Adam's theft of her father's painting which he had claimed, back in 1917, was a fake. 'Why then are you opening a new gallery with my father's work to be unveiled as a genuine masterpiece?' the letter asked, its writer claiming to have heard news of the grand opening from 'friendly ears and eyes'.

The letter continued:

I beseech you for the last time, Adam, to hand back my cottage and land so I can give it to Angie as her rightful inheritance. I promise that you will never see or hear from me again if you right this wrong. I will exit your life forever and leave you and Adelina in peace.

I have appealed to your conscience and better nature before. I have pursued my rights in the courts and been denied justice. You know I cannot let this matter rest. What choice do you leave me, a poor woman so grievously wronged? With nothing left to lose, I am forced to consider desperate measures that will damage us both – but you most of all.

If you deny my request for the cottage, you leave me little alternative. Ignore my appeal and persist with this exhibition of my father's painting, obtained by deceit, and I will make our secret dealings over this painting public and accuse you of being a thief and liar. I will insist the authenticity of the painting be tested by an independent authority. Either you've lied to me about this painting or you are lying to the world. Let us find out once and for all, shall we?

'Do you love me?' asked Adam playfully, trying to keep his voice as noncommittal as possible as he followed Laura in her idle meandering around the gallery.

'Probably,' said Laura coolly. 'I barely know you. Do you love *me*?'

Adam nodded. 'Yes, I think I do.' He trotted a little faster to catch up to her.

'Well, that is as it should be!' said Laura, laughing as she ducked to avoid Adam's outstretched hand. Their wandering had turned into a childish game of chasings. For a while, they did not speak but wove in and out of the marble busts and statues like two naughty children, breathless with laughter and the effort of running.

At last, Adam caught Laura by the wrist and reeled her gently in. She allowed herself to be kissed on the mouth. 'Does it bother you that I love you?'

'No. That's perfectly fine,' she said. And then her expression became more wistful and serious. 'It's all fine. But you have to admit, it's just a nice fantasy, isn't it, my Silver Fox?' This was her pet name for her older lover with his crop of silvery-grey hair that she now ruffled with her fingers.

'What do you mean?' Adam tried not to look hurt.

'It's like Mr Longford's film,' said Laura. 'We get to play

our roles for a little while, pretending we are people we are not. And when we take off our costumes, what then? I'm a girl from Mount Victoria who Mr Longford saw by accident one day and put in his film. Just the maid, remember? It's only a small part in a bigger story but I'm still having fun. I want to enjoy it while it lasts. That's all.'

Laura pecked him on the cheek and pirouetted across the carpet. Adam stood still for a few moments, his hands in his pockets, leaning slightly on his left leg. He was trying to work out what he felt: the state of his heart was so much harder to calculate than the state of his fortune. He had been in love with Adelina once, long ago. And then Freya. How could things have altered so profoundly? How could he dare trust his feelings at all?

He suddenly felt very old. He realised he had fallen for this woman not just for her beauty and youth but because he looked on her as a possible route of escape from his life. His affair was a crazy kind of throwing of the dice to start over. Part of him knew it was impossible and insane. There was no escape. He was as desperate to change the past as was his poor wife. And just as pathetic.

In a darkly comic moment, Adam saw himself as a character trapped inside a melodrama, *A Blue Mountains Mystery*, a tense tale of love, tragedy and betrayal. The blackmailing ex-lover, the mad wife, the ghost son. What would he be when the story finished? The rich and loyal husband, held hostage for a time but happily reunited with his wife in the end? Or his cruel doppelganger, the calculating, cold-blooded gangster who winds up dead? It was not a great choice.

He heard a gasp from Laura as she twitched a gold drape to look out one of the gallery windows. Hand-numbing coldness seeped through the glass and the light outside had deepened to that hypnotic underwater blue of early evening.

'Look,' she said. 'It's beginning to snow.'

CHAPTER 20

Adelina
Meadow Springs, July 1921

There was no tapping at her door that night, no lights in the corridor, no small anxious voice from the end of the passageway, but Adelina could not sleep. And so she pulled on her dressing gown and slippers and left her hotel room.

The moon was three-quarters full over the valley: a bowl of silvery light glittering from the gum trees in the distance. She had not found the depth of courage or despair to step off the cliff at Sensation Point that afternoon. But the vertigo of the abyss had entered her soul and scooped her clean.

She was empty now, fleshless, a ghost of her former self, already waiting for fate to deliver whatever blow it had in store. While the rest of humanity slept, Adelina floated down the corridors of the Palace, directionless, without will or intent, like the snowflakes outside, borne on flurries, whirling slowly through the mercurial liquid of the moon-soaked sky. Outside, the cries of night birds and low moan of retreating trains were muffled by the huge eiderdown of snow-heavy cloud.

Except for the moonlight pouring in at the windows on the valley side and the warm glow of the fireplaces and a few table lamps, the Palace was sunk into almost total darkness. Adelina knew there would be lights on in the night auditor's office downstairs where Mr Franklin worked, reconciling the day's takings, and the night manager's office where Mr Bosely was probably stealing a nap. Outside, a narrow triangle of light would swing through the gloom as Joe, the security guard, wrapped in overcoat, scarf, cap and gloves, did his hourly rounds with his torch and truncheon. Apart from those three, it felt as if she was the only person alive in the whole world.

Adelina was in no hurry as she padded noiselessly through the labyrinth of her husband's hotel. The moonlight and her melancholy mood made everything seem alien. How vulgar it all is, thought Adelina as she drifted from room to room. How ridiculous. Without a single atom of refinement or restraint in his bog-Irish soul, her parvenu of a husband had conspired with his builder to indiscriminately pile architectural style upon style for the creation of this quixotic palace. As a result, it had grown higgledy-piggledy along the cliff top until it stretched into a rambling cavalcade of Art Nouveau, Edwardian, Federation and Queen Anne-style pavilions, wings and galleries, nearly a quarter of a mile long. A magnificent mess. Fox's Folly.

The interiors fared no better. Take the casino, for example, this absurd room with its bizarre dome and skylight, its heavily draped proscenium stage, fake gold-leafed Corinthian columns and bright crimson walls hung with monumental canvases. A brand new Steinway grand stood off to one side, in aloof isolation from the clutter of potted palms, giant cloisonné vases, buttoned-down velvet chairs and S-shaped sweetheart sofas.

And what about the billiard room next door? Dominated by two giant stout-legged, blue-felted monsters, it featured a cavernous brick fireplace in red and white, and those peculiar asymmetrical arches over the doorways with their wooden fretwork screens, all held up by triads of liquorice-twist pillars. Standing on guard amid the smog of cigar smoke and brattle of ricocheting ivory was Adam's most recent acquisition: a seventeenth-century mock-bronze Venetian page clutching his flambeau, its flame a sculpted-glass lamp with a flickering electric light bulb to mimic fire. Adelina shivered with disgust just thinking about it.

There was no attempt at balance or harmony; all was clutter and chaos. In the vast marble-floored lobby, the modish slickness of the Art Deco grille over the front-office windows clashed with the swirling ironwork of the Art Nouveau railings on the stairs and the mock Italian marble balustrade outside on the terrace. Arched leadlight doors – more fitting to a vicarage or country railway station – connected the general manager's offices to the smoking lounge.

In every room Adelina picked her way past the dark-brown chesterfields, bookcases and cabinets, huddled together like brooding herds of cattle. Clocks ticked either sombrely – the ponderous brass-faced grandfathers sulking in corners – or impatiently, like the neurotic little ormolus on mantelpieces and console tables. The walls themselves were crammed with paintings, a sickening profusion of canvases, their varnish browning a shade darker every year. And then there was the statuary: a frozen bacchanalia in marble, bronze and plaster of satyrs, nymphs, nudes and goddesses. Adelina wondered why her husband even felt the need for a separate gallery when he had stuffed so much art into the Palace itself. It was all about excess: ostentatious, intemperate excess. Her husband's Achilles heel.

The library boasted a huge oak table, a reproduction of the one on which Queen Victoria had signed the Commonwealth charter that gave birth to Australian nationhood. It was jam-packed with convict, Aboriginal and bushranger memorabilia: pistols, leg irons, boomerangs, woomeras. Tall glass cabinets displayed hideous vases and grotesque masks: souvenirs from Adam's travels abroad. No inch of wall space was left unoccupied by antique weaponry, glass-eyed animal heads and mirrors of every conceivable shape, size and concavity.

It was in the merciless surface of one of the latter that Adelina caught a glimpse of herself as she passed through the lobby. She stopped to absorb this pitiful sight. Before her stood a creature she barely recognised. The last six months of worry had undone her looks entirely. Her once-glossy chestnut hair was as coarse as straw, hanging in unpinned disorder about her face. Her pale skin, which she had often likened to alabaster, was as dull as wax with livid marks of fatigue and sorrow. Her eyes were lustreless and downcast, her cheeks gaunt, her forehead lined with indelible furrows. And her body, once lissom and angular, was a wretched, half-starved thing of bony joints and stringy muscle. She was a ruin, a corpse, a white witch. How could anyone love this pathetic, moribund animal, halfway to becoming a spirit already?

Adam had once. He had loved her so fervently that it had taken a substantial bribe from his father Patrick Fox to engineer the alliance of their two families. Proud Adelina was the younger daughter of Thomas T. Musgrave, scion of an English dynasty with ancestral estates in Surrey, a country seat in rural Victoria and factories and warehouses in Port Melbourne. The Foxes were latecomers to wealth: Irish upstarts who had made their fortune in one generation with the largest store in Sydney dominating the retail trade of the city.

Haughtily aware of these differences, Adelina had dismissed Adam Fox's advances at first. She succumbed in the end to his charm, passion and good looks. Not to mention his persistence as her suitor, driven by the same refusal to admit defeat that saw his unstoppable rise as Sydney's richest retail entrepreneur. Even so, Adelina Musgrave was surprised when her father agreed to Adam's proposal of marriage, learning only later about his secret dealings to seal a Fox–Musgrove business alliance.

Adelina's older sister, Genevieve, died unwed and unexpectedly of pulmonary fever a year later, making Adelina sole heiress to the Musgrave fortune. This was settled on her less than three years later when her widowed father was struck down with cancer. Despite her own family's grubby involvement in commerce, Adelina's air of genteel superiority never really deserted her, even though nobody could deny she truly loved Adam. If Adelina were brutally honest, she was just as insufferable a snob at heart as her nemesis, Freya.

But she was not thinking about Freya now. Only herself. 'Sad old chook,' Adelina murmured to the image in the mirror. 'Ready for the chop.'

A flash of light in the distance caught her eye. Was it Joe doing his rounds out in the gardens? Shuffling to the high arched window overlooking the courtyard and west wing, she could see that it was coming from inside the new gallery.

'That's odd,' Adelina whispered to herself.

With the slenderest hope that the light was her beloved Robbie, Adelina pushed open a side door and began walking across the moonlit courtyard towards the dark outline of the gallery. Snow crunched underfoot. The wind was freshening, light powdery flakes prancing on its invisible currents and sparkling in the lunar brilliance. Adelina's hair thrashed in wild confusion about her face, obscuring her view at times and raking at her eyes and cheeks. She quickly became numbed by the cold except for her face and hands, which began to burn.

As she drew closer to the gallery she could make out the shadows of figures moving about inside, even though the building was in almost total darkness. The only source of light was a wavering glow of orange, probably from a lamp. Thieves, guessed Adelina. It was a natural assumption given the contents of the gallery. But how had they gained entry without raising the alarm? Presumably Adam had taken every precaution to lock the gallery up securely and protect it.

Adelina looked behind her, wondering where Joe was on his rounds. In the distance she spotted the wedge of torch-light moving steadily through the row of pines opposite the Apartments. If she called out now, she would most likely alert the intruders and fail to be heard by Joe at such a distance, over the rush of wind. It occurred to her that Joe's routine was probably known to these thieves and the timing of their intrusion planned in advance.

To be honest, Adelina was not interested in protecting Adam's precious artworks. What did she care? He had hardly earned her loyalty as far as that went. It was curiosity that drew her on, the impulse to discover what strange intervention fate had in store. She felt no fear, only a compelling conviction that, no matter who it was in the gallery, this meeting was preordained.

At the western end of the building she could see that a door had been chocked open with a brick. Someone had unbolted it from the inside and left it ajar deliberately. Stepping through the flowerbeds that abutted the gallery, Adelina stole up to the door and squeezed herself through the gap.

With all the windows clothed in thick drapes, the interior was pitch-black. The feeble light she had seen earlier was not visible from where she stood near the door. Adam had shown Adelina the plans for this building months ago but she had steadfastly refused to visit it in person, which meant she now had no way of getting her bearings easily. The room smelled of that unmistakeable oily odour of drying paint and the more pleasant aroma of fresh varnish. Adelina closed her eyes tightly for a minute and let her eyes adjust to the dark. With her eyes shut tight, her hearing became more acute and she detected the rise and fall of low voices, away to her right.

'Steady now. Take it slowly,' a woman urged in a voice that Adelina knew well but could not yet identify. 'Give me a hand,' replied another female, also in an uncannily familiar voice. Who on earth were they?

Adelina crept forward a few more feet and collided with a piece of sculpture. Thankfully neither the plinth nor its contents moved or made a sound and Adelina had the presence of mind not to cry out.

Proceeding with small, careful steps, Adelina made her way through the gallery towards the voices which continued their low whispered dialogue. From out of the grainy dark, there blossomed a bubble of light as Adelina approached the edge of what turned out to be an alcove.

In the smoky orange light of a kerosene lamp propped up on an empty plinth stood two women, both wearing cloaks from which the snow had long melted. They had their backs turned to Adelina and were looking up at a large painting on the inner wall of the alcove, hung in a richly carved gold frame. Adelina had never seen this painting before but she knew immediately who the artist was. Wolfgang von Gettner.

Fantastic surmises swarmed in Adelina's head as her eyes took in other details of the scene: a stepladder propped against the wall next to the von Gettner painting and several tools scattered on the floor beside a tradesman's leather bag. And over there, leaning against the wainscoting, a second large canvas, unframed and angled, so that its painted surface was hidden from her view. Before Adelina could form any theories, the elder of the two strangers turned and looked Adelina full in the face.

'Dear God!' Adelina heard a hoarse voice utter these words in horror. And then realised the voice was her own. Her head was filled with a high-pitched wail of rage and grief. A scream climbed out of Adelina's throat like a crazed, caged animal seeking release and filled the room.

The older woman's face drained white. She stepped back, raising her hands as if to ward off a blow. As she backed away she knocked the plinth supporting the kerosene lamp which then toppled to the floor and shattered. The room was momentarily plunged into Stygian blackness, blinding all three women.

But then a bright stream of burning kerosene ran across the carpet and latched onto the hem of the older woman's cloak, forming an eerie ring of blue light that shone on her panic-stricken face. Adelina heard boots stamping at the flames as the woman shouted at her startled companion: 'Quick, quick! Save the painting!'

Within seconds, the ring of fire had spread. It lapped at the new paint on the walls and liked what it found there, sucking more fuel into its hot mouth and spewing a fountain of flame up to the ceiling. 'Save it, save it!' screeched the older woman, her voice rising sharply now as she began to disappear inside a thickening mantle of smoke and battled to shed her cloak, which was well ablaze.

Adelina was rooted to the spot for what seemed an eternity despite the intense heat that threatened to overwhelm her. She saw the second, younger woman walk into the maelstrom of smoke that enveloped her older companion and heard her desperate cries of, 'Where are you?'

The gallery was now so brightly illuminated that Adelina could see the artworks all around her as clear as day. Paintings by Longstaff, Bunny, Lister and Ashton, the glossy varnished surface inside each gilt frame reflecting in miniature the dance of the flames. With a deep-throated roar, the fire clambered eagerly up the maroon walls, ripping at the wallpaper frieze of blood-red waratahs with its long talons. Adelina watched in amazement as it seized painting after painting in its bright maw, wolfing down each offering of paint and varnish into its black gullet. It was breathtaking to behold: the racket of splintering wood and the gleeful, lustful abandon of the flames were both compellingly obscene.

Adelina's hair began to burn from the sparks that whirled through the gallery. Though her will to live was at its lowest ebb, an instinctive engine for survival stirred inside her, fuelled by adrenaline, and dragged her away from the conflagration. The fire had already surged across the floor and walls and crested up to the ceiling, rolling over like a breaking wave to form a tunnel of flame. Adelina could hear pitiful screams from the far side of the gallery as she fled, not towards the exterior door which was blocked by flame as far as she could see, but in the opposite direction, towards the Palace. Smoke clawed at her eyes and lungs making it impossible to see a foot in front of her face or draw a proper breath until, at last, she fell against another door and tumbled, choking and weeping, into the night air.

It was freezing outside. Snow was falling more thickly now and had begun to settle on bushes like a dusting of caster sugar. In the distance she heard urgent male voices and loud alarm bells. She recognised the figure of Joe running across the lawn. When she looked back, she saw the full calamity of the burning building, its ear-splitting groans of torment punctuated by smaller crescendos of destruction as Adam's artworks toppled and exploded. On her knees in the garden, Adelina swatted at her hair where sparks stung her scalp like angry wasps. She had regained her breath but that was not what preoccupied her.

Seared into her mind was the scene of the two women who had surely perished in the fire. Robbie's prophecy was now half fulfilled. There was no mistaking the face of the woman who had turned towards her, the woman she had struggled so hard to forgive. But too late.

Freya.

CHAPTER 21

Adam
Meadow Springs, July 1921

Adam awoke from a nightmare of being trapped in a cave, water lapping at his chest and threatening to rise over his head. Still holding his breath, he heard the phone ringing incessantly downstairs with no staff on duty at the Meadow Springs house to answer it. As he slipped out of bed and pulled on his dressing gown, he noticed from his bedroom window an unusual glow in the sky to the west.

A tremor of misgiving quickened his pulse as he descended the stairs to the study. The hands of the hall clock stood at three twenty-eight. 'Who could be ringing at this hour?' he wondered aloud, though the house was empty. For one absurd moment, he thought it might be Freya, phoning from the other side of the world to settle her score with him directly. Or maybe it was Adelina, woken from sleep at the hotel by one of her bad dreams, wanting to hear his voice.

'I'm sorry to disturb you, sir,' said the man on the other end. It took Adam several seconds to recognise the night manager, Mr Bosely. 'A fire has broken out in the gallery. The brigade is on its way from Katoomba.'

'How bad is it?' asked Fox.

There was a second's pause. 'It's bad, sir. I have ordered the evacuation of the hotel. Just in case.'

'I'm coming over.'

The Vauxhall was slow to turn over in the cold but Fox eventually got it running. The snowfall was fast becoming a blizzard as the wind picked up and smacked the sides of the car, causing it to skid on the icy road as he drove west.

When he came over the brow of the hill at Meadow Springs and saw the fire, he felt his chest constrict with anguish. The outline of the gallery was dwarfed by a giant, ragged pillar of flame that could be seen for miles around. The hotel itself was shrouded in an eerie yellowish-grey pall that rendered it almost invisible. It was obvious the gallery was lost and the battle was now on to save the Palace.

On the crenellated rooftop of the hotel and in the surrounding gardens and outhouses, embers had started spot fires. Adam could see figures crisscrossing the front lawns urgently and running over the hotel's battlements with stirrup pumps, buckets and blankets, trying to bring these smaller outbreaks under control.

The vision of these twin storms of fire and snow, intermingled and overlaid against a silver-white, moon-washed sky, was nothing short of surreal: a spectacle of sublime beauty and terror. Each gust that whipped the blizzard into a greater frenzy also fanned the vortex of flames. Around the turret of fire, sparks and snowflakes cavorted as partners in a macabre jig. Hissing clouds of steam shot up as the crust of newly laid snow was pelted with cinders and burning debris.

At the eastern end of the hotel, Adam saw the crowd of guests, many wearing jackets and cloaks over their nightclothes, gathered in the clearing in front of the boiler house. They were all craning their necks in one direction. Mr Carson, Mrs Bosely and Dr Liebermeister were among the staff who had been roused from their beds and were now providing succour to the hotel's guests with blankets, eiderdowns, hot-water bottles and flasks of coffee as they escorted them to neighbouring houses.

As he pulled up in the gravel driveway, Adam checked his watch: ten past four. Still no sign of the Katoomba fire brigade. Where in God's name were they? He saw Bosely in shirtsleeves near the front steps of the casino, shouting directions over the roar of flames. He marched towards him.

'Good evening, sir.'

'Can we save her?' shouted Fox, pointing at the tongues of flame licking the outer wall of the Megalong Wing, where smoke poured in under the eaves.

'Only if this wind drops and the fire crew arrives soon.'

As if in answer to their prayers, within minutes sirens came blaring out of the darkness and the crew of the Katoomba fire brigade were rolling out their hoses. The snow and ice had made it hazardous on the road from Katoomba to Meadow Springs, which explained the delay. Now the firemen faced a different problem: adding to the challenge of the stiff westerly fanning the flames, it soon became clear that either the water pressure at the Palace was very poor or the pipes had frozen. The commander ordered his men to run their hoses to hydrants further back and they eventually found one nearly a quarter of a mile from the hotel that produced sufficient water pressure.

Adam joined his staff in bucket lines to put out the spot fires that sprang up everywhere. He turned at one point to see Laura, her face gaunt and smeared with soot, at the far end of a line, passing a heavy pail of water from hand to hand. She looked quite distraught at the sight of the conflagration. Their eyes met briefly and he half smiled to reassure her that his heart was not completely crushed. She managed only a small nod of her head, her eyes vacant and distant.

The battle to save the hotel took over two hours. When all the drama of the fire had subsided, Adam stood a few feet from the hot, smouldering ruins of the gallery, his hands thrust into his pockets, seeing if he could make out anything familiar. Temperatures had soared so high, there were pools of molten glass glistening among the pulverised remains of brick and plaster. Everything was lost, it seemed, reduced to rubble and ash. Adam could not let his mind fix on the reality of this catastrophe yet or it would undo him.

A strange chill crept up the back of Adam's neck. He suddenly realised that the entire time he had been watching this calamity unfold, his wife – who was staying at the hotel that night – had not come anywhere near him. He knew they had argued but, under the circumstances, this seemed extremely odd behaviour. Where was she?

'Has anyone seen Mrs Fox?' he asked Bosely.

'I haven't. Let me check with Carson. He supervised the evacuation.'

Adam began to wander back towards the hotel, looking around the thinning crowd of guests, hoping to see Adelina's familiar face. He was in an uncharacteristically fragile state of mind. This was not so hard to understand, except that his darkening mood went deeper than any grief over his gallery. He had the impression that he was teetering on the brink of a nameless abyss, the urge to let himself fall so strong it made him fear for the stable footing of his entire happiness and sanity. Where was Adelina? He was angry with her. How could she be so selfish as to abandon him tonight of all nights?

The giddy excitement of his infatuation with Laura was all very well. But in the grip of such profound vulnerability, Adam reached out for Adelina. For better or worse, as the priest had said all those years ago, they were bonded by life's trials and disappointments. Only Adelina could understand the depth of his suffering. Only she knew the intimate history of his sadness. It was the insouciance of youth that attracted Adam to Laura and was the same reason he did not turn to her now. He was a middle-aged, wounded man in need of a haven, a safe place to tie up and shelter in the coming storm.

Bosely and Carson reported to Adam that his wife did not appear to be among the evacuees. They had checked her room, which they discovered had been locked from the outside. The bed appeared to have been slept in and it was clear that her dressing gown and slippers were missing. They were still checking all the other guest rooms of the hotel but so far there was no sign of Mrs Fox.

The police, who had been called to the scene of the fire, quickly turned their attention to the search for the missing woman. Dr Liebermeister confirmed he had finished treating Adelina that afternoon around four o'clock. Mr Carson said that she had rung down to the front desk to ask that a light supper be brought to her room around seven-thirty as she was retiring early. Concern grew into alarm when Joe the security guard told Adam and Sergeant Brownlow that he thought he had seen a female figure near the burning gallery 'in her dressing gown'.

Adam paced the floor of the general manager's office, a mug of cold tea clutched in his hand. His hotel had been saved but his wife was now missing. Fear stalked him like a chill shadow. Two firemen had already begun the grim job of combing the ruins of the gallery. Several staff were dispatched to begin knocking on doors around the immediate neighbourhood in case Mrs Fox had sought shelter there.

Brownlow coughed apologetically as he and his deputy officer entered. 'I'm sorry to have to ask you this, Mr Fox, but has there been anything about your wife's behaviour recently that should give us any cause for concern?' Adam shrugged.

How could be even begin to explain his wife to these gentlemen? What scenario were they considering? he wondered. Suicide, murder, arson, kidnapping?

There was a shout from the direction of the gallery. 'Over here!'

'Please wait here, sir,' said the police sergeant as he and the fire chief rushed towards the smoking ruin, which had been cordoned off by ropes.

Bosely placed a firm hand on Fox's shoulder to comfort and restrain him. They waited in silence.

Adam's face was a mask of graven stone as the two men approached him some time later. The remains of a human body had been found among the rubble, charred and crushed beyond recognition, close to the mangled relic of a kerosene lamp and burned scraps of clothing. 'Impossible to identify at this point but it appears to have been wearing a long cloak. We found this close by. Do you recognise it?'

Adam inspected the rag of red tartan. 'No, I've never seen it before.'

Why would Adelina go into the gallery at night alone? It made no sense at all. Terror and hope wrestled desperately inside Adam, crashing about in his chest as they tried to throw each other over. His hand shook as he handed the cloth back to the police sergeant. 'Thank you, gentlemen.'

The fire chief explained that the presence of the kerosene lamp was highly suggestive as to the cause of the fire; establishing the identity of the intruder and their intentions would require much more detailed investigation. The two men were about to ask Mr Fox some more questions when there was a knock at the office door.

It was Dr Liebermeister. 'We have found her.'

Adam seized the doctor by the shoulders. 'Is she . . . ?'

Liebermeister lowered his head and took off his glasses. When he looked up again, Adam could not remember ever seeing the man's eyes this clearly before. They were shining with tears. 'I'm sorry, Herr Fox.'

A moan came from Adam's mouth and his body convulsed. 'Take me to her.'

Out of respect, the policeman and the fire chief followed at a distance as the German doctor led his employer across the terrace and into the darkened lobby of the Hydrotherapy Establishment, where Freya's plump mermaids still swam up the walls.

'Can we have a moment?' Liebermeister asked the two officials.

'Of course,' said the policeman.

A single lamp shone in the innermost of the echoing maze of rooms. It was here, accompanied by Dr Liebermeister, that Adam Fox looked upon his wife.

Adelina lay, arms crossed over a pale rectangle of stone, at the bottom of a tub of dark water, one of the continuous baths that had failed to heal her. The rectangle was Robbie's memorial plaque, its weight pressing down on her chest, stilling the agitation of her heart. The whiteness of her arms, legs, feet, toes was shocking in the blackness of the water, but most startling of all was the delicacy of her face, a porcelain mask ringed with a halo of floating hair. She could have been asleep except that her eyes remained wide open, shining green marbles, seeing straight through her husband across the Great Chasm.

Adam Fox kneeled by the tub and wept for his past.

CHAPTER 22

Angie
July 1921

Angie lay on her unmade bed in the dark. The curtains were pulled tight and the oil heater turned up so high that the room felt like a stifling cave, sealed to allow not one scintilla of light to enter or atom of heat to escape. Most people would have found the atmosphere of such a room oppressive but Angie welcomed the way the darkness and heat crushed her with its almost palpable weight and shut out the entire world beyond. She was hiding from everyone just like she had when she was a child in her hedge.

On the pillow next to her face lay a letter. It had arrived that afternoon and her hands had trembled as she tore open the envelope. The letter described the unexpected encounter with Adelina Fox and the accident that led to Freya perishing in the fire that destroyed the gallery at the Palace. Its writer had been there at the very end. She had tried to save Freya but had failed.

I know there is little I can offer you by way of comfort or consolation except to reassure you that your mother succumbed quickly, overcome by smoke; her suffering was brief and she was spared the agonies of the fire. There was nothing I could do to revive or rescue her though God be my witness I tried. I want you to know this so you will not torment yourself with unwarranted nightmares about her final moments.

Angie had stopped herself from tearing the letter to shreds in a fit of despair. Instead, she squeezed it into a ball inside her fist which she then used to punch the mattress over and over again as she buried her face in her pillow. 'Stupid! Stupid!' she shouted, smothering her cries so she would not be heard by anyone outside.

Her rage was only partly directed at her mother for this final act of abandonment and only partly at Adelina Fox for being the cause of the fire. Its real argument was with the malign force of fate that seemed bent on destroying her family. At the white-hot centre of this rage burned the resentment that her mother's death was the last act of a drama that had nothing much to do with Angie at all.

For so long she had blamed herself for her family's misfortunes. And then Freya had revealed the shameful secret of their past so that Angie could stop feeling responsible for Robbie's death. While this released her from self-recrimination, it also pushed her to the edge of the stage, out of the spotlight. Angie was just an unfortunate victim, a bit player in a battle of wills between Freya, Adam and Adelina.

Angie, it is natural for you to be angry with your mother for the dreadful way this has all turned out. But please understand, she is not to blame for what happened. As you know, I shared her conviction that justice only comes to those who are willing to fight for it and I admired her courage and determination to do so. Never doubt for a moment that she loved you deeply and that her efforts to reclaim the cottage were always motivated by her desire to secure your future happiness. Please try to forgive her and remember her for her best qualities and the great love she bore you.

'Lies! Lies! Lies!' Angie yelled, but without real conviction. She knew the letter-writer told the truth about her mother but she had to vent her anger even so. It was the only scrap of power she had left: to scream profanities into the void.

For what seemed like hours, she shouted and punched and writhed on her narrow bed until her throat was hoarse, her tears exhausted and her body spent. She then smoothed out the crumpled letter again and lay it next to her tear-stained face on the pillow. She would keep it as the last tissue-thin connection with her mother that she possessed: a memento whose value might become clearer and greater over time.

She wished she could lie in this dark, hot hole of a room forever and ever and never leave. On the edge of her exhausted calm, there loomed another crisis that she did not have the strength to face – might never have the strength to face. Was it up to her to tell her father the news that would surely kill him? Please God, spare me that, thought Angie. Poor Freddie. How cruelly fate had dealt with him. He had waited so patiently for Freya, believed in her plans and reassurances that they would return to their old life in Australia. He deserved a better end than this.

And what should she do now? Angie asked herself, lying in the dark. Her whole life had been lived in the shadow of a lie, its meaning changed by her mother's secret. Was she condemned to live the rest of her life in that shadow?

A streak of light leaked through the curtains. Angie sat up. She realised that she was free. She had paid off her debt to God and to her mother and could now choose her own path. It was not how she had ever imagined freedom. This freedom was a vast lonely ocean, bleak, soulless, with no compass or map to show her the way. It demanded a journey into the unknown, the unimaginable. For the first time in her young life Angie did not have her mother to guide and instruct her. She had to decide what it was she really wanted. Freya had fought for her independence, her land, her dignity. What was Angie willing to fight for?

Angie stood on the cliff edge of this uncertain future and felt its irresistible, vertiginous force, both seductive and terrifying.

She decided she would begin again. Begin her life all over again.

CHAPTER 23

Lisa

Canberra, June 2013

Sometimes everything changes all at once.

Lisa had been bushwalking one day up at Blackheath, following the cliff-top track from Govett's Leap. She was alone, carrying a light daypack with her camera, some water and a few chocolate bars, on the lookout for unusual and striking shots as always. On such a perfect day, she had mused on how the mountains were so rewarding and at the same time challenging for a photographer. Or any artist for that matter. They offered too much beauty. Images beckoned from every side, tantalising glimpses of the sublime in every distant blue and gold silhouette of ridgeline, every expressive sinew of gum branch or liquid dance of creek water or totemic rock face. Were she and her camera up to capturing even a fraction of it?

She was a good half-hour into her walk when she heard a crack. A frisson of fear ran up her spine and she looked up quickly to check if one of the great gum branches overhead had split off. 'Widow-makers' they called some of these trees. A good friend of her father's had been killed on a windless day from being struck down by a branch. But the crack had come from behind her. She turned around just in time to see something very few people ever see.

A geyser of powdery dust exploded from the cliff opposite where she stood. She saw the grey and apricot-coloured precipice slump like the flesh on a human face afflicted by stroke. The tremor was almost imperceptible at first but then the landslide built momentum with incredible speed. A giant slab of rock detached itself, sliding and tipping with a crash into the valley. The initial crack echoed like a gunshot around the curve of the ridge, followed by the thunder of the avalanche. The forest on the slope continued to tremble violently in the aftermath.

It all happened so fast Lisa did not have time to think of her camera. It was possible she was the only person in the valley to witness this scene and she immediately called National Parks to let them know where the rockfall had occurred. The tracks down below might now be impassable.

For days afterwards she thought about this landslide. How long ago had the processes begun that climaxed in those few seconds of destruction? She tried to imagine the long accumulation of a thousand subtle actions: rainwater gathering in fissures drop by drop to freeze, expand and prise open cracks; the invisible onslaught of wind over and over, sculpting, abrading, gouging; the insistence of tree roots, probing, pushing, altering the weight of soil and stone; and the play of gravity itself, shifting and tugging. All these forces and movements on and on until, with that single loud crack, the point of crisis arrives with frightening swiftness and is over in the blink of an eye.

Lisa had no sense of foreboding when Luke rang her at the Hotel Kurrajong on Wednesday to see how her research was going. Her only surprise was how pleased she felt to hear his voice. Much as she loved staying in hotels, especially those she knew well, there always came a time when she felt adrift and alone, wishing she were back in her familiar surroundings.

'I have something I have to tell you,' said Luke. She could hear the note of urgency in his voice. 'Two things, actually.' He sounded both excited and nervous.

'What? What is it?' She sat on her hotel bed and lay back against the cushions. She was tired. She had spent three long days in the archives.

'Well, I was at the Land Titles Office last week and I realised I hadn't cross-referenced Freya Wood as the heir to her father. The name on the title deed to the cottage land would have been changed when he died.'

'Yes, of course.'

'The title did not pass to Freddie Wood when he married Freya, as the law of coverture had been superseded by 1902. It stayed with Freya for her to dispose of as she thought fit.'

'I understand.'

Luke took a deep breath. 'It appears Freya transferred the title of her land to your grandfather under some obscure legal instrument before the Great War. And then her lawyers Mendel and Sons tried to challenge the transfer in a court case in 1920. She lost. I don't know what it means exactly, but it looks like Freya sold her land to Fox and then changed her mind.'

There was a moment's silence on the other end of the phone. Lisa knew that Luke was being diplomatic. She knew there was a much simpler explanation that was not flattering to Fox.

'So when did she transfer the title to Grandad?' asked Lisa.

'January 1917,' said Luke.

'Wasn't that after she and Angie left the cottage and moved to Liverpool to be near Freddie at the internment camp? And, according to Mrs Wells, Fox gave her cash to help her with the move and the rent?'

'Yes, it was. But that doesn't necessarily mean . . .' Luke sounded defensive.

'No,' Lisa cut him off, her voice tinged with irritation, even anger. 'But let's be honest, Luke, it doesn't look good.'

'No. No, it doesn't.'

'Hey, listen,' she said more gently. 'You don't have to protect my grandfather, Luke. Or me. That's not your job.'

'Well, we could have an interesting discussion about what my job is, Lisa,' Luke said quietly. 'I guess we just have to see where the trail leads.'

'I guess.'

'Which brings me to the other thing I have to talk to you about,' said Luke, sounding excited again. 'I've been contacted by a Beth Greenwood. She's the great-niece of Jane Blunt, the Foxes' governess. Remember her? The one Mrs Wells said was dismissed unfairly when Robert died? It turns out that Mrs Greenwood saw my ads in the local paper months ago and has been thinking about talking to me. She says there are some private papers we might be interested in looking at. They're in the National Archives. I rang her and she's sent written permission for you and me to access them. I've already emailed the permission letter direct to the Archives, filled out the call slips and spoken to one of the curators. I'll send you the references.'

This new lead seemed a very tenuous one to Lisa but Luke was convinced it was worth investigating. 'I have an appointment at the Archives on Friday morning. Are they're filed under Blunt or Greenwood?' asked Lisa.

'They're under Glanville-Smith. Beth gave me a quick potted history. After she left the Foxes, Jane Blunt did a short stint as a Sunday schoolteacher. She then became involved in Spiritualism and adopted a new name as a successful medium with the Spiritualist temple in Springwood. She even wrote a pamphlet with Mrs Foster Turner, Australia's most famous medium.'

'Well, that is bizarre. Thank you for all this.' Lisa smiled. 'You sound tired.'

'You too.'

There was another silence. Lisa realised how much their conversation sounded like that of two friends. Was that what they were? Or more than that?

'Listen, Luke . . .'

'Yes?'

'When I get back, let's have dinner. My treat. I'll cook us something at the bungalow. I can show you some of the diary entries if you like.'

Lisa held her breath. Was this too forward? Did this break the unspoken rules of their collaboration or were the diaries sufficient pretext for a dinner at her house?

'Sure. That would be great.' Luke sounded happy. 'Let me know when you've gone through the Glanville-Smith material. Mrs Greenwood said the relevant documents relate to 1921. Copies of letters, mostly.'

'Okay, I'll call you on Friday. Take care. Bye.'

When Lisa sat in the booth at the National Archives on Friday morning, she did not hear the crack coming. She began flicking through the correspondence files for 1920–21, including spirit photos – photocopies, of course, as the originals were held in proper archival albums. They were clever, these early photographic manipulations – simple double exposures using glass plates – but creepy and convincing nonetheless, especially for those who sorely needed to believe.

As she flicked, Lisa's eyes fell on one photo captioned *The Palace, Meadow Springs, January 1921.* She gasped. There was her grandfather Adam, sitting at a table with Adelina on his left. Someone had helpfully labelled all the faces in the photo in pencil. Lisa had never seen a photo of Adelina before; it was as if she had been erased from the Fox family history except as a name on a headstone at South Head. She appeared as delicate and white as stories about her suggested, but much more beautiful in this photo than Lisa had ever heard tell. A fragile and radiant beauty. Floating in a halo of light next to Adelina's shoulder was the face of a young boy. Robbie Fox.

What did this mean? Had Adelina tried to communicate with her son? It was not so surprising. A whole generation had turned to spiritual mediums for consolation. But what was the intention of this dismissed ex-governess returning to the Palace as a medium under an assumed name? Now, that was definitely strange, if not sinister.

Lisa's finger lighted on a sheet of faintly ruled blue stationery. It was a copy of a letter with the name of the intended reader but no address. The letter was dated 14 July 1921. But what immediately caught Lisa's eye was the name: 'Dearest Angie.'

Lisa felt her heart bolt and her pulse surge. She took a deep breath. 'Dearest Angie.' A letter addressed to the mysterious, vanished girl, the girl at the centre of her family's heartbreak. Angie, poor Angie. If she had been listening carefully, Lisa would have heard the crack of a landslide as she read:

Dearest Angie,

This is a difficult letter for me to write.

I cannot begin to describe the pain it causes me to have to tell you that your mother has died in the fire that destroyed the new gallery at the Palace on the night of 13th July. The police may or may not successfully identify her remains and determine the cause of the catastrophe, but I believe you should not be left wondering about the truth and deserve to know the circumstances of your mother's death.

Let me begin at the beginning. I know you and Freya discussed her plans, but to be honest I do not know how much she told you. Some things you will know, others perhaps not. Because I believe you deserve to know the entire truth, I will try to clarify the whole story. Forgive me if I traverse territory already familiar to you.

When Freya first sought my help, she told me that as far back as 1914, not long after poor Robbie's death, she had formed a plan to punish Adam Fox for his cruel treatment of her. She had hidden her father's last oil painting, The Valley, *bequeathed to her as a gift, inside the walls of the cottage. As a skilled artist familiar with her father's style, she made an exact facsimile and planned to sell this forgery to Fox. Her intention was that, when the painting was exposed as a fake, his name would be permanently tarnished and the resulting scandal might even ruin his hotel.*

I do not have to tell you how clever your mother was. She knew Fox would get the painting authenticated. So she gave him the original, which would pass that test and encourage him to show it off to the world when the time came. She then planned to steal into his gallery at night and substitute her forged copy for the real one. Then she would start rumours that Fox was passing off a fake as the last von Gettner.

The war came and Freya was driven from the mountains. She tried to protect her cottage by offering the painting to Fox.

She did not anticipate the depth of his ruthlessness. He took the original painting, had it authenticated as she intended, but then lied and said it had been identified as a fake. He cut off all payments. As a penniless and despised German outcast with her husband interned, Freya had no choice but to agree to surrender her title to the cottage and land.

As you may know, she wrote to him again this year threatening to make public their secret deal and his theft of her painting, in the hope of negotiating the return of her cottage. Adam ignored her. So Freya decided to go ahead with her plan in time for the grand unveiling of the von Gettner for the admiration of the world. That is why she and I stole into the gallery at night to replace the original work with its copy.

We had almost completed the substitution when we came face to face with the last person we ever expected to see: Adelina. She came creeping into the gallery and startled your mother, causing her to knock over the kerosene lamp we were using. The freshly painted chamber was soon alight.

I know there is little I can offer you by way of comfort or consolation except to reassure you that your mother succumbed quickly, overcome by smoke; her suffering was brief and she was spared the agonies of the fire. There was nothing I could do to revive or rescue her though God be my witness I tried. I want you to know this so you will not torment yourself with unwarranted nightmares about her final moments. I managed to escape with the original painting as she begged me to do with her dying breath. It is hidden away safely, back where it belongs. It is rightfully yours.

Angie, it is natural for you to be angry with your mother for the dreadful way this has all turned out. But please understand, she is not to blame for what happened. As you know, I shared her conviction that justice only comes to those who are willing to fight for it and I admired her courage and determination to do so. Never doubt for a moment that she loved you deeply and that her efforts to reclaim the cottage were always motivated by her desire to secure your future happiness.

Please try to forgive her and remember her for her best qualities and the great love she bore you. Angie, I do not think we shall ever meet again and so I wish you all the best for your future.

Miss Jane Emma Blunt alias Vera Glanville-Smith

Lisa had heard the story of the 1921 fire which had remained unsolved, despite vicious gossip about 'arson' and 'an insurance job'. But *this* . . . this strange story of deceit and double-crossing that led to the tragic death of Freya. This was heartbreaking.

If its contents were true, this letter also revealed a very different Adam Fox to the one she had heard about in her childhood and imagined from the photos. Who was he really? The larrikin in his wife's floral hat at the Annual Staff Ball, laughing and pouring champagne for his gardener? The man of action in the smart trilby and pinstriped suit, standing proudly in front of the Hudson? The sad, vulnerable man, with his staff gathered around him like a family, grieving for his hotel that was about to close, possibly forever? She knew this Adam Fox well.

Could this possibly be the same man who tormented Freya so cruelly that she had been driven to this elaborate act of madness? Who bought a valuable painting from her and then as good as stole it? Who took advantage of anti-German hysteria to force the Wood family off their property and bully Freya into surrendering her title? Who was *this* Adam Fox?

Once, and only once, Monika had spoken of a different man. The family was at Laura's apartment, looking through the albums, listening to Grandma's stories again. Monika appeared in the doorway of the kitchen, unsteady, a little drunk. It was not like her. 'For God's sake,' she yelled. 'Stop these endless fairytales. Tell them the truth, Laura. Tell them what a bastard he really was!'

Lisa had not thought about this for many years. And there it was – the memory of that outburst as vivid as the day she first heard it. That was when she heard the crack of the landslide, felt the sickening drag of the abyss. Nothing would be the same ever again. She understood for the first time the bitterness in the locals' names for their town's famous hotel, this monument to her grandfather's monstrous and ruthless ego. Fox's Folly. The Palace of Tears.

PART 3

Laura

CHAPTER 24

Adam
Meadow Springs, August 1928

This would be the last time Dame Nellie sang at the Palace. In fact, this evening's concert was one of the last three public performances she would ever give in Australia. Nobody could quite believe that the diva's notoriously long farewell was almost over. The most famous Australian in the world was about to exit the stage, this time for good. Except for some crackly recordings that failed miserably to capture its perfection, the purest operatic voice in history would soon be silenced. Forever.

No wonder then, this evening, the Palace was packed with its largest, most resplendent assembly in living memory. The lobby reverberated with a buzz of anticipation and preening self-importance unlike anything Adam could recall. Every chair, sofa, lounge and foot stool that could be found had been crammed into the casino as well as the adjoining billiard room and the smoking lounge. 'Fire regulations be damned!' Fox muttered to his general manager.

The silver-haired hotelier now stood on the front steps with his lovely young wife, Laura, on his arm. They nodded and smiled in greeting to the ceaseless flood of gentlemen in gleaming white shirt fronts, glossy top hats and silk scarves. And the women – what a parade of female splendour. It did Adam's heart good to see it. Creamy bare shoulders and satin-gloved forearms, midnight-blue gowns and evening coats of violet georgette and gold lamé, black opera cloaks embroidered with silver rhinestones and trimmed with fur, all with the added ornamentation of baroque pearls, diamond brooches, and corsages of lilies and orchids.

At Adam's left hand stood Hugh Ward, with his usual lopsided half-smile. He was still the comic actor at heart, waiting for his cue, and one of Adam's oldest friends. As the managing director of J.C. Williamson's, he had partnered the theatre company with Melba and her hand-picked cast of Italian opera singers for this triumphant farewell tour. Under Hugh's direction, the hotel's Steinway had been rolled out of the casino that morning and Melba's own grand piano, trucked up from Sydney, had been rolled in and tuned for tonight's concert. Melba herself arrived in her private train carriage in time for lunch and Hugh then helped her settle into the hotel's Delmonte Suite overlooking the valley.

At this very moment, the diva was upstairs, preparing. Adam had made sure her suite overflowed with cascades of daffodils, her favourites, as did the casino's proscenium stage, awash in so many of these golden blooms that the entire room glowed butter-yellow right up to the dome. The suite's four-poster bed had been fitted with Melba's own monogrammed silk sheets and cushions and a large Louis XV mirror hung on the opposite wall. It was no secret Nell's tastes tended towards the opulent. Her house in London had been decorated in the style of Versailles and her clothes and jewellery were renowned for their exaggerated size and brilliance: large hats and pearls as big as pigeon eggs. Let them snigger at her vulgarity, what did she care? Nothing changed the fact she was the highest-paid opera singer in history and, thanks to the advice of her good friend Baron Rothschild, she had amassed a staggering fortune.

'So *you* are the infamous Mr Fox,' she growled at him the first time they met, in 1909. Taking a break from her supreme reign at Covent Garden, she was back home on one of her 'sentimental tours' through the small towns of country Australia. Thanks to Hugh Ward, she had been persuaded to stop off at Meadow Springs for a concert at the Palace. She was much shorter than she appeared on stage, Adam thought, and more imperious than beautiful, but there was no mistaking her charisma. Her large brown eyes fixed on Adam with a mischievous twinkle. 'I've knocked around a few of Europe's finest hotels, my dear Mr Fox, but this bloody great pile of yours pisses on them all!'

Fox had guffawed at that. Hugh had warned him about the diva's swearing, learned from shearers and the like when Nell was growing up in outback Victoria. Still, it was quite something to hear such words come out of the same mouth that poured forth music so sublime, it made grown men weep for joy.

The 1909 concert at the Palace had been a sell-out success. In 1922, the diva was home again for concerts in Melbourne and Sydney which had each drawn a crowd of seventy thousand. Fox invited Melba back to perform at his hotel with her good friend, the English contralto Clara Butt. It was just what the hotel needed that year to restore its reputation for grandeur and celebrity and dispel the pall of gloom that hung over 'the Palace of Tears' after the tragic fire and Adelina's death the previous year.

Fox found much to like and admire in Dame Nellie. Just as Adam had done, she had invented herself from modest origins through the sheer force of her will and intelligence: a Scottish builder's daughter from country Victoria, hobnobbing with European aristocracy and royalty, and captivating audiences on both sides of the Atlantic. Like him, she had bullied and manipulated when necessary and shown immense generosity and loyalty when warranted. And she had made serious sacrifices. Because of a newspaper scandal that threatened to ruin her career, she had given up the Duc d'Orléans, her only true love. Adam had continued to follow her glittering public life with interest. And now, six years later, she was back.

'I hear you've done alright for yourself, you bloody cradle-snatcher!' she'd exclaimed when Adam went up to her room to pay his respects that afternoon. 'So when do I get to meet the lucky lady? I hear she's a bit of a looker. Keeps you awake at night, I bet!'

'I have a baby daughter to do that now,' said Adam, grinning. 'Little Lottie. The way she bawls her lungs out, I was hoping you might give her lessons.'

Melba's eyebrows arched. 'You know my golden rule.' She smiled slyly. 'I'll teach her everything I know as long as she has absolutely no talent.' Despite the rumours that she would stop at nothing to make sure no upcoming singers threatened her supremacy, she had in fact sponsored several young protégées at Covent Garden and set up an all-female singing school in Melbourne.

At the age of sixty-seven, Melba looked tired, thought Adam – which was hardly surprising given the rigours of touring and performance. She had also put on weight. Still the mistress of her own public image, she swathed herself dramatically in cloaks and furs to disguise her matron's figure. She knew the critics circled like vultures, waiting to pick over the bones of her ruined reputation if her voice faltered. But to date, she had defied them all. Her last concert at Convent Garden in 1926 had been a critical triumph.

And now they made fun of her long goodbye: three years of 'final' concerts. 'More farewells than Melba' became the mocking expression. But why should she go? Adam argued in her defence. The struggle to the top of the mountain had taken such courage and cost so much. She was the most famous Australian in the world. Why should she be in any hurry to leave the spotlight for someone else?

Adam himself had turned fifty-three in July. With his exceptional fitness and obsession over diets and health, he felt like a much younger man, full of the juice and muscle of life, fizzing with ideas. And Nellie was right that his young wife kept him up at night. Adam Fox had discovered the kind of excitement and stamina in the bedroom that he had never suspected was possible.

There were calls from some quarters for Adam Fox to slow down and start thinking about retirement and succession planning. He still kept a position on the board of the department store in Sydney that bore his name and maintained an active interest in the Palace, which had enjoyed a decade of record occupancy rates and steeply rising profits.

'You are a *rich* man,' well-meaning friends reminded Adam. 'And you have so many other interests. The store and the hotel are in good shape. They don't need your hand on the tiller anymore.' But the truth was he needed an heir to take over the family business. He didn't want to see everything he had built end up in someone else's hands. Back in 1921, with the death of Adelina, the loss of Robbie had struck him even more profoundly. He had no ties to the past and no connections to the future. Even the ghost of Freya seemed to have faded away to an incomprehensible silence. He was utterly alone in the world – except, of course, for the young woman whose beauty had captivated him. Though Laura was less than half his age, her soul was ageless and mysterious. Adam could not see why he should not be given a second chance at happiness.

As Mr Longford's film shoot at the Palace rapidly drew to its conclusion, Adam had to make a decision. That fateful night in the gallery, Laura had described their romance as 'a nice fantasy' which must inevitably come to an end. Adam dared hope for more. Lesser men would have been daunted by Laura's youth and beauty and the scandal of their affair, but Fox was not so easily discouraged. He had taken risks before in the face of public ridicule and disapproval and they had paid off handsomely

On 12 August 1921, less than a month after Adelina's death, Adam Fox proposed to Laura. She gave him her answer the next day. In December, they were married in a private ceremony at St Canice's in Katoomba and headed off on their honeymoon, travelling first class on the S.S. *Ormuz* to London, followed by a week at the Hotel de Crillon in Paris and three more weeks touring the Continent.

'You look supremely lovely tonight, my dear,' he murmured now in Laura's gold-and pearl-studded ear as she stood at his side, greeting guests with that enigmatic smile of hers. She looked stunning in an embroidered white silk, satin and chiffon evening gown by Lucien Lelong, its low-cut neckline showing off her shoulders, neck and breasts to perfection. Over this, Laura wore a garnet velvet evening wrap with a dark mink fur collar and ruched cuffs. The whole ensemble was a gift from Adam on their most recent sojourn abroad. It looked exotic and expensive and flattered Laura's voluptuous figure, little altered from her pregnancy last year with Lottie. 'You do this hotel proud.'

She beamed back at him. 'You look pretty presentable yourself.'

There was no doubt about it, thought Adam. Laura and the Palace were destined for each other. Maybe not the old, swank Edwardian Palace of chandeliers, waltzes and palm court orchestras. Pale, aristocratic and snobbish Adelina had been the perfect mascot for that Palace, though she despised it.

Tonight's concert evoked memories of that slower, more elegant, self-regarding time when barons of commerce back-slapped each other in the billiard room while, next door, their fine-boned wives, seated in lounges, sniggered discreetly at the *nouveau riche* ladies passing before them like penny arcade shooting ducks. But time does not stand still. Adam was shocked to realise how quickly his beloved hotel, boasting every modern convenience and innovation at its birth, had acquired the mildewy whiff of quaintness. Everything changed faster than ever before. The Palace had to change too.

The new post-war Palace was about naughtiness. Laura and Adam knew all about that: they had begun their affair behind his wife's back. In this new Palace, the hijinks, the bed-hopping, the madcap licentiousness that had once been the preserve of the very rich was now on offer to anyone with a little cash. Sex, ever-present but discreetly hidden by the hotel's Edwardian guests, now took centre stage.

After the war years, thousands of newlyweds flocked to the mountains, flush with money and aching to embrace life with a reckless urgency. The locals' nickname for the steam train service from Sydney was 'The Honeymoon Express'. Fancy dress parties at the Palace offered prizes for the best Valentino sheik, Clara Bow flapper and Fairbanks swashbuckler. The Jazz Age had arrived in the Blue Mountains.

Adam had always had a weakness for rule-breaking and merrymaking. Even before the Great War, he had instituted the Annual Staff Ball, a formal banquet held every June in the grand dining room. All the hotel staff, from the general manager down to the gardeners, kitchen hands and drivers, were seated in their Sunday best and waited on by the hotel's guests dressed in waiters' jackets and maids' pinafores. Everybody had fun playacting at being their opposite.

Including Fox himself. At the 1924 Staff Ball, Adam had gone one step further. He pulled on one of his wife's evening gowns, donned a large floral hat and swanned around the grand dining room batting his eyelids and blowing kisses. Pleasantly squiffy on beer and wine, the staff roared with laughter at the sight of their employer in drag and blew kisses back. A photographer captured the mood as Fox poured a flute of bubbly for the gardener, Stanley Hicks.

Fox's drag act opened a floodgate. Cross-dressing and play-acting became the flavour of all the Palace's parties, whether New Years', Christmas, Easter, Melbourne Cup or the King's Birthday. The photos told it all: a gaggle of lanky boys in identical white tennis dresses, Alice bands and cotton socks; pretty girls wearing boaters, ill-fitting suits and ties and with moustaches pencilled on their upper lips; men with blacked-up faces, flouncy swimsuits and paper Japanese umbrellas parading as bathing beauties. 'The Palace of Queers' some local wags came to call it.

At every party all eyes were drawn to Laura. Sheathed in the latest Lanvin or Patou dress from Paris and with her glossy Louise Brooks bob, Laura was impossible to ignore, out-drinking, out-dancing, outshining all the women in the room.

There had been only one source of disquiet in this perfect existence, the blowfly in the golden syrup tin, so to speak: it took Laura over five years to fall pregnant. Doctors were consulted to make sure there were no mechanical problems. She even went on special diets and regimes of pills. And yet still no baby came. In his darker moments, Fox wondered if this was God's punishment for his past sins. Lottie's eventual safe arrival was welcomed with a mix of joy and relief, compromised only by Adam's unspoken disappointment that he still had no son. But that would come. It would all come in good time. Laura was only twenty-six. The future looked bright.

'We have a serious problem.'

Mr Bosely's face was ashen. He had politely pushed his way through the human tide in the lobby to reach the Foxes. With less than an hour until Melba's concert – to be followed by a gala banquet for four hundred featuring Melba toast and Pêche Melba among other diva-inspired dishes – a major crisis had emerged.

'What is it?' Fox kept his voice steady.

'Dame Melba is *indisposed*. She tells me she cannot . . . *will not* go on.' The general manager looked like a man who had just done battle with a superior foe and lost. 'It appears she has read something in the *Daily Telegraph* that has upset her.'

'Shit,' said Hugh loudly enough to cause guests' heads to turn in his direction. He appeared to know what this was about. 'I thought we agreed not let any newspapers near her, Mr Bosely.'

'I know. I'm sorry, sir. It appears that one of the household staff didn't get the message and slipped the evening edition under her door. I'm so dreadfully sorry.'

'Okay.' Hugh sighed. He turned to Laura and Adam. 'Come with me. This is not going to be easy.'

When they reached the suite in the Delmonte Wing, they could hear two loud voices on the far side of the door. One of them belonged to Beverley Nichols, the secretary and biographer who travelled everywhere with Melba.

'You're making far too much of this,' they heard him scream. 'It's a storm in a bloody teacup, for crying out loud!'

Hugh knocked on the door. 'It's me, Nell. We need to talk. I have Adam and Laura with me.'

'Go away!' came the reply. A loud thump suggested something had been hurled at the door.

'Jesus wept. Calm down, you silly woman!' screeched the alarmed secretary. 'You have to talk to Hugh.'

Adam looked at his wife and rolled his eyes. Nell had a reputation for tantrums and paranoia. She was convinced, for example, that the Germans wanted to assassinate her because she had been rude to the Kaiser before the war and then raised so much money for the Allies' war effort with her patriotic concerts.

They heard the lock click and the door swung open.

Inside, the great diva was already in her finery, a stunning green satin gown covered by a long plush cloak of deepest purple with silver threads depicting flowers, birds and stars. She paced back and forth, her eyes ablaze.

'Have you seen this?' she shouted at Hugh, hurling a newspaper at his head. 'Go on, read it. Read it out loud so everyone can share in my humiliation.'

Hugh had seen the piece but decided to indulge her. He read:

WHAT DID MELBA REALLY SAY?

Today, English contralto Dame Clara Butt has told the Daily Telegraph *that she has sent a cable expressing her deepest regrets and apologies to her good friend Dame Nellie Melba for a story appearing in Dame Clara's biography, released yesterday in London. The story describes how Dame Nellie advised Dame Clara on the eve of her tour of Australia twenty-two years ago to* ***'sing 'em muck: it's all they understand.'***

Dame Clara Butt denies the truth of this account. The cable sent to Dame Nellie Melba reads as follows: 'Being on tour in India I unfortunately did not see proofs before the book was published. Am sure, knowing me, you'll understand. So sorry for causing you annoyance, especially while you are carrying out your usual wonderful work in our much-loved Australia.'

Whatever the truth, we urge both ladies to keep calm. Muck-raking is a more suitable pastime for politicians than for Dames of the British Empire.

'"Keep calm" they say,' yelled Nell, 'Bastards! Scumbags! Pouring petrol on the fire like they always do.'

'Forget about them,' admonished Hugh. 'Think of your audience, Nell. They love you. You can't let them down. You never have.'

'Maybe there's a first time for everything.'

For a moment, the diva's proud carriage slumped and her head bowed. Everyone in the room heard her sigh. Despite the artful panache of her hair and make-up and the exuberance of her costume, Nell appeared frail and frightened.

Laura stepped forward. She fell to one knee and took one of the grand lady's hands in hers. In a gesture that seemed as natural as it was quick, Laura kissed the opera singer's fingers. 'Please, Dame Nellie. I beg you.'

Tears ran down Nell's cheeks. She looked at Hugh. 'Remember Melbourne?'

Hugh nodded. He remembered. September 1902. The most famous Australian in the world, who had taken her stage name 'Melba' from the city of her girlhood, had returned for a royal tour by train through Victoria. This triumphal procession was to be followed by red-carpet gala dinners, a concert at the town hall and a public holiday declared in her honour. But when the train pulled into Albury on the first day of the tour, Melba discovered her father had suffered a stroke. She wanted to cancel the whole circus but he refused to allow it and so the iron-willed diva performed for her adoring public, while her heart broke for the father whom she had not seen in years.

Melba looked down at Laura. Her eyes glistened and the magnificent voice cracked with emotion. 'Let no one say I ever gave my second best to Australia. These jackals have tried to tear me down before. I will not let them have the last word.' She then became businesslike. 'All out, please, I have to finish my vocal exercises. There will be a ten-minute delay.'

The concert in the casino that evening was sublime. Melba sang her most famous arias from *La Boheme*, *Rigoletto* and *Lucia di Lammermoor* as well as several of her most popular ballads. Hugh, Laura and Adam exchanged meaningful looks as Melba finished the concert with the sweet, silvery rendition of 'Home, Sweet Home' that reduced audiences to tears.

The whole house stood up, one and all, and erupted into applause, accompanied by the wild tossing of top hats into the air and heaping of floral tributes onto the stage. The great chorus of bejewelled ladies and silk-scarved gents clapped and cheered and wept until their hands were chafed and their voices hoarse. Dame Nellie stood still, her face wet with tears, her arms outspread in a seemingly endless embrace. At last she lowered her arms and an attentive silence fell on the crowd.

She spoke. 'I have done my best. I have tried to keep faith with my art. For all that Australia has done for me, for all the beauty she has shown me, for all the love she has offered,

I wish to say thank you from the bottom of my heart. I never was prouder than I am tonight to be an Australian woman.'

In the dark, Adam Fox looked at his beautiful young wife, Laura, who had so graciously asked Dame Nellie to face the fickle world with courage one more time. Laura gave *him* that same courage, day after day. He loved her passionately, this mysterious woman. She was not like Freya or Adelina. She asked so little of him, made so few demands. And the mystery was that Adam found himself, more than he ever had with Freya and Adelina, wanting to please her in whatever way he could. Not to keep the peace or to impress her or to seal some bargain, but because he craved her attention and love.

Laura sensed her husband's gaze. She turned and bestowed that sweet, puzzling smile which had hooked Adam the very first time he laid eyes on her.

CHAPTER 25

Lisa
Leura and Katoomba, June 2013

Lisa arrived back from Canberra and sat alone in the bungalow with her laptop, wondering how to start making sense of it all.

With a glass of red at her elbow, Lisa sat, clicking through the files on her laptop. Apart from Jane Blunt's letter to Angie about Freya, she had found several other pieces of the jigsaw. She opened a story that was tabbed in the National Library's newspaper database. The *Katoomba Daily*, Saturday, 7 December 1937. Taking a deep gulp of shiraz, Lisa began to read:

MIRACLE BUSH SURVIVAL
After being lost for nearly two days in bushland around Asgard Swamp near Mount Victoria, Miss Monika Fox, 7, youngest daughter of hotelier Adam Fox, was found just

before sunset, unharmed except for a sprained ankle, near Thor's Head. It is thought she became separated at a family picnic on Wednesday afternoon. Grave concerns were raised for her safety during this week's heatwave, with temperatures reaching a summer record of 101 degrees. A bushfire near Mount Victoria also threatened to enter the Grose Valley.

'Given the extreme heat and fire danger, it is a miracle she survived,' said Inspector Frank Redding of Katoomba Police, who supervised the search effort. 'She made a camp in the Asgard mine kilns near the only water on the ridge not dried up after eight months of drought.'

Lisa drained her glass and poured a second. She did not believe in ghosts. Or miracles. But there it was: 'a miracle she survived . . . a camp in the Asgard mine kilns . . . the only water on the ridge not dried up after eight months of drought.'

What on earth could this mean? Was this 'miracle' thanks to the bushcraft Monika had been taught by her father and their family friend, 'Uncle' Mel Ward? Or was it something else altogether: divine intervention? destiny? dumb luck? Lisa was stunned that this story had remained hidden from her for so long. She pulled up the page she had bookmarked in her mother's childhood diaries, the only reference she had found to this episode so far. Monika and her sister Lottie had been fighting.

Lottie made a promise to never tell lies about me ever again – after that horrible time when I ran off into the bush for two days and poor Mama thought I was surely dead and everyone came looking for me. It was even in the paper. Papa was so angry and shouted a lot. But he kept hugging me, saying how brave and clever I was. I had never seen him cry like that before. He made me promise to never run away again. And I said, only if Lottie promises not to tell lies about me. So Papa made us both swear an oath on his Bible.

Lies, lies, so many lies. Lies of omission. Lies of commission. Elaborate acts of deception. Fake paintings, secret agreements, hidden cruelty, forbidden love. The more she uncovered the past, the more Lisa became lost herself. Her mother was a complete stranger to her: this little girl who survived the bush in a heatwave, fired a gun at her parents' gramophone records and broke into an American military hospital.

Lisa was more confused than ever about how much of her mother's past to share with Luke over dinner tomorrow night. He had taken time out from his own heavy workload and she felt she owed him something for that. And to be honest, she felt more alone than ever with this mystery. Who else did she trust to help her make sense of it all but Luke?

'What have you done to your *hair*?'

Lisa could not believe her ears. She had been at the hairdressers that morning for a cut and dye. Ella had done a wonderful job with the colour, a rich glossy chestnut that managed to avoid looking harsh or artificial, bringing out the blue sheen of her eyes. The cut was a chic, asymmetrical bob that framed her face in a seductive way, accentuating her cheekbones. Sally, the head nurse on duty at the Ritz that morning, gave her a conspiratorial grin when she walked in. Women always knew these things. Yes, alright, it was because she was having dinner with Luke. She wanted to look her best. Was that a crime?

Monika was staring at her daughter with a look of curiosity that Lisa had not seen directed at her for as long as she could remember. When Lisa sat down with her customary offering of chocolates, her mother usually bestowed on her a vague little smile no different to that she gave to each nurse and orderly as they arrived with her meds and trays of food.

But this was different. This time she actually looked at Lisa.

'I – I got it done this morning,' stuttered Lisa, taken aback.

'It suits you. You should keep it like that,' said Monika, already fishing in the chocolate box.

Tears pricked at the corner of Lisa's eyes. 'Thanks, Mum, I will,' she said. 'You up for some Scrabble?'

'Is the Pope Polish?' Monika was evidently not up to date on pontiffs since John Paul II, but her meaning was perfectly clear.

They played, and as usual Monika won.

'Was Mum okay while I was in Canberra?' Lisa asked Fiona, who came on shift as Lisa was packing up the Scrabble board. She was one of the few nurses that Lisa trusted, one of the few who retained some shred of empathy for the empty human shells in their care.

Fiona's eyes darted sideways. 'Hasn't anyone told you yet?'

'Told me? Told me what?' Lisa felt a bubble of panic expanding in her chest.

Fiona beckoned to Lisa to step into a quiet corner out of line of sight of the nurses' station.

'About yesterday,' said the nurse. 'Someone should have texted you.'

Lisa shook her head. Maybe she had missed it. She started thumbing through the log on her phone.

Fiona lowered her voice. 'We lost her. For about two hours.'

'What? I don't understand.' How could they 'lose' her mother?

'She wandered off. Put on her coat and walked out through the front garden. Nobody saw her leave. It happens sometimes. We were about to contact the police when someone found her at Bloome Park, sitting on a bench. Crying. She said she was looking for Brian – I think that was the name.'

Lisa shook her head. 'Brian? I've never heard her mention a Brian.'

'I'm sorry. I'm sure they would have texted you,' said Fiona, placing her hand on Lisa's shoulder. 'She refused her meds last night as well, which she's never done before. There's sure to be some paperwork on it. Let me go and check it out.'

Fiona and Lisa both knew these were bad signs. Big steps along the route to late-stage Alzheimer's. How quickly Monika's mind would unravel was impossible to predict but there was always the possibility of her brain function deteriorating rapidly over a few weeks. Did this latest news signal a deterioration?

And yet her mother had seemed more alert than usual today, even noticing Lisa's new hairdo.

Monika had dozed off when Lisa tiptoed back to her bedside to give her a kiss goodbye. She stood for a moment, studying her mother's face. She thought of seven-year-old Monika, so 'clever and brave' as Adam had called her, finding shelter in mountain bushland where fire and heat raged all around her. She thought of Monika at thirteen, watching like a hawk for signs of her mother's infidelity. She thought of her mother at forty-five, discovering her body had betrayed her with an unwanted pregnancy as her brilliant writing career was hitting its stride, but tolerating, if not welcoming, the fact of little Lisa for the sake of her marriage. She thought about her now, trying to find herself in a disintegrating world of memories, 'lost' all over again but with no reliable compass to find her way home.

Monika's life had always been about survival. There had been so many tough decisions she'd had to make on her own. Where was Laura, her mother, when Monika needed her at these times? It occurred to Lisa for the first time in her life that her own mother had probably faced the kind of loneliness that Lisa had suffered; the same longing to be able to depend on her parents' love and the same disappointment when they could not provide it. Was it enough for Lisa to find forgiveness in her own heart? Not yet. But it was a start.

Lisa picked out her most flattering dress – a low-cut little black number – and decided on a pearl necklace and small silver earrings. As she rummaged through her jewellery box, her hand alighted on something shining in a velvet case.

Her grandmother's gift. A silver mermaid with emerald hair set against a lapis lazuli wave. She held it up to the light. It was so beautiful. In all the years since Grandma Laura had given it to her, Lisa had never found the right moment to wear it. But she was in no doubt now. Tonight, Laura's mermaid would be her lucky charm. Its song, reawakened from the past, would unlock the mysteries of her own heart.

Luke arrived at seven-thirty with a box of chocolates. 'A ritual threshold gift,' he joked as he handed them over at the front door of the bungalow. 'And they're *all* for you!'

Lisa laughed. My God! She couldn't believe he had remembered a confidence from one of their first conversations: about how guilty she felt stealing from the box of chocolates she took to the Ritz every visit. And how much that guilt annoyed her. It was one of the things she liked most about Luke. He had a rare talent for listening. And remembering. Unlike just about every man she had ever dated, he was actually interested in *her*. And her family. But then, that *was* his job.

'Wow. You look wonderful!' he exclaimed. His face lit up with undisguised admiration. 'Your hair, right?'

Lisa laughed. 'Yes, my hair.'

She ushered him into the kitchen, where she poured a glass of wine for them both. 'My timing is a bit out.' Luke sipped and watched her as she talked and stirred. He asked if he could help and she gave him some parmesan to grate. She spooned him some of the sauce she was making. He nodded his approval.

Luke also looked different tonight, thought Lisa. The boyish air was gone, replaced by something more manly. He was wearing a dark cotton shirt, caramel chinos and a smart jacket that showed off his broad shoulders and back, the curves of his muscular neck and upper arms. His short, black, bristling hair and smooth, olive skin smelled good, with hints of coconut shampoo and leather aftershave. But most startling of all was the fact he had swapped his Elvis Costello glasses for contact lenses. She complimented him on the new look. He seemed pleased. 'And I can see so much better as well.'

They headed into the living-cum-dining room, its walls crowded with artworks, including original Kitty Koala illustrations and framed photographs.

'Are these yours?' he asked, looking at a series of large colour prints on the far wall as he helped her lay out the bowls and plates. They were studies Lisa had done two years earlier of the Cockatoo Island dockyards in Sydney Harbour: dinosaur carcasses of towering industrial cranes, frozen mid-swing; giant ship-making sheds like corrugated-iron cathedrals streaming greenish-blue light; and massive rust-red beam benders, with their heads arched back as if looking at the sky, arranged in monumental rows like Easter Island statues.

'These are fantastic!' said Luke. 'They really capture the atmosphere of the place. I must get back there one day. It's one of my favourite spots on the harbour.'

'Mine too,' said Lisa as she served the entree. 'I want to go camping there.'

The promise of fire was in the air that evening. It was the first time a man – apart from tradesmen – had stepped inside Lisa's house in years. Since the end of her relationship with Paul, really. She had opened her door again to the fickle winds of opportunity and the sparks of attraction. No wonder she was feeling nervous, despite the easy companionship that had grown up between her and Luke. This was different. They had both taken care with their appearance tonight. They both knew what this was about.

She had downed most of a preparatory glass of wine while she tended to the cooking. It soothed her nerves. There was no denying she was attracted to Luke. She had decided she would accept whichever way the evening flowed. But, of course, the truth was she secretly hoped Luke was attracted to her as well.

Luke had brought his laptop and it sat, waiting, on the coffee table while Lisa's perched on the couch. For later. They had a lot to discuss about the strange twists and turns of the Foxes' secret history. The thrill of it hung there like a ripe peach, waiting to be picked and savoured. But by some unspoken agreement, Lisa and Luke decided to not 'talk shop' over dinner.

Instead, Lisa asked Luke about his childhood in the mountains. He told her about his love of bushwalking, camping trips with his parents out to Lake Lyell and Dunn's Swamp and the Gardens of Stone. He even confessed sheepishly to being a bit of an amateur shutterbug when he was a kid and joining a camera club at school. More wine flowed. They talked about their favourite photographers, exhibitions they liked, art galleries, museums, trips they'd taken and trips they wanted to take, the most interesting people they had met, the strangest experience they'd ever had in a hotel. Apart from the Palace. They laughed – as loudly as each other – at the same jokes.

There was a lull in the conversation. It was late. A night train went rumbling through the darkness outside.

'I was looking at the photos again today,' said Luke.

'Which ones?'

'The ones of your grandmother. Laura.' He had a sly look on his face.

'And . . . ?'

'You are much more beautiful than she was.'

Lisa looked down, laughing, dismissing it as another joke.

'No, I mean it.' Luke was serious, she could tell. She sensed his dark eyes studying her face, hands, body. There was an attentiveness in his gaze that sounded a note of deep desire inside Lisa that she could not ignore.

He leaned closer and took her face in his hands. 'Ah, *Lisa*.' He spoke her name with such fervour. Like a confession. They kissed, tenderly at first and then with more urgent passion.

Lisa pulled away, breathless. 'Is it me you want, Luke?' she asked.

He looked at her, puzzled.

'Or my family?' She had not anticipated the question. It burst out of her, unbidden, like a self-protective trap, sprung from some well of self-doubt and suspicion. Luke looked at her solemnly for a moment. Had she offended him? Scared him off? Stupid, stupid Lisa.

'I could ask you the same question,' said Luke. 'What do *you* want?'

'I – I want you.'

'Because I'm the historian of your family's hotel?'

'No. No, not at all.'

'Well, there's your answer. Because that's not all I am. Like you're not just one of the Fox family. These are parts of who we are. Important parts, but not the whole story. It's *you* I want to get to know, Lisa. *You.* Not anyone else.'

He grabbed her then more forcefully than before, his hands clasping her head, his fingers entwined in her hair. Lisa uttered a cry of delight and surrender as Luke's deep kisses explored the sweetness of her mouth. How long, how long, how long she had waited for this feeling again! To be desired.

When they reached the couch, Lisa felt the laptop dig into her back. Luke dropped it onto the floor. 'I thought we could leave that to the morning. Over breakfast,' he said. Lisa laughed.

She could not remember the last time she had felt this good.

Luke made the coffee and toast and Lisa the scrambled eggs. They set up their laptops on the dining table.

'You first,' said Luke.

She showed him the letter from Miss Glanville-Smith.

He looked stunned on finishing it. 'Well, that changes everything. The fire wasn't arson after all. And Freya wasn't in Germany in 1921, she was here. But she went back on the boat with Angie in 1920. I have the record from the shipping lists.'

'Maybe she came back. Maybe she heard about Adam's plans to display her father's painting – probably through Miss Blunt – and decided it was time for revenge. But why? That's the question that haunts me. Is it because Adam stole the painting and her land? Or was there more to it than that?'

'I think you already know the answer,' said Luke. 'Why else would a woman spend so long plotting revenge? The painting and the land would be reasons enough, but there's an obsessiveness in this. It suggests something more. She was his lover.'

'Another reason for Adam to get rid of her and her family,' Lisa mused. Her eyes widened. 'Oh my God! You don't think . . . ?'

'What?'

'You don't think Angie was his illegitimate daughter? It would make sense. "The girl who broke all our hearts."'

Luke let out his breath. 'It's entirely possible. In most cases like this, the whole thing was covered up. The woman was either bullied or bribed into silence and the child adopted out or sent to an orphanage. Sometimes, rarely, the father would adopt the child under his own name.'

'Hard to imagine Adelina agreeing to that.'

'Yes. Why would she? So if Fox refused to acknowledge Angie as his daughter, it would give Freya another reason to hate him.'

'Whichever way you look at it, it's not flattering to my grandfather.' Lisa sighed. 'I was so naive. I just wanted to believe the fairytales about him. The ones my grandmother told. The great man, the visionary, trying to bring something new and exciting to the mountains. And now this . . .'

There was a long silence. They both watched the clouds of steam rise from their coffee cups in the shaft of sunlight on the dining table. It was a fresh, early-winter morning. Lisa had lit a fire in the slow-combustion heater in the lounge room. The wood fire crackled and popped, imploding every now and then in a shower of sparks. The bungalow had begun to warm up but they could both feel the chill air pressing at the windows and under the doors.

Luke idly stroked the wrist of Lisa's left hand, admiring the softness of her skin there, its blue-veined creaminess. How quickly this intimacy came, the afterglow from the roaring fire of last night. They both basked in its warmth.

Luke spoke at last. He did not look at Lisa at first but stared at the table, at her wrist, distracted, puzzled. 'You can't be *so* surprised about your grandfather. Can you? Did you honestly expect him to be a *nice* man?'

Lisa felt a blush rise to her cheeks. It sounded like a reprimand. She felt ashamed of her confession of girlish hero-worship. 'No, not *nice*,' she said tartly. 'Please give me some credit!'

Luke winced. 'I'm sorry if that sounded harsh. All I meant was . . . well, men like Fox are not unusual. They have big visions, big ideas. They push hard for what they want. People get hurt along the way. Used up, cast aside. It's not right, perhaps. Not fair. But it's the way the world works.'

Lisa pulled her hand away. 'In business, yes. In war. In politics. Yes, I get that. But we're talking about him disowning his daughter. His own flesh and blood. Cheating her out of her inheritance, her future, her rightful name. Is that justifiable?'

Luke looked at her. 'We're arguing over a hypothetical. We have no proof.'

'I guess I'm just curious how far you're prepared to go to protect the Adam Fox legend. You are the Palace's *official* historian after all. I assume they're not paying you to dig up dirt on the great man. To make him look bad.'

Luke frowned. 'Believe me, Lisa, as long as Fox hasn't murdered anyone, any acts of bastardry on his part will only add colour to his legend. Sins never look so bad at a distance.'

'Don't they? Maybe for the idle reader of history. The curious bystander.' Lisa was getting agitated. 'But it's a bit different when the bastard in question is your grandfather. When his sins affected the lives of everyone around him. Laura, Lottie, Alan, Monika. Me and Tom.'

Tears were falling now. What was she doing? Luke would run a mile if he had any sense. She was screwing up the best thing that had happened to her in years. Far from releasing herself from the Fox curse, she was letting it destroy her, rob her of any chance of happiness.

'I'm sorry, Luke. I don't know what's wrong with me.'

Luke put his arm around Lisa's shoulders. 'No, I'm the one

who should apologise. This is much harder for you. Of course it is. I'm the one being naive. I'm sorry, Lisa.'

They kissed again: their first 'make-up' kiss.

Lisa realised it was time for her to share everything. It was possible Monika was losing her battle with oblivion. Lisa didn't want her mother to slip away before she knew her story.

And Luke? If she did not let him into her life fully, with all its shameful secrets, well what was the point of this whole night? Lisa was thirty-eight, alone, adrift. She had to let go of her pride. Monika's diaries were the key. 'Let me read you something.'

Luke cancelled the rest of his day. So did Lisa. They sat in the lounge room of Monika Fox's bungalow while Lisa read pages she had bookmarked in her mother's diaries. About the midget sub raid, the move to the mountains, the trials of Osborne College, the closing of the hotel. She showed him the staff photo taken on the steps. 'Have you seen this?'

Luke had not. He agreed with Lisa that her grandfather looked sad.

'I guess he had no idea if it would ever reopen,' said Luke. 'The US Army handed it back in late 1943 and paid for damages. Even so, he had a lot of work to do to rehire staff and refurbish the place when the Yanks left. He finally reopened the hotel in July 1945. He turned seventy that year and combined the relaunch with his birthday celebrations. But some people say the glory days were over by then.'

Lisa turned over another page of her mother's diary and read aloud.

CHAPTER 26

Monika
Leura and Meadow Springs, February–July 1945

The war was nearly over. At least the war with Germany. But there was another war going on inside the Fox family that was not over.

The big rambling house on Jersey Avenue held a thousand happy memories. Childhood games with Captain Pogo on the well-rolled lawns and hide-and-seek on the creaking verandas. Birthday parties with clowns and jugglers, Aeroplane jelly and pass-the-parcel. Her parents playing tennis or croquet with friends on seemingly endless sunny weekends. Cocktail parties with paper lanterns in the trees and the convivial babbling stream of music and conversation late into the night, their parents' laughter occasionally bursting above the hubbub to comfort the dozing children upstairs.

But in the last two years this same house had become a battlefield where Adam and Laura waged a subtle war of small resentments and withering glances. At home from boarding school on weekends, Monika noted her father's little jabs and her mother's tearful silences with growing alarm. This was all much scarier than the real war. What was going wrong with her parents and their once blissful family life?

During 1943, the VADs had taken on more shifts to deal with the flood of wounded from the battlefields of the Pacific. Laura worked until late most days. When she *was* home, she talked openly about her visits to the US 118th General Hospital up at the Palace and how much she admired the hard-working doctors, brave soldiers and long-suffering nurses. She was proud of her work and her colleagues, despite her exhaustion and the moments of genuine despair when her patients died.

Monika scrutinised her mother's face for any signs of her hidden love for the American medical officer she had seen Laura with that day at the hospital, but failed to detect any telltale changes or signs. But then her mother had always been a gifted actress. Adam listened to Laura's talk about the hospital with a pained expression, grunting sulkily. Did he suspect anything? He must, Monika reasoned, or why else the sullen temper and sour looks?

The conversation always ended the same way. Laura sighed and made a point of asking Adam about his squad of Retreads and their drills down at the Valley Farm.

'Please don't patronise me,' Adam fumed. 'No one gives a toss about the Retreads. They're a bloody joke. The Japs are never going to invade us now.' He would storm out of the room and lock himself in his study. Or take the Hudson for a spin and not come home until late. It was not hard to guess the angst that ate at his heart: it was a young man's war now and Adam Fox had been left behind.

But by 1944, when the Palace had been returned to the Foxes and all the doctors and patients transferred to the new hospital complex at Herne Bay, Adam was busy again. He spent days at a time up at the cottage, supervising the refurbishment of his hotel and looking for reliable staff.

Now it was Laura's turn to sulk. She retired to her bedroom for long stretches with her door closed. One afternoon Monika knocked, impatient to share a story with her mother. When no reply came, she burst into the room to discover Laura bent over her writing desk. She was deep in thought, pen in hand. She started at the intrusion and quickly folded the letter she was writing in half – but not before Monika spied the bright red 'V . . . _ MAIL' logo with its Morse code 'V' for Victory. Maggie Bosely had shown Monika one of these V-mails from her American sweetheart sergeant. It was the US Army's free airmail service, nicknamed 'Funny Mail'. Letters handwritten onto V-mail forms were photographed onto microfilm which was then flown all over the world by aeroplane and reprinted in miniature for delivery to soldiers in the field and loved ones back home.

Her gaze rapidly took in the other contents of the desktop: a stack of V-mails with the censor's red stamp on the front; envelopes bearing the Red Cross flag in the corner and postmarked Geneva; aerogrammes, torn and resealed with sticky tape, marked RETURN TO SENDER. And, most startling of all, a bright pink postcard with the words: CARD OF CAPTURE FOR PRISONERS OF WAR.

'Out! Out!' Laura shouted at her, sweeping everything on the hinged desktop into the desk's inner chamber of pigeon holes and tiny drawers. Her mother slammed the desk closed and locked it. She then grabbed Monika roughly by the shoulders and steered her out of the room. 'How many times do I have to tell you to knock before you come in? This room is *private*.'

Monika saw that her mother's cheeks were wet with tears which Laura hastily wiped away with the back of her hand.

'Are you alright, Mama?' Monika asked.

'Don't be silly. I'm fine, darling,' said her mother in a more conciliatory tone as she closed the bedroom door behind them. She kissed Monika on the forehead. 'Sorry I got so cross. I'm just overtired, that's all. Now, what did you want to tell me?'

Monika had worked it all out. Over and over she replayed the scene she had seen at the hospital nearly a year ago: the handsome American officer with blue eyes and short blond hair, Laura's laughter, the touch on the arm, the letter passing from hand to hand. Mama's lover had been reposted somewhere in the Pacific or Europe. Laura pined for him, wrote him letters. He had stopped writing back. Maybe he had stormed the beaches of Normandy, liberated Paris and seen the destruction of Berlin. Or maybe he had ended up in a POW camp like poor Roger Merewether, whose parents fretted their hearts out, praying he was still alive.

Little wonder her mother was so sad and full of fear. Monika pitied her. But she hated her as well for bringing this terrible secret into the middle of their family. Like an undetonated bomb, hidden in the broom cupboard under the stairs or tucked away under the sofa, it waited to blow Monika's world to pieces.

Every now and then its ticking grew so loud, Monika was sure the explosion was only seconds away. It was a Saturday morning in mid-February 1945 with the whole family at breakfast, one of the rare occasions that saw everyone gathered together. Adam perused the news stories in the *Herald* while the children studied their comic books: *Captain Atom*, *The Panther* and *Tim Valour.* Laura poured a fresh cup of tea and flicked through the society columns.

'Listen to this,' Adam said, folding the newspaper to the headlines:

DRESDEN BURNS AFTER DOUBLE RAID
Wednesday's daylight attack on Dresden by 1350 American Flying Fortresses and Liberators followed last night's smash at the city by 800 R.A.F. heavy bombers. Fires started were still blazing when the American bombers arrived to drop hundreds of tons of high explosives and thousands of incendiaries. The glare could be seen for 200 miles. In addition to Dresden's normal population of 600,000, thousands of refugees from

other parts of the Reich have sought shelter here. The 2250 planes in this attack included two Lancaster squadrons and one Halifax squadron of the Royal Australian Air Force.

Monika saw the colour drain from her mother's face. The hand that held the milk jug for the tea was trembling. She put the jug down on the table so as not to drop it. She struggled to hide her emotions but the expression of grief on her face was impossible to conceal.

Adam continued, oblivious to Laura's reaction:

A Berlin military spokesman said that the world famous museum, the art gallery, the castle, the opera house, and other famous buildings were destroyed.

An eye-witness reported that the authorities in Dresden had been forced to wall in 1000 corpses lying in the ruins because there was no one to bury them, estimating there were between 400,000 and 600,000 dead and homeless in the city.

Adam folded the paper and tossed it on the table in a gesture of triumph. 'Well, that'll even the score for what those bastards dropped on Coventry.'

'*Enough!*' Laura stood up, her face chalky white, fists clenched. 'Do you think it's right for our children to hear this kind of thing?'

Monika had never seen her mother so upset.

Adam looked shaken but remained defiant. 'What? Do you think I should protect them from the truth? Pretend that this war costs nothing? Australian pilots flew that mission. Who knows how many have sacrificed their lives to bring an end to this slaughter?'

Laura glared at Adam with a mix of anger and contempt. 'Don't you lecture me about the truth,' she said in a low voice. 'And sacrifice! What do you know about that? What have you *ever* given up? For *anyone*?'

Laura's words seemed to hit her husband with the force of a slap. As she rushed from the room, she bumped the table. The milk jug toppled, spilled its contents and rolled off the edge, smashing on the tiled floor.

The ticking in Monika's ears was deafening.

'Hitler dead,' Monika recorded in her diary in early May, a footnote to the far weightier drama of her parents' unhappiness.

Her father disappeared into his work. While painters and carpenters swarmed all over the Palace, Fox was making plans for the relaunch of the hotel in July. It was to be done with his usual showman's panache. In the study at his house, he briefed his GM, Mr Merewether, the new food and beverages manager, Mr Nicholson, and the new chef, Pierre Fabrice. The relaunch would also be a celebration of Fox's seventieth birthday, a calculated nose-thumbing to those who had insisted he retire years ago.

In the quiet of his study as he sat alone, Adam tried not to dwell on the past. But at nearly seventy, it was difficult to do anything else. So many good people gone. Lottie Lyell was only half Adam's age when she succumbed to TB in December 1925, two weeks before her lover, Longford, was finally granted a divorce by his wife. Poor Raymond, whose brilliant film career crumbled after Lottie's death, had ended up as a nightwatchman on the wharves in Sydney during the war, always dapper and proud. In 1930 Sir Arthur Conan Doyle's great lion-heart had stopped with his final words for his beloved wife, Jean: 'You are wonderful.' In 1931, not long after she sang at the Palace, dear Nellie was silenced forever, dying in St Vincent's in Sydney from septicaemia after botched facelift surgery in Baden-Baden. The mistress of her looks to the bitter end.

Adam tried not to look back for fear of being overwhelmed by a sense of failure. His son Alan had turned thirteen in March: the same age as Robbie when he died. In seven years' time Adam would resign and give Alan the keys to the kingdom. He would be twenty, the same age as Adam when he took on responsibility for the family business. He had no doubts about his son's abilities: smart, hard-working, dependable. But the shameful truth that Adam kept locked in his heart was how much he missed Robbie's bald-faced cheek. It had reminded Adam so much of himself at the same age. It was not there in Alan, that reckless passion. Maybe that was a good thing. Passion and risk built empires but cooler heads kept them safe.

How he cherished his two daughters, both with an intelligence and independent spirit that reminded him of their mother. Lottie was the more stolid of the two, even timid at times, despite being the older sister, but she had a good and tender heart and for many years had always stood up for Monika, who was the natural troublemaker. In the last two years she had also blossomed into a beauty.

If that spirit of risk and rebellion that was missing in Alan had found an outlet, then its vessel was his youngest daughter, Monika. There was a fearlessness in Monika that impressed and, at times, even scared Adam. He knew instinctively that her fate, for better or worse, would not be that of a dutiful wife and mother. The unspoken truth that Adam struggled and largely failed to conceal was that Monika was his favourite.

Adam looked at the photograph he kept of Laura on his desk. His proud Queen of the Palace. He was deeply saddened by his own distrust of her. Once, like Conan Doyle, he would have died happily with the words 'you are wonderful' on his lips for his beautiful wife. If death came to claim him this very minute, he would still declare his love for her without hesitation. But did *she* still love him? That was the question that tormented him: the canker in the bloom of his near-perfect life, the crack in the mirror of his self-image. Why had she changed, become so withdrawn and secretive? What was she hiding from him? He did not dare put his greatest fear into words for it would surely break his heart and make a mockery of their whole marriage.

Adam made a vow not to let any of these private worries spoil the plans for his grand show. The people of Meadow Springs and beyond would have their party: a banquet for four hundred with a brass band on the terrace to welcome them and a chamber orchestra to accompany dinner. The occasion would mix the elegance of the Edwardian Palace with the sassiness of the Jazz Age hotel. The Palace would rise from the ashes of the war years as magnificent as ever.

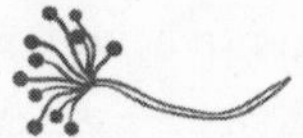

On 4 July 1945, the night sky was crisp with the promise of snow. The American and Australian flags rippled smartly side by side over the casino dome. The brass band on the terrace played 'The Stars and Stripes' followed by 'God Save the King' before ripping into raucous big-band swing numbers and foot-thumping Dixieland rags. Adam's guests were war-weary and sick to their stomachs of penny-pinching for Austerity. They welcomed the chance to kick up their heels. Hell, they'd just defeated Hitler and Mussolini: weren't they entitled to one night of celebration? For the sake of public appearances, Adam had donated a princely sum to the next War Loan and guests bought raffle tickets to raise money for starving refugees in Europe.

Adam had also invited a contingent of distinguished Yanks, including the American consul and a rear-admiral from the US navy. In the spirit of the fourth of July, fireworks tore the starry blackness open in waterfalls of red, white and blue. Guests crowded the terrace, clutching champagne glasses and admiring the spectacle overhead.

Laura stood at her husband's elbow, resplendent in a crimson Hattie Carnegie gown, straight off the boat from New York and sparkling like the fireworks above. Adam's heart ached at his wife's beauty. At forty-four, Laura was still the unrivalled Queen of the Palace. She had dressed her hair into a jet-black curve, swept high off her pale forehead in rich, wavy curls, with a glossy cascade of Victory rolls down to her shoulders. A cloud of spotted gauze seemed to float of its own will above her head, like balls of black pollen suspended on a breeze. She wore six long loops of cultured pearls with a studied insouciance that would have delighted Coco Chanel. Their lustre drew Adam's eye to the flesh of her throat. He remembered kissing that throat when they were both much younger. In his new gallery, the night of the fire, all those years ago. His most precious artwork. He remembered how insanely he had craved her then. He still craved her now.

Laura drained her glass of champagne and reached for a second as a waiter passed close by. Whatever rancour or suspicion had dogged her and Adam these last two years seemed a distant memory tonight. She smiled at him without the slightest hint of reserve. For a moment, Adam dared imagine Laura looked happy. Maybe this evening would recapture some of the carefree mood of parties past.

'Congratulations,' she toasted her husband. 'And many happy returns.'

'Thank you, my dear.' Adam smiled. 'It feels good to see the place back to her old self again.'

'She ages very graciously. Like her owner.' Laura adjusted the lapel of Adam's jacket in an intimate wifely way. 'Why are you so good at this?' she asked.

'At what?'

'All this.' She swept her hand over the scene: the gleaming sea of dinner suits and ball gowns, rippling with excited chatter and laughter. 'Making people happy. Giving them these moments of escape. From life's dullness. And disappointments.'

'Who knows? Born with it, I guess. Gift of the blarney and all that. Freya used to call me "the ringmaster". And not as a compliment either.' Adam laughed at the memory of Freya's scowl. 'Mind you, she loved the parties at the Palace back then just as much as I did.'

'She loved *you* too, didn't she?'

Laura drained the second glass. She looked directly at Adam. There was a puzzling expression in her eyes, one he could not decipher clearly. They had spoken of Freya of course. And Adelina. Many times. How could they not? Adam's past was not a closed book, though he chose not to dwell on it in a maudlin way. This relaunch of the Palace naturally brought back memories.

'Yes. She did.'

He was surprised to hear the tremor in his own voice. Where did it come from? Guilt over his dealings with Freya? Or did it arise from something else? A more general sadness and regret that came from the awful realisation that the story of his life was almost written and, in the words of the Persian poet, 'nor all thy Tears wash out a Word of it'. His history would one day lie open for all to read and judge: the strokes of luck, the lost opportunities, the triumphal decisions, the catastrophic mistakes, the people he'd protected and those he had betrayed.

'Yes. She did.' Laura echoed. She grabbed a third glass from a passing tray and held it aloft, proposing a toast. 'Here's to happiness! Adam Fox's gift to the world!'

There was a note of careless abandon in her voice and her eyes blazed with a reckless, wild light that Adam remembered well from her youth. She spilled some of the glass but did not seem to care or notice. Several guests within earshot joined Laura's toast. 'To happiness! And to Mr Fox!' they chorused, the clouds of bubbles in their raised champagne glasses reflecting the explosions of silver light overhead.

The dinner was a triumph. Instructed to prepare a banquet in celebration of Australia and America's wartime friendship, Chef Fabrice had conjured gourmet variations on popular American dishes: glazed pork ribs flambéed in Calvados, minced venison terrine moulded to resemble a meatloaf with hand-cut *pommes frites* 'on the side', and miniature pumpkin pies with Chantilly cream. A chamber orchestra accompanied the meal with selections from Gershwin, Barber, Copland and Grainger.

The crowning glory of the seven-course extravaganza was wheeled out on a trolley, illuminated by ranks of fizzing sparklers and proclaimed by the trumpets of Copland's *Fanfare for the Common Man*. Fabrice had excelled himself. All eyes were drawn to the replica of the casino dome as a very large bombe Alaska: a mound of frozen peanut-brittle ice-cream surrounded by sponge cake and meringue, sculpted to resemble the dome and baked to a golden honey-brown.

'Bravo!' someone cried. Others joined in. Soon, the crowd of diners were cheering and clapping and stamping their feet loud enough to make the floorboards thrum. Amid this tumult, Adam Fox stood up and walked to the bombe. As a treat, the three Fox offspring – Lottie, Monika and Alan – had been ushered in to watch their father light his birthday cake.

The lights in the casino were turned down. In the artificial gloom, the audience could make out Chef Fabrice in his chef whites striding to the table to assist the hotelier. The crowd's clapping became a chant – 'Fox! Fox! Fox!' – as the septuagenarian stepped forward with a burning taper held high. Flourishing a flask of brandy, he splashed it over the dessert and lit the brandy vapour. It caught with a *woof* and the dome was engulfed, waves of unearthly blue flame flowing over its surface. The audience began to applaud.

Only Adam heard the chair fall, pushed over backwards as its occupant struggled to escape. His face spasmed, white with rage, which he did his best to conceal. He looked up and saw her, Laura, hurrying out, her mouth covered to stifle a sob. She swept past her three children without so much as a backward glance.

The applause continued to rise to a deafening crescendo and Adam grinned and took a bow. It was unclear how many of the audience had seen Laura's dramatic exit, if any, or would notice her absence at his side when he resumed his seat. Even so, the moment of Adam's triumph was spoiled. *I will never forgive you for this* was the first thought that erupted into his mind as he struggled to control his temper.

Back in his seat, Adam Fox acknowledged the admiration and congratulations of the throng of well-wishers that crowded around him. The nanny had already ushered the children back home. Maybe their mother had joined them in the waiting car. He knew he should probably rush away now to see what it was that had upset Laura. Nobody could accuse him of not being a loving and dutiful husband. It was just that he wanted this evening to be perfect. Was that so wrong?

At that precise moment, Adam's mind reeled back to a similar night long ago in the library. Adelina weeping in the darkness. The looks of horror and pity on his guests' faces. The past reaching out again and again to punish him. Dear God, when would he *ever* be rid of these ghosts?

CHAPTER 27

Monika
Leura and Meadow Springs,
August 1945–July 1946

Now Monika had a secret and it was the greatest secret of her life.

The war had come to an end in August 1945 but it continued to cast long shadows. In June, Monika's friend Maggie Merewether had got her last V-mail from her sergeant, one of the fourteen thousand American soldiers killed on Okinawa only weeks before two atom bombs forced the surrender of Japan. Maggie withdrew from the world with a shattered heart and vanished from Monika and Lottie's lives. The following January, her brother, Roger – the boofhead and drongo – finally made it home from Singapore, reduced to a pitiful skeleton after his trials on the Burma–Thailand railway but alive at least and recovering in Concord Repat.

Monika went to visit him with her mother and they both came away shaken.

Monika barely saw her father, who spent most of his days on the golf links at Blackheath or Leura, or having lunch or drinks with friends in the city. She missed him dreadfully and was jealous of her brother, Alan, who was now the focus of the old man's attention. Alan was being groomed as Adam's successor and had recently started lessons behind the wheel of the Hudson under his father's watchful eye.

Matriculating from Osborne College in November with high marks in her leaving exams, Monika began her diploma at Sydney Teachers College in January 1946. She and Lottie shared rooms in a family friend's house at Darling Point. Lottie was also a student: of shorthand and typing during the day and the dance steps, smooth banter and spending power of eligible Sydney bachelors at night. Monika tagged along as chaperone on some of these evenings and wound up feeling resentful that Lottie, extroverted and glamorous, drew all the attention. Who would have thought timid little Lottie would turn out just like Mother? mused Monika as she watched her older sister bewitching all her dance partners.

Monika returned home to visit her parents on weekends to play tennis and croquet, go for walks and show off her father's hotel to her new girlfriends from college. Out of class, she had taken to wearing bright red lipstick, a silk headscarf and Gene Tierney sunglasses to acquire some of that femme fatale's dangerous allure. Which was how one hot, windy afternoon in early February she came to meet Brün Faber.

Her secret love.

Monika wrote in her diary:

The Palace! The last place on earth I imagined meeting anyone, least of all someone like him. There I was on the terrace with Lucy and Di from college when the wind snatched the scarf off my head and blew it halfway down the slope to Sun Bath Road. This tall bloke appeared out of nowhere, retrieved my scarf and brought it to me like a chivalrous knight bearing a gift to his lady love. 'I believe this is yours,' he said solemnly and bowed. 'How did you know?' I asked. He had blushed then, confessing he had been watching me on the terrace. 'You are the daughter of Mr Fox, yes?'

I swear I have never laid eyes on a man so handsome in my whole life. His hair is spun gold and his eyes are slivers of turquoise. I still find it hard to believe he is real. So gallant. So exotic. So forbidden. My very own German. Brün. His family are refugees who came on one of the first boats out of Europe. They now live in Lithgow where his father runs the brewery and Brün delivers the beer to my family's hotel. He asked to see me again. Next week. Is this not fate? My parents must never know. Especially my father.

There were probably many reasons for Monika's attraction to Brün which ignited so swiftly into romantic love. But the simplest of these reasons was Brün's beauty and bearing. Six foot two inches tall, he had an athletic physique: broad shoulders, wide chest and muscular legs and arms from the daily demands of loading and unloading crates of beer. His face had the symmetry and flawless complexion of golden youth while his blond hair, cropped close to his skull, had the sheen of polished brass.

Beyond that surface beauty, but at the same time suffusing it with injured nobility, was the fact that Brün had *suffered.* At the age of seventeen, he had seen and done and heard things that were beyond the darkest and most lurid imaginings of a young girl from the Blue Mountains. Brün had grown up as a boy in Hitler's Germany, watched its rise to glory and witnessed its utter ruin. His family had fled east from Berlin to Dresden and survived the fire-bombing there. To Monika he was a Teutonic knight, scarred from the flames of a modern-day *Götterdämmerung.*

With only a tentative command of English and the reticence to be expected of a wartime refugee, especially one from a former enemy nation, Brün did not surrender his story all at once. It took intimacy and trust for that story to find its voice and for the writer within Monika to listen without judgement. And so, over the next five months, Brün and Monika discovered each other slowly and tantalisingly in their clandestine meetings every Saturday afternoon.

Monika cloaked these encounters in the guise of enrolment in a camera club that met for regular bushwalks in the upper mountains on weekends. Laura was delighted to hear that her daughter had taken up a hobby dear to her own heart but that also gave her an excuse to visit. With the tense atmosphere at home, Monika was a welcome companion for her mother and a distraction from her troubles. Adam usually absented himself at the golf club while Laura and Monika sat on the veranda reading magazines, listening to songs on the radio, drinking tea and nibbling biscuits.

Countless times Monika felt the urge to confess her secret love to her mother but fear held her back; not so much the fear of her mother's disapproval, though that was a potent and intimidating prospect, but fear of the even worse possibility that Laura would confess her own secret love.

That would be too much to bear.

And so for nearly five blissful months, Monika's simple deception was sustained. Her best friend, Di, would take Monika's camera on the photographic club's expeditions and return with a full roll of photos to be printed and shown off to Laura if she asked. It didn't take Monika long to work out the best place for her and Brün to steal a blissful half-hour or longer together from his weekend delivery run. She had seen where her father hid the key for the cottage in a downpipe of the old painter's studio and knew a way through the hedge to avoid being seen by anyone at the hotel. Unknown to Monika, this was the second time that young forbidden love had perfected its repertoire of caresses and kisses in Freya von Gettner's humble cottage.

Monika's diary waxed lyrical about her new love with all its attendant ecstasies and anxieties. Brün loved Monika's philosophical frame of mind and they talked about life and death and art with great earnestness. He was an honourable young man from a Catholic family and so his repeated declarations of love and his intention to marry Monika were pure-hearted.

Monika trusted all this to be true but she was still torn. She loved Brün passionately. She wanted their cottage-time of hugging, holding, stroking, kissing, touching to never end. But she did not want to think beyond that. She was greedy for him. And greedy for his stories, which were unlike anything she had ever heard or imagined.

One afternoon, Brün finally told Monika about Dresden. He described the night the bombers came, turning the city into a manmade hell where everything burned: the streets burned, the buildings burned, the people burned. He had seen men and women drop dead at his feet, asphyxiated as the fire sucked the oxygen from the air. He had seen a young mother stumble and let the bundle in her arms fly in an arc into the flames. He had seen the hot wind seize people like dead leaves and pull them back inside the burning buildings. He had seen cremated adults shrunk to the size of children, whole families burned in a huddle. He had whispered to himself over and over: 'Please don't let me burn. Please don't let me burn. Please don't let me burn.' He had lost his aunt and uncle and one of his sisters.

Afterwards, they cried together and held each other. That afternoon, Monika let Brün make love to her. Not because she felt sorry for him but because this was what she chose. He used a condom, of course, but she felt reckless even so, willing to plunge into this forbidden world of pleasure and blissful forgetfulness to escape the chill shadow of so much death and cruelty.

By chance, Monika had kept her camera with her that day. She took Brün's photo as he sat by the window of the cottage, his hair shining in the sunlight, his face turned away in profile as he looked at something in the garden. A handsome satin bowerbird performing his dance for a female.

Monika wrote all this down later in her diary. Feverishly. Even though she was training to be a school teacher, she still harboured secret ambitions to become a writer. She recalled her English teacher at Osborne's, Mrs Wickham, who had thought Monika had a bright future as a writer but warned her that 'suffering is essential . . . to be a novelist of any note'.

But did that suffering include other people's? As she recorded Brün's story in her diary she felt a queasiness at stealing something intensely personal from him, a precious fragment of his soul. 'I am only borrowing these memories, not taking them,' she reassured herself uncertainly. And then wondered for one vertiginous moment whether she only loved Brün for his unusual history and forbidden otherness. Was that wrong? Would she be punished?

In March the governor-general – Prince Henry, the Duke of Gloucester – arrived with his wife in his private plane at Blackheath aerodrome to open a new wing of the district hospital in Katoomba. The good citizens turned out in force, a flock of hats and gloves, to greet the two British royals as they took a stroll down the main street with Prime Minister Chifley and Mr Freelander, the mayor, close behind. As a prominent public figure, Adam Fox joined the official party for the civic lunch at the Carrington that day and was photographed shaking hands with the duke and duchess.

Not surprisingly there was a great upwelling of patriotic sentiment, bolstered by the sight of Union Jacks hung from every shop awning and an honour guard of ex-servicemen, proudly wearing their medals, in front of the Carrington's steps. None of this made much impression on Monika Fox as she was at college in Sydney. But there was to be an ugly consequence.

When Brün arrived at the cottage the following Saturday afternoon, he was wearing a cap pulled down low over his forehead. Monika teased him about looking like a 'navvy' and playfully snatched it away. She gasped at the deep cut on his temple. Brün was cross at first but then explained how he had been attacked by three men outside a pub on Wednesday night. Two of them were returned soldiers. Calling him a Nazi, they kicked and punched him to the ground. He managed to inflict some damage before he went down and, luckily, the three men took off quickly when a car approached.

The Fabers were aware of the undercurrents of loathing among the townsfolk of Lithgow that bubbled up every now and then into acts of open hostility, but the Fabers had their supporters too: fellow churchgoers and small-business owners and other families from the Lithgow migrant hostel. These 'refos' included the hundreds of 'Balts' and Germans working at the Kandos cement works. The final judgement of the town came in the bars and lounges of the local hotels where drinkers took to the Fabers' lagers with a thirsty zeal. 'You got to hand it to Krauts, they know how to make beer' was the general verdict.

As if Monika's tender feelings for Brün could be inflamed any more, she now felt fearful and protective and outraged at the injustice of this attack. She kissed his wound. They made love again and she held him in her arms for a long time afterwards, wishing she could kill the men who had dared to hurt her German.

'How could you be so crass?' Laura had asked Adam after the drama of the bombe Alaska at the party to reopen the Palace. Adam denied there was anything sinister in the presentation of the fiery dessert but for Laura the vision of the Palace in flames had triggered painful memories of that fateful night so many years ago.

'I think that night haunts *you* more than it haunts *me*!' Adam had said petulantly. 'You can't still feel responsible for Adelina's death, surely?' They had raked over these ashes many times and Adam had explicitly exonerated Laura of any blame for his poor wife's breakdown and suicide. 'It was grief for Robbie that killed my wife,' Adam had explained to her. 'Not my love affair with you.'

But it was not Laura's guilt that poisoned the atmosphere of their marriage. It was Adam's own jealous and paranoid conviction, despite repeated denials from Laura, that she was being unfaithful. He confronted her more than once with this accusation and she begged him to trust her. 'Please, Adam, please believe that I still love you,' she said. 'You have nothing to fear.'

To ease the tension between them and gather his thoughts, Adam stayed in the cottage for short periods. Here, he sat on the veranda in the evenings, smoking and listening to 78s on the RCA Victor or the night songs of the bush, the violin-sawing of crickets and the cackle of tree frogs. He thought about Adelina and the fervour with which he had courted her as a young man in Melbourne, dazzling her with his vision for a grand hotel. He thought about Freya and their lovemaking here and in the studio, and his heartbreak one morning in this garden while baby Angie played. He thought about the first time he had shown this cottage to Laura and how she had fallen in love with it and talked him out of his plans to tear it down.

Ah, Laura, Laura, Laura. You should be sitting next to me here, my proud Queen of the Palace. Over the top of the hedge, Adam could see the grey slated casino dome and the crenellated rooftop with its fresh coat of white paint. The old lady looked as good as new since the Yanks had pulled out, and business was brisk again within weeks of her rebirth. There were several generations of guests who had given their hearts to this hotel. Like pilgrims before a shrine, men and women stood arm in arm in the lobby, their eyes misting over as they recalled the distant romantic highlights of their youth. No wonder locals still called it the Palace of Tears.

Adam struggled with the storm of emotions inside his head. Were his romantic feelings for Laura also now destined to be no more than memories? He was determined not to be consumed by the suspicious rage that brewed in his heart, telling himself it was an expression of his own weakness and self-doubt. There is a crisis in your marriage, he admonished his better nature, and you must find the courage to see it through. So Adam bargained with himself. Even if Laura was involved with another man, he reasoned, he refused to believe that she would ultimately choose him over her husband. Their marriage would somehow survive.

He had tried to be strong as he watched his wife's evasiveness, her sadness and silent torment grow over the last two years. Laura apologised again and again for her strange moods and insisted they meant nothing and would be overcome. He tried to forgive her for the sake of their love and for their three children. But it was hard.

The tension at the Fox family home had grown in intensity over the last six months. By the middle of the year they could all feel its presence like a cloud of flammable vapour that hung over the house, awaiting only a single spark to set it off. Monika managed to remain aloof as she only came back for weekends. Brün was the haven she escaped to from the misery of her family.

But the whole family knew it was just a matter of time before it would all go up. The disaster struck with full force one Sunday afternoon in July with everyone home for a family lunch. Laura had spent most of the weekend in bed, falling into bouts of weeping for no apparent reason and refusing to come down for meals. Something had triggered this latest fit of despair, something terrible. Adam had tried to talk to her but to no avail. Monika, too, had tried, with similar results.

Adam sat at the head of the table with Alan, Lottie and Monika as they watched the meal their cook, Sarah, had prepared go cold. Adam had sent Sarah up to fetch Mrs Fox and would not let them touch a mouthful until their mother came down. No one spoke a word. The only sound was the tap of Adam's glass of water on the table top like a metronome keeping time.

It grew louder and louder until, without warning, he hurled it against the opposite wall. Everyone froze in terror. Adam stood up and stormed out of the room. He mounted the stairs and began pounding on Laura's bedroom door with his fists. Monika felt her stomach lurch and her body went numb. This was it, the detonation she had waited for.

'What are you hiding from me, Laura? What are you keeping secret?'

Behind the door, Laura was crying. 'Go away!'

'Why won't you tell me what's going on? What is it you are hiding from me?'

'Go away! Go back to your bloody hotel. It's all you've ever loved. More than me. More than your children. I wish it had burned down that night of the fire. It killed poor Adelina and now it will kill me!'

Monika did not recognise this voice; it belonged to another woman, a wretched madwoman howling in distress. And the words made no sense at all, though they evidently wounded her father deeply, for he cried out as if in pain.

'How dare you! How dare you say such things! Open this door!' yelled Adam.

This rage was more terrifying than anything Monika had witnessed before. Alan, shamefaced and trembling, and Lottie, paralysed with fear, hung back in the dining room. But Monika tiptoed to the doorway to listen. Floorboards creaked overhead and they all heard something explode: an object thrown against a wall upstairs.

'Go away!' Laura shouted.

'Open the door now or I'll break it down!'

'I don't love you! You're a monster! Go away!'

'You're lying to me, I know it. You've been lying to me for years!'

Adam bellowed like a wounded animal and went crashing down the stairs and out the back door. Monika ran to the dining-room window. She saw a thick-necked old man, his scalp glowing bright pink through his thinning hair, wrestling with the door of the garden shed. She could not believe this was the same man she had hero-worshipped all these years.

There was an ominous silence. The house itself seemed to tense as they all waited. 'Mama, are you alright?' Monika called out. There was only the sound of weeping from behind the closed door. And then the loud bang of the back door slamming open and her father's heavy tread as he mounted the stairs again. Monika came out of the dining room and saw him. His face was a mask of cold, white rage.

He was carrying an axe.

Monika screamed, 'Stop!' She rushed at him but it was as if he did not see her. His hand went up and shoved her hard in the chest, throwing her back against the wall. He continued along the corridor towards Laura's room. The first swing of the axe bit deep and the bedroom door shuddered on its hinges. The second splintered the top panel and took an effort for Adam to pull it out.

'Open the door!' Adam bellowed.

Monika heard the snick of the lock and the turn of the handle. Adam surged forward into the room. 'Give me the letters! I know about the letters!' he yelled.

'No!'

The children heard a scream and the sound of more objects breaking; china or glass or wood, they could not say what. They were consumed by terror.

'No, no!' Laura begged in a pitiful voice drowned out by her husband's angry shouts and the repeated sounds of heavy blows.

Monika had to act. She looked at Lottie, quivering with anger and fear, and her brother, Alan, his fists squeezed tight against his temples, sobbing with rage. 'He'll kill her!' he cried. 'We have to do something.'

'Phone the police,' Lottie hissed. 'Or get one of the neighbours.'

'No, wait,' commanded Monika. Impelled more by desperation than any conscious act of courage, she ran outside to the shed. Alan had already picked up the telephone receiver when he and Lottie heard Monika's feet pounding up the stairs .What was she going to do?

When Monika stepped through the doorway she saw her mother cowering in the far corner of the room. Her father had split her mother's writing desk almost in two, spewing its contents all over the carpet: books, pens, bundles of letters, small boxes, all crushed, shredded, stained with ink from shattered bottles. Adam had his axe raised for the final blow.

She pointed the barrel of her rifle at the back of her father's head.

'Stop. Stop now. Or I'll shoot.'

CHAPTER 28

Lisa
Katoomba, June 2013

When Lisa had finished reading, she and Luke sat in the bungalow in silence for some time, listening to sparks rattling up the stovepipe of the slow-combustion heater and the soft implosions of embers in the firebox. Raindrops tapping against the windows and roof made a delicate accompaniment.

'Thank you,' Luke said at last.

Lisa sat, dry-eyed, next to him on the couch. She had expected to feel exposed and ashamed but she did not. She felt, instead, surprisingly at peace, as if an invisible burden had been lifted from her chest, allowing her to breathe more freely.

Luke gently caressed the fingers of her left hand. 'And you wonder why I feel a little protective towards you and your family? There's so much to understand here, so much that is still hidden.'

Lisa nodded. She had read to the last entry in the final volume of Monika's marbled-cover diaries: 25 August 1946. Here, the story ended abruptly with not a single jot on the succeeding pages. It was as if Monika's childhood had plummeted into a blank hole, vanished into a space beyond words.

Lisa sighed. 'And I'm running out of time, Luke. I want to understand all this before I lose her.' She told him about Monika wandering off from the nursing home and refusing her meds. If the disease took off, it could be only weeks before Monika's memory flushed away everything, including her daughter's name and face.

'The nurse said they found her down at Bloome Park. Apparently she was looking for someone called Brian. Unless the nurse got it wrong, and it was Brün she was looking for. Is that possible?'

'Yes. It's perfectly possible. He may still be alive and might even have stayed in – or returned to – the district. Just like your mother. I'll give my friend Naomi a ring out at the Lithgow Historical Society to see if there's anything about the Fabers in the archives.'

'Thank you. You are so . . .' She struggled to find the right word. 'Wonderful.'

'Yes, I am.' Luke kissed her tenderly on the forehead. 'I promise to help you as best as I can. Not because I am the historian of the Palace, but because I want you to know about your past. Before it's too late.'

He looked at his watch. 'Speaking of which, I have to go.

I have a meeting tonight up at the hotel with the owners and the architects. Progress report.'

'I suppose you won't be mentioning you had several hours of sex with the youngest living descendant of Adam Fox.'

'I'm not sure that it would be strictly relevant.' Luke laughed as he pulled on his jacket and closed his laptop. 'In fact, I'm pretty sure I should *not* mention it.'

'When will I see you?' Lisa asked, wincing at the cliché of her anxiety as he headed for the door.

'Soon,' he offered, already checking his iPhone for messages. 'I'll text you.' And with a farewell kiss, he was gone, leaving Lisa in the familiar silence of her mother's bungalow. Except *that* silence was now all the more profound for the strange void left by her lover's absence.

She switched on the naked electric bulb in the basement. Why was she standing here again? Lisa had a powerful impulse to revisit the contents of her mother's well-managed 'tomb'. She turned the key in the padlock and opened up the trunk. She might be back where the journey had begun, but she had learned so much since she first stood here in early May, nearly two months ago.

She stared into the trunk, and inhaled its sickly musk of mothballs and dust. There were Monika's childhood treasures. Horse-riding and clay-pigeon shooting ribbons from the

Lithgow Show. A drawing of her cocker spaniel, Captain Pogo, signed by her brother, Alan. A pile of dogeared children's books. A battered tin with a pearl earring. And a little girl's Start-Rite Mary Jane shoe – just the one – its white patent leather all scuffed and the buckle rusted. What did these objects mean to Monika?

Lisa had removed some of the contents of the trunk onto the shelves opposite. These included two more photo albums, mostly of Laura and Adam's trips abroad. Lisa had studied these again with interest, particularly the photos of a trip through France, Germany and South America in 1937. The children had been left in the care of their nannies for two months while Adam showed off some of his favourite places to Laura. The travel snaps included photos of the happy couple enjoying afternoon tea on luxury German airships as they travelled between Hamburg, Frankfurt, Dresden and Leipzig before embarking on a flight to Rio on the LZ 127 *Graf Zeppelin*.

Photos of their one day in Dresden showed Adam posing in front of the city's baroque marvels: the landmark Frauenkirche with its distinctive 'stone bell' dome and the three-tier wedding-cake Semperoper opera house. No doubt this was when they had bought Laura's new SLR camera, her Kine Exacta.

There was one package inside the trunk she had neglected to look at, that did not fit the pattern of nostalgic items from childhood. Wrapped in clear plastic, it lay underneath the stack of diaries and battered books. Lisa scooped it out.

It was Monika's typewritten manuscript: the one she had laboured over for six years. Publishers had rejected it as 'too strange' and 'unexpected' from the famous author of the Kitty Koala series. Her mother had never shown it to Lisa. It did not belong on the tidy shelves with all the celebrated books and photos and merchandise. Instead, it had been buried here, an object of shame, a stillborn book. She had spied this unwanted, unloved thing when she first dug into the trunk but hadn't thought to pay it any attention.

Now Lisa tucked the plastic-wrapped package under her arm, closed and relocked the trunk, and went back upstairs. The blue light of evening had settled over the house and garden, and through the window she saw the half-sphere of the moon. In one week it would be the winter solstice, the shortest day of the year. The streets of Katoomba would be filled with people dressed as mythical beasts and monsters for the town's popular Winter Magic Festival, a modern-day Neo-Druidic celebration. Ulrich would be in the mountains by then; maybe he would think it was fun.

She poured herself a glass of red and sat by the fire, then took out the manuscript and laid it on the coffee table. The pages had begun to yellow and the typewriter text had faded to a lighter shade of purplish-black.

'The Castle of Ice'
For Brün and Peggy

Lisa started. A story for Brün. And Peggy? Who on earth was Peggy? She began to read:

Once upon a time, a young princess named Sparrow lived in a castle on a cliff above a great forest. From the giant blue-green blocks of its foundations to its finely carved finials and flagpoles, the castle was made entirely of ice. 'What fool builds a castle out of ice?' whispered the townsfolk. 'One day a fire will melt it to the ground.'

Cursed by a terrible enchantment, the castle lacked all love and warmth. The king was old and his young queen dreamed of the day she would take a new husband. The old king so cherished his daughter that he had made her a pretty garden with a roof of ice and ice-carved trees and flowers and rabbits and squirrels. But Sparrow longed to feel the sun on her face and be among living creatures.

On the morning of her twelfth birthday, the princess was greeted in her garden by a handsome satin bowerbird who dropped a blue petal at her feet. 'How did you get here?' she gasped. The handsome bird then hopped away to the garden wall and tapped three times. A crack appeared and Princess Sparrow squeezed through the narrow space which closed up behind her.

Across the snow-blanketed ground she followed the trail of blue petals down the rocky precipice into the vast, whispering forest below. The Wald. Here, silver-white trees flowed like forked lightning up to the sky. Insects zinged and hummed in the sun's warmth and parrots screeched in blurs of cochineal and Prussian blue.

In the midst of a grove of the lightning trees stood a cottage with a roof thatched from paperbark. An old blind woman stacked firewood at the door. She was the Witch of the Wald and her wisdom about this land and its animals was legendary.

'Come live with me for one year and be my eyes and hands, and I will show you the secrets of the Wald. At the end of that year, you will be free to go. But you must make me one promise: you will not speak a word to anyone but me.'

The princess agreed and lived with the old blind woman. She collected kindling from windfall and chopped firewood for the stove. She fetched water from the small brown creek and trapped rabbits for their supper. She harvested greens from the garden and scared birds away from the fruit trees.

The old woman kept her promise. She showed Sparrow all the secrets of the Wald. The sleeping hollows of the snakes, their coils of muscled beauty in copper, chocolate and bronze. The basking spots of the lizards with their blue tongues, frilled collars and thorny skulls. The meeting places of the kookaburras, competing like sideshow spruikers with luminescent vests and raucous laughter. She taught Sparrow the secret language of these creatures and for months at a time Sparrow heard no human voice, only the voices of the forest.

And then one day, as Sparrow was fetching water at the creek, she saw the reflection of a young man, tall and handsome with hair the colour of sunlight and eyes the colour of sky. He spoke to her in a foreign tongue she did not understand. She pressed her finger to her lips to show him she must not speak. The young man took her in his arms and kissed her. They both heard the distant baying of hounds and the horns of the royal huntsmen who roamed the Wald looking for the princess. The young man kissed her again and fled. The princess never spoke a word of her secret love to the Witch of the Wald and she never broke her vow of silence.

She met her love by the creek every day and their silent passion grew stronger. The young man gave her a golden ring to make her his wife. She became big with child and gave birth to a daughter. With only one day left till her year with the witch expired, she left her swaddled infant with her husband and returned to prepare the witch's supper. Tomorrow she would leave the Wald forever to begin a new life.

The following morning she went to the creek with her few possessions packed for the journey. Little did she know that the bowerbird followed her, dropping a trail of petals.

Overjoyed at the sight of her husband and baby, Sparrow called out 'Over here, my loves!'

The witch stepped out from behind a tree and removed her cowl.

It was not the old blind woman under the cowl but Sparrow's mother. 'Your love has betrayed you!' cried the cruel queen, revealing herself to be a powerful witch who years ago enchanted the king and his castle. 'The Witch of the Wald was my wicked sister who lured you into her forest so you would take over my reign. She has paid for her treason!'

The queen's guards dragged out the body of the dead witch and laid it before the grief-stricken princess.

'And now let me show you the true face of your unnatural love!' The Queen cast a spell on the handsome young man

and the infant girl surrounded by her huntsmen. In the blink of an eye, father and child turned into a giant bear and baby cub, with eyes of blue and fur of golden-brown. The bear bellowed in anger, snatching up his cub and fleeing.

'Please call off the hunters,' the princess begged her mother.

'Only if you surrender your child-cub to me and renounce your right to the throne,' demanded the queen.

But it was already too late. The head huntsman raised his crossbow and the bolt pierced the giant bear's heart. The princess cradled her husband's head as he died.

In his own tongue Sparrow told the satin bowerbird to pluck out the eyes of the wicked queen who had killed his mistress and deceived him. She called to the crows and currawongs and commanded them to snatch hot coals from the cottage stove and drop them like petals along the winding paths of the Wald. The birds did her bidding and soon the entire ocean of trees was ablaze. As the flames roared over the snowy berg, the battlements and turrets of the magnificent castle gushed with tears. Then all the courtiers heard a crack like the fusillade of a thousand cannons. The giant blue-green blocks of the foundations split asunder and the castle came tumbling down, crushing all inside and drowning the rest in the deluge that flowed over the precipice. The blinded queen, her guards and huntsmen all perished.

With the queen's spell broken by her death, the young cub was transformed back into a baby girl. The whispering forest came back to life too, reborn from the flood. The bear-prince's spirit could still be heard, roaring in the woods, every winter.

Within earshot of the mighty waterfall and by the banks of the new river that flowed through the Wald, Sparrow and her daughter made their home in the witch's cottage, where they lived together happily ever after.

As Lisa turned over the final page, she found a black-and-white photo tucked between it and a sheet of plain cardboard. It was a photo of a young man looking out a window. His blond hair flared slightly in the strong sunlight that flooded the room behind him. There was no doubt who it was. Brün. Her mother's German boyfriend. Her first love.

Lisa sat in the deafening quiet of her mother's house, thunderstruck. This strange tale over which her mother had laboured with love for six years was unlike anything else Monika Fox had ever written. A universe away from the cosy, comic world of Kitty Koala and her furry friends. Why had Monika spent so much time crafting such a dark story with its barely disguised allegory of the Palace and her parents' troubled marriage? What did it mean to her, this odd tale which she had finally found the courage to write in her late sixties? In her heart, Lisa knew exactly what this fable was: an act of public confession safely hidden behind the veil of a fairytale. Such tales always told the truth.

Monika had always loved fairytales and fables, the stories of Aesop, the Brothers Grimm and Perrault. She had read them aloud to her children when they were small. Lisa recalled the name Bruin, the character of the brown bear in *Reynard the*

Fox, a collection of French and German fairytales that Monika kept on the bookshelf in her study.

A pile of these treasured books from Monika's own childhood had also turned up in the trunk with their well-thumbed pages, creased spines and handwritten messages in fountain pen over the frontispiece: *With Love to My Clever Story-Teller, from Mama, Christmas 1941* and *To the Girl Who Got Lost in The Woods And Was Found Again, Happy 8th Birthday Monz, January 1938.*

So what to make of 'The Castle of Ice'? The two sisters, the blind woman and the queen, were both powerful witches who acted in the role of 'mother' to the girl. They were clearly twin aspects of the one person, thought Lisa, a very dark portrait of Laura, the self-admiring beauty, married to an older man over whom she cast a spell.

But that was not the clue Lisa was interested in. At the heart of Monika's strange fairytale was a vow of silence around a secret love and a pregnancy. This part of the story climaxed with the demand to surrender an illegitimate child, the result of an unnatural union between the princess and a bear. This Bruin is an outsider who does not belong in the Wald and must be banished or killed. The story was not only dedicated to Monika's young German lover but she had even hidden a photo of him inside the manuscript.

And then there was the dedication: 'For Brün and Peggy'. The child in the story was a little girl, a female bear cub that the queen demanded be given away. The ending saw this child and her mother reunited to live in the cottage 'happily ever after'.

Lisa felt a door fly open inside her mind. What else could this story mean? This had to be the story of Monika's pregnancy to Brün. Her mother's diary ended abruptly in August 1946. From that day on, Brün vanished, never to be mentioned again. Until this story.

'For Brün and Peggy'. If Peggy was the little girl in the story who had to be given up, Monika was not alone in a generation of women who had been forced to surrender their babies. It would explain so much, Lisa thought, her mind racing ahead, desperate to piece the entire mystery together. Why her mother could not love Lisa and Tom properly. Why she could not risk exposing herself again to the pain of loss. Why the only children she could love were her distant readers.

Lisa sat back. Of course, the existence of Peggy, her half-sister who was now either dead or a woman in her sixties, was pure conjecture, based on an unpublished fairy story hidden in a trunk. But it had a ring of truth that Lisa felt reverberate in her bones and skin, in her heart and her head.

Who could she share this mad, half-guessed secret with? Her brother? Luke? Or was it finally the moment for her to confront Monika? To learn the truth before time ran out. Whatever the cost.

CHAPTER 29

Monika
Benedict Street Maternity Home, January 1947

She awoke to the squeak of shoes on linoleum and the smack of Dettol and bleach in her nostrils. Her left hand still clung to the white iron bedhead behind her. She remembered clutching it, like a drowning woman clutching a life buoy, as she began to drift into nothingness. Was it last night? Yesterday? When was it? She couldn't recall exactly. Her eyelids fluttered open. The room was semi-dark, silent. A breeze knocked the blinds about, rippling through the tall, barred windows of the dorm. She felt its coolness, as welcome as a wet compress against her forehead.

It was going be a long, hot summer. When the brown-brick hostel grew too stifling and the breezes arrived, the sisters took the babies into the garden for some fresh air. They draped blankets and netting over the cribs in the shade of the giant pine trees. With the breeze lifting the gull-wings of their white caps, they patrolled the cribs to make sure no insects dropped onto their charges.

A tremendous throng of cicadas had gathered in the pines. They pulsed their mating thrum, falling in and out of rhythm with each other like the string section of a symphonic orchestra. How old was she the last time she'd heard this music? Five? Six? It was so easy to forget how loud and maddening this drone became, day after bloody day.

Monika had been unconscious for a long time. She moved her head to one side. Slow. Heavy, foggy. She wondered if any of the other girls were in the dorm today. The curtains were pulled shut on either side of her bed. She could not see or hear anyone. They came and went so often. Monika would be going home soon, they told her. Once the paperwork was done. What was that? A shadow flickering at the back of her mind. The ghost of her dream. Her memory.

The bush, hot and dry. Asgard Swamp. December 1937. Six weeks before her eighth birthday. A picnic near the big rock, pink granite and sandstone, shaded by gums. A rock with all the right footholds and finger holes for children to climb. A fort for playing cowboys and Indians, a hideout for bushies and bobbies, a castle for crusaders and Saracens. Perfect for battles, chasings, hide-and-seek. Her sister, Lottie, just turned nine, in plaits and a new dress. Her brother, Alan, four, still in dungarees. Their two best friends, Maggie Bosely and Dottie Wilson. And the adults: the two nannies, Meg and Joan; the housekeeper, Mrs Moxham, and the driver, Charlie Pyke.

Mama and Papa are away on a trip in Europe. They'll be back before Christmas. 'We'll take you to Jervis Bay for the hols,' Papa promised. Monika is still not impressed she didn't get to fly in a giant Zeppelin like the one in the postcard.

After lunch, comes the big fight. Some stupid thing. Lottie demanding her sister's favourite golliwog, Mr Allsorts. *'I'll tell Papa you bunged up his tennis racquet practising with rocks!' 'No, I didn't. Liar!' 'You're the liar!'*

Monika running off through the long, scratchy grass, away from the rock, away from the fire trail. Hiding behind a pyramid of purple stone. Hearing the adults calling, calling. Voices growing more urgent and desperate. Running off again when Charlie comes too close. Breaking the buckle on one of her brand-new pair of white Mary Janes. Taking them off and tucking them into her pockets, with her socks balled up inside. Mama would kill her if she lost those. Don't think about what she'd do to Monika for scaring the wits out of Mrs Moxham and poor Meg and Joan. *'It's all Lottie's fault. For telling lies!'* That's what she'd say. And they'd be so cross with Lottie for upsetting her.

Scrub, rocks, gum trees, the same scene everywhere she turns. She stops thinking about how cross she is with Lottie and starts looking for the way back. Not sure where the fire trail is. Voices have all died, drowned out by waves of cicada-drone. A party of painted skippers dances past her head. Ants are biting the soft flesh between her toes like hot needles and she picks them out urgently. Crushes them.

She realises this is not a game anymore. She's really lost. She cups her mouth and calls, '*Coo-ee!*' Waits. Silence. Calls again, louder this time, sounding a bit scared, even to herself. '*Coo-ee!*' There is a cockatoo screech in the distance and the sound of the wind passing through the canopy. 'Help! Charlie! Help!' she screams. Her voice sounds puny and weak. Silence.

She begins to run, barefoot, through the scrub. She stumbles and twists her ankle. The dream speeds everything up, chops bits out. She is sitting on a low rock, out of breath, rubbing her ankle which begins to swell. Her hair is soaked. She takes off her straw hat and feels how damp it is. She is feeling sick from the heat. She is dirty, sticky with sweat. Her dress is torn. Her ankle is very sore. She is tempted to cry but tells herself, *Don't be a baby!*

What time is it? She looks up at the sun to see how far it has slid down the sky. Uncle Mel tried to teach her the compass points and how to find directions by the sun. Put a stick in the ground. Mark the shortest shadow at midday. That'll give you a line north–south: the shadow points south and the base of the stick north. And then you have to work out east and west. Easier when Mel explains it.

He's not her real uncle, of course. His name is Melbourne Ward and he's the son of Papa's best friend, Mr Hugh Ward. He was an actor once like his father and then became the biggest collector of crabs in the whole world. Now he's mostly collecting the skulls and bones of Aborigines, and masks and paintings and stuff. As long as Monika's papa agrees, he plans to build a museum for his crabs and bones next door to the Palace. Her papa calls him 'the Wild Man' and says someone should put *him* in a museum. Even so, Monz likes spending time in the bush with Mel, who knows the names of all the flowers and animals. She wishes he was here now.

The dream speeds up again. Monika is feeling dizzy. Her lips are parched and her temples throb. It has not rained for weeks. She has to find water. Mel has told her to watch the birds. Birds always know where water is. She sees a flock of wild pigeons flying over the swamp grasses, dipping low as if ready to drink. She will follow the path of their flight. She walks but she is limping now as her ankle hurts.

At the top of the next rise, she turns left and staggers down a narrow trail. In the distance are cliffs, gold in the afternoon light. Monika stops and looks down into a sea of gum trees, lapping the great fractured ramparts of rock. Ridge piled up behind ridge. And then she smells it. The sting in her nostrils. Smoke. She looks to the horizon. A pillar of dark grey smoke is being pumped into the sky. It is a bushfire in the next valley. It is heading this way.

A surge of terror washes through her body. Now tears come, salt against her lips. *Stupid, stupid, stupid girl!* she tells herself. *You're going to die out here all alone. Will Mama and Papa cry when they find you dead? Or will they just hate you for running away?* Monika pictures her grave in the blackened bush, an ash pile smothered in pink flannel flowers; they are the prettiest and rarest of the flannel flowers, Uncle Mel told her, and they only come to life after a bushfire.

The grizzling of a baby, somewhere outside, brought Monika back. The breeze, billowing the curtains at her bedside, rattled the daffodil stalks still tied with twine in the cloudy water of a jar on her table. Who brought those? The almoner would be here again soon. To talk. Talk, talk, talk. She was so tired of talking.

When she began feeling sick and knew for certain she must be pregnant, she had just wanted it to all go away. She knew the instant she let her secret out into the world, the silence would be shattered forever. And who could she tell? There was only one person she could trust. Monika knew the shame unmarried mothers brought on their families. When Maggie fell pregnant last year, the Boselys had tried to avoid becoming outcasts by sending her off to a maternity home in Victoria. She had still not returned. Those who knew the truth blamed them for raising 'a bad girl'. *Dated a Yank, they say. Always knew she was trouble, that one.*

Laura cried gently and hugged her tight. But she didn't play her role as 'distraught mother' quite the way Monika had hoped. She was meant to be outraged. *Stupid girl! My God, you're only sixteen! You're throwing your life away!* She was meant to put her foot down and insist they get rid of the baby. Monika had rehearsed it all in her head. She realised this was what she herself wanted. Laura was heartbroken but she did not sound angry. Just tired.

'Do you love him?' she asked.

'Yes, but . . .' Monika looked away. Brün was such a very beautiful young man. Her Wagnerian knight who loved Beethoven and Brahms, played the piano a little and still struggled with his English. The real problem was he had no ambitions beyond his father's brewery and a quiet life in the mountains. Monika knew she wanted more, much more. 'Yes, but . . .' was as good as a confession that she did not love Brün enough to throw away her hopes for a different future.

Laura nodded. She understood.

'Well, we don't have many choices,' said Laura. 'If you don't want to marry Brün, then you face a very hard life as an unwed mother. Unless . . .'

Monika wanted to shout at her the monstrous truth in her heart: *Don't you get it? I don't want the baby! Make it go away! Please!* She knew it wasn't that simple. This was not one of those fairytales where women handed over their children to witches or dwarves to fulfil a bargain or prevent a curse. This was brute reality. There was the life of a human being at stake.

Laura spoke. 'There is one possibility. I could raise the child as my own. A change-of-life baby. Not uncommon even in the mid-forties. The child need never know. It would have a perfectly good life and avoid the stigma of illegitimacy.'

Monika did not know what to think. She could never imagine her father agreeing. It was a pretty threadbare disguise for a bastard pregnancy, she thought: doomed to failure if it was meant to protect the Foxes from gossip. 'I – I'll think about it,' Monika mumbled, burying her face in her mother's shoulder and weeping until she thought her heart would break.

Adam had moved out to the cottage, his usual refuge, for a short while after the incident of the axed desk and the gun. The gun had not been loaded, of course, but that did not change the fact that a line had been crossed. Adam had dropped the axe, crashed to his knees like a wounded bull and shuddered with deep sobs in the arms of his wife. 'Please, please forgive me.' Monika would never forget the sight of her father's face distorted with shame and desolation and the sound of her mother's voice – 'It's alright, my love, it's alright' – over and over. She did not know who she hated the most that day for frightening Lottie and Alan so badly and forcing her to resort to such a desperate course. She had flung the gun aside, packed her bags and caught the next train back to Darling Point, taking Lottie and Alan with her and leaving her parents to sort out their own tortured lives.

Adam had begged his children's forgiveness but soon resumed the mantle of the family patriarch as if nothing had changed. When Laura explained Monika's situation, he stormed up and down the hallway, shouting. *Pregnant to a German brewer's son, for crying out loud!* He would call the police and charge the boy with 'carnal knowledge', threaten the Fabers with lawyers, cut off their contract to the hotel, get their business boycotted all over the district.

'Yes, that's brilliant. Let's take out a big advertisement in the newspaper too while we're at it! It's better if the boy – and his family – never know,' counselled Laura.

Adam calmed down and decided it was time to involve the expert advice of the family's doctor, solicitor and priest. Any decision about Monika's future was to be taken out of the hands of the Fox women – what would they know of these matters, after all? – and put into the competent hands of professional men.

The paramount consideration was secrecy, urged all three professionals, and the easiest, quickest and least painful solution was a 'closed adoption'. As a result, it was decided that, in the last six months or so of her pregnancy, Monika would be sent away to the Benedict Street Maternity Home in Sydney, operated by the Catholic Church. Here, she would board with thirty-six other unmarried mothers, hidden from public scrutiny until her baby was delivered and put up for adoption through Martin Street Maternity Hospital. All done with discretion and care.

It was clear to both Monika and her mother that this plan to exile her from the family was intended as a punishment. Laura tried to explain to Adam the cruelty of his decision but he refused to listen. She realised that this was a test of her loyalty and love after the recent crisis. She would have to sacrifice Monika and Monika's unborn child to save her marriage – or so she told herself.

Monika was surprisingly stoic. At least her father and his male experts had made the dreadful decision for her. She had survived the strictures of Osborne College and she would survive this. In six months' time the nightmare would be over.

She missed Brün so much: her lips, breasts, body still ached for his touch. Tears spilled from her eyes when she lay in bed and thought of their final parting. She had sent him a letter: 'Ours is an impossible love and cannot continue, my brave Bear. We are so young and from such different worlds. I know you will find happiness again. I promise I will never forget you, Brün.' It was a good letter, she thought, melodramatic and self-aggrandising as all such letters should be.

Brün came to the house in Jersey Avenue one night soon after and threw gravel at her bedroom window. 'We can go away. Just you and me. No one can tell us how to live.'

Again her father spared her the agony of making a decision, storming out of the house and yelling, 'She does not want to see you. Come here again and I will ruin your father's business, do you understand? This is my final warning!'

For six months she endured the stern solicitude of the nuns at Benedict Street Maternity Home. Some were kinder than others but the general mission was clear: to shepherd the souls of the poor women who had fallen into sin down the path of redemption. It was like school all over again but even lonelier. Monika had never thought she would pine for Lottie's company so much.

The Benedict Street girls were addressed only by their first names in order to protect their privacy. There were few opportunities during the day for private conversation anyway as they were all expected to perform 'light duties', including shifts in the kitchen, the office and the nursery, as part-payment for their board. Given her father's wealth, this was absurd and decidedly a punishment in Monika's case. It was made very clear that she was to receive no 'special treatment'.

The afternoons were given over to chapel and then cookery, craft, and gardening classes. *Idle hands are the devil's tools.* While chopping food, sewing, weeding, and washing and ironing bed linen were onerous enough, it was the time spent in the nursery that was by far the worst of Monika's tasks. From the day she arrived, Monika had made a firm decision to give her child up for adoption, so she could not understand why the nuns tormented her by forcing her to care for other women's babies in the nursery.

Except for distant memories of her baby brother, Alan, Monika was unfamiliar with babies. These defenceless creatures gurgled, cooed, smiled and ogled her from their cribs. She was shocked at how very small they were: such tiny pink hands with fingers that wiggled like the soft horns of snails probing the air; chests as fragile as those of little birds that shuddered with each breath; eyes that drank in the world with a permanent gaze of wonderment. How was this meant to help stiffen her resolve to give up her child? It was cruel and perverse.

As she felt the stirrings of her own unborn child within her, that firm resolve began to flag even more. The sisters were well-practised at detecting these moments of morose fixation and they swooped down to shore up weak wills. Every day, the company of girls was ushered into the chapel where the sisters gently berated them for their sinfulness before offering the salve of Jesus's love and mercy, followed by a hymn or two to the whine of the harmonium.

Every week, the almoner, Mrs Richards from the Child Welfare Department, visited with her own government-approved version of salvation to counsel Monika about adoption. 'I have many good families waiting to give a new life to illegitimate babies like yours. The adoption of these babies removes the legal stigma of illegitimacy. It legitimises these babies' births again. If you truly love your child, you will give it the opportunity for a fresh start and the chance to grow up in a good family with a mother and father.' Just as baptism washed babies free of sin, adoption would wipe away the stain of illegitimacy.

All this talk had the opposite effect to that intended. By the last month of her pregnancy, nothing could stop or change the building storm of emotions that had taken hold of Monika during her period of confinement at Benedict Street. It was a combination of growing defiance against the insistent brainwashing she endured and the softening of the boundaries between her own self and the mysterious but unmistakeably present *other person* inside her.

She suffered through lower back pain, dizziness, high blood pressure, nausea, loss of appetite, skin rashes, pimples and hot flushes. Her hips unlocked and her back unhinged, leaving her feeling unstable and vulnerable. She avoided mirrors but felt unsightly and ridiculous some days and expansive and glorious on others. Her belly swelled so big and taut it was hard to find a comfortable position in which to sit or lie. As she read on her side in bed, she felt her baby stirring and saw her flesh ripple with the imprint of a hand or foot.

Was she still confident she could surrender this child to someone else so easily? Monika was haunted by the thought of that moment of surrender as she stroked her taut belly, imagining she was cradling the head of her child. The sisters forbade the girls to give their baby a name. They could reprimand her for saying a name out loud, perhaps, but they could not stop her thinking it. Her secret name. *Rosie.*

Visitors were screened by the sisters and confined to the immediate family. Adam or Laura visited but never together. Papa was brisk and businesslike, fiddling with his hat nervously in his lap. He came bearing gifts of books and sweets to assuage his guilt and ended each visit with a tender peck on her forehead. One day, leaning over, he whispered, 'My clever girl. You have such a bright future ahead of you. So much to achieve. I hope you'll forgive me. Some day.'

Laura came bearing fruit baskets, flowers and Mr Allsorts, Monz's golliwog from when she was little. She found it hard to hide her anger from the sisters, though Monika begged her not to make her time here any harder. She clung to Monika when the visit ended, stifling her sobs with difficulty. It seemed the nuns had a word with Adam, because Laura did not come again for the last two months.

To her surprise, the only person in whom Monika could confide without fear of judgement, advice or emotion was Lottie. Her big sister brought her gossip and magazines, chocolates and cheeriness. It was to Lottie she told the secret name. It was to Lottie she confessed: 'I think I have fallen in love with my little Rosie.'

Her breasts had swollen too and her nipples leaked milk. In the last week before her due date, she was sent to the single mothers' ward at Martin Street Maternity. She was surrounded by sullen, silent women, all about her own age. A young doctor came and wrote in her file, marked B.F.A. – Baby For Adoption – even though Monika had not yet signed any consent forms. Dr Stevens did not look much older than her, maybe early twenties, anaemic, thin, aloof. She heard one nurse refer to him as an intern. He patted her here and there, wrote up her notes, and started her on a daily regime of pills and needles. Her wrists were strapped with thongs to the bed rails and she was injected two, sometimes three, times a day. She saw the names on the bottles but no one explained what they were for. Amytal Sodium. Nembutal. DES. Her breasts stopped leaking. She felt odd, disoriented, trapped in a blurry torpor, and as the hours dragged slowly by, she lapsed into bouts of dreamless sleep.

When the day finally arrived, Monika did not know Lottie was outside in the waiting room, refused entry 'so as not to cause the patient any distress'. Monika's head felt cloudy, heavy. Her temples throbbed. She felt the spasms in her uterus coming closer and closer together, grinding her up in relentless waves of pain. How would she ever get through this birth?

She was trolleyed into the labour ward on her back, a drip in her arm. The hastily tied, thin cotton gown flapped open. The lights were too bright. The room was cold. White tiles like a butcher's shop. The nurses made no eye contact. Their mouths were covered with masks. They offered no kind or reassuring words.

Monika felt scared now. And so sad. Wasn't birth supposed to be something special, sacred? This was all so impersonal, so clinical, so rushed. Where was Laura? Why did she not come? Why did nobody hold her hand? The pain was crushing all the breath out of her. She cried out. 'Shut up! Silly girl!' An older woman, stern-faced.

A bedsheet blocked her view of the birth itself. All she could feel was the surging tide of the contractions and the pressure of her baby's head. On and on and on and on. And then the moment of release. She heard a baby's cry. A sob escaped her own mouth.

'What is it? A girl or boy?' she whimpered. But nobody heard her. There was the bang of a door and the sound of the newborn's cries receding into the distance. The neon lights overhead were extinguished. 'All done!' a nurse announced brightly. Monika felt the sting of a needle in her arm. 'You won't remember a thing!'

And Monika slipped into a dark, empty place.

At the bottom of the narrow trail she finds a creek. The drought has reduced it to a trickle but it still runs clean and Monika scoops up its water greedily. It has no particular flavour so she knows it is safe. Her lips are healed, her throat slaked. *You will*

live! says a voice inside her head. She follows this trickle to a larger creek, running fast but shallow. She drinks again and splashes across to the further bank. She must find some shelter from the sun soon. Her skin burns and her eyes itch. Monika hobbles up the far side of the creek and follows the trail along the cliff line. She ducks under a log and sees a hole cut into the side of the sandstone cliff face. It is the low entrance to an abandoned coal mine.

Maybe she can rest here. The walls are slimy and overgrown with lichen and ferns. She sees frozen drips of orange wax – stalactites – suspended from the ceiling. She peers inside but it gets dark only a short way in and she can hear hundreds of creatures rustling about. One of them alights on her bare foot, a big, brown, cave cricket. She shrieks and shakes it off.

She must sit down soon as she can barely keep the weight on her sprained left ankle. She looks across the valley to where the golden afternoon light is retreating up the cliffs. Bruises of blue-grey storm cloud spread across the pale flesh of the sky. If only these clouds would drop their cargo of rain, she would no longer be in any danger from the fire. She stumbles on a while longer, following the trail that hugs the cliff face. As she rounds a corner, she sees a hole in the thick foliage: a doorway made of bricks. It is like something from one of her mother's fairytales and looks completely out of place here in the rugged scrub of Asgard Plateau.

It must be a goblin's hut, thinks Monika. The hut is overgrown with vines, bushes and clumps of grass. Monika peers inside. Satisfied it is safe, she crawls on her hands and knees through the arched doorway. There are no crickets here, no slime or ferns or stalactites. Inside is a small, domed room, lined with bricks from the floor to the round skylight in its roof. Monika is surprised at how clean it appears; she imagines a short bearded fellow with a broom giving it a good sweep out. She has no idea it is a coke kiln built by coal miners many years ago. To a little girl lost in the bush, it is a miracle.

Monika takes her Mary Janes and her balled-up socks out of her pockets and arranges them near the doorway, making house. She presses her swollen, discoloured ankle against the smooth brick lining of the room. The coolness is a balm.

Birds are starting to fall silent now as the copper-pink light of dusk slides up the cliff faces opposite. And then, unexpectedly, she hears a medley of bird calls in quick succession: the staccato cackle of a kookaburra, the long liquid flute-note and snap of a whipbird, the swooping throaty carol of a currawong and the squeaky chirrups and tinkling of a crimson rosella. These calls ring out over the valley with the clarity of church bells, each run of notes dropping into the still air of the long dusk like pebbles dropped into silver water.

Monika crawls to the door to listen. She knows what this is. A superb lyrebird, a male, is giving his evening concert, showing off his mastery as a mimic of every sound in the bush. Her heart skips to a lighter beat to hear such beauty. It feels as if he is performing just for her.

The sky begins to darken to a velvet blue as the storm clouds roll away to the east, propelled by a wind that drives the heat off the cliff tops. Monika sits on the front step of her new bush home.

She watches the line of fire from the next valley snake up the far ridge. Its fiery glow lights up the patch of sky above the ridge and she can smell the smoke. She prays that the fire will not descend into this valley overnight and race up the steep gully beneath her while she sleeps. Hunger whines in her belly but, thankfully, fatigue dulls the pain. It has been the strangest day of her short life.

The night is still except for the creaking of frogs. She turns her weary gaze to the sky. She sighs and her soul is unburdened for a moment at the sight of the Milky Way making its steady progress over the horizon, a river of incandescent white with its countless shining droplets of stars. *I must tell Mama and Papa about this*, she murmurs before nodding off to sleep.

'So, I think you know what this is,' said Mrs Richards from Child Welfare. Monika was well acquainted with this plump, cheery woman with her Brillo steel-wool hair, large cotton print dresses and cardigans with pearl buttons. She made herself comfortable at the formica table. Monika heard the cushion of the chair exhale and its hollow, chrome legs creak under Mrs Richard's ampleness.

That morning, Sister Kate had helped Monika into her blouse and skirt and escorted her downstairs for her interview.

Every night, just before they turned the lights out, it was Sister Kate who gave her an injection. It had been three days since they took her baby away and she had drifted on a becalmed sea, fogbound and silent.

Now the day of truth had arrived.

Monika sat down opposite the almoner and Mrs Richards put a one-page form on the table between them. She turned it around so Monika could read the printed text. Mrs Richards had a pleasant, singsong voice that made everything sound simple and straightforward.

'Now, as I have explained to you, this is the consent form. As a Justice of the Peace, I am empowered to witness the fact that you have signed this form, fully informed of what your signature on this document means. This form is the basis for an adoption order by which a court will transfer all parental rights from you, the birth mother, to your child's adoptive parents. The adoption order means you are no longer your child's legal guardian and will be totally and permanently deprived of all parental rights. In the interest of the child's welfare, you will have no contact for the rest of its adult life. Do you understand?'

Mrs Richards had gone over all these details before, explaining how Monika's decision, while painful and difficult of course, was an act of 'true love' and self-sacrifice, 'ensuring a better life for your baby than you could ever provide'.

Monika folded her arms across her chest. 'I want to see my baby,' she said, '*before* I can decide.'

Mrs Richards sighed. This was a not-uncommon bump in the road. Tedious but able to be negotiated with her usual professional patience and care. 'I think that is a very bad idea. It will only make things much harder for you, my dear.'

'Why has nobody let me see her? I just don't understand.'

Monika began to feel agitated. She turned her back on the almoner and squared her shoulders. Mrs Richards coughed. She went to the door, opened it and called down the corridor in her loud, cheery voice. 'Sister Kate! Are you there?'

The sister came running. Squeak-squeak-squeak.

The almoner resumed her seat. 'There, there, dear,' said Mrs Richards, patting Monika on the arm. 'I understand exactly how you feel.' She turned to the sister. 'Miss Fox is quite naturally upset. Can we give her something to help her calm down a bit?'

'Of course.' The nurse smiled and hurried out.

'I'll tell you what, Monika,' said Mrs Richards. 'I'm prepared to bend the rules. But you have to agree to what I ask. This is for your own sake, you understand? If you sign the adoption papers today, then I will make sure you can see your baby.'

'I – I don't know. I want more time to think about it,' said Monika, standing up and then sitting down again. She was confused, angry, lost.

Sister Kate returned with a paper cup of water and a pill held in her open palm.

'I don't even know if she's a girl or a boy,' mumbled Monika, tears running down her cheeks. 'I want to see Rosie.'

The sister winced at the use of a name but Mrs Richards gave her a warning look. 'Of course you do, poor child,' crooned the almoner. 'Here, take this. It will make you feel better. We can work this out. Sit down.'

Mrs Richards handed her the water and pill and Monika swallowed it automatically with one quick gulp. She sat down again.

'It's natural for you to want to see your baby. But, for your own sake, you must be clear about your decision before you do so. Otherwise, it will just make the whole situation much, much harder on you. Do you understand what I'm saying?'

Monika blinked and nodded. She looked at the form again.

'It's for the best,' prompted Mrs Richards, stroking her client's arm. 'I promise you.'

'Where do I sign?' muttered Monika, the taste of salt in her mouth.

'Here.' Mrs Richards handed her the biro.

Monika H. Fox. It was done.

She felt tired now, very tired. 'Time for some rest,' soothed Sister Kate. 'You've had a big day.'

The dream fast-forwards to the next morning. The sun comes up early. Monika is sitting in the cool of her brick hut watching the stars wink out as the sky grows light. She is so hungry that all she can think about is food but she knows she cannot roam too far on her swollen ankle. She'll just have to sit out the heat of the middle of the day inside her hut. The air is filled with the acrid tang of bushfire smoke and the sky over the valley is white with its haze. But the fire hasn't come any closer overnight. Maybe the wind has changed direction. Maybe the clouds will come back and drop their rain. Maybe someone will find her before the fire does. Maybe she won't die today.

She makes slow painful progress back up the track to drink her fill at the creek. She soaks her socks and her dress in the water and sucks on them back at her hut. Perspiration seeps from her temples. The heat is already oppressive with the sun still low in the sky. On the way back, she picks what she hopes are some purple geebung berries. She peels them the way Uncle Mel showed her and sucks out the sugary pulp. She hopes her memory is good and she hasn't just poisoned herself. She wishes she'd learned some more blackfella bushcraft. She is like every other white person in the mountains – still a stranger in a strange country after all these years.

She will be dizzy with hunger again in an hour or so and, if she has the strength and can bear the pain, she'll creep back to the creek for another drink in the evening. As the sun reaches its zenith, she sits in her hut. She sings out loud. To keep her spirits up. To alert any searchers. To remind herself she is still alive.

The songs she sings are from her parents' record collection. Bing Crosby, Al Bowlly, Rudy Vallée, Cliff Edwards. 'Singing a Song to the Stars.' 'It's Only a Paper Moon.' 'I Love to See the Evenin' Sun Go Down.' She thinks about her father and mother all dressed up for one of their fancy parties at the Palace. She is resigned to the fact she is not as beautiful as her mother and sister, but she does have some of her parents' smarts. She knows, even at the tender age of almost eight, that she is destined to be *someone*. Her father sometimes picks her up and swings her into the air in his strong arms, exclaiming, *One day everyone's gonna know all about Monika Fox!*

She looks up at the sickly feverish sky that pulses with the hypnotic beat of a thousand cicadas and the unremitting glare of the sun through white smoke. The odds of her survival do not feel good today. 'If you let me live,' she shouts to this cruel sky, 'I promise to make my life extraordinary!'

Monika was woken in the middle of the night by a tap on her shoulder. It was Sister Kate, holding an index finger to her lips to signal the need for secrecy. She beckoned to her with the same finger. Monika had been dreaming about the bush, the fire and the stars, when she was lost as a little girl. She was still groggy from the drugs and unsteady on her feet as she slid out of bed. The sister put one arm around her waist and the other under her left arm to support her.

'Be very quiet,' the sister hissed in her ear. They moved along the corridor of the hostel as slowly as possible so as not to squeak on the linoleum. The lights were all out in the other dormitories and the black-and-white-checked floor was dimly illuminated by a pool of light at the far end of the corridor.

'If anyone asks where we're going, you need to use the toilet, alright?' whispered Sister Kate.

When they reached the bottom of the flight of stairs to the second storey, Monika realised something strange was going on.

'Up here,' said the sister, and they began to climb.

The nursery was in near total darkness. The room fluttered with the delicate rhythm of sleeping infants, a soft cyclic hum of breathing. Sister Kate tugged Monika gently along the row of cribs. Monika could feel the young woman, not much older than herself, shaking like a leaf. If she was discovered breaking the rules like this, she would probably be expelled from the hostel.

'Mrs Richards is a liar. She is sending your baby away tomorrow,' murmured the sister. 'Here she is.'

They stopped at the third crib from the end. Sister Kate took a torch out from her pocket and shone it off to one side so only the pale edge of its circle of light fell on the sleeping child in the crib. Monika looked down.

The baby was swaddled tightly but she could see her face clearly. A head of charcoal-black hair, a chubby pink oval, flickering eyelids as translucent as petals, a broad nose, dimpled chin and surprisingly large mouth. Monika's heart ached at the sight of this perfect fusion of her and Brün.

'Have they given her a name yet?'

'Peggy,' said the sister, checking the chart at the end of the bed. The torch went out. 'We have to go. I'm sorry.'

Was it better or worse that she had seen her daughter? That she knew what she looked like and what her name was? Was it kinder or crueller this way? As Monika walked back through the darkened nursery, she could not possibly say.

As the sun begins to slide down the western slope of the sky on Monika's second day in the bush, she hobbles slowly along the cliff line away from her hut. It takes her hours and she has to grit her teeth against the throbbing pain in her ankle. It is this sprain, she realises, that will be the death of her as she will never be able to walk out of this bush, even if she can find her bearings.

Having drunk her fill, she crosses the creek again and makes her way back up the rise to the ridgeline to see if she can spot any movement of people in the distance. She prays that search parties are out today looking for her. She has kept an ear open for any shouts or whistles bouncing off the cliffs. Apart from the rise and fall of the cicada song and the squeals of parrots, she has heard nothing.

In the distance she sees a rocky knoll and heads in its direction. Every five minutes or so she stops and cups her mouth for a loud 'coo-ee'. The view is breathtaking: a sparkling sea of gums in the molten afternoon light as far as the eye can see. In front of her, there is a steep descent to a pillar that stands alone, split off from the main plateau. Several skinny gums grow there, looking forlorn, as if aware of their pathetic isolation on this narrow island of rock. Thor's Head it is called on the map, though Monika doesn't know this. Even so, she feels drawn by its sublime beauty. She imagines scaling to the top to stand, arms outspread in the dying light of sunset, screaming her name into the valley. A final shout of defiance. '*Monika!*'

If nobody finds her today or tomorrow, she will surely die. A handful of berries and creek water don't fill her belly for long and she can feel herself growing weak. Her ankle is the size of a cricket ball. The drum of cicadas bores through her skull like a drill. Her head is splitting and the skin on her face and arms, blistered and red from sunburn, pulses waves of heat.

She knows she is in deep trouble when her vision begins to blur. All she can think about is lying on the ground and not moving anymore. Even the idea of ants crawling over her inert body is not enough to dissuade her from curling up in a ball on the sand and stones and clutching her temples to still the incessant buzzing inside her head. Maybe if she lies still long enough, the pain will go away.

And then she hears a faint cry, off to the right. 'Coo-ee!'

She shakes her head in disbelief. The cry comes again, but fainter this time. Moving away. Dear God! She must not let them escape. She will never catch up with her busted ankle. This is her last chance.

She stumbles to her feet, dizzy, unsteady, wincing in pain. She is determined not to die. Not today. She cups her mouth and hopes her voice has not withered in her parched throat. She replies as loudly as she can. 'Coo-ee!'

The cries ricochet back and forth, overlapping as the other caller gets closer, Monika's growing hoarser and more desperate. 'Over here! Over here!' shouts a male voice and Monika hears boots crashing through the scrub close by.

'Thank you,' she says, casting her eyes to the sky, as a man in a dark-blue uniform appears in front of her. Now, at last, she allows herself to cry. She has been given a second chance. To make an extraordinary life.

When Monika woke the following morning, she sensed a familiar presence on the other side of the cotton curtains. Sister Kate, who was about to finish her night shift, yanked them aside to reveal Laura sitting in a blue chair, her hat in her lap. She looked pale and fragile but calm. She smiled nervously at her daughter.

'Are you alright, my sweet? I have missed you so much.'

'Oh, Mama,' cried Monika. 'They're taking my baby away.'

Laura scooped up her daughter in her arms. She hugged her tight to comfort her like she used to when she was small and frightened from a terrible nightmare.

'Then we must stop them,' her mother said. 'If that's what you want.'

'I'm afraid that is not possible, Mrs Fox,' said a loud voice behind them. It was Mrs Richards. 'Monika has given her consent and the adoption order has been issued. The child has already been collected by its adoptive parents.'

'That's not true!' shouted Monika, before realising that she could not possibly know this. Sister Kate's face drained white and she looked at Monika in terror.

'Are you calling me a liar, Miss Fox?' said Mrs Richards, her habitual cheeriness now replaced by a crescendo of anger.

'No, of course not.' Monika almost choked on the words. 'I'm sorry.'

'Just as well. Official visiting hours are not until midday,' said Mrs Richards, glaring at Laura. 'But as you're here now, you can take your daughter home. The Department of Child Welfare has no more business with her.' The almoner walked off briskly, her face still burning red with indignation.

'Your father doesn't know I'm here,' explained Laura as she helped Monika to dress. 'But I couldn't leave you alone any longer. I'm sorry, my love.'

Laura kissed her brave daughter on the cheek. She helped pack Monika's suitcase and together they walked out of the brown-brick building where, upstairs in the nursery, baby Peggy still lay sleeping.

CHAPTER 30

Lisa
Katoomba, June 2013

Lisa sat at the coffee table with an empty wine glass. Her mother's manuscript and the photo of Brün lay in front of her. It was late and she had begun to drift off to sleep when the phone rang. Could it be Luke, leaving his meeting at the Palace?

'I hope I didn't wake you. I checked the time zones so it wouldn't be too late.' She didn't recognise the caller at first. A young male voice with soft, round vowels rolled between precise consonants. A German accent. Her mind stirred. Ulrich.

'No, no, it's fine. Nice to hear from you. I got your email. How are you, Ulrich?'

'Please. All my friends call me Ulli.'

Ulli was ringing to confirm that he was due to arrive in Sydney on Friday morning. He had reserved a room at the

Carrington Hotel for three days. It was just as well as the entire town of Katoomba was booked solid for the Winter Magic Festival that weekend. 'I should arrive late afternoon. Can we meet at the hotel?'

'Sure, no problem. We can have a look at the festival, if you like, and then have dinner. I was thinking of inviting my friend Luke – he's the historian I mentioned. Is that okay with you?'

'Yes, yes, of course. That will be great, Lisa. Thank you. I am looking forward to it. And to meeting Monika, too. See you soon.'

Lisa climbed into bed. She propped the photo of Brün against the stack of books on her bedside table and stared at it, wondering at the coincidence that this photo and a story dedicated to her mother's secret lover turned up the same week a young man arrives from Germany, claiming a connection with her family. Lisa's eyes closed and she tumbled into a night of long strange dreams.

It is summertime at the Palace. Everyone is here. Monika and Lottie are down on the terrace with their rifles, shooting gramophone records. Adam is in the empty casino, dressed in an evening gown and floral hat, dancing with Laura, both lost in each other's eyes. Wrapped in a white robe, Adelina lies on her deckchair outside the spa, reading a psychic magazine. Freya is in her garden, painting in the shade. Freddie and his boys haul large blocks of ice that sweat in the blazing sun. There is a marquee on the lawn and musicians. A party.

'Where are all the guests?' Lisa asks Uncle Alan, who brings her a big bowl of ice-cream and jelly. It is her sixth birthday and he has invited her to the Palace for a treat. Her brother, Tom, will not be coming today, nor her father, Michael. As usual. And then she sees something odd in the distance. Four children standing on the track leading down to Sensation Point. Two boys and two girls. There is a forlorn air about this group, a sense they have been deliberately excluded from the celebrations.

'Who are they, Uncle?' Lisa asks, but Uncle Alan pretends he cannot see them.

Lisa insists. At last he relents. 'If you really must know, they're Robbie, Angie, Brün and Peggy. The ones we never talk about.'

Lisa woke to the sound of her mobile ringing. She had overslept.

'You sound terrible! Are you okay?'

Lisa couldn't stop herself from smiling at Luke's frankness. She loved the sound of his voice and realised how much she had longed to hear it again.

'Thanks a lot.' She laughed. 'Well, to be honest, I've had a shocking night's sleep. The weirdest dreams.'

'I guess that's not so surprising,' said Luke. 'Under the circumstances.'

'I spoke to Ulli last night. He'll be here on Friday. Are you okay to join us for dinner at my place? Maybe have a drink first up at the Carrington and watch the fireworks?'

'Yes, of course. I'll bring dessert or something if you like.' Luke sounded a bit strained. Could he be jealous? Of Ulli? How silly was that! The thought cheered Lisa immensely.

'I just wanted to let you know I made a call today to my friend out at Lithgow, about Brün Faber,' Luke continued. He could have emailed her this information but had rung instead. Maybe he too ached to hear her voice and this gave him the perfect excuse for a phone call. Did they need excuses anymore?

'That's great.'

'She sent me some excellent information. I'll bring it with me on Friday. But in a nutshell, Brün took over the brewery from his father and ran it until he sold the business in the 1990s. He had a family of his own and died of a heart attack in 2004.'

Poor Monika. She would not meet her love again.

'I have some interesting news too. I think.' She realised even as she said this that Peggy's existence was still only conjecture. 'But it can wait.' They chatted a little longer about their plans for the week until Lisa looked at the clock and realised it was time to get ready for her morning visit to Monika. 'See you Friday then!'

What Lisa hardly dared utter was her strong suspicion that this coming Friday she would be meeting her cousin:

her half-sister Peggy's son, Monika and Brün's grandson. The thought both excited and terrified her.

Ulli had made it clear how eager he was to meet Monika. He was coming all the way from Germany for this meeting. And then it hit Lisa: if Ulli was in fact Monika's grandson, she had to be forewarned. It was time for Lisa to gently tug at the veil that had for so long hidden Monika's past.

'How is she doing today?' Lisa asked Fiona as soon as she arrived, shaking out her umbrella and unwinding her scarf as she entered the soupy warmth of the nursing home. It was cold and wet outside and everyone was predicting snow again for the weekend. It would not be the first time there had been snow on a Winter Magic Festival weekend. People flocked from Sydney whenever it began snowing in the upper mountains, so if anything it would boost the number of people attending.

'She's doing really well,' Fiona said. 'She's talking, making jokes. Even writing again. I haven't seen her this good for quite a while.'

Lisa discovered her mother writing in her notebook in the library. Most of the other residents must have decided to spend the morning in bed or in the TV room, as Monika had the sombre, bookshelf-lined room to herself.

She sat with one elbow on the heavy oak table while the other arm pivoted busily back and forth, her silver fountain pen hovering and skimming over the pages like a small bird over water. She was writing in her favourite lined notebook, the one she kept by her side at all times.

'What are you working on, Mum?' Lisa asked.

She could recall so many scenes identical to this one, repeated in endless variations, over the years of her life with Monika. How often she had seen her mother like this, eyes focused elsewhere, brow furrowed, tongue clicking against the roof of her mouth, breathing slightly rapid, as her pen raced over a page or her fingers over her keyboard. And then pausing, contemplative, with her right hand cupping her chin and her index finger resting against her cheek.

'A story,' Monika replied with a sly smile, like the cat with the proverbial cream, savouring the unique pleasure of cornering such an elusive, secretive thing. Monika was never happier than when her writing was flowing well. Sometimes, when her children had been small, she had read one of her stories out loud to them, partly to test its robustness and the music of its language but also just to see their amusement. Lisa included these among her favourite memories, these scenes of her and Tom tucked inside Monika's arms as she performed the voices of all her characters, chuckling at her own jokes and her children's peals of laughter.

'I am one of the luckiest women alive,' she had told journalists who interviewed her about her success. 'My job is my greatest love. Bringing pleasure to my readers is my greatest joy.'

Given her mother's considerable international reputation and success, one thing had always mystified Lisa. After the divorce had gone through and the Beecroft house was sold, Monika had the means to live anywhere in the world she chose. But having always made it clear how glad she was to escape her childhood, she then surprised everyone by deciding to buy a bungalow in Katoomba. 'For the quiet and solitude,' she said. But that had never convinced Lisa. There were plenty of quiet and remote spots. No, there was something else that drew her back. And Lisa wondered if she now held the key to the mystery. Brün, Monika's first love, had wanted her to live here with him. Maybe she came back for the memory of him: the young man who had loved her without compromise or betrayal. Or maybe it was the bush itself – the bush that had almost killed her when she was little and had never really let her go.

Lisa sat down and produced the box of chocolates. 'I think you've earned a cup of tea and a break,' she suggested. As if on cue, Fiona wheeled in a trolley with the makings of a nice hot cup of Earl Grey.

Monika nodded. 'I agree. Here, you should have one too.' Monika had already slipped off the ribbon and lifted the lid. She proffered the open box. A laugh escaped Lisa's lips. She studied her mother's face with disbelief. Was this the same woman she had left here two days ago? The woman who had refused her meds and wandered off to Bloome Park?

Given everything that had transpired since she last saw Monika – the night with Luke, the reading of the diary, the discovery of the fairy story and the photo, the lurid dreams

– this meeting of mother and daughter took place in a greatly altered world.

They both thanked Fiona for the tea and she withdrew with her trolley, leaving them in peace.

'I have something I want to show you, Mum,' said Lisa, pulling a package out of her bag. 'It's another story. One of yours.'

Monika smiled with mild curiosity.

'Can I read it to you?' Lisa asked.

'Why, yes. That would be nice.'

With her heart beating faster, Lisa skipped the dedication and began to read the story aloud. She devoutly hoped that Monika wouldn't feel ambushed or betrayed. She watched her mother's face as she read, alert to any signs of distress.

Monika listened closely, a half-smile on her lips. She seemed genuinely entranced. Did she recognise the story? Did she have any comprehension of what it had meant to her once?

Lisa read the final sentences: '"The bear-prince's spirit could still be heard, roaring in the woods, every winter. Within earshot of the mighty waterfall and by the banks of the new river that flowed through the Wald, Sparrow and her daughter made their home in the witch's cottage, where they lived together happily ever after."'

Monika closed her eyes and sighed. 'Fairytales always have such happy endings.'

'Do you remember this story, Mum? I found it hidden away. Inside your trunk.' There, Lisa had made her confession. The truth was out. It fluttered anxiously about the room like a bird newly freed from its cage.

Monika put down her cup of tea. She looked straight at Lisa and there was a different kind of light in her pale blue eyes. An unwavering light of understanding.

'Well, well, well,' Monika whispered. 'And what else did you find?'

'This.'

Lisa pulled out the photo of Brün and placed it on the table before her.

Monika's hand flew to her mouth. The cry she uttered expressed surprise and delight, grief and tenderness.

'Ah, my Brün, my *liebchen*. I had almost forgotten you.'

CHAPTER 31

Adam

Leura, December 1957

Adam gestured to the drinks waiter. 'Another round here, please.' He clipped his Henry Clay cigar and threw the finished tip into the fireplace. Adam's guests – his son Alan and fellow hotelier Jimmy Sparks – sat opposite in oxblood leather armchairs. Haloed in smoke, the three men puffed contentedly on their cigars and sipped tumblers of Scotland's finest single malt, both indulgences courtesy of Adam. They had gathered in the smoking lounge at the Chateau Napier in Leura to raise a toast to the coming year even though it was still only the first day of December.

'To 1958,' declared Adam when the waiter had poured a second round from Fox's precious bottle of imported whisky.

'To 1958,' the other two echoed, raising their glasses. The

present year had proved to be one of exhausting highs and lows for all three and, ever hopeful, they looked eagerly to the opportunities offered by the future.

Adam had handed the keys of the Palace to his son two years earlier. The fact was he had been enjoying life with Laura so much he was ready to let someone else worry about the hotel. Adam and Laura's marriage had weathered the crisis of his jealousy and her bitter grief over the forced adoption of Monika's baby. Now their marital fortunes prospered and thrived. As Adam surrendered his control of the business, he and Laura resumed one of their greatest passions: travel.

There had been trips to Japan, Canada, Alaska, Scandinavia, Italy and Russia, revealing more wonders than could ever sate photographer Laura's appetite for beauty. She and Adam realised they shared the collector's tireless impulse to possess the world entire, through curios and souvenirs for Adam, and pictures for Laura. He built her a darkroom at the Jersey Avenue house and ordered the best German camera bodies and lenses.

Adam's adoration and generosity knew no bounds when it came to his beloved queen. They ate and slept in first-class comfort on flights along the Kangaroo Route to London, with stops in Bombay, Tehran and Zurich. They took suites at the Savoy and the Dorchester and dined at Mirabelle in Mayfair. Now in her fifties, Laura still commanded attention in her custom-made suits and gowns by Dior, Givenchy and Balenciaga.

'You look supremely lovely tonight, my dear,' Adam would whisper in her diamond-studded ear as they made their entrance.

'You look pretty presentable yourself,' she would reply.

Adam looked around at the Napier's heavy chesterfields and armchairs, the quaint Art Nouveau reading lamps and the reproduction landscape paintings. The four-storey guesthouse, opened in 1910, had become a picture-postcard treasure like the Palace. She was a grand old dame and Adam loved her dearly. But every time he returned from overseas, the more the hotels and guesthouses of the mountains looked tired and twee, relics of a bygone era.

By the middle of the decade, it was clear that even the Palace needed to spruik herself harder than ever. She could not survive on nostalgia alone. To Adam's surprise, Alan had inherited some of his father's flair for showmanship. It was his idea to build an in-ground swimming pool with a concrete mermaid diving into the deep end, suspended for eternity inches above the water. It was also his idea to use the pool to host bathing-beauty competitions and swimsuit parades.

Adam was impressed when Cinesound sent a camera crew up to film a swimsuit fashion show at the Palace. Wearing their alluring smiles and cats-eye sunglasses and admired by a large holiday crowd, the models strutted and twirled around the pool in bathing costumes with names like 'Sweet Talker', 'Modern Miss' and 'Moulin Rouge'. The newsreel was seen by thousands of cinemagoers who chuckled when the narrator admonished, 'No wolf-whistles, please, gents. Echo Point is just around the corner and those whistles will just go on and on!'

Adam was greatly respected by the local aristocracy of business leaders. A 'tourism pioneer' they called him. He did care deeply about the survival of the Blue Mountains and generously supported new ideas. In 1953, the prime minister's wife had come to Blackheath to launch the town's inaugural Rhododendron Festival. Adam sponsored the street parade led by a district beauty, crowned as Rhododendron Queen and enthroned on a float carpeted in blossoms. The following year, thousands gathered to see another queen – recently crowned at Westminster Cathedral and now on a royal tour of Australia – as she made a half-hour stop in Katoomba, blessing the lookout platform at Echo Point with her presence.

Once upon a time, the mountains' natural beauty – its views, clean air, tranquillity and bushwalks – had been enough to lure visitors. Was it enough anymore? Nubile maidens in swimsuits and floral crowns were the latest novel attraction, but by the summer of 1957, Adam Fox and his son had serious doubts that even this was enough.

So where had everyone gone? The answer was simple: they were at the beach. Adam had watched as seven gold medals at the 1956 Melbourne Olympics gave birth to a new national hero: the swimmer. Now families packed their cars and sped along highways up and down the coast for summer holidays, staying in cheap motels and caravan parks or visiting the blue rectangles of Olympic pools dotting every suburb.

They built public pools in the mountains, too, but tried to find other good reasons for people to visit. Mel Ward moved his thirty-thousand crabs and God-knew-what-else into a long fibro shack up the road from the Palace. Tourists flocked to this eccentric Gallery of Natural History and Indigenous Arts, stuffed to the rafters with 'native curios', fossilised remains and vast collections of insects, reptiles and shells. Meanwhile Mr Harry Hammon started construction of his Skyway, a viewing cabin suspended on a steel cable over the cliffs at Katoomba Falls.

Horrie Gates' amusement park in the big gully behind Katoomba boasted fairground rides, a Ferris wheel and a 'giggle house'. But the main attraction was a Catalina Flying Boat anchored in a manmade lake; inside, 'passengers' watched aerial footage while a speedboat made choppy circles to rock the Catalina from side to side. The park folded after four years. Now Adam was excited by a new project: a motor-racing track like the one at Bathurst. He was convinced this would bring thousands of tourists to the mountains. Bulldozers had already started clearing the trees and shanty dwellings of the blackfellas who had been living in the old gully for years.

'For years!' Monika had protested loudly at a recent dinner with the family. 'That's their home. How can you allow this?' She had remonstrated with her father but the conversation had been nimbly switched to another topic.

Adam took another gulp of his whisky and studied his son. Alan was a conscientious chap but he worried far too much. It would drive him mad. All three of his children had inherited his drive and his appetite for hard work. How Adam wished he could teach them one further lesson: all the worry in the world changes nothing.

He still had a special place in his heart for Monika. She was one of the great joys of his life even when they argued.

She was still a sentimental girl in many ways, despite some tough times in her childhood. But he was immensely proud of her success as a writer. And her marriage to that smart young fellow Michael, who'd just taken up a job as a solicitor at Gordon and Hines. He seemed to have his head screwed on right. Adam knew he would always look after Monika.

They had met at her publisher's head office in North Sydney over a year ago. A member of the company's legal team, Michael Evans had dark eyes, black hair and a dimple in his chin, all of which was a promising start, improved by the fact he was also intelligent, well-read, charming and cosmopolitan. The attraction was instant on both sides. Michael invited the author out to lunch and told her, 'If we do this again, someone else will have to work on your contracts.'

When it was published last year, *Kitty Koala's Furry Adventure* had proved an instant success both critically and in the Christmas sales. Everyone fell in love with soft-hearted, scatter-brained Kitty and her bush gang, including Lottie Lyrebird and Billy Blue-Tongue. Monika had dragged her big sister from store to store to admire the displays in the windows. Neither of them could have foreseen the wave of fame that was about to carry Monika away.

Monika and Michael married in the spring. It was the high point of 1957 as far as Adam was concerned. Despite Monika's protests, Adam organised a lavish wedding at St Mary's and a reception at the Palace. 'Come on, Monz, it's not every day I have a daughter get married. You know this is the way I like to show my love. It will be a day to remember!' She hugged her father. He would never change and, as he had rightly pointed out, this was the way he showed his love.

The ceremony and reception made the social pages of all the major papers. For better or worse, the Foxes had always lived in the spotlight. Monika accepted that the wedding was inevitably going to be a piece of public theatre to impress Sydney's rich and powerful. It was all just part of being a Fox. Laura cried as Adam gave Monika away in the crowded cathedral. She rejoiced to see her daughter made strong and happy by her new love. Adam choked back tears that day too and felt truly blessed to be Monika's father.

The conversation in the smoking lounge had inevitably come round to one of the lowest points of the year. It had happened back in October and was still the talk of the mountains. A world-famous Australian archaeologist, Professor Vere Gordon Childe, had plummeted to his death from a well-known lookout. He had stayed overnight at the Carrington, and the following day caught a taxi to Govett's Leap, where he asked the driver to wait. Four hours later, the poor driver discovered a jacket and wallet on a rock alongside the path and then a hat, glasses and a compass on the ledge outside the safety fence. The professor's body was discovered at the base of the cliff. The coronial inquest made a finding of accidental death but gossip continued to insist that Childe had stage-managed this 'accident' around a well-planned suicide.

Adam knew the stories from the local police officers who drank at the Palace. Suicide was alarmingly common in the mountains. People made pilgrimages, some of them from as far away as Europe and Japan, to end their lives at the scenic lookouts, leaving shoes, bankbooks, coats, handbags, pipes and spectacles as their final calling card. Suicide was a tourist market all of its own.

'He was a communist, a spy for the Soviets,' said Jimmy confidently, blowing – in his imagination – an 'atom bomb' ring of smoke towards the ceiling. 'ASIO had been watching him for years. He knew the game was up so he took the only way out.'

Adam was not convinced but nodded politely. Jimmy was full of crank conspiracy theories. It was a symptom of the times.

'Whatever the reason, this kind of tragedy is bad for business,' said Alan, jiggling the ice in his tumbler. 'It gives people the creeps.'

'I'm not so sure,' mused Adam, staring moodily into the fireplace and feeling philosophical after his second whisky. 'When Robbie died, Adelina insisted on erecting a plaque at the lookout and I respected her wishes. I was worried it would be bad for the hotel, scare people away.'

'And did it?' Alan rarely heard his father talk about Robbie, the brother he never knew. The family ghost. To be honest, he preferred it that way.

'No, strangely enough, it did not. In fact, some people came to Sensation Point just to look at the plaque and the spot where my son fell.'

'So why is that, do you think?' Jimmy asked.

'We're all fascinated by death, I guess.' Adam shrugged. 'Especially other people's. It's the safest way to confront our own. Despite our best efforts to put the whole thing out of our minds for as long as possible.'

He patted Alan on the shoulder. 'Ah, sweet arrogance of youth! How I miss it! Not to have to contemplate the end.' He paused, then added, 'Except for that gloomy, dramatic lot, young poets and painters and the like.'

He knew that wasn't fair. In his experience, painters had given Adam some of the most exalted, life-affirming moments of his own trek from cradle to grave. He thought of Freya's watercolour of a grevillea on his study wall. He thought of her father's oil painting *The Valley*, now no more than a magnificent memory. They were assertions of life's beauty and preciousness, shouted into the dark abyss.

Adam had been thinking a great deal recently about the Blue Mountains and the fact that, despite his impulse to travel the world and bring back souvenirs, he had never wanted to live anywhere else. The appeal of this long sandstone plateau, carved by waterfalls into rugged ridges and deep valleys, was at times elusive and subtle, at others melodramatic. It drew countless people here to savour its melancholic splendour. It forced others, like him, to find reasons and ways to make the place home.

Nothing was achieved without risk and cost. The allure of the mountains had taught Adam that lesson. The place gave up its riches readily enough: its panoramas, its bracing air, its waterfalls and forests and cliffs. But it exacted a cost as well: the ever-present threat of danger. Venomous snakes and spiders. Visitors lost in the bush, vanishing without trace. Tourists falling or jumping to their death. The regular trials by fire as the bush was engulfed in flames which swept towards the townships.

Why did Adam love it so? He had no definitive answer.

The mountains offered up vistas of inspiration, horizons of wonder where the mind dared to leap and the imagination soar. It enriched the spirit, breathed hope back into the wounded heart. Yet there was always that reminder of the fall: vertigo's strange seduction that dragged you down the bright waterfall into the valley of shadow below. Mortality, failure, despair – all these must be acknowledged. Adam realised, over time, that his beloved mountains expressed the inner drama of his own soul. It was possible, even probable, others felt the same.

'By my age, of course, death becomes just a matter of time,' said Adam with a chuckle. He drained his glass. 'Another round, gents?'

Laura lay in her bed, half asleep. Adam was up at the cottage tonight so she was alone. It was still his favourite retreat: quiet, cosy, hidden away. He had been out drinking late with Alan and Jimmy Sparks at the Chateau Napier and they had then gone on to the Palace for a nightcap. He decided not to drive back to Leura. He rang her around eleven, his voice honeyed and hoarse with affection.

'I just wanted to wish you sweet dreams, my darling,' he said, apologising for the lateness of the hour and not coming home to warm their bed.

'Did you and Alan have a good time?' she asked.

'Yes, yes. He's growing into a fine young man. I'm so proud of him. I have left the Palace in good hands.'

'Night, night, Adam. Get a good night's sleep.'

'You too, my darling.'

Laura could not sleep, however. After tossing and turning for an hour, she rolled over and switched on the bedside lamp. The postcard from New York stood on her bedside table.

I love this place. I want to travel and write and never stop. Michael is the most wonderful husband anyone could wish for. My life is perfect right now. I love you, Mum. Take care.

Monika xxxxx

Laura was pleased for Monika. She and her daughter had grown closer over the last year or two. She deserved to be happy after the misery she had endured as a young woman. Fortune seemed to be smiling on Lottie as well. She had found an administrative job in an advertising agency and was dating a young man from Melbourne. There were hints of an impending engagement.

Laura thought fondly of her own honeymoon in Europe, the first of her many trips abroad, thanks to Adam. Travel had not just given Laura a wider window on the world but also an artistic calling. She loved the fact Adam took her photography so seriously.

Her skill as a photographer had made her the family archivist. It was she who took, printed, arranged and captioned the photos of family life in Moroccan leather-bound volumes. A few days earlier she had sat flicking through these albums. Photo after photo that told a story of marital harmony and carefree prosperity. Children playing games on the lawn. Captain Pogo in a pram. Adam in front of the Hudson 8. It was a true story as far as it went. She and Adam and the children had enjoyed a privileged life. But it was not the whole story. The missing faces, the shameful secrets, the life-changing events outside the photo frame, they told another story.

Would there ever be a right time to tell that story? Would these revelations ever do more good than harm? This decision required a careful and delicate calculation. Monika was making a new life as a young wife and successful writer. Lottie and Alan were making their own way in the world with bright prospects. Laura could not imagine any justification for burdening her children with a past they did not need to understand. She would keep her vow of silence.

Laura placed the postcard from Monika back on her bedside table, switched out the light and went to sleep.

There was a light rap on the window and Adam woke up. Probably a leaf blown against the glass. Except that he couldn't hear a puff of wind outside. The night was calm. He had grown accustomed to the bed at the cottage but his back was playing up, making for a night of broken sleep. He had only just drifted off again after readjusting his position to relieve the pain in his lower spine. He had also had one too many tumblers of Scotch and his head was foggy and full of broken thoughts.

Woken out of this doze, Adam swore. He decided to get up and make sure the latch was properly secure. He would not be able to relax and get back to sleep if he did not perform this ritual. He tightened the latch. Through the black square of the window pane, he saw something moving in the garden. The moon, a blue-white scimitar, was half buried in a bank of cloud so that the cottage garden was bathed in a dim light that provided little helpful detail. Even so, there was no mistaking the movement in the middle distance. A figure in white.

'Thief!' murmured Adam, his lips forming the word even before his mind had fully fleshed out any possible scenario.

According to his wristwatch it was ten minutes shy of four o'clock. He dragged on a pair of trousers and tucked in his nightshirt. The figure in the garden moved to the left, towards the hedge. It then stopped and began to move back. Adam stepped into his boots and pulled on a light jacket. He could feel a chill in the air as he opened the door of the cottage and came out onto the veranda. He picked up the hatchet that was leaning against the woodpile near the front stairs. He sincerely hoped that the intruder was not armed. He carried the hatchet more as a prop, a gesture of bravado, than a weapon.

'Hello! Who's there? Can I help you?'

Adam tried to sound businesslike, even friendly, rather than jumping straight to a tone of confrontation. He would give this stranger the benefit of the doubt. Maybe they were lost. A drunk from the hotel. A guest sleepwalking. Such things were possible. He hoped that, if it were a thief, he might have the common sense and decency to run off, saving them both an unpleasant encounter.

'Hello there!'

The figure, obscured by foliage, continued to drift to the right under the big old gums that Adam had never had the heart to chop down. He had cleared away the rest of Freya's native cottage garden but he had left this stand of Blue Mountain ash. Almost comically, Adam was irritated now that the figure did not bother to stop or slow down or respond in any way. His irritation threatened to boil over into anger. 'Hey, you! What are you doing here? What do you want?'

As Adam closed in on the stranger, the figure halted. Adam gripped the handle of the hatchet more firmly to steady his nerves. Then the mysterious figure moved off again, further under the trees. Its outline appeared to blur like a moving image in a photograph, leaving a cloud of streaky phosphorescence in its wake.

Adam stumbled forward. His heart broke into a gallop. Was he losing his mind? He did not believe in ghosts. This must be a dream, so extraordinarily vivid that he felt as if he was standing in the chill air of a summer night. He knew this familiar and, at the same time, utterly strange cottage garden where all the tortured history of his life had begun. And now – it seemed inevitable – where it would end.

The figure stepped away through the garden towards the cliffs in the distance. Adam knew it was insane but he could not resist the impulse to follow. Was it *her*? *Freya?* He whispered the name to himself. He wanted to look on her face one more time. Just like her son's. How could anyone have failed to see Freya's face in Robbie, the same fire in the eyes, the same insolent grin and intelligent brow?

Adam dropped the hatchet and staggered through the long native grass, oblivious to the rocks and overgrown stone borders under his feet. His hands clawed and his legs and thighs pressed against branches of straggling wattle and grevillea in this wilder part of the garden where the bush had pushed its way in.

'Is it you?' He realised he had spoken out loud; was this an admission of madness? He was speaking to a figment of his own mind. Did he want to confess his love, his guilt? Was this the meaning of this dream, this sleepwalk, a last chance to repent for his cruel sins? When would he wake up? Soon. Soon.

The moon emerged from behind the cloud bank. Ahead of him, Adam saw the needles of the she-oaks glisten as moonlight flooded the valley. Adam gasped to see the beauty of it. Beyond, the snaking ridgeline flamed orange and Adam caught a whiff of smoke. A path led away and down towards Sensation Point. Was this the fate intended for him, for history to repeat itself? He was sorry for the past but he refused to atone for it in this way. To follow in Robbie's footsteps. Or Adelina's. He would not give in to despair. He would turn back now. In defiance.

Adam's right boot caught on something sharp and angular in the grass underfoot. His leg twisted severely and he heard the sound of bone cracking. Dear God, the pain was excruciating. It filled his head with lightning and blood, driving a bolt of electricity through his left hip. He crashed forward, his arms flung out, falling too fast to save himself. At the last moment, before blackness mercifully swallowed up his mind, Adam saw what he had stumbled on. His lips twitched into a grim smile.

It was Robbie's memorial plaque. The marble rectangle that Adelina had hugged to her chest and that Adam had ordered be thrown away into the bush, banished from his sight, so he would not ever have to lay his eyes on it again.

Adam was unconscious when the security guard from the hotel found him the following morning, his lips blue, his face chalk-white. An ambulance took the stricken hotelier to the Blue Mountains Anzac Memorial Hospital in Katoomba, where he was rushed into the emergency department.

The doctor on duty rang Mrs Fox at her home. 'I'm afraid there's been an accident. Your husband is in a serious condition and I urge you to come to the hospital immediately.'

The meaning of this statement was clear. Laura steadied herself for a moment as the house shifted under her feet and she thought she would pass out. It was the moment she had rehearsed in her head and dreaded for a long time.

The phone rang again. It was Alan, who had just arrived at the Palace to learn the news of his father's accident from the duty manager. 'I'm coming right now. I've already rung Lottie and told to her to catch a taxi up here.'

'Thank you, Alan.'

This will be hard on the children, she thought. What a shame she should have to tell Monika in the middle of her honeymoon. But she would never be forgiven if she did not give her daughter a chance to see Adam one last time.

It is the second day of December, 1957. Just before eleven-thirty am, Laura Fox stands by the bed of her husband Adam in the emergency ward. His eyes are closed and he is as white as wax. At her side, Alan and Lottie squeeze their mother's hands in spasms of grief and affection. Adam Fox's own personal doctor, Dr Karl Hertz, arrives soon afterwards and is briefed on his patient's condition. The registrar explains that Adam has fractured his hip in an accidental fall. There has been some internal bleeding and organ damage which they are still investigating. His condition is critical but stable.

Just before lunchtime, a man runs into the emergency ward shouting, 'There's a big fire coming from North Katoomba. It's moving fast just behind the hospital and is headed for Queens Road. We may have to evacuate.'

Alan runs through the corridors to find a public phone to ring Jimmy Sparks, who lives on Queens Road, only a few streets away. Out the windows of the hospital, he can see a large plume of grey smoke, like a filthy ruffled blanket, smothering Katoomba. There's also a brassy glare, that ominous light that comes with bushfire. A large fire is out there alright, but how close is it to the town? Hard to say. Alan can't hear any sirens so it seems the brigades have not been alerted yet.

'Hi, Jimmy. Is that you?'

Alan hears a voice on the other end. It is shouting. 'I've got to go, Alan! It's coming! It's coming fast!' The line goes dead.

Alan runs back to the ward.

'We have to get back to the house. The hospital will look after Papa. But I think something big is headed towards Leura.' Laura and Lottie look at him in mute astonishment. When they get to the car park, the eerie light, thick as syrup, makes every metal surface glint like hot embers. Smoke stings their nostrils and the wind whips up dust into their eyes. As they climb into Alan's Jaguar, Laura sees the giant plume, taller than any storm front, towering over north Leura.

Alan grips the steering wheel, white-knuckled, as they head east along the highway. Several houses between Queens Road and the intersection are already on fire, smoke streaming from their roofs and eaves like blood gushing from a dying animal. A couple of homes have already had their exterior walls stripped away and they can see flames gnawing at the black skeletons of their frames.

'Dear God, it's happening! It's happening!' Laura moans over and over, as if she has imagined this cataclysm before but cannot bring herself to believe it has finally arrived. As they drive up the hill towards the intersection, a sea of flame has completely engulfed the houses along Highland Road. There are people running along the highway, girls in uniforms from the local Catholic school and nuns in their black habits, flapping absurdly in the hot wind, heading into the village of Leura itself.

As they approach the top of the hill, the familiar scenery of the town has changed into a war zone. On the north side of Leura Mall, the shops with the big 'Peters Ice Cream' advertisement on the side wall and the La Rana block of flats next door are well ablaze. Cars parked in the street are burning, oily black smoke pouring from their petrol tanks. Telegraph poles are on fire, turning black as their ceramic insulators detonate in the heat. The sky has disappeared behind a vast cloud of thick greyish-white smoke which casts a torrent of hot molten light over the whole scene.

Most shocking of all is the sight of the Chateau Napier high on the hill on the corner of the highway. As the Jaguar speeds through the intersection, everyone in the car sees flames ignite the row of cypress and radiata pine trees at the rear of the guesthouse. The trees flare like giant torches. When flames leap onto the guesthouse itself, the explosion that follows sounds like air being sucked through a tube, a great *woof* that reverberates in their ears. ('It went up like a bomb!' Lottie would say later.) They watch in horror as a bright orange ball of flame consumes the entire guesthouse and its grounds. Out of the pyre of collapsing walls and burning roof timbers, a pyramid of glowing embers is thrust into the sky, leaving the building an incandescent ruin.

Lottie is sobbing and gulping for air. Laura cannot speak. The car windows and doors are hot to the touch. Alan leans forward, trying to see through the choking smoke and blinding dust powered by high winds. 'The fire front's right behind us,' he shouts over the deafening din of flames and wind. 'It's crossing the highway.'

As the Jaguar heads towards the railway bridge, Alan sees embers starting to rain down on the Baptist church on the opposite corner. They can all hear the sirens now and see fire trucks pulling into the main street of the village.

There is chaos in the village as fire sweeps in from all directions. The Alexandra Hotel, right by the railway line opposite Leura station, is spared while the Baptist Church of Christ on the corner is burned down. The hairdressing salon, the electrician's shop, the ladies' hat shop succumb to a fire that sneaks up from the gully behind the Mall. Without warning, tongues of flame shoot out of the shopfronts, shattering the glass and driving the firemen back into the street. Flames have also caught inside the toyshop and the Presbyterian church on the next corner.

Out of the dirty, boiling cloud of smoke that overshadows the whole town, ash and cinders come raining down, a blizzard of grey snow and flaming sleet. It falls on people's hair and clothes, it gathers in the trees, starting more fires. Laura looks out the car window at the staring, stricken people, the rain of ash and cinders, the flames licking at the shopfronts. She thinks of Dresden.

In their smart woollen jackets with double pairs of brass buttons and their stiff-peaked caps, the men of the town fire brigade battle smoke inhalation and heat exhaustion. In its wisdom, the government had disbanded the local volunteer rural fire brigades two years earlier, dispensing with years of experience fighting bushfires. Instead, the defence of these villages is left in the hands of the town brigades who have never before faced a fire of this magnitude or ferocity.

Other men arrive, stripped down to their singlets with wet handkerchiefs tied across their mouths. They wrestle with long canvas hoses and strap on Indian-tank backpacks, harnessed across their shoulders, as they furiously hand-pump jets of water at the flames. Men in khaki slouch hats and open jackets thrash at burning grass, shrubs and fences with wet flour sacks and gum branches to extinguish smaller outbreaks. All around her, Laura sees people acting with tremendous courage. She thinks how sad it is that all this effort has an air of futility and manic desperation, as if swatting at some enormous fire-breathing monster.

When Alan, Laura and Lottie reach the family house in Jersey Avenue, the gum trees in the garden are already alight from embers. Laura races inside, scoops up an armful of photo albums and heads back to the car in the driveway. She makes several more of these trips. Alan has stripped off his jacket and tie and is hosing down the roof of the house and attempting to put out the fires in the gums. Embers are raining down all around him.

'What do you want me to take?' shouts Lottie, her mind buzzing with panic. She runs into her childhood bedroom and starts throwing things into a cardboard grocery carton: sports medals, a 'treasure box' she and Monika had once buried in the back garden with one of her mother's pearl earrings, a fairy costume Laura made for a school play. She suddenly remembers something and runs into the room next door, pulling objects off shelves. 'Where are they, where are they?' At last she finds what she is looking for: Monika's diaries hidden behind the bookcase. Her sister will be grateful one day that Lottie used to spy on her at night. She scoops up some more mementoes, including Mr Allsorts, Monz's favourite gollywog and her old Mary Jane with the broken buckle.

The town is so deeply enshrouded in smoke it is hard to see more than one or two blocks away. In houses up and down Jersey Avenue, women and men are ferrying armfuls of clothing, paintings, clocks, rugs, chairs, side tables, vases, whatever they deem precious, to the open boots of their cars or leaving them in disordered piles on the pavement like a series of impromptu garage sales.

Then the first explosion occurs two blocks away. A fireball lobs into the back garden of the Frenches' house on the corner.

Laura and Alan hear the screams of terror. Within minutes another fireball leaps over three houses and picks out another property, the Williamsons'. The blizzard of embers grows thicker and faster. The front fence of the Fox house is now on fire.

'We have to go!' Alan shouts at his mother and sister. It appears that the town's water supply has run dry as the water from his garden hose slows to a trickle and stops. He watches a fireball consume another house only a block away, sending out another shockwave of heat that is now past endurance.

The roar of the next fireball is deafening, as loud as the locomotives of the coal trains that rumble past the village day and night. Laura feels terror grip her whole body, crushing her chest and filling up her head with static. She screams.

'Get in the car!' shouts Alan. He is pushing her and Lottie towards the Jag. 'There's nothing we can do now!'

Alan starts the engine and backs out of the driveway. Laura looks behind her. She steels herself for what she is about to see. But nothing can prepare her for the sight of her home's destruction. The fire has punched out the windows of the old sandstone two-storey mansion and found its way inside. It flows triumphantly from room to room, pillaging with abandon, putting out its bright pennants of flame through every shattered window frame. The new writing desk in her study burns. The lawn burns, the hedge burns. The veranda where her children played hide-and-seek is submerged in fire. The pavilion by the tennis court, the scene of so many summer parties, burns. Her married life with Adam, her children, their friends, it all burns and is carried away in flame and smoke and ash.

Laura cannot speak for others who have lost their homes and businesses this day: one hundred and thirty properties destroyed in Leura in less than two hours and another forty buildings in the neighbouring village of Wentworth Falls, the worst fires in those towns' history. That night, as she stands in a hospital ward and watches her husband losing his struggle to live, Laura knows she will not rebuild her house. She will leave the mountains forever. Her life here is over. She says nothing to Adam about the fire or their home. She must bear that grief alone now, readying herself for a future without him. For the great, never-ending loneliness.

Adam stirs in the bed, his breathing laboured and his face drained of all colour. He tries to speak. She leans in close.

'Thank you,' he says.

'For what?'

'For giving me a second chance.'

He drifts away and seems to sleep. He wakes again and looks at her. He speaks to Laura for the last time.

'You look supremely lovely tonight, my dear.'

Laura touches his face. 'You look pretty presentable yourself,' she says.

CHAPTER 32

Lisa

Katoomba, June 2013

Katoomba's main street swarmed with dragons, vampires, witches and wizards in record numbers. Winter Magic, the annual winter solstice festival, was in full swing.

Lisa met Ulli at the station and escorted him up the grand driveway to the Carrington. He checked in, dropped his luggage in his room and met Lisa back downstairs in the bar.

'Are you too tired for a walk around?' she asked, mindful that he was not long off a flight from Germany.

'It's just what I need after all that time sitting on a plane!' Ulli smiled.

Lisa wondered what her friends and acquaintances in the mountains would make of Ulli. Lisa had done a double take as he came off the train, humping his backpack and wearing a beanie. Six foot three inches tall with the wiry physique of a mountaineer, he had golden-blond hair, high cheekbones and piercing blue eyes. A Nordic god. Even so, he didn't look as much like Brün as she had anticipated from her mother's description. He had, instead, the large eyes and aristocratic face of her grandmother, Laura.

Lisa and Ulli made their way through the packed crowd. Looking down the long dip of Katoomba Street, they beheld a river of brightly coloured humanity swirling noisily past rows of white-tented market stalls. The crowd was an all-day, non-stop, free-form street theatre, perfect for people-watching.

Re-enactment buffs from every era of history mingled freely with characters from every well-known sci-fi and fantasy franchise. The street buzzed with buskers, drag queens, druids, steampunk Victorians, demons, goddesses, *Star Wars* princesses and stormtroopers, Buddhist nuns, fire-eaters and flame-twirlers, monocyclists, medieval maidens, magicians, Dr Whos, ninjas, knights, mermaids, and beasts, insects and birds with painted faces, wired wings and padded tails. Everywhere one looked, people showed off the brilliance and humour of their costumes, their make-up and masks, their hats, helmets and other exotic headgear. They paraded their alternate creative selves, exhibited their inner superhero or villain. It was a carnival of the id, a communal remembering of a pagan past.

Ulli laughed. 'This is wonderful! Who would have thought such a thing possible in a small town in Australia?'

Lisa decided not to be insulted by this arguably patronising observation as there was not the slightest hint of a sneer in

Ulli's tone. He was just being honest. Who knew what view he had of Australia all the way from Stuttgart?

'I'm glad you're enjoying it,' she said.

A man with a white goatee, dressed in a pith helmet, gold-braided jacket and jodhpurs, came prancing by and stopped in front of Ulli.

'Now that, dear fellow, is a fashion crime!' he declared, waving his swagger-stick reproachfully at Ulli.

'I am sorry. I have done something wrong?' Ulli seemed a little alarmed.

'Brown jacket, faded blue jeans, Nike trainers. At Winter Magic?! I'm going to have to write you a ticket for your fashion infringement and tag you as a sartorial offender,' insisted the mock military man.

'I think it's a joke,' whispered Lisa, trying to put Ulli at his ease.

'It most certainly is not!' piped the pith-helmeted fashion policeman. Several of his colleagues, also in carnivalesque Edwardian costume, were handing out infringement notices to members of the crowd. Realising it was in jest, Ulli relaxed, even proffering a wrist for the red-and-yellow-striped 'convict' tag to be tied on.

'I'm told they call themselves the Katoomba Amusements Company,' Lisa explained as they walked on. 'Named after a madcap bunch who set up an entertainment club here decades ago. Movie theatre, roller-skating rink, all-female orchestra, roof garden. The latest in fun in 1911. Just over there.'

She pointed to the corner of Katoomba and Main streets,

where a real-estate agency now stood, a few doors down from the old Savoy cinema building.

'You seem to know a lot of local history.'

'I've started to take an interest, thanks to my friend Luke.'

Just before seven o'clock they met up with Luke for a drink at the Carrington's Art Nouveau cocktail bar. The historian seemed eager to meet the mysterious Ulli, but Lisa soon noticed that he was acting quite defensively. Thankfully, Ulli was either oblivious or extremely polite. Luke ordered another drink and knocked it back before they headed out to the front lawn to watch the fireworks. Snowflakes drifted lazily from the sky leaving a crust of ice on the street.

'Well, this is most unexpected!' Ulli caught a snowflake on his tongue. 'I thought I was coming to the tropics!'

A large crowd had gathered outside for music and dance performances on the Edwardian hotel's main balcony followed by the fireworks display from the rooftop.

'Katoomba's always had a history of merry-making,' said Luke, having to raise his voice over the hubbub of the crowd. 'Back in the 1930s, New Year's Eve was a really big deal up here. Thousands of people came and the guesthouses would compete with costumes and floats in a street parade. At midnight the trains in the station would all sound their horns and the crowd would sing "Auld Lang Syne".'

'It sounds extremely jolly,' said Ulli, nodding politely.

Lisa couldn't help smiling. Luke was being competitive with their German visitor and defensive of his own turf. She knew exactly why: he was jealous. It was silly, of course, as Ulli was probably related to her, but the sweeter and more civil this young German became, the more restless and threatened Luke appeared. Lisa wished she knew an easy way to put him out of his misery. Maybe it had been a mistake inviting him.

Above them on the hotel's balcony, members of the local Gundungarra and Darug communities performed a welcome-to-country ceremony followed by traditional dances. Bare-chested except for white handprints on their backs and shoulders, a group of eight men stamped their feet in unison and transformed their bodies and hands into fluid mimicry of birds and animals, accompanied by the deep drone of a didgeridoo and percussive beats of clap sticks. The crowd cheered and applauded. Lisa explained how welcome-to-country was standard practice for public events as a way of acknowledging an ongoing Aboriginal presence and connection.

'Every country has its difficult past to deal with, yes? So this is very impressive,' said Ulli.

Their conversation was cut short by loud cheers as the first rockets screeched from the hotel roof and exploded in crimson and silver bursts. Lisa looked around her. She was surrounded by faces of all colours, people of many cultures and faiths. Lesbians and gay men hugged and danced, fathers and mothers, dark-skinned and fair, held their children aloft on their shoulders or let them run through the forest of legs.

It was true Australia was still dealing with its difficult past. In the last two months, Lisa had learned about shocking episodes in her own family history. Stories of government-legislated and socially sanctioned cruelty that she could barely believe were true or possible. Upheavals and separations that caused needless suffering. But in this place, surrounded by these people, she felt hopeful Australians could be absolved from those past sins if they were willing. Already great changes had been achieved from one generation to the next. Perhaps, with generosity and courage, more could be done.

The jubilant mood was infectious. As the snowfall thickened and the fireworks display approached its climax, Lisa, Luke and Ulli cheered and clapped.

'It's good you came!' Lisa shouted at Ulli.

'What?' Ulli was laughing, unable to hear her over the crowd.

'I said we're glad you came!' she repeated. Even Luke nodded, a little more relaxed now as Lisa's kisses and hugs had made it perfectly clear to the good-looking German that Luke was much more than just a 'friend'.

He nodded and grinned. 'Me too! I'm glad I came.'

This strange triangle was complete. It was a scene Lisa could not even have imagined was possible weeks ago. Her life had changed, was changing. It would never be the same again.

What would happen now?

'Okay, let me show you what I've found,' said Ulli, opening his laptop. 'I know I could have just emailed you these documents. But I felt it was important we discover this link between our families face to face. If you know what I mean.'

After the fireworks, Ulli, Lisa and Luke had picked up some Thai takeaway and a couple of bottles of wine. Over dinner at the bungalow they talked about Luke's history of the Palace, which was only weeks away from a final draft. They looked at Lisa's recent photographs of the hotel as it assumed its new, young face again with the reconstruction. They looked at Ulli's rock-climbing and travel photos from his trips around the world.

As Lisa served coffee, the time came to talk about the past.

Ulli turned around his laptop so they could see the screen. It displayed a scanned handwritten letter in German.

'I never met my mother properly,' Ulli began. 'She and my father broke up soon after I was born. My father remarried and I grew up with a new mother whom I loved very much.

'But I was curious. I wanted to know about my birth mother. Who was she? I overheard conversations I was not meant to hear. I learned that even though she was called Saskia, that was not her birth name. I heard that she had been adopted into a new family. That her own birth mother came from Australia.'

Lisa's grip on Luke's hand tightened. All of this was consistent with the possibility that Ulli's mother was Monika's child, Peggy. But there were so many questions. How had she ended up in Germany? Did her new family move there? Why did she change her name?

'When my father was diagnosed this year with terminal cancer, I realised this could be my last chance. I asked him to tell me about Saskia. He did not want to tell me anything at first. He had loved Saskia very much and it wounded him to drag up the past. But I persuaded him it was time for me to know the truth.'

Lisa nodded. How true that was. Luke tightened his hold on her hand. He looked as nervous as she did.

Ulli continued. 'He told me that Saskia suffered for many years from disturbing memories. Nightmares. She was haunted by terrible things that happened in her childhood. She tried to come to terms with her suffering. But she could not. One day, when I was still a baby, she walked out the front door and vanished. She disappeared from our lives forever. All efforts to find her failed.'

Lisa was shocked. 'That's awful, Ulli. I'm so sorry.'

Ulli sighed. 'It was very hard. As a child I thought she must have left because I was bad. But at last I have stopped blaming myself, thanks to what my father told me. And then he gave me these letters which Saskia had left behind with all her other things. They are letters from Saskia's mother.'

'Saskia's mother?'

'Yes, that's right. Who was born in Australia.'

Lisa drew in her breath. This was the moment of truth. Were those letters from Monika? Had Peggy, who became Saskia, sought out her mother in Australia? Was this the story that Monika had withheld for so long?

When she had shown her mother the photo of Brün two days before, Monika had touched it like some precious long-lost treasure.

'What else do you know, Lisa?' her mother had asked.

'Bits and pieces. So little. I want to know more,' Lisa replied, still anxious about revealing too much.

Monika put down her cup of tea. She looked at Lisa with tears in her eyes. 'Perhaps you're right. My mind gives me so much trouble these days. I seem to be forgetting things.'

'You dedicated this story to Brün and Peggy,' Lisa said. 'Who's Peggy, Mum?'

Monika looked down at the table for a long time. She had become as still and quiet as a statue. Lisa waited, unsure if her mother had slipped back into her Alzheimer's fog or shut herself away. At last she heard her mother speak in a low voice. 'Peggy was my first child. They made me give her away.'

Monika wept quietly for some minutes and then recovered her composure, wiping her eyes with a tissue. 'I can't tell you this all at once. But I will, I promise. Next time.'

Lisa kissed her mother. 'Please forgive me,' she said.

'I'm the one who should ask forgiveness,' said Monika.

As Lisa left, she saw Monika pick up her pen and resume her writing.

So now the moment of truth was at hand.

'This is a letter to Saskia's mother. My grandmother. It is from her cousin in Australia. There are many of these letters. They wrote to each other often. See here: "Dear Spatzi". That was my grandmother's nickname. *Spatzi.* Sparrow.'

Lisa sat up straight. Spatzi? That made no sense at all. 'I don't understand,' she said. 'Spatzi was the friend of Laura – my grandmother – who visited her from Germany in 1936. Monika wrote about it in her diary.'

'Yes, yes.' Ulli was excited. 'That's her. She did come to Australia then. Only for a short while. She visited her cousin. Your grandmother. Here, I have a photo of them together during Spatzi's visit.'

Ulli tapped at the keyboard and a photo appeared on the screen, a grainy snapshot of two women with their arms around each other. One of them was young, perhaps twenty, with fair hair and a sweet smile. But it was the other woman who made Lisa gasp. There was no mistaking that glossy black shoulder-length hair, thick-lashed eyes, and full red lips. Her glamorous grandmother. Laura. Lisa pointed at this familiar face on the screen.

'So who's that ?' she asked Ulli.

'My grandmother's cousin. Angie.'

Angie? Had Ulli just said *Angie*? Luke looked at Lisa with undisguised shock. 'I'm sorry, Ulrich, what did you say her name was?'

'Spatzi called her Angie. I believe her real name was Angela. Angela Wood. There, you can see her signature at the bottom of the letter. She always wrote to Spatzi using that name. But in Australia everyone called her Laura. Laura Fox.'

Luke and Lisa look at each other dumbfounded. *Whatever happened to Angie, poor Angie? Whatever happened to her?* Lisa's head reeled. How could Laura and Angie be the same person? *The girl who broke your father's heart.* There must be some mistake.

'Are you alright, Lisa?' Ulli asked.

'Yes, yes. This is just . . . a bit confusing.' She laughed a little crazily. That had to be the understatement of all time. 'Please. Please, go on.'

'This is what I found out. Spatzi was born in Australia. Her real name was Greta. Her mother was Eveline, the daughter of a famous landscape painter. Wolfgang von Gettner. Eveline had a sister named Freya who also had a daughter. Angela. Angie. My grandmother's cousin. I understand Eveline married an Australian who was killed in the First World War. And then, after the war, she and her baby daughter, Greta, came to Germany and settled with Eveline's uncle in Dusseldorf.'

This was extraordinary. Lisa had been so moved by what she had learned about Freddie Wood's internment and the deportations. She had not imagined for a minute that this tragedy was possibly part of her own family history.

Lisa looked at Luke. He appeared completely flummoxed. He had checked the shipping lists that registered Mrs F. Wood and Miss A. Wood as booked on a passage from Australia for Germany. He had seen no records for Eveline or Greta. But then he had not looked for them.

Ulli continued his story. 'As she grew up, Spatzi kept in touch with her cousin Angie. Angie even came to Germany on her honeymoon with her husband. She wanted to see Eveline and Greta but she could not. So many years later Angie paid for Spatzi to visit her in Australia.'

Lisa was wide-eyed. Her mother's diary had described her: 'Spatzi, a good friend of Mama's all the way from Germany, stayed the whole week. Very pretty, lots of fun.' Lisa recalled that Adam had been away on business. Now all the familiar pieces of the jigsaw had been moved once more to tell a whole new story.

'So . . . so what happened to Spatzi?' she asked.

'Well, that is a very sad story. She met a young man, Stefan, just before the war. They married and she fell pregnant with a little girl. My mother. They named her Ingrid. Stefan went off to fight in the war and was killed. Meanwhile, Dusseldorf was heavily bombed so Eveline took Spatzi and little Ingrid and decided to seek safety somewhere else. They chose Dresden.'

Lisa gasped. Her hands flew to her mouth.

'Yes, I'm afraid so. Eveline and Spatzi were both killed in the raid, but by some miracle, Ingrid survived. She was only five years old.'

Lisa stifled a sob. She thought of her mother's diary again. She remembered poor Brün's tale of survival. She remembered Laura's distress over the story Adam read from the newspaper. When did Laura learn the fate of her aunt and cousin?

'Yes, it's hard to imagine.' Ulli sighed. 'My mother was then adopted by a family in Stuttgart where she grew up greatly loved but haunted by memories. A year later, her uncle Karl in Dusseldorf tracked her down and handed over most of her mother's belongings, which she had left behind, planning to return. These included the letters from her cousin in Australia. Angie.'

Tears were now trickling down Lisa's face. She kept shaking her head in disbelief, trying to piece together everything she knew into a different pattern.

'Trying to forget her past, Ingrid changed her name to Saskia. Strangely, though, she kept these letters of her mother's. She met and married my father, Markus, and I came along a few years later. Which makes us third cousins, I believe,' said Ulli. 'It is a very curious story, don't you think?'

'Incredible,' said Lisa. *Incredible.* 'Thank you.'

'I have only been here a few hours but I think Ingrid would have liked Australia,' said Ulli. 'I'm only sorry she never made it here like her mother did.'

Lisa and Ulli hugged. 'Thank you, thank you,' she kept saying, unable to find the right words to express the depths of her emotion.

She could not stop staring at the photo on the laptop screen. Her grandmother, Laura, with her movie-star good looks, her cryptic smile. She thought of the mermaid brooch, the gift from Laura on her twenty-first birthday. 'A gift from *my* mother.' Freya, the painter. *Angie was Laura. Laura was Angie.* How was it possible?

And then a realisation came to Lisa with shocking clarity and certainty.

Monika had known this story all along. She had held the key to this secret past the whole time. And right now she walked along a cliff edge, clutching that key in her hand, likely to miss a step at any moment and fall into an abyss of oblivion, taking the whole story of her family's past with her. One thing was clear. *That could not happen.*

CHAPTER 33

Laura
Mosman, April 1996

Laura sat at her favourite writing desk, a copy of the one she had been given by Adam as a present before the fire destroyed their home. She looked in the mirror on the other side of the apartment. At ninety-four years of age, *she* looked like the White Witch now, she laughed to herself. That name she and Freya had made up for poor Adelina.

It was ten years since Alan had died in a car crash and twelve since Monika's marriage failed. The punishment of the Foxes seemed to have no end. But why should these children, these innocents, pay the price of their parents' sins? That she could never understand. Until she realised that it was her responsibility to be honest. The past could not be forgiven if it was not known or understood.

She finally let go of the Palace after Alan's death. Adam's will had left her the sole shareholder and executor with provisions for the three children to inherit equal shares from any sale of the property, with poor Alan's share to be divided between his siblings. Lottie used her inheritance to start a dance school for kids in Chicago. Monika was able to pursue her faltering writing career in comfort as a single mother. Laura bought a nice big apartment in Mosman and lived off her investments. Nobody could accuse Adam of not providing well for his family.

Laura's heart had been torn in two by a deep grief but also a sense of liberation when she signed the papers to transfer the hotel to its new owners. They intended to appoint a well-established hotel chain to manage the property as they had no experience in running hotels. If the Palace had any future at all, then it was hopefully now in good hands. She felt she owed Adam that much.

She had been diagnosed with aggressive late-stage liver cancer six months earlier and the doctors had told her it was inoperable. She had decided to keep it secret from family and friends until the very end to spare everyone the drama. Her life had been filled with far too much of that and she wanted it to end with peace and dignity.

Her plans to slip quietly away were slightly derailed by her granddaughter's unexpected twenty-first birthday invitation. She had loved the visits from Tom and Lisa when they were little but relations with Monika had grown impossible, especially after Michael left. Ah, my dearest Monika, always so determined to be independent but so very proud and unforgiving at times.

She blamed herself too. She had interfered, given advice when it was not wanted. She had made this mistake too many times.

But going to the party was not a mistake. It was quite something to meet her grown-up granddaughter Lisa. The arts student who loved photography of all things. It was enough to make you believe in destiny. Laura smiled to herself. She recognised something of her young self in this girl. A quiet determination. An insistence on doing things her own way. It was a quality that could either be a blessing or a curse, depending on what opportunities life offered.

She had given Lisa her mermaid brooch. It was a precious thing, made by a friend of Freya's to commemorate the wonderful mural she had painted in the spa at the Palace. Freya had given it to her when she thought she was going to die from the Spanish flu in Liverpool in 1919. It was time to hand it on, a kind of baton or torch from the woman artist of one generation to the next. Laura had no need of it now.

And then her granddaughter had asked her if she loved Adam Fox. *At the end.* What a question! Asked so solemnly. It seemed vital for Lisa that she should know the truth. So Laura had told her the truth as she remembered it. Yes, she had loved Adam to the very end and he had loved her. Despite everything. And then she had let slip her secret: '*It was Angie who broke all our hearts, poor girl.*'

Angie, poor Angie. Her secret self. Left behind so long ago, it was as if she were another person altogether. Abandoned, forgotten, lost in the dark. She, Laura, had chosen a new name, a new life. She thought she could leave Angie behind.

But she found out – just as Adam had – that the past really never goes away.

So now it was time to tell her secret. At last. She would write a letter to Monika. A letter that undid the lie, set the record straight. A letter that hopefully threw some light into the shadows of Monika's own life. It would be up to Monika if she was willing to share it with Tom and Lisa. She would not interfere ever again between a mother and her child. It would be Monika's decision.

Was she a coward for doing it this way: a posthumous letter? Maybe, but it was better than no explanation at all. So Laura arranged herself at her beautiful desk and began to write.

CHAPTER 34

Monika
The Ritz, June 2013

'Did you remind her I'm bringing a visitor?' asked Lisa as they arrived at the Ritz.

'Yes. She asked me to help her get all dressed up,' said Fiona.

'Give me a few minutes first, then I'll come and get you,' said Lisa to Ulli. She had no intention of ambushing Monika. She'd dropped in the day before and sought her mother out in the library, which had virtually become her private study. Nobody else seemed to spend time there so Monika was left alone to do her writing. Lisa had explained that she had a visitor from Germany who was the grandson of Spatzi. Sparrow. He wanted to meet her.

'What did he tell you about Spatzi?' Monika asked.

'That she was a cousin to Angela Wood,' said Lisa, watching

her mother carefully. 'Freya's daughter. The painter from the cottage.'

'Ah yes. Angie. So what does he want to meet me for?'

'He has letters from Angie to Spatzi. He thought you might want to see them.'

Monika's face paled a little and her eyes misted with tears. 'I guess the time has come,' she said. 'I always knew it would. Yes, tell him to come. With the letters.'

So Monika was expecting Ulli's visit today and, Lisa saw, had put on her best silk blouse, dark skirt, smart jacket, make-up, pearls, stockings. Fiona had brushed her grey hair into a tight shiny knot that made her look aristocratic rather than grim.

'Of course I'm ready,' she said when Lisa enquired, with a touch of her old impatience. 'Don't be silly.'

They sat down with cups of tea and an extra large box of chocolates which Ulli had brought as a gift. Lisa could tell Monika was quite taken with the young German's good looks and manners. She had not seen her mother so animated for as long as she could remember.

Ulli told the story of his mother, Saskia, and his grandmother, Spatzi. Monika sat and listened with close attention. And then he mentioned Angie. He asked Monika if she wanted to see a photograph. She nodded. The photo came up on the screen. She sighed and nodded again.

'So, there she is,' said Monika. She looked at her mother with an odd mix of fondness that struggled with a note of bitter sadness. 'Her secret is out. It is what she would have wanted.' She put down her cup. 'She was quite something, that Angie.

The beauty, the actress. Made herself up like a character from a book. It takes courage to be a writer. To invent a person out of nothing. But it takes something else to invent *yourself*.'

Monika picked up her notebook, the one she had been writing in for the last week or so. The one she locked in her bedside drawer every night. That never left her sight. She opened it to the last page and pulled out an envelope, tired and worn. With hands that shook slightly she unfolded a letter and handed it to Lisa.

'It is from your grandmother. She wrote it just before she died. Perhaps I should have shown it to you before. I didn't know what was the right thing to do. Now you've made that choice for me.'

Lisa took the delicate onion-skinned paper in her hands. The handwriting was strong and clear and in dark fountain-pen ink that had not faded. She began to read aloud:

My darling Monz,

I am no writer like you, my clever daughter, so I ask you to forgive any failings of style in this letter. What I am about to tell you does not require much style. It is simply the story of a girl who decided to change her life without realising the cost to herself or others. I do not ask for your forgiveness for what I did; that would be too much to expect. But I hope you will forgive me for telling it to you now I am gone. I have thought about this a great deal and finally I decided it was better this way.

I am and always will be your mother. Who gave birth to

you and raised you and loved you with a fierce and unfaltering love. Still do, as I draw breath. Nothing in this story changes that fundamental truth.

For years during and after the Great War, the schoolchildren in Meadow Springs sang a playground song: 'Whatever happened to Angie, poor Angie? Whatever happened to her? She loved a boy as rich as rich though he did not love her.'

I am the answer to that song, my darling. My real name is not Laura. I was born Angela Wood and for most of my childhood I was called Angie. I am the girl from the cottage next door to the Palace, the daughter of Freya von Gettner and Freddie Wood. You have heard stories about me, of course: stories that have been told in the village for years. That I was in love with Adam Fox's first son, Robbie, and that on his thirteenth birthday I led him down to Sensation Point where he fell to his death.

That story is true. I did love Robbie even though I was only eleven and he was only thirteen. It is easy to mistake intense secret friendship for love when you are that young. What I truly loved was the Palace. I spent most of my childhood dreaming of being part of that forbidden world. It was a world that had once belonged to my mother, before her father lost his fortune. It was a world I felt entitled to but for a cruel twist of fate. My mother shared my sense of entitlement. Robbie was going to be my ticket to that world. When he died, my dream died with him.

When I was nearly seventeen, I found out that Robbie was in fact Freya and Adam Fox's son – my half-brother.

Lisa gasped and looked at her mother in astonishment. Monika nodded.

When Adam was building his hotel, he and Freya had a passionate affair. She fell pregnant. Adam arranged for Robbie to be raised as his and Adelina's son. This secret was a burden that Freya carried for years and one that I watched tear away at her soul.

You may understand now why I wanted us to adopt your baby girl and bring her up as our own. Because I had seen the cost of giving away a child. I had seen what it does to a mother. Twice Adam arranged for a woman he loved to give up her baby: first Freya and then you, his own daughter. Men have no idea what it is to make that kind of sacrifice or they would never allow it. I don't think Freya ever forgave Adam for abandoning her the way he did. For betraying their love.

'Good God! So that's what happened,' exclaimed Lisa, shaking her head. She and Luke had strayed close to the truth, even suspecting that Angie was Adam's illegitimate daughter, but never for a moment thinking of Robbie. Monika's eyes glistened brightly. 'So much to learn,' she sighed. 'Too late.'

Lisa read on:

In the meantime, Freddie Wood had fallen in love with Freya and, alone and heartbroken, she accepted his proposal of marriage. Soon afterwards I was born. My family paid a heavy price for Robbie's death. And we paid an even higher one for being German when the war came. I still believe Adam did his best to protect us from the hatred of people we thought we could trust. He frightened off an angry mob who burned the hotel's German piano and wanted to hurt me and Freddie. But he could not stop the military taking my father away to a camp.

My mother believed to her dying day that Adam used that hatred of our family to his advantage. With Freddie interned, Freya and I were poor and alone. Freya sold Adam the last painting of my grandfather's so she would not have to sell the title to her cottage. In the end, Adam took the painting and the cottage. He wanted us to disappear so he could wipe away the pain of Robbie's death, to make poor Adelina happy and erase his own guilt.

What changed everything for me was when my mother nearly died from the Spanish flu in Liverpool. My father was about to be deported to Germany. My best friend, Astrid, was dying and Oskar, the German boy I loved – like your Brün – was also to be deported with his family. I was alone. When Freya recovered, she told me the truth about Robbie. I realised then I would do anything she asked of me.

Freya had plans to get our cottage back. It meant she and I would have to stay in Australia for a while longer and we would act secretly, in the shadows. Poor Freddie would have to wait for us. Aunty Eveline and baby Greta, who had no future here, took our places on the boat to Germany, their passage paid for by the government. They joined Freddie in Dusseldorf with our relatives there. It required forgery of birth and marriage certificates so they became Mrs Freya and Miss Angela Wood, all easily done with help from Uncle Karl's printing works and my mother's exceptional artistic skill. I learned that all talented painters make talented forgers.

That explained the names on the shipping list, thought Lisa. She imagined Freya hoped to bring them all home to Australia once she got her cottage and land back. If that failed, presumably she and Angie had intended to go to Germany to join Freddie, Eveline and Greta.

Having failed to win back the cottage by legal means, Freya knew the only way to change Adam's mind was through Adelina. She was the key. Adelina would persuade Adam he should give back the cottage. Through his devotion and sense of duty to his wife, we would unlock whatever decency there was left in Adam Fox in order that he make amends for the past and surrender the cottage.

We had two allies in this plan. The first was Jane Blunt, the ex-governess who hated Adelina for sacking her and felt sorry for me and Freya. Since leaving the Foxes, Jane had become a well-known medium in the mountains under the name of Vera Glanville-Smith. She lived in a remote cottage at Mount Victoria, and it was here that my mother and I hid ourselves away. The second was my devoted childhood protector from school, Simon Rushworth. Since leaving school, this gentle and clever fellow had begun an apprenticeship as assistant to postcard photographer Harry Phillips.

When we learned about the visit of Sir Arthur Conan Doyle to the Palace, the timing was perfect. Miss Vera Glanville-Smith sowed the idea of a séance in the mind of the head housekeeper, Mrs Wells, who we knew had introduced Adelina to Spiritualism. Vera Glanville-Smith then staged a séance in which the spirit of Robbie demanded that Adelina 'forgive'. A copy of the postcard that I had shown Robbie the day of his death was used to unsettle Adam and Adelina. Late at night in Harry Phillips' studio, Simon made the 'spirit' photos of Robbie that Mrs Wells gave to Adelina.

We sincerely hoped the séance and photos would be provocation enough to change Adelina's mind about the cottage and she would persuade Adam to give them back. We waited and waited but with no results. So we decided to take the next step.

Everyone knew a film was going to be shot around the mountains, including at the Palace. The director was hiring locals for small roles as cast and crew. Simon got a job as a runner and introduced me to Mr Longford. My appearance had changed a great deal since leaving Meadow Springs and there was no one at the hotel who had laid eyes on me since I was eleven. With my new name, Laura, I was soon working on the film and Simon and I were both accommodated inside the Palace.

Here, Simon and I executed our boldest plan. With leftover ends of film stock, Simon filmed a boy dressed up as Robbie. We projected this onto a column of dry ice in the hotel, convincing guests, Mrs Wells and later Adelina that they saw a ghost. It was the same trick Mr Longford had used for the 'Spider's Web' dance in his film.

Adelina was so moved by the sight of Robbie that I feared she might lose her mind. I persuaded Freya that one haunting was enough. We would achieve nothing by driving Adelina mad. The message from Robbie was clear: 'make things right'. We were convinced Adelina would now persuade Adam to give back the cottage. The plan might well have worked, but Adam would not be moved.

And there was one other complication no one had counted on. Adam began to fall in love with 'Laura', the girl who didn't exist. It all started as harmless flirting at first and I played along so as not to arouse suspicion. I even hoped I could use this turn of events to our advantage: to learn more about what Adam thought and to influence him if possible. He talked to me of his plans to tear down the cottage and extend the hotel. I told him he must never destroy such a sweet place.

As I realised his feelings towards me were becoming more serious, I dared not tell Freya for fear of breaking her heart. Imagine her sense of betrayal! I only hoped our plot to get back the cottage would be successful and I would be able to cast off my disguise and vanish into thin air. If that broke Adam Fox's heart, so be it!

Freya had one other plan up her sleeve. To threaten to expose as a forgery the von Gettner painting Adam had stolen from her. The only problem was she and Jane Blunt had the forged copy of the painting hidden in the cottage. They had to sneak inside the new art gallery Adam had built and substitute it for the real painting on the wall. I asked Adam to show me around his new gallery, and as he did I turned off the alarms and left the external door unlocked so Freya and Jane could enter.

Lisa felt tears pricking at her eyes. She knew how this part of the story turned out from Jane Blunt's letter to Angie. How poor Freya's plan for revenge killed her.

This plan too went horribly wrong. Adelina wandered the hotel that night looking for her son's ghost and discovered my mother and Jane inside the gallery. She startled my mother, who upset a kerosene lamp and caused a fire to break out. The original painting was saved, Jane later told me, but my mother perished, all her plans in ruins. Now you will understand why Adam's igniting a cake in the shape of the hotel upset me so much all those years later at his birthday party. I still have nightmares about Freya's death.

As you know, Adelina committed suicide on the night of the fire. Because of the séance's prophecy? Out of grief for her son? Her husband's infidelity? I do not know. Did I feel guilty? Yes, I did, and that guilt grew over the years as I became a wife and mother. But also, no. She spared my family no kindness or mercy when I was a girl accused of killing Robbie and when we were driven from our property during the war.

Back in Germany, my poor father, already a broken man from his time in the internment camp, was crushed by the news of Freya's death. He died of a heart attack soon afterwards. I was now all alone in the world. I could have asked for Uncle Karl's help, I suppose, and made my way to Germany to be with Eveline and Greta. But Adam Fox had fallen in love with me – with the woman I pretended to be. And that was when Adam proposed marriage.

'Good God! This is one of the strangest stories I've ever heard!' Ulli looked at Lisa and Monika in amazement. His face was ashen with emotion. 'That poor girl!'

'Yes, that poor girl,' echoed Lisa, unable to imagine what she would have done at age nineteen faced with the same choices.

Here was a strange dilemma. My mother had been Adam's true love and he had thrown her over for the sake of his respectable marriage and his magnificent hotel. She had borne him a son, my half-brother Robbie, who would have been the heir to the Palace had he not died. And here was Adam asking me, Robbie's half-sister, to be Mrs Fox. Handing me my childhood dream on a plate. Perverse as it sounds, it felt like destiny.

I was the only member left in Australia of those clever von Gettners, the family who did whatever it took to survive. I was being offered the chance to make a new life. My mother had been forced to lie about her own child. My own childhood had been rewritten because of that lie. Freya and I had woven an elaborate web of lies to catch Adam. Becoming Laura Fox would be the most ambitious, the most monstrous lie of all.

But with this lie, I would save the cottage. I would become the queen of the Palace that neither Freya nor Adelina had ever been. My children – Freya's grandchildren, Wolfgang's great-grandchildren – would have the life that had been so unfairly taken from Freya and Wolfgang. I would avenge my mother's death by taking her rightful place, having the life Adam should have given her. That is what I told myself when I said 'yes'.

Some might think it strange I could love a man like Adam. I confess at first my love was more about the Palace and everything it offered. But your father was not a monster. He was no saint either. He was charming and passionate and devoted. Eventually I fell in love with the best qualities of the man himself. Generous, funny, imaginative, daring. He was a loving father too. You, Lottie and Alan know that. We managed to make a happy life together, a good and exciting life.

'Are you okay, Mum?' asked Lisa, as her mother dabbed at her eyes with a handkerchief.

Monika nodded. 'Yes, yes. I know the contents of this letter off by heart.'

So what went wrong? I could not forget about the past. When Adam suggested we go to Germany for our honeymoon, it seemed as if God was playing a cruel joke. Freddie had died just two months earlier in Dusseldorf. I wanted to see Aunty Eveline and my cousin Greta, little Spatzi, but there was no opportunity to do so. We wrote to each other for years. Adam was generous with gifts and money, so I sent Eveline and Spatzi help whenever I could manage it.

I saved up enough to pay for a passage by ship for Spatzi to visit me while Adam was away on business in 1936. She had grown into such a beautiful young woman and had fallen in love with a 'junge' *called Stefan. They wanted to marry but his parents did not approve of a* 'fremde', *a foreign-born, non-German. The injustice of this prejudice, given the deportation of thousands of 'Germans' from Australia, defied words.*

Spatzi and I spent a wonderful eight days together, talking about the past and her future. She adored you children. Do you remember her? How I wished she had been able to stay. Especially given how things turned out.

I thought I had made my peace with my life and with Adam. But then the second war with Germany broke out. So many bad memories came flooding back. German Australians were interned again and here was I, living a lie, safe from hatred. I fretted terribly for Eveline and Spatzi. I even began to think about Oskar, my childhood sweetheart, who I had not heard from since his family was deported.

When I began working as a VAD nurse, I met a doctor at the American military hospital that took over the Palace. His name was Frederick, the same as my father. And he told me his secret: that his grandparents were German migrants to the USA, something he had managed to keep quiet so he could enlist. Your father had become withdrawn with the closing of the hotel. I was lonely and troubled by the fate of my family back in Germany. Frederick and I did not become lovers but we shared something intensely private and painful: the burden of a secret past.

Lisa glanced at Monika. Little Monz, the trespasser at the hospital, had imagined a love affair between this man and her own mother. The fear of its discovery had filled pages of her diary.

Frederick promised to help me get letters to my family in Dusseldorf. There were US Army mail channels that went through Switzerland, where the von Gettners had sympathetic friends who were willing to forward mail. The letters from Dusseldorf were infrequent and heavily censored but they were better than silence. I read that Stefan defied his parents. He and Spatzi married and she was expecting. Love flourished in the midst of war. I even wondered if the Red Cross might be able to track down Oskar, my long-lost sweetheart, who I knew would be fighting somewhere. It was absurd but I was convinced he would not be dead; maybe he was a prisoner-of-war. I thought about Freya a lot. I wished she was alive to see her grandchildren.

Adam was convinced I had a lover of course and that all the letters I was writing were to him – which was why he lost his mind and split my desk open with an axe to discover my secret. We drifted apart and, yes, there were times I did hate him for what he had done to my family. That part of me that blamed him for Freddie and Freya's suffering had been buried for so long. It all came to a head when I received a letter from Dusseldorf in July 1946. It had taken months to reach me. The letter said that Eveline, Spatzi and her child Ingrid had fled to Dresden to escape the bombing. Eveline and Spatzi were both killed in the firestorm. I blamed Adam for their deaths. Ingrid survived – now the only living link to my family.

This all happened around the time you and Brün fell in love. I felt as if the past would never let me go. My own daughter had fallen in love with a young German boy. And then you fell pregnant. Difficult as this was, I seized it as a chance to make amends, to heal the wounds of the past. To save an unwanted child rather than give it away. To openly embrace a German family in Australia without shame.

But Adam would not permit this to happen. I did hate him then and I slid into suppressed rage and depression. I let you and your baby down and I will never forgive myself for that. I thought about ending it all then, one way or another. Divorce, death. But I knew how it felt to be alone and terrified in the world, to have my family torn apart. And I swore I would not let that happen to my children.

Lisa wiped the tears from her eyes so she could continue to read. Her voice was hoarse with emotion but she was determined to finish the letter.

The war ended. Alan took over the hotel. I tried to find out more about Ingrid, the little girl who had survived Dresden.

But I had no luck. And then I made a decision. There had to be an end to mourning the dead: Freya, Freddie, Eveline, Spatzi. I owed it to my children and my marriage to find a way back from this despair. I had to forgive Adam. My mother had not been able to do this and it had killed her.

Adam and I did find each other again and the next ten years of our life together were genuinely happy. And then fate decided the slate should be wiped clean. Adam had the accident in the cottage garden that ended his life. And the fires came and picked out our home for destruction, leaving houses untouched on either side. It felt like God's judgement.

I have lived a lie. It is time for that lie to end. And so I have written you this letter. I started out pretending to be someone I was not. But my love for you, my children, and for my husband was real. Is real. I have truly become Laura, Adam Fox's wife and your mother. I lived and I die as Laura Fox.

I leave it up to you to choose whom you share this letter with now I am gone.

With all my love,

Mum

Lisa put down the last page of the letter and looked up at Monika.

Her face was streaked with tears. But she was smiling and nodding. She seemed to be proud of her remarkable mother.

'Quite something that Angie,' she said.

EPILOGUE

Lisa
October 2013

Lisa had rung Tom the night of her visit to the Ritz and the reading of the letter from Angie. Monika had allowed her to photocopy the tissue-thin paper and Lisa then scanned and sent it to Tom.

'Well, how do you feel?' he asked her when she had finished telling him about Brün and Peggy. And Ulrich and Ingrid. And Laura and Angie.

'I don't know yet,' she said. 'It will take some time to sink in. But overall, I feel . . . amazed. Amazed to be part of such an extraordinary family.'

'Yes, that much is true.' Tom laughed. 'Not always a good thing, necessarily. But amazing.'

'Yes.' Lisa understood what he meant. They had both paid

dearly for this dramatic legacy of silence and secrets. It was something at least to understand what had made Monika such a distant, injured mother, unable to love them fully. But it was another thing to let go of childhood pain and self-blame. That would come but it would take time.

'How *is* Mum?' Tom asked.

'She's different,' said Lisa. 'It's hard to explain. She looks at me with real curiosity. She asks me things about my life. I actually feel closer to her than I could have ever thought possible. I only wish it would last. I even introduced her to Luke.'

'Ah, yes, Luke! Now when do we get to meet him?' asked Tom.

'When you bring Natalie and the kids up for the party the owners are throwing at the Palace in October. It's kind of a celebration of their progress. Very exclusive. They've invited all the Foxes. Make sure you put it in the diary. They'll even put you all up in the hotel for free.'

'Well that's a date, I guess,' said Tom. 'I look forward to it.'

Monika arrived in the black limousine which had collected her from the Ritz, much to the surprise of the staff and fellow residents. She had 'dressed up' for the occasion in a frock in crimson and grey, a light silk shawl in mercury silver with delicate drop earrings and a pearl necklace. She waved at the flashing cameras as she exited the car with her father's beautiful wooden cane in one hand to support her and Luke

Davis holding her other arm, beaming from ear to ear. He and Lisa had pulled off a miracle: they had persuaded Monika Fox to come back to the Palace after fifty-six years.

A hot dry wind whipped up willy-willies of dust and tiny chips of gravel as men in their suits and women in their hats and finery made their way from the car park to the entrance. There was talk of a bushfire burning out of control out past Lithgow, heading towards Mount Victoria and the Grose Valley. It was unseasonally early for a fire incident and there were good reasons to be vigilant as the bush was very dry with a big spike in temperatures and drop in humidity. But there was no cause for panic.

Nothing was going to spoil today's party, thought Lisa as she watched her mother walk up the front stairs. The first stage of the refurbished hotel was a revelation. The main casino building, the lobby and the conservatory had been given a complete facelift, the stunning recreations of the original colour schemes paired with fresh modern touches in the furnishings and artworks. Lisa loved these adaptations and the overall ambience of grandeur, light and space. She studied Monika's face as she entered the lobby. Her mother looked around in astonishment. Her face lit up with delight. Adam Fox would have been as pleased as punch to see his hotel restored to a state that won such an approving smile from his Monz.

Lisa had been away on commercial photo shoots for the last six weeks so she was pleasantly surprised at how much the hotel had progressed for the celebration. She had also been busy preparing for an exhibition of photos about the Palace and the Fox family that was to be held at the State Library of New South Wales. It would be guest curated by Luke. She was still working with him on a final selection and was looking for an image that would make a fitting closing statement. She had brought her cameras with her, of course. It was not every day that Monika, Tom and Lisa were in the same room, let alone at the resurrection of the family's famous hotel.

A model of the entire project was mounted on a table in the middle of the lobby. A crowd had gathered around to play with the interactive display buttons that illuminated areas of the proposed development with artist's impressions, film clips with music and effects, fly-throughs of the interiors made startlingly vivid with CGI animations, and photos of historical objects that had been found on the building site.

In the long curving expanse of the conservatory, a generous buffet luncheon had been laid out on white damask-covered tables along the interior wall with ice carvings of the Palace logo, a modernised version of the original scrolled P that had graced all the hotel's cutlery in the early days. A line of waiters in smart white Edwardian jackets with brass buttons stood to attention by the picture windows with trays of champagne flutes and cocktail glasses.

Lisa could not believe this was the same room where she had eaten a bowl of ice-cream when she was six, surrounded by a coachload of retirees in anoraks and cardigans. The ornate cream plaster ceiling had been re-created with exquisite attention to detail but also luscious new highlights of gold, aqua, pistachio and coral for the roses, cornices and friezes.

The magnificent floral carpet underfoot was glossy perfection with its thick fairytale forest of rose brambles, all its buds, leaves, thorns and blossoms in buttercup yellow and carnation red on a dark field of navy blue.

Tom stood nervously with his family at the other side of the room. Monika approached him slowly. Lisa had warned him that their mother had slipped backwards over the last month, the Alzheimer's taking its usual zigzag, but inevitably downward, path. He must not be unduly distressed if she had trouble recognising him or Natalie and the kids. It had been over two years since they had last laid eyes on each other.

'Tom?' Monika whispered, her eyes sparkling with tears as she approached.

'Mum?'

They hugged and kissed. Monika beamed at her daughter-in-law and grandchildren. Lisa could not have wished for more.

The other guests gradually took chairs at the front of the room. They included the heritage architects, business associates of the owners, academic consultants from the University of Western Sydney, journalists, photographers, the mayor and other local dignitaries. There were several speeches. Luke said a few words about his official history and then introduced Monika Fox. The audience burst into warm applause as she made her way to the lectern with Lisa at her side.

'I am very proud to be here today,' said Monika looking down at her notes, her voice a little shaky at first but quickly settling into an easy, light tempo. The professional writer's mastery of words and love of an audience had overcome any nerves. Even the shadow of her stroke and Alzheimer's seemed banished today.

'My father had a good sense of humour, as some of you may know. He knew what the wags called his extravagant hotel in the bush. He even joked about putting a sign out the front: "Fox's Folly. Lunatics Welcome at Discount Rates. Breakfast Included." He was the kind of man who liked to prove other people wrong. He watched his hotel boom through the good times and struggle through the bad, wondering if the sceptics would have the final say.

'Well, I can reassure you that if my father was alive today to see what you have achieved in this new incarnation of his vision, he would be the first to raise a glass and say: "Three cheers for Fox's Folly. Long may she live!"'

There was much laughter and a big round of applause. Monika and the mayor were then handed a pair of golden scissors and together they cut the red ribbon strung across the doorway between the conservatory and the casino. The mayor announced: 'I declare stage one of the Palace open!' Cameras clicked madly and the crowd applauded again. Guests were then invited to mingle and enjoy drinks and food.

Lisa and Tom smiled at each other as people came up to get their official programs autographed by Monika Fox.

'Remind you of anything?' said Lisa.

'Oh yes.' Tom nodded.

'Wait, wait, I want these two in the photo as well,' protested Monika, grabbing Lisa's hand as a press photographer assembled several VIPs for a publicity shot in the casino.

Sunlight poured through the overhead dome and stained-glass windows, illuminating the brilliant white walls and columns in sharp contrast with the black lacquered woodwork and charcoal Art Deco carpet.

Lisa could not have felt happier as she stood with her arms around her brother and mother and smiled for the camera. Not all the sadness of the past could be healed overnight but this family reunion was an astonishing first step. For her and Tom. And for Monika, too. To stand up in public and speak with pride about Adam Fox meant she must have forgiven her father a little.

The clink of champagne glasses, the chatter of voices and bright bubbles of laughter, the polite nods and smiles of the wait staff . . . this scene, played out countless times in these rooms, seemed to have revived the soul of this elegant old hotel, reborn to inspire delight and pleasure once more just as Adam Fox intended.

The past was acknowledged in other ways, too.

'The owners have agreed to include an art gallery in the hotel,' Luke had informed Lisa that morning. 'It will be called the Von Gettner Wing, featuring a work by Wolfgang, sketches and paintings by Freya, and family photographs by Laura. And your photographs of the hotel too, if you agree. Four generations of talent in one place. My idea.'

Lisa was overjoyed. She kissed her clever historian passionately to show her appreciation.

There remained only one ghost still not laid to rest at this banquet. Peggy. Lisa thought about her half-sister nearly every day, hoping that somewhere, out there in the world, Peggy had found a fulfilling, happy life. It seemed fitting that this act of remembrance had now been passed on to Lisa. In the last few weeks, Monika's mind had started to drift again, letting go of Peggy and all the painful memories of her past.

Lisa heard a sharp bang from another room. She looked at Luke. 'What was that?' A gust had slammed a door shut. The wind was rising outside. Through the giant picture windows, Lisa could see the canopy of the gums in the valley beginning to toss violently like waves in a storm-lashed sea.

Lisa's breath caught in her throat. In the far distance, over the purple ridge at the far end of the valley, she saw the grey haze of smoke on the horizon.

Mobile phones started ringing in the crowd around her. She heard urgent, hushed conversations and saw people's faces grow agitated or gravely still.

Tom came over with Luke at his side. 'It looks like the Lithgow fire has broken containment lines and is heading towards Mount Victoria. They say it could cross into this valley.'

'I think it already has.' Lisa pointed to the distant haze that was rapidly darkening and solidifying into a cumulus of smoke. 'We should think about getting Monika back to the Ritz. Who knows how quickly that fire is moving?'

'What do you want to do?' Luke asked Tom. Tom and his family had driven up from Canberra the day before and were among the few guests who had been given rooms in the half-finished hotel.

'We'll be fine here for now, thanks, Luke,' said Tom, who had lived through the 2003 fires in Canberra. 'If they ask us to evacuate, we'll make a move then.'

The wail of sirens was audible in the distance, no doubt fire trucks heading up the highway to Mount Victoria. Lisa saw the mayor in a huddle with his deputy, another councillor and the council's communications manager, all on their phones. They looked sombre. It appeared events were moving fast and in the wrong direction. The official party shook hands with the hotel owners and made a quick exit.

The sky over the valley was a dirty yellowish-grey. That telltale bushfire light suffused everything with its queasy, yellow glare. More sirens screamed up the highway and the buzz of helicopter rotors came chopping through the air overhead.

'Mum, are you okay?'

Lisa noticed Monika looking flustered as people began drifting away, preoccupied with their phones. Half-empty champagne flutes sat next to abandoned plates of finger food.

'What's happening?' she asked.

'There's a bushfire heading towards Mount Victoria. People are a bit concerned.'

'Well, we'll be perfectly safe here, won't we?' said Monika.

Luke had told Lisa that the hotel was fitted with the most sophisticated anti-bushfire technology available. Triple-glazed windows with metal shutters. Giant underground tanks. Roof-mounted spray systems that threw a curtain of water over the entire building. Lisa nodded. 'We'll be fine for now, I guess.'

'They're about to close the highway at Mount Victoria,' they heard someone call out. The last few guests began shaking hands, patting shoulders, wishing each other 'good luck' and heading towards their cars.

'Well, I'm not leaving my family,' Monika said. 'I'm staying right here with you and Tom.' She found a nearby chair to sit in.

'Okay,' said Lisa, 'I'll be right back.'

Natalie kindly brought Monika a plate of food and sat with her.

Lisa found Luke standing by the windows of the conservatory.

'That fire is coming right this way. Who knows how far ahead it will start spotting?' said Luke.

With winds gusting up to ninety kilometres per hour, embers could be carried a long way ahead of the fire front, starting spot fires anywhere. They could both see the towering smoke clouds gathering menacingly over the valley and heard the wind and sirens reaching a new crescendo of urgency outside.

'Today of all days. Long live Fox's Folly, eh?' Luke shook his head in disbelief. 'I hope I don't have to write another chapter about this poor bloody hotel.'

'The story never ends,' said Lisa. She tucked herself in close to him and placed her right hand on the nape of his neck, stroking it gently.

'Let's just hope you're right.' He turned and took her in his arms then and kissed her tenderly. 'For you and me, Lisa, I hope it's just the beginning.'

'Luke?' Lisa looked at him curiously.

'I love you,' he whispered in her ear. 'I want to spend my life with you.'

'That's what I want too,' she said.

'Sorry to interrupt,' said Tom, 'but the fire brigades are here in force. They want us to move our cars away from the hotel.'

Over the next two hours the firefront made its steady progress. Through the picture windows of the conservatory, the Foxes had ringside seats for the coming conflagration. They watched the choppers make their runs with their belly buckets swinging, cheering as plumes of white water cascaded into the treetops. The sky grew darker and the sirens louder as the fire moved towards them.

'Embers are landing in the garden!' called out Tom. Lisa was outside taking photos from the terrace, making sure to stay well away from the firies who had set up three trucks on the road in front of the hotel. She had heard reports that nine houses in Mount Victoria had been destroyed despite intense efforts to save them.

Lisa ran to the front of the hotel where Luke stood in the gravel driveway near the big hedge. Burning gum leaves, their curled edges glowing red hot, rained down onto the drive and the lawn. The air was almost too hot to breathe.

A gum tree exploded on the far side of the hedge, its canopy bursting into a giant torch flame. 'Over here! Over here!!' screamed Lisa.

Firies started running towards the door in the hedge.

'Get hoses in there!' shouted one of the fire captains. He looked at Lisa and Luke. 'You two, back inside!'

The wind was gusting ferociously, carrying a blizzard of sparks, dust, smoke and debris. Smoke poured from the hedge and Lisa saw flames licking at its innards. It was lost; fire would consume it hungrily in no time at all. She began taking photos, pulling her jacket over her head to protect herself from embers.

'Get back inside!' shouted the fire captain. 'It's too dangerous!'

'Just one more minute,' pleaded Lisa. The white pylons of Blue Mountain ash in the cottage garden were burning brightly. This was her story, her life, her past.

'Lisa! Lisa!' It was Luke, waving at her urgently. 'Come back!'

Under the onslaught of the giant wind, the cottage groaned, threatening to lift off its foundations. There was a crack as sharp as a rifle shot and the building screamed in pain. With a loud popping sound like a round of machine-gun fire, the corrugated-iron roof peeled back, spitting out its nails like old teeth. Lisa heard the shattering of window glass, the splintering of wood. Embers began their deadly work inside, flames blossoming within seconds.

And then she saw it. Propped up inside the roof rafters of the cottage, a bright rectangle of colour, an epiphany of beauty, its canvas wrappings falling away. Lisa knew immediately what it was: *The Valley*. Wolfgang von Gettner's final painting. The original. Returned to 'where it belongs' just as Jane Blunt had told Angie in her letter. And in her wisdom, Angie had chosen to leave it there, the painting that had brought such joy to Adam Fox but such suffering to her and Freya.

'Dear God!' cried Lisa as she took photo after photo. She watched the hidden masterpiece burn like the valley it portrayed.

Behind her, a curtain of water fell with a crash in front of the Palace. She heard the thunder of the hoses from the fire trucks.

She knew the hotel would be saved but the cottage would be sacrificed. Her eyes blurred with tears for its passing but she also felt a sense of rightness. Of relief.

Angie's story was ended. Angie, poor Angie, who broke all our hearts.

ACKNOWLEDGEMENTS

While *Palace of Tears* is a work of fiction, parts of its story are inspired by the intriguing history of the Hydro Majestic hotel in the Blue Mountains. I have dramatically adapted historic events such as its opening in a snowstorm, a visit in 1921 by Sir Arthur Conan Doyle, the filming of *The Blue Mountains Mystery*, a fire that destroyed the gallery, and its wartime conversion to a military hospital.

My own research owes much to the National Library of Australia's brilliant Trove online newspaper archive. I am also grateful to John Merriman, Local Studies Librarian at Blue Mountains City Library and to the Sydney staff of the National Film and Sound Archives for their professional help.

I owe a special thanks to my friends Peter and Bobbie Rushforth for drawing my attention to Mary Shaw, granddaughter of the Hydro Majestic's visionary founder Mark Foy and a rich source of stories. I am also grateful to Steve Tucker for a personal tour of the hotel while it was still under refurbishment in 2013.

I acknowledge my adaptation of a 1920s chef's table menu recreated for The Savoy Grill and reviewed in Stylist.co.uk. Valued resources included John Low's lavishly illustrated *Pictorial Memories: Blue Mountains* (Kingsclear Books, 1991) and Dr Martin Thomas's superb *The Artificial Horizon: Imagining the Blue Mountains* (University of Melbourne Press, 2003).

My enduring interest in the internment of German-Australians during the First World War was first sparked by Gerhard Fischer's *Enemy Aliens: Internment and the Homefront Experience in Australia 1914–1920* (University of Queensland Press, 1989) and recently rekindled by *The Enemy at Home*, co-written with Nadine Helmi (University of NSW Press, 2011). Many years ago I watched film footage of the internment camps archived at the Australian War Memorial and knew I wanted more people to be aware of this story.

My heartfelt thanks go to my agent Selwa Anthony for her encouragement, guidance and wisdom. I am especially indebted to my publisher, Annette Barlow, and editor, Ali Lavau, for their passionate support and uncompromising advice. My thanks to Kirby Armstrong for her luscious cover and elegant internal design. My thanks also to Christa Munns and the rest of the Allen & Unwin team who have brought this book to life.

My greatest thanks are reserved for my wife, Claire, who shares and understands the challenges – and rewards – of the writer's life. She not only provided critical insights and much-valued advice but gave me the space and time to write this book and the courage and faith to finish it.